NOT JUST A SOLDIER'S WAR

Betty Burton is the author of *Jude, Jaen, Hard Loves, Easy Riches, The Consequences of War, Goodbye Piccadilly, Long, Hot Summer, Falling in Love Again* and *The Girl Now Leaving*, as well as the collection of short stories, *Women Are Bloody Marvellous!* She has written for both television and radio and won the Chichester Festival Theatre Award. Born in Romsey, Hampshire, she now lives in Southsea with her husband, Russ.

D1340550

BETTY BURTON

Not Just a Soldier's War

This edition published by Grafton Books, 1999

Grafton Books is an imprint of
HarperCollins*Publishers*
77–85 Fulham Palace Road,
Hammersmith, London W6 8JB

1 3 5 7 9 8 6 4 2

First published in Great Britain by
HarperCollins*Publishers* 1996

ISBN 0-261-67345-9

Set in Bembo at
Rowland Photosetting Ltd,
Bury St Edmunds, Suffolk

Printed and bound in Great Britain by
Caledonian International Book Manufacturing Ltd, Glasgow

For my father,
Leon Archer of Romsey,
in his eighty-eighth year
and
for my new grandson,
Joseph Burton of Hayling Island,
in his first.

Acknowledgements and Thanks

Not Just a Soldier's War is of course a fiction, but it stands upon the real lives of women volunteers who went to help the Republic of Spain when it was invaded in 1936.

Evelyn Hutchins was one of the few women volunteers to have driven a big truck in the Spanish Civil War.

Winifred Bates' recorded reminiscences provided my title.

Material, notes, help and encouragement for *Not Just a Soldier's War* were given very generously during the months of its writing from: Dave Goldman of Newcastle under Lyme, a journalist who is a veteran of the International Brigade; Abe Amorodin of New York, Secretary to the Veterans of the Abraham Lincoln Brigade; Jim Fyrth, whose books on the Spanish Civil War and suggested lines of research have been invaluable; Dr Keith Reed-Jones, who helped in the creation of Eugenia; and Frances Millard, Sue Bruley, Terry Smyth and Ken Lunn of the University of Portsmouth, who pointed me in the right direction at the start of my research. Not least of those who helped to shape this novel is my editor, Susan Opie. I thank her for her understanding and care.

'They came from the four corners of the world, for compassionate reasons and opposition to fascism — secretaries, nurses and medical aids, interpreters, drivers, administrators, relief workers, teachers and, in the early days, as front-line soldiers. Women of the best spirits of their generation' – Sally Alexander, *Women's Voices from the Spanish Civil War*

Prologue:

England 1937

'I say, have these. I feel a real Charlie carrying flowers.'

The golden-haired woman, the youngest of the group, took the flowers from a young man wearing a blazer and found herself, now holding a second bunch of flowers, pushed to the front to face the journalists and a battery of ciné-cameras and photographers.

'Everybody smile.'

They smiled.

'A nice big wave.'

They waved.

A nurse said, 'I wish I'd known that there was going to be such a to-do, I'd have given it a miss.' Her accent seemed to be rather too 'cut-glass' for a nurse. With a hunch of her shoulders, she went on, 'My mother doesn't know yet that I'm going back to Spain. *Fait accompli*. Best way with mothers who fuss, eh?'

The young woman agreed. 'I thought it would be just a photograph with the mayor.'

A man with a handsome Jewish face, wearing baggy corduroys and a tweed jacket and looking nothing like the popular image of the surgeon he was, said genially, 'Come along, you nurses, let's give these press chaps what they want,' and he put his left arm round the nurse's waist and the other round the woman with the golden hair.

The Real Charlie said, 'Right! Let's give them what they want and get the cause of the Spanish Republic in all the newsreels.' Holding aloft the hand of the woman who now clutched the embarrassing flowers, he shouted, '*¡No pasarán!*'

'Lord save us,' said the nurse, rolling her eyes. 'A patriot before he's even there.'

When the newsreel film of the Aid to Spain send-off was shown in cinemas, the belief of the group that they were part of a great and idealistic movement intent on saving the world from fascism showed clearly in their youthful eyes.

On the journey between Victoria Station and the Gare du Nord there was a gradual emergence of individuals. The nurse was called Crane, the Real Charlie was Phil Martin, a medical aide, the doctor was David Goldring, and the very young, golden-haired woman said her name was Eve Anders.

On that leg of the journey, Eve, although not unfriendly, kept to the fringes of the group, secretly revelling in her marvellous new freedom. These people were what she had hoped for. Not to be found in her own environment, they were radicals with revolutionary ideals and, she decided, they probably also believed in equality for women and free love. They seemed very red; she had never heard such left-of-left views expressed before.

What would Ray think of them? Ray was the elder of her two brothers, committed to working for his union; he would think she had better watch out, these were dangerous people. Ken, her other brother, had declared himself a Republican and was already in Spain, fighting with the International Brigade. So it was of Ken she thought when Dina Vandeck, one of the doctors, moved the talk on to Marx and then to the royal family.

'This is my second stint at the barricades,' Dina said, boasting, but maybe sending herself up a bit. 'I had intended travelling weeks ago, but my mother got herself so upset over the abdication that she made herself ill.'

Phil Martin hooted. 'Upset about those two parasites? Not a great chum of Harry Pollitt is she, then, your mother?'

Crane said, 'I *have* heard that they intend making their home in Germany.'

Goldring said, 'Hitler's welcome to them.'

'For my money,' Phil Martin said, 'they should all be cleared off to Germany, the whole bang shoot of them, back where

2

they came from. Monarchy is just fascism with knobs on, right?'

'Right!' Goldring said. 'Very far right,' and everybody laughed.

Eve Anders, who had thought her own views were quite advanced, was stimulated by the easy way they threw comments at one another, and wondered whether she happened to be travelling with an unusually leftist-thinking group. They were all in agreement that class consciousness was the bugbear of Britain, and that inherited privilege sprang from the top and the top was the king. She felt quite ashamed that she had seen the Silver Jubilee procession and had danced at a Coronation celebration party. But the shame soon dissolved into a kind of euphoria when, as they were speeding through France, she was occasionally drawn in to the conversation.

In what seemed like a very short time, they were drawing into the Gare du Nord. After brief farewells and wishing Eve good luck, the medical unit hurried off to catch another train to Barcelona.

Chapter One

Eve's contact was waiting for her. 'You are a driver?' Eve nodded. 'That's good news, you're an absolute godsend.' She shook hands firmly but briefly. 'I'm from Aid to Spain, of course. A friend of Charlotte Haldane. Charlotte is our inspiration.' Her distinct, cultured accent was the kind Eve longed for. 'I was beginning to think I should have to drive to Albacete myself, but I've hardly driven anything heavier than a shooting brake.'

Eve, a practised chameleon and mimic, slipped easily into the other woman's speech patterns as they left the concourse. 'I have an absolute passion for driving heavy vehicles,' she declared. 'Absolute passion' was an exaggeration, but she had learned to drive on heavy gears. She owned a Light Goods licence and was hoping that ambulances, which she expected to be driving, would be so classified. She was confident of her own ability. 'Is it right- or left-hand drive?'

'One of ours. Looks as though it might have been a Harvey Nichols delivery vehicle in a past life. All fitted out with seats now, used for ferrying men to the battle zones.'

'What is it doing here in Paris?'

'The driver dropped out – fatigue. So many volunteers try to do too much. He carried up a bunch of people going home for a spell of rest and recuperation, and was forced to join them. I suggest you put up here for tonight and set out in the morning. We have a place for you to stay.'

'Fine,' Eve said. 'Fine.' It was what she had hoped for: time to go over the maps once more and to memorize another list of useful Spanish words, then to start off first thing before too much traffic was about so that she could get used to driving on the right-hand side of the road.

As she walked through the streets with her guide, Eve gave only half of her mind to the inconsequential conversation.

'Do you know Paris?'

'Hardly at all. I did stay in a hotel quite close to the Ile de la Cité on one occasion. I still have a lovely dinner gown I took home from Lascelles'.' The couture gown of fine concertina silk was squashed into her sponge-bag because she hadn't been able to leave it behind.

'Wonderful! Beautiful things at Lascelles'. Awfully expensive.'

Eve briefly considered not showing off, then she thought: What the hell! Why shouldn't I?

It was the clichés that were the most exciting; there really were pavement cafés with parasols, and flower-sellers, and an old man wearing a black beret.

Again she reminded herself: I've got away. I'm free. Travelling light. She carried a few suitable clothes and shoes in a good, leather bag, as well as a canvas tote containing a camera, some maps, pencils, notebooks, rolls of film, money and cheques. Despite having volunteered to be a driver, she felt that she still had many choices: I can please myself. I don't actually *have* to go to Spain, nobody can make me. Briefly she wondered how her brother had coped with his own sudden freedom.

Her guide said something that Eve didn't catch, and laughed, showing teeth that were fine and well-cared-for. If there is one thing, Eve thought, more than any other, that sets the English lower and upper classes apart, it is our teeth. Not that Eve's teeth were any less fine.

The vehicle, with its bull-nose and oval windows in the back doors, did look like a shop delivery van. It was in the care of Francis and Frances O'Dell, a married couple known as Frankie and Fran, who were putting her up for the night.

The O'Dells made her welcome. It was obvious that they were used to providing for visitors who were passing through on their way to Spain, for they kept a couple of small rooms with single beds always ready. Although Eve was in Paris for only a few hours, she had intended to take another look at the Lascelles store, but having eaten ravenously her first-ever cassoulet, she was content to sit with Fran sorting through bags of clothing and supplies which were part of the aid she was to deliver, and window-shopping lost its appeal. She now saw she had a small part to play in the great drama being staged in Europe, an image inspired by Fran's suggestion that the German and Italian leaders were using Spain as a dress-rehearsal for an even greater show.

Eve asked the O'Dells if they had been to Spain.

'Oh yes,' said Fran. 'I came here after I got pregnant because Frankie thought I should see my own doctor. It's as well I did, because I lost the baby.'

Eve felt that to say she was sorry wasn't enough, but what else could she say?

'I'm sorry too, but had I miscarried in Madrid, Frankie would have blamed the bombing. In fact, I have a prolapsed womb, so I doubt if I shall ever be able to carry to term.'

It was peaceful in the comfortable apartment. Delicious scents of wine, garlic and tomato, reminders of the good meal, wafted across the room to the windows open to the summer evening.

'I like it here,' Eve said.

The older woman smiled. 'So do I. I wonder where you will be by this time tomorrow.'

'Forgive me,' Frankie said, 'but you are very young to be driving ambulances.'

'Trucks. I'm not an ambulance-driver.'

'I say, look at this, isn't it splendid?' Fran O'Dell held up a fancy waistcoat of peacock-blue brocade piped in silk cord. 'Very extravagant, just look at the buttons.'

Eve took the beautiful garment and felt the softness of its lining and the texture of the brocade. The buttons were little discs of porcelain rimmed in gold. 'Oh, they're little willow-pattern plates! They remind me of a doll's teaset my cousin Mary had.' Mary's teaset had not been of porcelain, however, but of mass-produced pottery splodged with a blue pattern and stamped 'Made in China' on every piece. Crude and cheap as it was, Mary had been the envy of every little girl who saw it.

Eve folded the waistcoat and wondered whether to pack it in the men's or the women's bundle. Women's. She loved extravagant and beautiful things; even as she scorned herself for doing so, she coveted the garment with its exquisite buttons.

'I think I remember seeing this before,' Fran said.

Eve smiled. 'It is memorable. I shan't forget it in a hurry.'

'Lord Lovecraft turned up at a fund-raising in just such a waistcoat.'

'There can hardly be two.'

Fran chuckled. 'You can be sure of that. Sweetheart as he is when it comes to worthy causes, Lovecraft would never appear in anything less than exclusive.'

Eve realized that this was one of those moments that she would always remember. Before the day was over she would write it up in her journal and was already anticipating what she would say about the contradictions of people like Lord Lovecraft and herself: he giving generously to charity while indulging himself with beautiful clothes, she, the idealist and supporter of equality, coveting the buttons and the fine fabric. 'Perhaps that's why he gave it away,' she suggested. 'He found that it wasn't exclusive.'

'I doubt if its exclusiveness will bother its recipient; it's more likely to be whether they dare to be seen wearing it.'

As she sat there sorting and chatting, it suddenly struck her that until now she had only ever known two socialists who were middle-class, but here she was sitting with a woman with a good accent deciding what to do with Lord Lovecraft's waistcoat. Momentarily she longed for someone from her own class with whom she could share what she was thinking. Then she dismissed the idea. 'I think if I were in need of a waistcoat, Fran, that would cheer me up no end.'

Oh, the things Eve remembered that she had worn when she was in need: the skirts and tops 'run up' out of remnants, the hand-me-down hats and shoes. She refused to let those memories come crashing in like this. She was no longer that girl. At

8

last she was doing what she had once only dreamed about: she had left home for good, leaving behind her mistakes, her old loves, and old guilts and embarrassments. She had abandoned her childish resentment of such unalterables as accidents of birth and environment, and, in cutting and running from people who loved her, she had freed herself of the conventional expectations they had of her. Above all else, she was throwing off the baggage of her class and from here on she knew that she could be anyone she chose to be.

Lost in her own thoughts she folded garments and gazed out into the warm summer evening sky.

Fran O'Dell, puzzled, glanced at the young woman from time to time. Eve seemed somehow to be both calm and energized. There was something deep and fascinating about her and Fran would have liked to know her better. Still, there was always a chance that they would meet again somewhere.

Eve, not noticing that she was being observed, continued to sort through her thoughts: I am travelling light, not even carrying my real name. This side of the English Channel, I am Eve Anders, a volunteer in the fight against fascism.

Well read and well spoken, she knew that she had a face and figure that, if she chose, could open doors and smooth her way. From the day that she had watched her home town receding she had been accepted for who she was. She was never going to say Lor, luv a duck, me bleedin' beads, or whatever it was Eliza Doolittle had said. She had been stepping over the class barrier for long enough now to know that she could stay over it. She knew that the trick was to be enigmatic, or, as some of her old friends would have said, to 'Keep your bloody mouth shut'.

Bringing her thoughts back to the room, Eve said, 'One could always sell them.'

'Sell what?'

'Lord Lovecraft's buttons, they look quite valuable.'

'Bartering would be the better course. One never knows with currency when there's a war going on.'

9

Later that night Eve lay in bed taking stock of her progress since leaving London. There seemed to be so much she didn't know, and she wanted to know it all.

Eve's first official stop was Perpignan, where she was due to pick up supplies to be dropped off in Barcelona. Even with the windows down, the inside of the cab became sweltering. Sweat dampened her hairline and trickled between her breasts, but oh she was happy, confident, independent and, most important, she was in control. The road signs were unfamiliar, but it did not take her long to adjust to the feel of the road. The van was no problem to drive, except that from time to time she was forced to stop to top up the radiator which she suspected of leaking. Good luck was with her when, stopping at a petrol pump not far from the border, her phrase-book French was recognized at once by the elderly ex-patriate English proprietor.

'I still call it home,' he said, from under the bonnet, 'though I've been here nearly twenty years – since the war.' As he tinkered with the radiator he bombarded her with questions, about unemployment, the abdication, the new king, and why England had taken against Spain: 'May as well be against as be neutral.' When Eve told him that she wasn't neutral and that she was going there to drive trucks, he emerged grinning from under the bonnet, fisted the air and said, '¡No pasarán!' He called for his wife to come and meet a compatriot. The woman insisted that Eve wait while she made fresh coffee, which she served with cold pork and bread.

'Might as well let me give her a quick once-over while you eat that,' the old man said. Anxious as she was to get on, Eve was touched by the couple's kindness.

'I got a reputation at Mons for being able to get anything with four wheels and an engine working,' he continued. '"Never fear, Townsend's here," they'd say. I'll not let you out of here with anything dodgy.'

He talked to her constantly as he worked. 'After I was invalided out after Mons, I vowed I would be a pacifist, tried to tell them back home, but nobody wanted to know. But I've had to change my views since Franco. I would never go to war over a bit of land same as we did in 1914 . . . us and the Bosch were killing each other in thousands over a bit of land hardly bigger than my orchard there, land that's been changing hands since Adam was a lad. But if I was young and healthy there's one thing I'd go to war over, and that's fascism. Look at this, your front off-side is losing air, and your spare needs repairing.' He looked quite gratified. 'You see – you could have been in trouble. France and England's both as bad as the other. They should come out against fascism. Fascism is a bad idea, terrible bad. If Franco isn't put down, we shall all be in it again, up to our necks. It's what the Blackshirts want, of course, nice little war in Spain to practise for the big one. It's criminal really, staying neutral when Hitler and Mussolini are pouring arms and men into Spain on Franco's side. You know why? If it's a choice between Russia and Germany, the British will side with Hitler . . . the French are no better.'

As soon as the old man had finished, Eve lost no time in getting back on the road again. The medics she had travelled with were miles ahead of her now. Had she known the route, she would have put her foot down in her eagerness to get going. The Paris stop-over had been a delay, the time spent fixing the engine had been another. But now, at last, Spain was just a few kilometres further along the road she was travelling. Kilometres, not miles; she had made the transition unconsciously. She smiled.

Just before she reached the border, she stopped her vehicle to eat by the roadside, savouring the moment when she would show her papers and drive into the Republic of Spain.

This is the beginning, she thought.

This was where she would part company with her slum child-hood and her factory job, guiding miles of firm fabric beneath flying needles, millions of stitches, year in year out. This was where she would leave behind her past as Lu Wilmott; leave behind Ray who had been more father than elder brother, and

Bar Barney, who had been her innocent first love and who was now Ray's wife.

This was where idealism would not lead to dismissal from a no-hope factory job. From here on she would declare her ideals, a red flag if she so chose.

This, she was sure, was the beginning of a life in which beautiful, urbane David Hatton, who could have had her virginity a long time before she gave it to Duke Barney, would play no part. David had given her a taste of the high life; he had found her magical and mysterious, but she was leaving him behind still not knowing her true identity.

This was also to be the beginning of a life in which Duke Barney had no place. He had been secretive, passionate, ambitious. Even when they were lovers, neither of them had thought of anything as mundane as love. Theirs was – still was – a powerful passion. Although he was out of her life, Duke Barney was not a man to be easily dismissed.

And this was where, no longer Louise Wilmott, she would start her new life as Eve Anders.

Her papers must have been unexceptional, for she had no trouble crossing the border.

Chapter Two

Eve longed to see something of Barcelona, but her instructions were to pick up a lorry and take some young Spanish men and one woman to Albacete, as well as a soldier, Pérez, who was going to Lérida and wanted a lift only as far as Tarragona. A tenth passenger she had to pick up outside the railway station: a French-Canadian in civilian clothes carrying a military kit-bag, François Le Bon.

Pérez, who had been sitting up front, handed over the route map and relinquished the passenger seat to the bilingual Le Bon. As they made their way further south, so the landscape changed. In the heat of the afternoon, Eve drew off the road into the shade of some trees and gave in to the necessity of *siesta*. When the sun was lower they set out again, but the air was still hotter than Eve had ever known. Her passengers, catching the through breeze, sang songs with stirring tunes, while Pérez pored attentively over newspapers or snoozed.

They stopped at Tarragona where Pérez arranged for Eve to stay the night at his sister's house. She had spoken very little to him on the journey, but in Tarragona he turned out to be a courteous man with a school-teacherish manner, or perhaps it was that he reminded her of a teacher at the night-school she had attended for several years. Pérez's sister, Señora Portillo, a teacher who spoke some English, ran a small *hostal* providing little more than accommodation, but Eve welcomed the atmosphere. Her husband Eduardo and son Paulo were away fighting.

Eve was up at dawn the next day to give the lorry a check before setting out on the long journey. The Señora pressed upon them a parting gift of some home-made oaty biscuits and bottles of fizzy drink, *la gaseosa*, a new word for Eve's rapidly expanding vocabulary. Knowing that they were headed south she asked them to enquire for Eduardo and Paulo, whom she had not heard from for weeks. They had been in the military barracks in Albacete, so perhaps they had not received her letters. 'I ask everyone,' she said. 'It may happen that your paths cross; these things happen in war.'

While the others were making themselves as comfortable as their rifles, gear and the wooden bed of the lorry would allow, François Le Bon spent a few minutes studying the map, as he had done the day before, then relaxed into the upright passenger seat. In minutes they were away, Señora Portillo standing forlornly in her yard, then returning the clenched-fist salute of the young people who were setting out as full of spirit as had the missing Eduardo and Paulo.

The little *hostal* was about halfway to their destination, so they were prepared for the best part of another day on the road. Again François Le Bon took on the role of tourist guide and interpreter for their inexperienced driver. Although Eve was quite content with her own company, she enjoyed his comments on the passing scene, as he recorded items of interest in a loose-leaf notebook.

'Zaragoza, the Balearics, Sierra Nevada, Andalucia, Granada,' she said. 'When I was a schoolgirl and geography was boring, I used to flip through the atlas looking for romantic names and Spain had such a lot of them. My imagination would be set on fire by them, especially the ones that ended with A: Yecla, Villena, Cieza, La Mancha, Andalucia, Granada.'

The militia woman known as Marguerite, the leader, leaned into the cab and said something too fast for Eve to understand, except for 'La Mancha'.

Eve turned her head briefly. '*No comprendo,*' she said, adding, with a smile, 'Don Quixote was from La Mancha.'

Marguerite shook Le Bon's shoulder, indicating that he should interpret, then repeated her eager message.

Le Bon understood. 'She asks if you have been to La Mancha.' Eve shook her head. 'It's where she's from, from the town of

Consuela. She says . . . *extranjeros* . . . ? foreigners? Yes . . . she's saying foreigners always know about Don Quixote but they don't know about the beautiful plains of La Mancha where the saffron crocuses grow.'

Eve nodded. 'Saffron . . . I understand.' She took her eyes off the road long enough to smile at Marguerite and grasp her hand briefly. '*Gracias*.' To Le Bon she said, 'I wish I'd had the good sense to have read languages.'

Le Bon tilted his head and took a long look at her. 'What did you read?'

She paused before answering, realizing that he was bound to think that she had been to university and that she half hoped he would, otherwise why had she said 'read' instead of 'learned'? She felt irritated by her own crassness. 'Nothing noteworthy.'

'Oh,' he said shortly, and closed his notebook. The silence that followed seemed all the more marked because the men in the back were all dozing.

Eventually, she said, 'Don't stop writing, I didn't mean noteworthy in that way. Sorry if I sounded prickly.'

'It's OK. It's just me, I've got the curiosity of a cat. When I'm back home I write a column for my hometown paper. That's what this is about,' he indicated his notebook.

'Oh. You're reporting on the war for a local paper?'

'No. Well, yes and no. I just send stuff back.'

'And you write about the war?'

'Not about the war; more about people, I guess.'

'What they call human interest stories?'

He smiled, 'Yeah, they do, they do. Which is why I was so curious about how a young English beauty comes to be driving a truck to Albacete with such an assorted bunch as we are.'

'Because about the only thing she could offer that was of any use was to drive.'

'Why on the side of the Republic?'

She was taken aback. 'Isn't it obvious?'

'To me yes, but not every English lady is on the side of the Republic. I heard one recently, doing a radio broadcast in Eng-

15

lish, describing how she felt about Spain, about life carrying on bravely with battles raging within ear-shot, how the fiestas and market-days carried on regardless, about the shining light – meaning Franco – that was guiding the youth of Spain.'

'That's just how they feel,' she indicated Marguerite and the others dozing in the back, 'from those songs they were singing: pretty inspirational, guided by a shining light.'

'She was Florence Farmborough, ever heard of her? A British fascist. On Sunday evenings she does radio talks from Salamanca, to English-speaking countries. She dedicates her account of her experiences in Spain "with pride and humility to Generalissimo Franco".'

'When I see a Western, I'm never on the side of the cowboys. The Indians were only fighting to keep their own land. So I would want to help Republican Spain, wouldn't I?'

By now they had almost reached Valencia, and started on that part of the journey on which Pérez had said they would probably hear shelling. Battles were raging between the Nationalist and Republican forces just to the east of the road on which they were driving. At the beginning of the year, the Nationalists had held Madrid, then the Republicans had taken it back, but now the two sides were preparing to fight for the city once again.

'Will we hear the guns from here?'

'We might –' François Le Bon didn't finish his sentence.

Eve didn't know which registered first, the clean hole in the shattered windscreen, the sense of movement of air by her cheek or the crack of rifle fire. She jumped on the brakes. The vehicle slewed, turned round, tyres squealing to a sliding halt. Her heart was pumping twenty to the dozen, and her fingers were locked to the steering wheel like the claws of a perching bird. Le Bon flung open the passenger door and rolled out. In a second he had gone round to the back of the van. Marguerite was there before him.

Eve crawled out of the passenger-side door and dropped to the ground. She had never felt so scared in her life. As she lay under the lorry, her pulse thumping in her ears, she became aware of the soldiers who were all silent and looking perplexed. Marguerite, her face red with anger, snatched a rifle from a very young soldier. The boy, looking stricken, suddenly rushed to some boulders and was sick. Le Bon helped Eve out from under the lorry. 'OK?'

'Yes. Is anyone hurt?'

François Le Bon rolled his eyes. 'Not that you'd notice. Some of these youngsters think these things are toys. He was cleaning his rifle, had a bullet up the spout and he didn't know . . . didn't know. Didn't know the bloody thing was loaded!'

The boy soldier was humiliated before his comrades, the worst of punishments. Having bawled him out, Marguerite gave him a brief brush on his peachy cheek with her knuckles and told them all to get back into the truck.

They continued on to Valencia, with hot air and the smell of oil coming in through the hole in the windscreen. Occasionally they caught a whiff of oranges, passing a pile of the bright fruits by the roadside, then another and another. Some piles were great mountains from which came the very pungent smell of orange oil and rotting fruits.

'Why is all this fruit going to waste?' Eve asked. Le Bon shrugged but turned to ask Marguerite.

'They say they are no good.'

They passed more and yet more oranges. When they saw a woman upending a cart and adding to an already enormous pile, Eve announced, 'I'm going to stop. Can somebody ask?'

Marguerite and Le Bon quizzed a woman. Yes, she said, the oranges were useless, rotting. Yes, there had been a very good crop, but there was no transport. The crop was for the juicing factory, and the juicing factory was waiting for the oranges, but the trucks did not come last season. There was no petrol . . . perhaps no trucks . . . perhaps no drivers. The woman knew only that the oranges had ripened and the trucks had not come. She said that she had orange concentrate for barter.

They offered her half a bar of soap, five cigarettes and the rest of Señora Portillo's oat biscuits. As an afterthought Eve climbed on to the van's roof and dragged out some of the clothes.

The woman, who had offered them the shade of the family grove for their *siesta*, went ahead of the van, leading her donkey, the square of carbolic soap slipped into the pocket of Lord Lovecraft's flamboyant brocade waistcoat.

Eve lay on her back resting but not sleeping, and in the sweltering heat, a little less powerful under the stumpy trees, she thought how strange it was that she had arrived with a medical team, was designated an ambulance-driver, yet here she was taking a *siesta* in an orange grove with members of the Spanish militia and a Canadian who wrote for a newspaper.

She looked through the pattern of strong, shiny leaves which scarcely moved. Of all places – an orange grove. A place she would have imagined to be full of mystery, full of the kind of energy and magnetism she had discovered in the depths of a woodland in England. There, she had once been as close to perfect happiness as she ever expected to get. There, she had seen ecstasy personified. There she had taken part in a ritual in which she and Bar – the girl who had been her heart-bound friend – had wound a spell for themselves. As she watched the leaves and smelled the sweet perfume of the orange blossom, she visualized the two of them as they had been on her twelfth birthday, two naked girls winding themselves like silkworms inside a cocoon of their own virginal spells, then, face to face and clutching one another, they leaped into a deep pool of cool green water.

When Bar had left their enchanted place and come to live in the city, she had wound another cocoon, but this time around herself and Ray and Ray's baby. A cocoon for three. The baby was due soon, and its aunt was lying flat on her back in an orange grove. This suddenly seemed so significant that Eve needed to record it lest she forget the essence of this, her first truly deep thoughts about things she had left behind, or run away from.

Although she had kept a diary since that summer in the birch woods with Bar, she had never felt so compelled to write as she did now. She withdrew from her haversack a leather-bound book of blank sheets as strong and light as air-mail paper. This was the only indulgence she had allowed herself when she was preparing to leave England, apart from the useless silk gown crushed into a sponge-bag. Paper was in very short supply here, so she was teaching herself to write tidily, clearly and minutely. It would not be easy, for it was in her nature to throw her heavy writing down on the page, dashing long crossings on Ts and finishing off with whips any letters that looped below the line.

After about two hours' rest they all returned to the lorry which was still uncomfortably hot. Before they set off again, Eve sat on the running-board where she could survey the whole scene: the orange mountain, Marguerite and the young members of the militia, and the valley in which neat orange groves were already growing next year's crop. About the only thing she had known about the growing of oranges was that the trees could hold fruit and blossom at the same time – and now she had seen that.

The boy who had fired off the bullet close to her face sat quietly, a little apart, rolling a green orange between his hands. He took off his cap and wiped the rim. He could hardly be out of school, no age to be a soldier. But he was at the age for idealism. Yes. She knew how it was to want to *do* something.

François Le Bon came over and offered a cigarette. Eve hesitated. 'I don't like taking yours, they're in short supply, aren't they?'

'You can say that again. It's OK, you can give me one next.' He leaned idly against the side of the hot van, looking across the lines of orange trees. 'This is how I always imagined Spain must be. Just because of the marmalade. You know, Seville oranges. I just love marmalade, so I know I would love Spain.'

'I think I know what you mean.'

'I saw you writing.'

Eve nodded. 'Just for myself. There are things I don't want to leave to memory in case they fade.'

'Do you write a lot?'

'Most days. I've been doing it since I was twelve . . . almost can't help it now.'

'Uh-huh, it's like that. I don't know what to do when I get near the end of a notebook and I can't find anywhere to get another. I've even taken to turning the book round and writing across that way in red pencil.'

'I suppose there's a shortage of a lot of things.'

'Quite a lot. Paper especially. I always buy essentials even when I haven't actually run out.'

'You can tell I'm new to Spain, can't you?'

'You're doing OK. None of us foreigners can call ourselves a veteran. The International Brigade wasn't formed till last October. What gives you away is this.' He touched the fold of her right arm just below where her shirt-sleeve was rolled up. She winced. 'Truck-drivers here get one arm browner than the other, right-hand drive truck, right arm suntanned. You want to take care. Takes a while for us fair ones to harden up. Sun gets me on the back of the neck. I guess I could do with one of those caps like they wear in the Foreign Legion. I carry a tin of cooking soda and a little bottle of water. Let me put some on for you?'

The cooking soda was cool. She liked Le Bon with his taciturn, unshakable manner. She liked Marguerite with her rolled-up sleeves, her neckerchief and tassled military cap. She liked the young soldiers, José, Diego, Miguel, Cip, Juan, Andreu and Marco, the careless boy.

'I was writing about the waistcoat, I was told it once belonged to Lord Lovecraft.'

' "Lord Lovecraft's Waistcoat" – a play in three acts. Is there a story?'

'Not really. I stopped over in Paris on my way here, to pick up a van and some clothes from one of the aid committees. The waistcoat stood out like a parakeet at a barn owl show.'

20

Had that happened only days ago? It seemed to be weeks since she had spent the evening sorting clothing in the O'Dells' Paris flat.

The soldiers were dropped off at a depot on the outskirts of Albacete. As the men were off-loading their gear and the bottles of concentrate, Marco hurriedly pushed a little package into her hand. '*Abuela, Abuela*,' he said, and was gone.

Le Bon examined the little kerchief. '*Abuela* means grandmother . . . I guess she must have made it for him. You're not Roman Catholic, then? It's the Sacred Heart. On a piece of cloth like this, it becomes a kind of talisman, lucky charm, worn close to the breast for protection.'

'I can't keep it. He believes in it.'

'Don't . . . he must want you to have it.'

She didn't like the idea of the boy going off to fight without his grandmother's charm.

She had reached Albacete at last.

Albacete is an ancient garrison town where General Franco was born, and in which he had succeeded in establishing power until he was overthrown by an uprising of local people. In spite of Albacete's fervently Republican spirit, there were still small enclaves of that other spirit in hiding, still believing in the Generalissimo as a Christian Nationalist, and not as a friend of the fascist countries. Still in the city, little pockets of his followers spread rumours and half-truths and truths about communist atrocities, anarchist desecrations and military command from Moscow. Spying, sniping from windows, the Albacete fascists had not given up.

Le Bon, no longer making notes, followed the street-plan. 'Will you just look at this place. Looks as though the streets haven't been swept for months.'

True, the streets were a mess, and roughly painted slogans and posters seemed to cover every bit of wall space. But it was of little consequence to Eve. She had made it! From home to London to Paris to Perpignan to Barcelona and now at last

Albacete. As she watched Le Bon, the last of her passengers, alight she experienced a sense of achievement. She had driven a big, heavy lorry with passengers and supplies, on roads that were strange to her, and arrived in Albacete in one piece. If she impressed no one else, she impressed herself.

The section of the transport depot to which she was to deliver her Aid to Spain gift truck was in the charge of a woman called Mrs Alexander. In another life, she might have appeared on the inside cover of *Country Life* magazine wearing a white dress and gardenias. In the depot, where Eve found her, she wore brown corduroy trousers, a man's shirt and tennis shoes. Her accent would have suited the BBC beautifully, but her drooping fag and raised oil-can were something else. Eve, with her tendency to make snap judgements, did not take to her. It was the accent which grated.

'Oh, you're the driver. Marvellous! Can we do with you.' She went to shake hands ('Christ, what a mess!'), and wiped her palm on her behind. 'Helan, with an "a" not an "e", Alexander. People call me Alex,' she said, removing her cigarette carefully with greasy thumb and fingertips.

'Eve Anders.'

'OK, Anders, any problems getting here?'

'No.'

'I gather you brought down one of our favourite doctors – François Le Bon.'

'A doctor? He said he wrote for his local paper.'

'Maybe he does, he's out here with a field unit. I believe that in Canada he's known best for the neat way he amputates. A specialist. Isn't wasted out here.'

All those hours spent together on the drive down yet, even in their moment of sharpness about what she did back home, he hadn't given a clue about what he really did himself.

'Beauties, aren't they?' Alexander patted the olive-coloured truck whose engine she had been tinkering with. 'Straight off the production line. Best of British engineering. Ever driven a Bedford?'

'No, but I wouldn't mind the chance.'

'Ha! The chaps wouldn't care for that.' She lovingly rubbed the headlamp glass with a clean rag.

'The roads I came on were very good. I didn't know what to expect. I would have guessed bad if anyone had asked me.'

'Doesn't do to pre-judge anything in this country. The main road and rail systems are mostly good, one of the great achievements of this government. Different in the remoter regions; mountain tracks are absolute hellers.'

She didn't smile much. Eve's first impression was that she might not be an easy person to work with, probably used to giving orders.

'Look inside. Hospitals on wheels. Aren't they super? A real bloody shame about the mud and blood. Will you be all right about that?'

'I shan't know until I'm in it, and then it won't be any use saying no. I'll manage.'

'No bloody good out here if you don't. Sit in, see how it feels.'

As soon as she got behind the wheel, Eve knew that she would have no trouble driving it. It was high seated and the steering wheel was large. There was a strange feeling of luxury, considering their purpose. 'I'd be all right with one of these. They're made for legs as long as mine.'

'Made for men. Can't take it to the local garage and have pedal blocks made. We don't get many women drivers . . . a couple of Americans, they're good, but they had to bash their way in. Their chaps got really fucked up about it. Might get you on delivering repaired vehicles.'

'Do you drive them yourself?'

'Mostly I push around bits of paper, essential to smooth running, of course. What I like is to just bugger about with a spanner and oil-rag. But we all have to do anything we can. Anything. I'll come out with you in the morning, see how things go with you. Better take your things over to the Starlight Hotel, bag your place in the dorm.'

'Starlight Hotel?'
'You'll see.'

In its more elegant days the Starlight Hotel, Eve decided, must have been a dance-hall or a cinema. The half-circle flight of marble steps and the chrome trim and push-bars to the swing doors were still in place, the foyer still echoed but now with heavier shoes and studs. The first-floor dormitories and rooms were reached by a curved stair with a brass handrail that was now kept shiny only by the many hands that skidded over its surface as young women hurried in and out.

It was not very clean, or convenient, the alterations having been made piecemeal and not always very well. Partitions had been erected, probably to give an impression of privacy, but as eight or ten women were housed, if that was the word, within each area, Eve wondered if it might have been less chaotic without them. One thing, though, putting up in a place like the Starlight Hotel reinforced the impression that this was a very different life.

She awakened just as the sky was growing light. Cool air carrying petrol and exhaust fumes blew across her from the open window, and although she hadn't been kept awake, she was aware that the sound of vehicles hadn't stopped all night. Alexander's warning that there were snipers active in the town wasn't an idle one; several times she was aroused briefly by the crack of a rifle.

Four of the other beds in the makeshift dormitory were now occupied but none of the occupants stirred. Last night they had come together briefly as they stepped round one another's gear, two Swedish administrative clerks and two English nurses, Smart and Haskell, old hands in Spain and long-time friends. None of them seemed particularly curious about the newcomer.

On each of the spare beds was a thin, rolled-up mattress, a brown blanket and a pillow. It was the first time in her life that Eve had slept in a room with strangers. Dormitories had been the centre of the action in the girls' school stories she had devoured as a child, but this one was dedicated to nothing but sleep and a quick wash and brush-up.

It was full daylight when Eve reached the depot for her test run. She turned the key in the ignition and the engine started at once. Alexander climbed into the passenger seat, Eve put the gears into reverse and carefully rolled the vehicle out of the line.

'Want me to see you out?' Alexander asked.

'I think I'll be all right.'

'Only think? This is a valuable piece of equipment.'

Eve gave her a sharp glance, refusing to be intimidated. 'No. I shall be all right.' And she was, although it was heavier than the van she had brought in from France and the truck she had driven down from Barcelona. Alexander gave her terse but straightforward directions out of the compound, through more of Albacete's unswept streets, then out of the town and on to roads which eventually became little more than unsurfaced rocky tracks.

Eve soon realized that as well as looking in the wing-mirror and keeping an eye on the road ahead, Alexander was watching her every manoeuvre. As they rounded a bend they were confronted by a mule drawing a little cart, bang in the centre of the road. She didn't brake hard, but slowed down a few yards behind and waited to see if a driver appeared. Alexander made no comment, seeming content for Eve to follow behind slowly. It wasn't by any means the first time that Eve had been in this situation; she had cut her driving teeth following some badly maintained tractor, or a herd of cows, or a hay wagon along English country lanes.

'Down here . . . turn off right at the next . . . that's it.'

Alexander kept Eve driving, reversing, tight turning in narrow lanes, for an hour. 'OK. Turn it off. Pretty good, Anders. Hop out, stretch your legs for ten minutes. It can get you in the calf muscles until you become used to it.'

Except for an occasional distant roll of thunder, everywhere was as quiet and peaceful as an English summer day, and the rural landscape quite as empty of people. But here there was no patchwork of fields neatly marked by hedges, here the undulations of the dry-looking, craggy land were not easily rolling like those at home. Yet it was beautiful.

'Sounds like a thunder-storm brewing.'

'Shelling – German big guns most likely – a good few kilometres from here. Sound carries on the dry air.'

Helan Alexander, unconcerned, put two fingers in her mouth and whistled shrilly. Hooves pounded, and the heads of a beautiful gelding and a mule appeared, snorting, over a low hedge. She pulled a couple of crusts from a pocket and fed them to the animals as she told them in a low voice what beautiful boys they were.

The big horse was certainly beautiful. When Eve fondled its muzzle, it quivered.

'You like horses, Anders?'

'Yes.'

'The Arab belonged to the big house up there, but when the owner pushed off to Africa, he had to leave his animals to fend for themselves. Well, just one old chappie sees to them. This is the last one, it's only a matter of time before he ends up in the pot. I'm surprised he's lasted so long.'

'He?'

'Why not? Never does to remind a male of the species he's lost his balls.'

In spite of her upbringing in a poor area of a poor city, it wasn't difficult to shock Eve Anders whose education had been in an Anglican Church school.

'Know much about them?'

'I like to ride.'

'Pity there's no saddle. I reconnoitred the stables, most of the tack has gone.'

'I didn't have a saddle when I learned to ride.'

Alexander turned and looked, as though seeing Eve for the first time. 'Now that, Anders, *really* impresses me.' She nodded to the horse and its companion mule. 'Why don't you?

26

He might be cottage pie the next time you see him.'

'Are you serious? You are.'

'Good protein, not a lot of it about. Go on, let's see what you can do.'

It seemed ages since Eve had been on a horse, but the curve of that beautiful back, even though it hadn't seen a curry comb in months, was inviting. The mule kept a close watch as Eve mounted from the gate. Holding the unkempt mane low down its neck, she kneed the well-behaved animal forward to a slow walk, rising and falling as easily as she had done six years ago, the little mule moving in and keeping close. Eve talked encouragingly in a low, quiet voice as Bar Barney had taught her, 'Good dobbin – good dobbin – good dobbin.' She didn't go far, aware of Alexander leaning over the gate watching, and the big Bedford heating up in the morning sunshine.

'You do it very prettily, Anders. Where did you learn to ride like that?'

Starting with a clean sheet, a new name and no past but confronted with a direct question, it was not easy to reply. 'Oh, I used to spend school holidays on my aunt's farm.'

Now, as she made her way to the depot to eat and receive her instructions, she thought about 'my aunt's farm', and wondered what Alexander had made of that. In the world of the Alexander family, a farm would mean several thousand acres, part of a large estate. But the truth about her aunt's farm had been in there somewhere. Mrs Alexander could think what she liked.

Chapter Three

Eve's first assignment was to drive the truck back to Barcelona, taking a load of vehicle spares that had been variously restored, rethreaded and reseated at the depot. She was disappointed not to have been sent on a more important mission, driving an ambulance, or a heavy-duty truck such as one of the big Bedfords. Yes, she would love to be given charge of one of those.

This time she saw a little more of the city. Barcelona had been defended by its people in bloody street skirmishes, and had been bombed until some parts of the ancient city were destroyed. Public buildings were occupied by various military groups and churches had been put to secular use, or in some cases destroyed in an orgy of revenge against old repression. As she made her way through the thronging, bustling streets, nothing she had heard about Barcelona or seen on newsreels had prepared her for the atmosphere of a city in the full flood of revolutionary fervour. Every building was festooned with flags – communist red, anarchist red-and-black – every wall was plastered with posters whose messages were clear: Defend the Republic! Smash the Fascist Invaders! Barcelona was a city that belonged to its people.

She delivered her boxes and was given new orders, not to return to Albacete with medical supplies as she had expected, but to report to a Dr Quemada who immediately made her responsible for the welfare of Sister Sophie Wineapple, an American nurse who was sick. Eve was to take her to a villa outside the city, stay with her for a week and then bring her back. It seemed a strange thing to be doing.

Throughout the short journey, Sister Wineapple sat silent and withdrawn, clutching her trembling hands.

The villa, stripped of its original contents and furnished with more functional items, was still to Eve's eyes the most splendid house she had ever entered. The huge bedrooms contained several beds, each of which had a bunched-up mosquito net at the head. All the beds were partitioned in the style of a hospital ward, but the divisions were made from an assortment of curtains of beautiful fabric. Eve's silent charge appeared to see none of this, for as soon as she had put her bag down, she simply collapsed with a huge sigh on to a narrow bed and fell at once into a deep sleep. Having taken off her shoes and covered her with the mosquito net, Eve returned to the ground floor where she was hailed by a woman's voice with a Scots accent.

'Are ye the one that's brought in the poor wee Sister that worked herself to a standstill?'

'Sister Wineapple? Yes. She's on her bed, dead to the world.'

'Awch, then she'll be fine. It's the ones who can't sleep ye need to keep an eye on. Have you eaten yet? Awch well, neither have I, let's see what we can find, I think I saw a packet of Kellogg's if they're not scoffed by now. I'm Polly Hurley. What are you called?'

Polly Hurley 'found' half a packet of cornflakes which, from the way she doled them out and briefly agonized about not taking too large a portion, Eve came to realize, must be a treat. 'Heaven,' she said with each savoured spoonful. A piece of bread and a cup of peculiar-tasting tea with watery evaporated milk completed the snack or, as Eve was to discover, the meal.

'It's so quiet, the place seems deserted.'

'Peace and quiet is the general idea. A breath of God's good air and a few afternoon *siestas* and a good sleep at night is all most of them need.'

'Who are they? What is this place? Look, I've only just arrived in Spain and I haven't an idea what I'm supposed to be doing.'

'Thrown in at the deep end like a good many of us. Don't fret, float on your back and let the tide carry you and before you know it, you'll be striking out on your own. You'll soon see, the nurses and doctors work themselves to a standstill, they're short of everything needed to do their job but it doesn't stop them.'

'Not until they drop, like the woman I brought here?'

'That's mostly it. Some get terrible diarrhoea from bad food, or wi' us and some of the Colonials it's the sudden change of diet – they say it's all the beans we eat, but I say it's all the oil and spices we aren't used to. We all experience getting the runs at some time or other. The Yanks call it getting the skitters, it's no' a bad description. If you're new, I'll gi' you your first bit of advice: get your folks to send you packets of toilet paper, and if it's a choice between that and the old ciggies, give up smoking I say.'

'Are you a nurse or what?'

'No, no. Ye'll find that a lot of the nurses are non-political . . . they just know they are against fascism, but I'm a life-long anarchist.' Eve had been going to say that she had always assumed that there wasn't much difference between anarchists and fascists, but she realized that what the Scots woman had said indicated the opposite. 'I do therapeutic massage.'

Eve, who had always considered herself well-informed, suddenly felt quite ignorant, and could only guess at what therapeutic massage might be.

'If you want to make yourself useful while you're here, you can help me. I've taught a good many the basics of how to use their hands.'

As Eve drank the last of the strange-tasting tea, she listened with fascinated attention to Polly Hurley saying in her delightful accent what she had obviously said many times before: 'Hands have the greatest power to heal, did ye know that? I don't mean the laying on of hands or a thing like that . . . no, heal and comfort. Human beings need to be touched by other human beings, long to be touched, but in a society like ours which of us can bring ourselves to ask?'

Eve nodded, not out of politeness, but because she agreed. Perhaps it was as much the feel of David Hatton's hands in contact with her skin that had left her wanting more when he had withdrawn; perhaps it was that same contact between herself and Duke Barney that had urged them on in their lust for one another. Touch and be touched. Yes, that was important.

'But it's OK if it's done by a professional like yourself.'

Polly Hurley nodded. 'Absolutely. And, of course, if you are away from home and in a situation like this where everyone is a stranger to everyone else, then there are only people like myself or prostitutes for the men and casual lovers for the women.'

That evening, once Eve had taken some food and drink to the exhausted Sister Wineapple, she put on one of Polly Hurley's white aprons and learned how to warm between her palms the small bottles of aromatic oil, and how much to drip on to bare shoulders and backs. As she watched, she was fascinated to see how knots of muscles appeared to dissolve under Polly Hurley's manipulative fingers, and when she rolled into bed that night, she thought: Of all things to learn on my first day here – anarchists are not sinister bombers. Any skill one had was valuable.

For four days, Sister Wineapple slept almost continuously. There was little Eve could do, so she helped Polly Hurley with the dozen or so stressed and overworked people who came into the neat little room where she worked; mostly in silence either because few spoke English or because they appreciated the quiet of the sweet-smelling room. She came to know the restful routine of the 'guests', as they were referred to. In the extensive grounds of the villa there was a tennis-court with odd lengths of mosquito nets tied to string for a net. And there was a stable with four horses, not well groomed or particularly well fed, but at least they were well exercised.

On the fifth day, Eve, rising early as she always did, found a transformed Sister Wineapple sitting on the edge of her bed, her hair wet from shampooing, scooping some pills into her mouth. 'Hell's teeth, that feels better. D'you know if they still keep horses here? Do you ride?'

Eve was astonished at the overnight resurgence of spirit in

the American nurse. 'Four. I saw them yesterday. They're very popular with the other guests.'

'Guests? Is that what they call us in the nut-house in these egalitarian times? Fair enough! Do you feel like a ride out?'

The morning was bright, brighter than any morning Eve could remember since the summers of her childhood in rural Hampshire, but much hotter. They rode in silence for perhaps an hour. The terrain was rocky and dry, something Eve had never experienced before, but the American nurse, sitting straight in the saddle, went easily with every movement of the spare-fleshed animal between her hooked-up knees. Eve was reminded at once of Bar Barney, the close friend of her childhood and now her sister-in-law.

Bar was good with horses, born with them and sat on them before she could walk, as were all the Barneys, especially Duke. Duke Barney did not so much ride a horse as give the horse the privilege of carrying him. Even in his barefoot boyhood, Duke had driven a pony trap standing up, like a Roman charioteer.

Duke still strode disturbingly into her sleep. So too did David Hatton. The gypsy and the gentleman. Together they sounded like a *Red Letter* magazine romance, but they were the only two men who had interested her sufficiently to arouse her to passion. They had each given her an insight into her nature. She was aware now how strong sexual desire could be, and how it was dangerous to a young woman who did not want to become entangled in romantic love, or tied down in marriage. She had a life to live, a future to make. She knew how to take care of herself if only she wasn't caught unawares, as she had been by Duke and David.

Sometimes separately, sometimes confusingly together, she dreamed of the two men. Each was trying to force his rival away, although in the real world neither knew of the other's existence. In other dreams they appeared in some mysterious kind of collusion, not exactly against her but more in league with one another. It was this latter image that disturbed her most, seeming to make her heart thump and swell, making it difficult to breathe and waking her before dawn.

When at last the two women dismounted in the shade of one of the few tree-sized shrubs of the rocky region, Eve said, 'You ride well.'

'I was born with a horse between my legs, almost literally. My ma was out ride'n when I started to come on her, she gee-d the horse up and got back in town just as I was coming out. Well, that's how she tells it, and I can believe it. Toughest man in town is my ma.' She burst into sudden exuberant laughter, then just as suddenly burst into tears. Eve sat close and did nothing to try to stop the tears, remembering Aunt May's advice: 'Let it all go.'

Eventually Wineapple said, 'If you can't stand watching a strong woman cry . . . sorry.'

'It's OK. Better out than in, my Aunt May would have said.'

'Have you got the makings?'

Eve handed her a tin containing tobacco and some papers – the nearest thing to a packet of cigarettes that she had been able to acquire in Albacete.

'Guess that means I'm getting back to normal.'

'I'm glad. You looked pretty dreadful when I picked you up.'

'Did I? I guess I must have. They tried to get me to have a spell in France or England, but all I needed was to catch up on some sleep. How long have we been here?'

'This is the fifth day.'

'Phew! A real sleep bender. Time I got out of the booby-hatch and back to work. OK if we get going today?'

'According to my instructions, I'm not supposed to take you back for another two days yet.'

'I'm needed. Every time a nurse or doctor goes down, it puts extra pressure on the rest of the team. Then they go down. You know how it is.'

'Actually, I don't. I've only been in Spain a few days. Bringing you here was my first job.'

As she drew hungrily on her cigarette, the nurse looked long and hard at Eve. 'If I had any sense I'd tell you to go back. If you had any sense, you'd go. But I guess good sense has no more to do with you being here than it has with me. Why'd you come?'

For a few moments Eve watched the smoke of her cigarette curl upwards in the dry, warm air. Why? No simple answer. A longing to get away; to see for herself what her brother Ken had described in his letters home; to be Eve Anders. 'I saw a boatload of Basque refugee children arrive. I think I felt ashamed that the government didn't appear to care ... it was left to ordinary people to care.'

'There are a lot of politicals in the medical aid service, non-politicals too, religious types, Quakers, all sorts of reasons to be here.'

'I'm not that much of a political type, you don't have to be. Just a democratic type, I suppose.'

'Not political? I'd say taking the law into your own hands when you believe in something is quite political enough for some folks.'

'I mean, I'm not an anarchist or anything. There's a woman here who is.'

Sophie Wineapple raised her head with a smile. 'And she wasn't hiding a bomb under her cloak?'

It suddenly occurred to Eve Anders that, to all intents and purposes, she *was* a political type: she carried a Communist Party card and she was sponsored by communists. 'Can you tell me something about ... about what it's like here? Do you mind talking about it?'

'I don't mind, but I don't know about you. It ain't no picnic.'

'I never expected it would be.'

'It's the most important thing I've ever done. That's why I wouldn't let them send me away to rest up, thought I might not be able to get back into the country if I left. Of course I could have, but when a body flakes out your brain ain't exactly

34

razor-sharp.' She smiled, her hollow eyes filling out, the dark rings fading. 'But I'm OK now.'

'Do you want to go back to the house?'

'Not yet. I'll be glad to talk if you can take it. Talking's necessary to recovery, it's often the best thing a nurse can do for a patient, sit and listen. Ain't much time for that in a front-line hospital.'

'So talk to me. It's my assignment to stay with you, remember?'

'For me, volunteering's been a bit like when you're a kid, and you set out with your best friends, all excitement and expectations on some adventure, some kind'a expedition that you sure as hell know is going to change your life. Know what I mean? Then it starts to go wrong. One of the kids falls in the creek, another gets into poison ivy, it starts to storm and you can't remember why in hell's name you thought it was so important. Ever done a thing like that?'

'A lot of things have fallen apart in my life.'

'Hey, you talk like your own grandma. You can't be more than . . . what?'

'I'm twenty.'

'Twenty. It's fifteen years since that happened to me.'

'Are you saying that you made a mistake in coming here?'

'Never! What I'm saying is, I didn't know how to pace myself, none of us does. What are you supposed to do when you've been sewing men back together for two days without sleep and they still keep coming?'

'You keep working without sleep?'

'You do, but there's times when you shouldn't. Thing is, I always had real heavy menses, y'know? Doctors, being men, never think of a thing like that. It's OK, you can keep going if you get the squitters – and boy, do you get the squitters or do you get the squitters! Hard to keep going if you got women's problems. Seems as though you can't hardly think of anything except the cramps. Men don't want to know. Doctors especially.'

35

'You'd think they'd understand better than ordinary men.'

'Who said doctors aren't ordinary men? They're often the worst, they get to see women's insides and they don't like what they see. Don't think I'm snivelling, just stating facts. Three months now, my cycle's been all to pot. Wasn't till I crashed in the theatre that I realized how bad things had got. God, I felt a failure, an absolute and utter failure. There's all these lads – legs off, ears shot away, bits of shell in them – and here's Sister Wineapple dropping in a heap on the floor and being sent to the booby-hatch because of belly cramps and loss of sleep.' Her mood changed in a second and she started to cry with long wrenching sobs and streams of tears.

Eve was non-plussed. Had her companion been Bar Barney or Kate Roles, her friends from childhood, she would have known how to offer comfort, but Sister Wineapple was an older woman, a tough-talking American, so she hesitated before putting her arm about the woman's shaking shoulders.

When at last the tears subsided, Eve said, 'I think we should go back to the house, and you should get some rest.' Sophie Wineapple nodded agreement, and they made their way back to the villa.

While Eve was kneeling down helping to unlace her charge's heavy shoes, Sophie Wineapple touched Eve's cheek. 'Hey,' she said, 'you're a real pal. If I said anything to put you off, take no notice. It's the right thing to do, you know, absolutely the right thing. There's no way those sons a' bitches are going to take back the freedom from these great people.' She made a fist. '¡No pasarán! You know that? "They shall not pass".' She sank back on to her bed.

'I know, and I'll do my best to see that they don't if you'll just get some rest.'

'OK, but sit and talk for a bit, d'you mind? It felt real good out there, you'd make a good psychiatric doctor. What are you when you aren't sitting nurses who've gone a bit nutty?'

So, what or who was Eve Anders? She was none of the things she used to be when she was Louise Vera Wilmott. She wasn't the schoolgirl who still smarted from not being able to continue at the grammar school. She wasn't the factory girl who had spent half her spare time at night-school and the other half in glamorous home-made dresses dancing her feet off. She was no longer Lu Wilmott, a poor kid from the back-streets of Portsmouth whose dreams could never be realized while her old class weighed down her ambitions. 'You aren't nutty. I'm a lorry-driver. I hope when I get to Albacete they'll give me an ambulance to drive.'

'Girl truck-drivers are rare as hen's teeth; I don't think I've met more 'n two. One especially, Eve, yeah, Eve Hutchins, an American, little person, raised hell when they said she couldn't enlist, they had to give in in the end, she shamed them for being chauvinists so she reckoned. Remember her if anyone tries to tell you it can't be done.'

'OK, I will.'

Without preamble, Sister Wineapple launched into a long monologue. 'I guess the last straw was on the day before you brought me here. Every day for weeks now, the hospital court-yard and all the corridors have been filled with the dead and dying. The ambulances can't even get near to unload. Everywhere we go we have to step over bodies. Some of the wounds are terrible but they have to wait because there's always others who are worse. I hadn't slept for days, just snatches here and there – how could you when you had to step over all those injuries? If anyone spoke to me, I felt like killing them. When I fell down in the theatre, the doctor ordered me to get some sleep.' She paused, and smiled wryly, her mind obviously else-where. 'There's a more equal relationship between us medics here, but I was trained to obey God when he ordered, it's not a thing you can untrain. So I went to the little room where the nurses used to flop down but both beds were occupied . . . severe head injury . . . awful bad one . . . brains oozing out, y' know, big pool of blood on the floor. The man in the other bed was dead, stomach shot to pieces. I had him removed, turned the mattress over and went out like a light. I couldn't have slept for long – there was a raid or shelling or something, I don't know, it gets so that you only notice when the walls shake – and I realized the boy in the next bed was dead, nothing I could do, so I left him, turned over and went back to sleep, for about an hour, I think, maybe more, I don't know, except that when somebody came and made me get up because they wanted a bed for a patient, I thought I should have screamed and never stopped. But of course I didn't, did I, too well trained for any show of emotion. So I splashed my face and went back into the theatre. I guess I must 'a looked a sight, shaking like I had the DTs or something, eyes and nose running like nobody's business – a real mad-woman scene, I guess. I don't really know. Somebody gave me a couple 'a pills, acted like a Mickey Finn. Last clear memory until you came for me.' She sighed heavily and smiled. 'Sounds like a mad-house, it's not really. It just don't do to abuse yourself. There's nearly always a food shortage, well that's OK, but shortage of sleep? That'll do for you in the end.'

'Maybe that's what you should be doing now.'

'I don't think so. I feel really quite good now. Sorry if I've been mingy to you, you just new here and all, but you've done a real job on me, better'n a psychiatrist's couch, off-loading on to somebody who don't have a stake in keeping you on your feet. Hope you don't ever need the same favour from me, but I'll be right here for you if you do, remember that.'

'Thanks.'

'Promise?'

The following day Eve returned a fresh and competent theatre sister to her hospital and picked up a message with new orders, which were to take the van to a transport depot and get a lift in a truck on the way south to the Auto-Parc at Albacete.

Sophie Wineapple said a formal thanks and, as Eve was leaving, added, '*Feixisme ¡No!* Stick to the beans.' *Feixisme ¡No!* was the anti-fascist slogan daubed everywhere in Barcelona.

*   *   *

Although Helan Alexander had not said so, she must have thought Eve competent, for her next assignment was to deliver a Bedford ambulance.

'The Bedfords are going up to El Goloso. D'you know El Goloso?' Alexander asked Eve when she reported to her.

'Near Madrid?'

'Yeah, near the Guadarrama mountains.'

The Guadarramas. Madrid. Madrid was now the front line.

The hospital trucks were for El Goloso. The rest of the convoy consisted of supply trucks and a personnel carrier with some soldiers in uniform, probably not regulars but older than those who had travelled with Eve to Albacete. These men wore bandoliers and carried their rifles with ease. The convoy leader was Captain Benito Delgado, a Spanish officer of the Republican army, a dark and handsome man who wore his cap at a jaunty angle. Another Spaniard and an Australian were also ambulance-drivers. Among the various medicos travelling to Madrid were Smart and Haskell, the nurses who had shared Eve's dormitory in the Starlight Hotel.

Captain Delgado said that the hospital trucks should be at the middle of the convoy, keeping within sight of one another. 'If there is sniping or shelling, you will stop and take cover only when ordered.' It seemed to Eve that he was speaking directly to her.

Nurse Haskell smiled at Eve and said quietly, 'He probably thinks women shouldn't be allowed loose with a precious hospital truck.'

Grinning, the Australian, who had overheard the comment, said, 'He don't mean noth'n by it, I know him. Anarchists can be a bit set in the old ways when it comes to the womenfolk, but he's a decent fella.' He gave Eve a hearty handshake. 'His name's Delgado, mine's Clive Lavender. They call me Ozz. You'll never guess why.'

Eve laughed and thanked the big, handsome Australian. 'Anders. Eve Anders.'

'OK, Andy, I'll be right behind you.'

It was another beautiful, cloudless day as the convoy rolled out of the Albacete Auto-Parc depot. Smart and Haskell travelled with Eve, a French doctor rode with the captain, and an untrained orderly and two more nurses rode with the Australian.

Smart and Haskell spent the first hour writing letters, enabling Eve to concentrate on keeping the correct distance from the ambulance ahead. Apart from a donkey and cart in the middle of the road, and a little girl with two frisky goats, the road was empty. Eve was able to enjoy the experience of seeing every-thing from a much higher vantage point than she had in the lorry. 'What are those trees? We passed a whole orchard of them back there, they seemed to be growing on rocks and sand.'

'Olives. You call them groves, not orchards. This is oil country, same as Texas.'

'Oh, I always expected olive trees would be enormous, like oaks. They sound so grand and important in the Bible.'

There was a moment of the kind of silence that can almost be felt, then Haskell said, 'How long have you been out here?'

'I'm pretty new – a couple of weeks.'

'Hey, Smarty, d'you hear that? This girl's straight from home and we've entrusted life and limb to her.'

'She seems a better bet than some I could remind you of. You came down by train?'

'I drove down.'

Haskell said, 'Brilliant railway system.'

'It'd be even better if the two unions were on better terms,' Smart replied.

'That'll never happen. The UGT and the CNT hate one another's guts. Red is red and black is black and never the twain, etcetera, etcetera.'

'Give it time, give it time.'

Eve didn't understand this exchange but she had begun to realize that the civil war was more complicated than she had supposed.

'You must have impressed Alex for her to have trusted you

with one of these treasures.' Haskell indicated the converted Bedford.

'She did a test run with me. We went miles and miles on little tracks.'

Smart laughed. 'Alex would. She's not as dotty as you'd think.'

'Is she dotty?'

'Unpredictable.'

'How's your Spanish, Anders?' Haskell asked.

'I've been learning it from a book, and I've picked up a smattering.'

Smart said, 'I think we owe it to the comrades to learn as much Spanish as we can, and about their new social order.'

'Don't sound so smug, Smarty, not everybody's got an ear for it like you.'

'It's important to know they've dropped *Don* and *Señor* in favour of Comrade or informal names.'

'Not everywhere, not everywhere. Trouble is,' Haskell went on, 'there's Spanish and there's Spanish. Some find Catalan is as difficult as Russian, and nobody understands Basque, not even other Spaniards.'

They drifted in and out of conversations. Haskell, who appeared to have a sixth sense for hazards, looked up from time to time: '*burro* – donkey', '*camion* – truck', and once, pointing to a picturesque castle in the distance, 'See? *Un castillo.*'

Eve replied, 'Yes, "castles in Spain".'

'Too damned many,' commented Smart. 'It's no wonder the peasants had had enough of the old system.'

'And knowing human nature, not so surprising Franco's determined to take them all back.'

'I have a brother out here. I keep wondering whether I might come across him.'

'So is Smarty's aunt, isn't she, Smarty?' Haskell seemed to find this quite funny, but Smart didn't rise to the bait. 'Oh, Smarty darling, don't get so po-faced over it, nobody can help their relations.'

'Just drop it!'

'I know you don't agree, but it's best to have these things out in the open.'

'You have anything you like in the open. Now shut up!'

Haskell did shut up, but one could have cut the atmosphere with a knife. Eve had worked in the close company of women for long enough to recognize that this was an old argument and that Haskell was using her to score points.

After about ten minutes had elapsed, Haskell shoved a piece of paper in front of Eve: 'On the side of the Nationalists!'

The silence was resumed until Smart said, 'You can be such a bitch, Rene.'

Haskell put an arm about Smart, who didn't brush her off. 'I know, darling, but better in the open. Look, Anders isn't shocked to death that your Aunt Flo thinks the sun shines out of Franco's arse.'

'And so coarse. Florence is not my aunt, as you very well know.'

'Good as, darling.'

'Look,' Eve said, 'could you both just shut up for a bit? I've never driven in a proper convoy before.' She sensed rather than saw the moue they made at one another, but they did shut up.

On the outskirts of a small village, the commander dropped the leading vehicle to a crawl and signalled them to slow down.

'More good old razzmatazz,' Haskell said.

'Don't pretend the old ennui, darling,' Smart said without rancour. 'You make a four-course dinner of it.'

Villagers came out of their homes and waved enthusiastically. In her wing-mirror Eve saw the Australian leaning out, trying to shake every hand that reached up to his. Still a bit wary of the huge Bedford, she hardly dared allow it to move ahead when people gathered round and offered their hands. Except for the distant shelling when she was out with Alexander, she had hardly been aware of the war, yet as she watched the commander and the Australian leaning out and touching every hand offered, she felt that she was taking part in a kind of triumphal parade. 'Is it always like this?'

Smart replied, 'A lot of the time. Poor sods, had centuries under the old system, not much better than slaves. These people aren't going back.'

Haskell said, 'Germany can send all the bombers it likes, the spirit of our comrades will keep them going. Right is on the side of the Republic, traa-raa!'

The convoy rolled into El Goloso without mishap. The two nurses took their bags and led the way into the hospital laughing and chatting, reminding Eve of days when she and her friends at work had forgotten any earlier friction as soon as they were free of their close confinement.

The hospital was alive with activity: busy people hurried to and fro carrying boxes, packets, drums, parcels, awkward and unwieldy cots, mattresses, straw-filled palliasses and kitchen equipment.

Tall and bearded, the head of the medical service greeted them briefly, shuffling their documents about. He signed some, then handed them back. 'Sorry, but there is a change to whatever orders you have. You've been seconded to us for a few days while we move in, then I think you're to collect vehicles from Madrid. A patrol truck and guards will travel with you.'

Ozz nodded. 'OK, doc, suits me.'

'Mrs Alexander wants you to telephone her, Miss Anders. Tell her we're grateful for letting us have a couple o' extra hands. Can I leave you to it? We're awfu' busy just now.' He banged on a wooden partition and a nurse popped her head round the door. 'Ah, nurse, find a wee corner for the young lady, will you?'

Eve followed the nurse, who turned out to be French, to a room full of packing cases with a couple of mattresses propped up on end. Leaving her bag, she was taken to where she and Ozz would help the nurses with the kitting-out of the Bedfords.

Ozz said, 'I wouldn't mind getting a chance to drive one of these to the front.'

'Is that where they are going?'

'It's what they are, mobile field-hospitals.'

'Where do you think they'll go?'

'La Granja, so I heard. Our side are launching an offensive.'

Ozz turned out to be a really good companion. He had a sixth sense about where everything might be found, and the smile on his face seemed to suggest that he found everything faintly entertaining. 'If you need the little girls' place, it's down along the hall there. When you come out, go down that corridor and I reckon you'll come to some kind of eating place. I'll be there. It won't be flash, but they'll feed us poor travellers.'

They were given bread, bully beef and some black tea. After they had eaten, they sat companionably on a couple of boxes. Eve liked Ozz, liked his easy-going manner, his open, rugged features, his broad brow made broader by hair clipped short above his ears and standing up in a high, unruly mop. It was his hair that gave the impression that he was a bit of a comic, but his deep-set eyes were intelligent and shrewd.

'Not often you see a woman driver. How long you been at the depot?'

'I'm pretty new. This is my first proper assignment.'

'That so? Y' done well, Andy. Nice roads, but driving on the wrong side can be a real pig when you're not used to it. Yeah, y' done well.'

She had done better than well. If she'd been a man, she bet he wouldn't have given her a pat on the head. 'It was nice driving through those villages. What a welcome!'

He nodded. 'A line of trucks always looks as though something's happening. I reckon it must be hell for them; it would be for me. The set-up here was bloody medieval before the Republic. I'd cheer too, whoever came to help me hang on to my nice new democracy.' He paused. 'D'you mind if I ask you something sort of personal?'

'That depends.'

'Why does a girl want to come out here and drive trucks?'

'Same reason you did, I imagine.'

'To run in the Olympics?'

'I thought I could do something useful. What d'you mean about the Olympics?'

'I'm a bit of a runner.' He raced two fingers across his knee. 'Y' know? Hundred yards sprint, hurdles. I was at the games.'

'In Berlin?'

'No, not them. The real ones, the games in Barcelona, the People's Games. You never heard about it?' Eve shook her head. 'They were held in Barcelona in the true Olympic spirit, not like that Berlin circus.' He laughed. 'All the good guys came to Barcelona,' he said. 'Ever hear of Sam Aarons?'

'I may have, my brothers were always talking about sport.'

'He's a good Aussie athlete. He ran at the People's Games, and stayed on too. I meet up with him sometimes. This is a place where you keep meeting up with the same people.'

'I hope so. My brother Ken is here.'

'Is that so? Which outfit is he with?'

'Fifteenth Brigade.'

'The British Battalion?'

'That's right.'

'They did good in Jarama, the Fifteenth.'

'Did they? I haven't heard from him in weeks.'

Ozz Lavender noticed the faintly sad smile that played about the lips of his beautiful comrade. Here, in this place where they were all strangers, no matter the extent of the camaraderie, or the emotions that escaped through the eyes, it didn't do to intrude.

Eve shrugged away her worry about Ken. 'Isn't it time we started work again, Ozz?'

She stubbed out her cigarette under her heavy shoe. At once Ozz picked it up. 'Smoking a whole ciggie, stomping it out, says "rookie". Here, keep it in an empty matchbox. You'll be glad when there's no ciggies for love or money.'

Eve couldn't imagine wanting a cigarette enough to be reduced to smoking dog-ends like a down-and-out.

That night Eve fell into the deep sleep of physical and mental exhaustion and awoke next morning refreshed and full of energy for a day of helping in the preparation of the field-hospital. Aware that Ken was most likely somewhere out there in the field of battle, she didn't allow herself to think too much about the scores of rolled-up stretchers and the hundreds of boxes stencilled: 'Sterile field-dressings. DO NOT BREAK OPEN UNTIL NEEDED FOR IMMEDIATE USE.'

Chapter Four

Lieutenant Kenneth Wilmott, International Brigader of the 15th Brigade, British Battalion, was moving over the hilly countryside towards Villanueva de la Cañada. He was accompanied by 50,000 men. This was the number committed by the Republic to prevent the fascists from taking Madrid. The offensive was on a small front and as the 50,000 progressed towards the new battle front, they fouled the very atmosphere in which they moved. Dust flew up at every step, encrusting their profusely sweating bodies. There was precious little water to drink, certainly none at all to wash in. It was not surprising that flies were everywhere.

Spanish soldiers from the south, many of whom worked in the vineyards and vegetable fields, were accustomed to working under the sun, but to the men of the 15th Brigade it was hot beyond anything they had ever thought possible. Their thirst was almost unbearable.

As they progressed slowly towards the battle, with shells from enemy guns falling all around them, Vallee, a Welsh sergeant of the 15th Brigade, who had been with Ken Wilmott since they had had their Jarama battle-wounds treated at La Pasionaria hospital, shouted, 'You know, boy, they say a pebble is the thing. You suck it like a boi-eld sweet.'

Ken Wilmott shouted over his shoulder to the NCO, whom he had grown to like for his humour and his generous nature, and to admire for his courage and intelligence, 'I've been sucking a bloody button the last half-hour, and I can't spit sixpence. Makes me think about water, buckets and buckets of it.' Here, in the sweltering mid-summer heat, there was none. If they weren't all to die of thirst they needed to take the fortified village. The young lieutenant couldn't imagine how they would keep going in the dreadful heat without water. 'If you can find a pebble that hasn't been peed or shat on, then help yourself, Vallee old son.'

Sergeant Vallee suddenly shouted, 'Bloody hell! Will you look at that, boy.'

Suddenly, as though by magic, a refugee family appeared on the battle field, their meagre belongings piled on to a cart drawn by two horses with rags binding their eyes. Atop their possessions were seated two small children and an ancient couple. A youth and a woman were hanging on like grim death to one horse, while a man and a girl tried to control the other. The grand-mother told her beads as she bent protectively over a baby, and the grandfather protected a couple of hens in a wicker cage without the aid of a rosary.

The little group halted. The soldiers shouted at them to get off the road. Go away. Get going, anywhere but here. The horses bucked and shied at every shell which made the exchange with the soldiers very difficult. Ken Wilmott patted the rump of one of the horses and gave the grandmother a friendly smile which she did not receive at all well. Vallee fared better with her. He produced three glacier mints from somewhere, one each for the children and one for the grumpy old lady. With forceful gesticulations the soldiers tried to tell the family that there was a battle going on.

'Hell's bells, Pedro, they know that. Let's get them off the road.' (Vallee, who called all Spanish soldiers Pedro, was in turn called Blanco which, because Vallee had the blackest of black skins, the Pedros thought was a very original and hilarious idea. 'I been called worse than that, boy. I been called a Taffy before now.')

Once the family had been moved away from the falling shells, the little group which had dealt with them turned its attention back to the objective of cutting off Villanueva de la Cañada where a fascist resistance force was holding fortified positions. As the Republican troops advanced they were subjected to continual machine-gun fire. Ken Wilmott, making his way a little ahead of his friend, called back, 'Suck a pebble you said, didn't you? And you had glacier mints all the time.'

'I was keeping them as a surprise. For after we have taken this place.'

Lieutenant Wilmott was about to reply when his left hand was knocked away from his rifle. He felt nothing, but from his previous experience he knew that he had been hit. Blood ran down his arm.

Crouching, Vallee ran forward. 'You been 'it, boy.'

'I know that, you dozy Welshman.'

Vallee pulled a dressing from his pouch and ripped it open with his teeth. Already flies were buzzing at the scent of blood.

As Vallee bound the wound, he read aloud from the packet, '"Sterile field-dressings. DO NOT BREAK OPEN UNTIL NEEDED FOR IMMEDIATE USE." Thank the Lord it was an Englishman needed this, boy. If it had been one of the Pedros, they wouldn't have known about that. Might have been ripping dressings open any old time.' He grinned, his large mouth pulling back over his large teeth.

Vallee was the first black man Ken had ever known, and he could still be surprised by the pinkness inside his friend's mouth and on the palms of his hands and soles of his feet. In their weeks together they had become good friends. They had promised one another that once the Republic had ousted the insurgents, the two of them would 'Go and have a dekko' at Africa. 'Land of my Fathers, you see, boy,' Vallee would say, demonstrating great Welshness in his vowels.

The wound dressed, they resumed their previous positions in the advancing line. Keeping his mind on the cover ahead, Ken supported his courage by shouting inconsequential banter at Vallee. 'What else . . . ?' A spray of machine-gun bullets ricocheted around them, cutting off sound.

Vallee, a few yards to the Lieutenant's rear, shouted, 'What else what?'

'What else you got stowed away, like the mints? A nice cold beer? How about it, old son?'

Ken Wilmott couldn't hear Vallee's reply in another hail of machine-gun bullets and artillery shells exploding very close to their positions. He looked back and saw Vallee half-concealed behind a little rise of rock. 'You all right, Vallee?'

Vallee did not reply.

When Ken Wilmott crawled back to his friend, he found the black Welshman face down in a pool of blood. He turned him over. The bullet must have gone straight into his mouth and out of the back of his neck. Already the flies were black swarms in his mouth, his ears and along the rims of his large open eyes. Wilmott closed the sergeant's eyes and tried to pull his tin hat over them, but in the urgency of battle there was no time for the dead. 'Sorry, old son, it's the best I can do.'

By now the pocket of Nationalists in Villanueva de la Cañada were within firing range, but the fascists had the advantage of machine-guns. To Ken Wilmott, as he lay in a ditch, just one in a line of men with rifles, the day seemed endless. Perhaps it was the loss of blood, perhaps it was the intense heat, or the raging thirst, but the battle took on a strange air of unreality. It was as though he was in a picture house watching a film, urging on the good guys. Then, quite suddenly, as dusk was falling, the firing petered out.

Something was happening in the village.

The brigade held their breath as a group of women and children moved towards them, shuffling along the road in close formation. Between the two lines of fire they came slowly forward, huddled, crouching, the kids wide-eyed and clinging, all of them obviously scared to death. In any number of different languages, the men of the brigade started to shout at them to move, to hurry, to get away, to get off the road. But still the group shuffled slowly forward.

Ken Wilmott raised his head and was about to rush forward to urge them on when, like others in the advance line of the brigade, he saw that the tight formation and the shuffling progress was because they were being used as a human shield, urged on by a group of Nationalist troops with bayonets fixed.

Both sides fired at once. Not all the women and children dropped to the ground of their own volition.

Perhaps the field-dressing acted as a target for a Nationalist sniper, or maybe it was coincidental, but the second wound Lieutenant Wilmott of the 15th Brigade received that day was hardly a couple of inches from the first. It didn't take him long to realize that he was out of this particular battle, so he reported to his leader who ordered him to make for the ambulances. He joined other walking wounded, had his arm looked at and dressed by an American nurse, and was pointed in the direction of an ambulance taking less seriously injured men to a hospital in Madrid.

At that moment Ken didn't care where he was taken; it was enough for now that he had been given a swig of water. It was warm, but it was water. Suddenly he remembered the leaking tap at home that had been his job to fix, but which in his excitement to leave he had forgotten. Had Ray fixed it? In his next letter he would tell Ray he was sorry he hadn't done the washer. He could hardly bear the thought of two years of water dripping away into the sink, down the drain, through the sewers and out into the Solent. He hoped Ray had fixed it. He vowed at that moment that he would never again waste a single drop of water.

It was dawn by the time Ken Wilmott's wound had been cleaned and strapped. He was right-handed, so he could still manage a rifle and not be away from his men for very long. As on the previous occasion when he had ended up in hospital, his mind became infested with little memories of his day-to-day life at home, the time after his parents had died and the three children had held on to the home, somehow remaining a family of sorts, and pooling their three wage-packets, of which only Ray's contained anything much. One of his chores had been to fetch and carry the bag-wash. Nobody knew how much he had hated that job, it was women's work, and he would do it only if the bag of clothes was put inside a potato sack.

As he looked now for somewhere to wash himself and his shirt, he thought about how things had changed. For over two years he had been doing his own washing, rubbing soap in with his knuckles, when there was any soap, sometimes sluicing his clothes in a stream, or a trough, and on occasions, as when he had worked his way down through France, washing out the field dirt in some commemorative stone bowl or fountain.

Having cleaned himself as well as he could with one arm, he sat outside on the hospital steps and savoured the only bit of the day when the heat was bearable, wondering briefly where Vallee's body would be buried. If the village had been taken by his own side, then he might be buried in a communal grave. It was possible that he was still there where he had fallen, the flies at work on him, as also might be the women and children who had been caught between the two sides as they fired. There, on the steps of the hospital, not far from the old gates of the city, for the first time since he had joined the Internationals, the young soldier – who had been catapulted into the rank of lieutenant at the battle of Jarama because he was next in line – wondered how Spain could possibly survive as one nation. Perhaps, like Ireland, they would have to partition the country: monarchy and Church ruling one part, Republic and people the other.

It was only when he was sorting through his haversack that he remembered the letter. Mail had been handed out almost at the same time as orders were given for the advance on Villanueva de la Cañada. The letter was from his sister. He smoothed it out and read: '*Salud!* Kenny. By the time that you receive this I too shall be in Spain.'

He read the sentence again.

I have offered myself as a driver. You remember Dad's friend Sidney Anderson? He has fixed me up with the necessary papers to get me into the Republic, which means that I have become a card-carrying communist. It is a complicated story, which with any luck I may be able to tell you, but for now suffice to say, not only have I left home, I have also left my old self there and from here on I function as someone new. I am determined to make something of myself and the first step is to leave behind all preconceptions and stereotypes that people have about the kind of people we come from. I am no longer a working-class girl. I am in the process of making myself classless.

I am now me, one Miss Eve Anders. That is who I am. I am a twenty-year-old truck driver who has volunteered to work to help keep Spain's democratically elected government in power. That is all that I am. I have no past which means that no one can enter there and classify me, by which I mean classify as in to see me by class and not by ability and character. My papers say that I am Eve Anders, niece of Sidney Anderson. How did I arrive at that name? At first I was to be Elvi Anders (LV from my old initials, see?). Then I tried E. V. Anders and so became Eve. Are you shocked? Probably not, because I believe that you may have had something similar in mind when you left home. You wanted to know what was out there. Since I came here, you have become 'My brother in the 15th Brigade of the International Brigade'. The IBs (or do you say brigaders?) do seem to be well thought of.

The greatest hurdle was to try to make Ray see that it was not that I was ashamed of what we were – are, and inside ourselves will always be – but that this bit of my life was over. My love for my two brothers will never diminish. I think that he did not entirely understand, but what with him now having Bar in his life and the baby coming, he was able to let me go. With his wife much of an age with me, how could he not admit that I was no longer his little sister, no longer the girl he had protected and provided for for so long, but that I had become a woman capable of going it alone.

I am not asking your blessing, Kenny, as I might once have done, feeling that I should explain and placate. You might be surprised to hear that I ever did that, but I did. For years I cleaned the old gas cooker and the lavs on Sunday morning in the hope that you and Ray wouldn't think I spent too much time at night-school or with my head in a book. If I have grown to be more forthright and independent than all the girls I went to school with ('with whom I went to school' as we both know from our years at Lampeter C of E, that most exclusive school for the children of the elite of the Pompey back-streets), then it is quite likely because I was brought up by a mother who had no husband to speak of, and by two brothers who had the vision to see a world beyond the end of Lampeter Street.

Please write to me, Ken. To Eve Anders, c/o Auto-Parc, Albacete, which is, of course, your own address. Odd thing that. I shall try to follow closely the fortunes of the 15th Brigade, so that if and when my orders take me anywhere near, then I shall search you out. Much love, Kenny. *¡Hasta la vista!*

Chapter Five

Eve Anders and Ozz Lavender were three days at the El Goloso hospital before they moved on. Now driving flat-bed supply trucks back to the depot for overhaul, they were guarded by the same small personnel carrier and some of the men who had accompanied them from Albacete. Armed guards. This time the leader was a short, dark Spaniard. He made a thumbs-up and Ozz signalled that the rest were ready. 'OK, chief, let wagons roll. You wan'a go next, Andy? I'll bring up the rear.'

Their journey took them back in the direction from which they had come, then towards the Sierra de Alcaraz to the south-west. They drove until evening when they reached a small town and followed the lead truck into the back of a *hostal* where Eve gladly climbed out of her cab to flex her aching knees.

Ozz said, 'Looks OK. Come on, follow the boys.'

Without ceremony their uniformed companions went inside. 'It looks like a regular hotel. What do we do about paying?'

'Leave it to our *compadres*, they know how it works. I guess they've stopped here before. There's petrol pumps across the road, we need to fill up.' He lit the stub of a cigarette and stood looking up at the yellow, sandy walls of the building.

An elderly woman in black appeared, bobbing her head and holding her palms apart in a gesture of welcome. The woman directed them to a back room where their Spanish companions were already removing their jackets and stretching their arms. Sharing with them was something Eve had not anticipated, but she placed her canvas bag against the wall, opened it and fetched out a comb and face-cloth which she held up to the woman, saying hesitantly, '*Lavar . . . por favor?*'

The woman smiled and indicated for Eve to pick up her bag

and follow her. Up two flights of narrow stairs Eve found herself in a narrow room with a narrow window and a narrow bed. The woman took her bag, deposited it on a cane chair and pointed to a jug and basin. Having taken a look into a narrow cupboard, which was empty, she smiled and left.

They had a satisfying meal of stew in which the beans overwhelmed the meat. The soldiers talked all through the meal, laughing with one another and with various people who came to lean against the door. Sometimes they engaged in a kind of quick-fire discussion which was entirely beyond Eve's understanding. Ozz interpreted, and it appeared that the conversation was not very different from what it would have been anywhere. Anything new? Where have you come from? How were the roads? Sierra de Alcaraz? You should take this road, not that, too many bends. No, I say they should keep to the new road.

The light went and no sooner were Eve's shoes and jacket off and her legs stretched out gratefully on the hard little mattress than she fell into a deep sleep. Before dawn she was woken by men's voices in the yard. The Spanish driver was already under the bonnet of his vehicle, topping up the radiator. She made her bed, took away her washing water and refilled the jug. They left the hotel with exchanges of salutes, and then drove out of the town in the first light of morning.

They stopped on a high point from where it was possible to see across an arid-looking plain to an even higher point.

Ozz gestured. 'The Sierra de Alcaraz.'

To Eve, the sight was breathtaking. The English landscape she was used to bore no comparison to the Alcaraz valley which appeared vast and infertile. But the barrenness was illusion, for the entire vista, including the slopes of the mountains, was practically one huge olive grove. A mule-cart trailed dust as it followed a narrow meandering road. The wider highway took a more direct route across the flat plain and then disappeared behind a wood of trees that were darker and much taller than the olives – spruce or pine perhaps. Except for these roadways, none of the land was left uncultivated.

This journey – Albacete to El Goloso to Ayna in the Sierra de Alcaraz – gave Eve Anders the confidence she needed. She was now sure that she could drive anything, anywhere. She had covered hundreds of kilometres, but where was the war? She had transported supplies and people, she had seen ravaged towns and she had heard, in the distance, the sound of shelling, but she fretted to be at the front. Whatever Helan Alexander had said about the importance of what she had been doing until now, it was not the kind of war work she had envisaged doing when she volunteered. There were women on the front line, nurses picking up the pieces and putting men back together again, there were ammunition lorries and ambulances to be driven. The extraordinary beauty of the Sierra de Alcaraz was well and good, and the quaintness of meandering mule-carts stirred emotions and gave an impression of being at one with the people, but they had nothing to do with the real events that were going on without her.

Another dawn. Another village. Eve was the first of their little group to be up and about. Dolores, a nurse, the daughter of the proprietors of the little *hostal* in which they had spent the night, had asked for a lift back to her medical unit. She had shared her narrow bed with Eve, sleeping one at each end. Eve looked forward to her company and had gone down early to clear any debris from the passenger seat. Dolores was neat as could be, with blue-black hair strained back into a shining bun, and Eve would have been ashamed to have offered her less than a spick-and-span cab. She checked the oil, it was low, topped up the radiator and refilled the jerry-can, wiped the tacky grime from the big steering wheel and tucked a wet face-flannel in a sponge-bag where she could reach it. She knew from experience that it would neither cool nor refresh once the heat of the roads started to rise and heat up the cab, but the moisture gave the impression that it did.

It was still hardly light when she had finished her check. The Spanish guard came down, his boots unlaced, wearing only his khaki trousers, the webbing braces hitched over his shoulders. He saluted, then swung round and slapped his forehead with the flat of his hand. In gestured English he apologized for not wearing a shirt.

'It's OK. I don't mind. I have brothers . . . *hermano* . . . two brothers.' She held up two fingers.

'I also. Antonio. Julian.' He gestured a query.

'Ralph. Kenneth.' She gestured, 'Bigger . . . older than me.'

He gestured: Antonio a bit taller than himself, Julian very tall, indicating with flicks of his bunched fingers that his brothers were eighteen and twenty. He grinned, seemingly as pleased as she at this exchange, then patted his own head, spreading his knees, making himself even shorter. 'Florentîn.'

It was a joke, for the name was so unsuited to such a squat and burly man, but it was also a breakthrough. Throughout the journey she had noticed him watching her manoeuvres with the flat-bed lorry very critically, and assumed that he disapproved of a woman doing a man's job. She had thought for some time that there were far too many barriers that kept ordinary people apart, and it was true.

She fetched water and topped up the radiator of his personnel-carrier, then washed the layer of insects and dust from the windscreen, while he removed the plugs and cleaned them.

Ozz came out to check his own lorry, so that by the time the smell of beans and chilli wafted across to them, the sky had lightened. Florentîn, who, Eve suspected, was probably the family clown, bent his knees and, twirling an imaginary cane, offered her his arm. He shuffled along with his feet at ten-to-two. 'Charlie Chaplin!' He made a sweeping bow. 'Dietrich.'

Ozz, who was following, wiping black greasy hands on a rag, said, 'Too right, Florrie! Marlene, but younger.' There were not making a pass, there was nothing to disturb Eve's feeling of security that had grown steadily. Growing up as she had in a military and naval town, she had developed a sixth sense about men, and she trusted these two completely.

Eve felt good. It was a beautiful morning and she was involved in something momentous. She and Ozz shared a cigarette while Florentîn and his men drove across the road to the petrol pump. Children who had gathered to wait for the school bus turned their attention to the soldiers and the lorry. All were black-haired and brown-eyed in this small village.

'What is it about Spanish children, aren't they beautiful?'

'Real little charmers.'

'And the young women, I don't think I've ever seen so many really lovely young women.'

'It don't last. They marry too young, have too many kids, work too hard.'

Eve mimicked his accent. 'Well ain't that the truth the world over.'

'So you ain't all goody-goody then, Andy?'

'I ain't goody-goody at all, Ozz. I have a bland face that tells lies. Don't be fooled by it.'

'You got Florrie going all right. He thinks you're the cat's whiskas.'

'We had a long talk. He has two brothers. I have two brothers. It took us ten minutes to exchange that bit of information.'

Ozz, as usual, filled waiting time making new smokes from old. Eve watched the guards teasing the children. A youth standing in a cart drawn by a blunt-faced mule flicked it up to the little shed which was hung about with an odd assortment of bald tyres. The mule drank from a bucket of water, a facility for filling radiators. Several of the smaller children went to pet the mule. A woman carrying a large basket sauntered along the road and called something to the young mule-driver. He frowned. Was she his mother wanting him to do something for her? Something too demeaning for him, such as giving her a lift into town?

The little girls' dresses, although clean, were unironed, threadbare and patched. Eve had gone to school like that for years, unaware that there was any other kind of school clothes. She had seldom actually been ragged, and never naked underneath as some of her classmates had been, but her skirts were made from remnants and the best bits of other skirts. That alone was reason enough for any girl with spirit and a liking for nice things to want to escape the drab meanness of that kind of life. And that, too, was one of the reasons why she had become Eve Anders, a free and independent woman. Now that she had lived in Spain, she was sure she could never go back and live under the dingy, dreary skies of England. She would stay here, where the sun shone, where bare-arsed children were not chilled to the marrow. She pinched out the cigarette and added it to Ozz's cache.

It must have been the sound of the tractor labouring in a field on the other side of the hedge that hid the sound of the aeroplanes.

Suddenly, air was sucked up around them. Without warning there was a devastating explosion. Eve's ear-drums hurt, yet she automatically turned towards the direction of the violence. Then, as the blast struck, she was knocked back into the open door of Ozz's lorry, hitting her spine on something hard. Unbelievable things were in flight. A mule's head. A basket. A child. She heard a bellow, but it was cut short when the little petrol station went up in a great sheet of flame. She got to her feet seconds before Ozz. The fierceness of the blazing petrol and oil made it impossible to get anywhere near the centre of the chaos. People came running from God knew where. She saw Dolores, still not in uniform, carrying a khaki haversack imprinted with a red cross which she unbuckled as she ran.

For a brief second Eve caught sight of Florentîn. The little clown who had been Charlie Chaplin was hanging, like a mangled scarecrow, in the fiercely burning debris of his vehicle, then in a second, as the petrol tank exploded, he was gone. There was no sign of the other guards. But there was of the children. Some of the children. Bits of the children. Perhaps the ones who had gone to pet the mule weighed less and were blown away from the fire by the bomb blast, perhaps it was luck, or fate, or even God. Three of them lay spread-eagled yards along the road, not moving. Pieces of the roof of the mechanic's little shack were draped across them like corrugated iron blankets. Eve ran to them and heaved the hot metal away. One moved, a little girl probably, but who could tell?

In seconds, it seemed, although it must have been longer, other people too were carrying the injured, conscious and unconscious, blistered, burned black, red raw, blood gushing, oozing, trickling, eyes open, eyes closed, eyes missing. It was a vivid silent horror movie, yet more horrific than anything a film-maker could fake. Silent. The child's mouth made a shape for screaming, but no sound came. One entire side of its body was burned from neck to ankle. Eve wanted to give comfort, but wherever she touched, skin and flesh came away.

Suddenly, Ozz, bare to the waist, came into her field of vision. He looked at the child on her lap, covered his eyes for a second and spread his hands in a helpless gesture. 'Ozz, find some water.' She said the words but no sound came. Even so he was there in seconds with a pail of water which she ladled over the child with her free hand. Ozz's face loomed again mouthing silent words. She seemed unable to make sense of anything. He pointed to her ears. Deaf!

Then Dolores, her half-made plait disintegrating, her white shirt filthy, brought a small bottle and a hypodermic needle. She said something. Ozz told her that Eve couldn't hear, so Dolores showed her the bottle. Morphine in any language is recognizable. It took effect at once, and as the child's mouth sagged Dolores picked the child up and handed it to Ozz who gestured, with a nod of his head, that Eve should follow. As she stood up, all hell was let loose. A dreadful explosion of sound, of cries, and screams, of voices shouting orders, of thin terrifying wails, loud crackling flames and falling timbers.

She would probably never know how long she had sat cradling the child, but while she had been doing so Dolores' mother and the other women of the place had dragged mattresses from the bedrooms and laid them in the backs of the flat-bed trucks. They now brought out pillows, towels and lengths of torn sheeting. One of the older women brought a black shawl and tied it around Eve's shoulders. Was it so that the man without a foot should not look on her brassiere? Or was it an old woman not knowing what else to do but what she had always done to protect an unclothed young woman. I'm mad. We're all insane, nothing is worth this. Nothing.

It was clear that neither she nor Ozz was in a fit state to drive such dreadfully injured casualties in the make-shift ambulances, but they could drive and the trucks were undamaged. Dolores did not travel in the cab, but, with the assistance of two elderly women, knelt doing what she could to alleviate the suffering. Where had they all come from? Standing by Ozz's truck, Eve had noticed only the soldiers, the boy and the children. There must have been people working in the fields. There had been a tractor. And there had been a woman with a basket, what had happened to her? From time to time, they had to stop to allow Dolores to change trucks. Ozz and Eve didn't speak. If she looked as dreadful as he did, then she must look tormented and half-dead. Before Dolores climbed into the back of Eve's truck, Eve pinned up the nurse's hair and gave her the wetted towel to wipe her face and arms.

'Not drive slow, now. Very quick. Villa Luna. Leetle few kilometres.' She pointed ahead.

Ozz leaned out, signalled that he was going on and called back, 'Fifteen minutes maximum, Andy.'

'I'm afraid to drive too quickly.'

'Quick, *doloroso, doloroso*, ah pain!' Dolores held up the morphine bottle which was empty. 'Villa Luna ees, ah, *Gran Bretaña*. Yes?'

'Yes. English hospital?'

Dolores climbed into the truck. 'We go.'

'OK. Dolores? The child?' She indicated the burns with a sweep of her hands.

Dolores' reply was incomprehensible. There was no time to make concessions to foreigners who needed a dictionary. Eve recognized something: *sangre*, blood. She shut out everything except her driving. The road was a good one, so they drove fast. Blood transfusion.

Someone had telephoned ahead, so that when they reached the Villa Luna nurses and orderlies were ready with stretchers. There were sixteen casualties. The last four to be lifted from the trucks went in with sheets covering their faces. None of them was a child.

As soon as the casualties had been taken inside, she and Ozz set about sponging the stained mattresses with salt water and putting them in the sun to dry. Silently they foraged for something to drink. Carrying their enamel mugs of tea into which spoonfuls of condensed milk had been stirred, they discovered, to their surprise, a most beautiful garden beyond the surfaced parking area. It was almost wild, untended except for a patch of grass that might once have been a small lawn which had been scythed like a hayfield, and on its hard terraces weeds fought garden plants for space. It was both welcoming and comforting. So, what with that and the scent of the hay and hot earth, Eve was momentarily stabbed by a memory from way back. She tried to ignore her thoughts and lifted the welcome mug of tea to her mouth, but when the scent of that too reached her, she found it difficult to swallow.

Every morning used to start with her elder brother brewing a large pot of tea into which they would stir condensed milk. Ray would give her the spoon to lick as she watched him fasten his shirt stud. Then Ken would rush down at the last minute, slopping tea over the oil-cloth table-cover in his haste, and dash out of the house holding a slice of thick bread between his teeth while he combed his hair. She would write home today. Maybe by now Ray would have heard from Ken and have some idea of where he was. Maybe by now Ken would have received her letter saying that she too was in Spain.

'OK, Andy?' Ozz's gentle voice broke into her thoughts.

'Yeah, yeah. I'm OK. How about you?'

'OK. I've done a fair old bit of driving ambulances. Never gets no better, and that's for sure.'

She looked at her wrist-watch, then put it to her ear. 'Is that all it is?'

'Yeah. Seems like it's been ages.'

'I suppose we should report in to Alex.'

'I gave the old guy at the hotel her number. I don't know if he understood, I asked him to ring the number and just say that Ozz had gone to the hospital at Huete. I think that's where we are. Let's scrounge something to eat. If we don't get a call by then, we'll ring her. Sure you're OK?'

'I'm fine.'

'I'll check with the admin, see if Alex has been on, then get a bit of something inside us then.'

More beans and chilli, but this time with generous sweet tomatoes, basil and garlic.

Although Villa Luna was an English base hospital, it seemed to be staffed with a representative of every one of the United Nations. While they were waiting for their food, a woman's voice with a Yorkshire accent came from behind them. 'It looks like you two have been in a bit of a ruck.' A middle-aged woman with straight, iron-grey hair clipped back unceremoniously looked directly at them from behind round, heavy lenses. She held out a hand. 'Jean Pook.'

Eve looked down at herself, then ran her fingers through her hair. 'A bomb on some petrol pumps.'

'Were that it? I took the call. They're saying it was Eyetie planes, shouldn't wonder. If that's how Mussolini is training this crack air-force of his, shows what a dirty lot they are. It's one thing dropping bombs where the fighting is, it's a dirty dog that uses a village for target practice.'

'What is this place?' Ozz asked.

As soon as her behind hit the bench, Jean Pook started to eat with great gusto. 'I think it were once a monastery, but before it was given over to us lot it was called a presbytery. I think that's a school for lads who want to be priests. A lot of dormitories, just right for a hospital.'

'I thought it didn't look much like a villa.'

'Aye, well, that's the English for you. Story goes, the advance party took down the sign, and because there were larks singing some romantic joker decided to call it House of Larks. I think that was it. Anyway, like the rest of us Brits who can't talk to foreigners without our pocket dictionaries, this lad couldn't tell his *luna*s from his *alondra*s. Bie! This farty food gets fiercer by the day. I love it. Know now why they say, feeling full of beans. Well that's me! Look, me lass, you've never seen nowt like some of the ablutions here, especially in the part used for staff and the like, but if you want to have a pee and a wash-up, best place is end of corridor on first floor. Mostly urinals there, but there's some of our sort. Tek no notice who comes in, man or beast, just carry on wi' what you're doing. It's called egalitarianism − or equality if you're in the fourpenny seats. Well, I'd better get back to work.'

When she had gone, Eve and Ozz looked at one another and smiled a little. Ozz said, 'I feel better. Do you reckon it was the sweet tea or her?'

'Treatment for shock? Oh, her. Definitely her. I'm going to try and get through to Alex.'

In the best peeing and washing place on the first floor, Eve filled a hand-basin with cold water and washed her face and head in it, unnoticed by man or beast. She ran a comb through her wet hair.

'That's better.' Jean Pook, the woman who liked beans, was operating the small telephone switchboard. 'Is your name Lavender?'

'No, that's the other driver.'

'OK, one of you is to call this Albacete number. Want me to get it for you?'

It was the Auto-Parc and Alexander's extension number. Eve nodded. Jean spoke fluent Spanish. She was no dozy Brit in need of a pocket dictionary. Eve was. She had been pretty useless in the emergency.

'You're through.'

The line to Albacete was clear, as was Alex's upper-class voice. 'Anders? This is Alex.'

'Yes, Alex.'

'Are you and Ozz OK?'

'Yes.'

'Thank God! Some old chappie phoned here, said what happened. Pretty bloody awful.'

'It was, and if you don't mind I don't want to talk about it just now.'

'OK. Good thing Ozz had the second truck, he's a good chum when things get hot. Now listen, you leave the lorries at Villa Luna. They're to hold on to them pending news from Madrid.'

'God above, Alex! Why is it that every order is countermanded?'

'It's war, darling.'

In the short silence that followed, Eve saw Alexander in her mind's eye, one eye closed against the smoke, sucking on the flattened end of her cigarette. 'I don't need you to remind me, I've got it all over my shirt. Darling.'

'If there isn't a shower, get somebody to pour a bowl of water over you. Put on some clean knickers and socks. Wash what you were wearing this morning and lay it in the sun. The stains won't go, but it will get rid of the stink. Do it. That's an order. Are you still there? Good! And for God's sake, Anders, don't get so touchy about taking orders. Sure as hell, I'm not the one to give them, but that's how it works for now. Perhaps you'd like to try deciding which of the ten demands for transport gets the one free truck that's fit to be on the road. Now, put Ozz on.'

Eve would probably have burst into tears had she tried to answer, so she just thrust the earpiece back at the switchboard operator.

'Want me to call your man on the Tannoy?'

Eve realized that Jean Pook had heard Alexander's dressing down. She nodded. 'Ozz Lavender.'

She sat on the stairs facing the desk where Ozz was taking the call. Every now and then he would glance in her direction and he smiled a lot, but Eve would have bet that he was getting agitated by whatever Alex was saying. He dived into his shirt pocket and took out a new cigarette, feeling about his other pockets absently for a light. She was about to offer her own lighter, but Jean got there first. She winked at Eve, then raised her eyebrows and made a moue, obviously listening in to the Albacete call, all the while pulling out some plugs and inserting others.

When he finished, Jean started to say something but Ozz put up a stiff and commanding hand. 'Don't! If y'don't mind, I'll handle it.' She smiled and shrugged.

'What was that all about?' asked Eve.

'You don't want to know.'

'What do you mean, I don't want to know?'

'Alex give you orders? Instructions?'

'She told me to take off my dirty clothes and get somebody to pour water over me.'

'She's right, Andy, it's what you should do.'

He handed her his cigarette upon which she drew thankfully and didn't hand it back. 'I want to find out about those people we brought in. We can't just go.'

'We can. Now, are you going to let me have another drag on the ciggie?'

'Ciggie is such a damned silly word for a grown man to use.'

'Well, sweetheart, it's an uncontrovertible fact of life that Aussies smoke ciggies because of the mozzies. Y'see, cigarettes just don't scan.'

She didn't want to see herself as only a gun-runner; she wanted to be involved in what they did. She scowled at him, unwilling to give up her mood. 'That little kid. I have to find out whether it . . . if it . . . if they saved it.'

'It's not what we do, Andy. We ferry the bully-beef, we run the guns, sometimes we get to drive the ambulances. We don't cook the stew or shoot off the rifles. We just off-load the goods, turn around and go back for more. It's called truck-driving, Andy. It's what we do.' They were back outside again, and the heat from the stone terrace leaped up at them.

'For God's sake, Clive, those were injured people, not goods.'

'Bloody sure they were! You think I don't know it! What do you think one of them left behind in my truck? A finger. Not a very big one it's true, but a finger. An injured person's finger, most likely left behind by the woman with the basket. She threw herself around a bit before she got her shot from Dolores. I thought she might miss it, so I took it to a nurse. Sorry, she said, we'd put it back if we could, but the finger would only die and drop off again.'

His bitter put-down was the worst she had ever experienced. She had grown up knowing how to ignore the intended hurt. But this was not the same. This was rejection by a friend, an attack on her for insensitivity, for not seeing that his way of dealing with what they did was no less valid than her own. She felt sick at the thought. She had not realized how much she had grown to like him in such a short time. But she stalked on towards the scythed grass, now bleached and dry, not knowing what to do.

Ozz threw himself down on the grass and stretched out flat on his back. She stood before him like a penitent. 'When my mother was buried, I ran away from the graveside. The police came looking for me. My brothers were distraught and other people worried. I had a reputation for going off like a fire-cracker. It seemed OK till then. After that I saw that there was a dark side, a self-indulgent side. I vowed then that I would never go off in all directions without thinking. You can hurt people that way. And I've done it again. I'm sorry.'

He raised himself up on his elbows and looked at her. 'You're an OK kinda girl, Andy. My mam would have you round for Sunday tea like a shot.'

'I mean it. I'm really sorry, Ozz.'

'It's OK, I was a bit hard on you. I got my black side too.'

They sat in silence for a few minutes. 'Andy? Whyn't you do as Alex says, and go get water poured over you? Your clobber's a touch high.'

She sniffed her shirt. 'Is it?'

'Not so's you'd notice.'

'OK.'

'Just go fetch your bag, and if you go round the end of that building with the tin roof, there's a set-up of water and buckets that'll just do the trick.'

Eve had the old Ozz back again.

The soap was so thin as to be almost transparent, but the water was soft and created a foamy lather.

For the first time Eve noticed how white her torso was compared to the skin that had been exposed to the sun – as Duke Barney's had been that time when they were both young and she had seen him dive naked into the pool of green water. The sacred pool had been hers and Bar Barney's till then. A surge of desire ran through her, and she was shocked that she had so little control over herself when only hours before she had been part of the most horrific scene imaginable. She closed her eyes and pulled gently on the rope, allowing a steady trickle of cool water to hit the crown of her head.

Not long before she left home, she and her old head-teacher, who had become her trusted friend, had talked for the first time as equals. They had exchanged confidences about sexual desire and lust without reaching any clear conclusions. Sexual desire, they decided, was such that one could manipulate it a little if one wished, encourage it. But lust, the older woman had postulated, lust was unstable, unpredictable; it was the first Mrs Rochester as Jane Eyre had encountered her, a creature of nature, of necessity best kept locked away, for if left unguarded it would burst out and destroy the happy home.

Letting go the bit of rope, she looked down at her white breasts. The cold trickle had done no good, she would have to put on a cotton bra under her shirt. Sex on the brain! There was no getting dry in the humid atmosphere of the shower-stalls. Trousers would stick to her legs, so she opted for a green cotton skirt and one of her checked shirts. The clothes that Ozz had complained of she had been squeezing under her feet as she showered. Now, as she was hanging them out over a make-shift washing line, along with a variety of men's underpants, cotton petticoats, canvas trousers of unknown gender and an assortment of dark socks, she wondered what instructions Alex had given Ozz.

She found him chatting to a couple of men in white coats and a woman in nurse's uniform. The four of them were standing beside the two flat-bed trucks, one of which was now piled high with what looked like the bedding they had brought with them. The medics moved off.

Without preamble Ozz said, 'Now listen, Andy, you may not like this, and if you don't then go and make your beef to Alex. It's her idea.'

'May not like what?'

'Drive a big Mercedes.'

'A what?'

'A Mercedes saloon car.'

'I don't know what you're talking about. What's a Mercedes?'

'Want to see one?' She followed him to one of the many outhouses. 'There! What d'you think?'

Garaged there was the largest and grandest car Eve had ever seen. Beneath mud and dust it was easy to see that the dull gleam of the radiator-grille and metal trims was of a high quality, but the bodywork had been sprayed or painted in red and black. Ozz opened the passenger door and bounced on the sprung seat. 'Come on, get in.'

Sitting behind the leather-covered steering wheel she looked along the bonnet and then at the interior. Nothing had been done to spoil the hide covering or the walnut panels in which the many instruments were set. Eve's experience of expensive motors was limited to a few drives with David and later with Duke, neither of whom had driven anything this luxurious. As with the Bedford lorries, one could see without turning the engine over that there was power under the bonnet, which was why she loved driving the big ambulances. Holding the steering wheel at '9.15', she glanced in all the mirrors and touched the gear lever. Then she remembered that it was more than likely that Alex was about to move her about again, and began to feel irritated at Ozz for aiding and abetting.

'Why didn't Alex speak to me?'

'You were in the shower-stalls.'

'And she couldn't wait, so she got you to soften me up for whatever it is she wants me to do. What, for Heaven's sake, could anybody do with a thing like this.' She smiled, trying to show Ozz that she didn't blame him. 'Come on, come on, I shan't bite your head off.'

'Well, I'm real glad of that. It's going to be used for the ferrying of official visitors.'

'What the hell kind of official visitors?'

'MPs on fact-finding visits, Aid to Spain people, film people . . .'

Her first suspicion had not been wrong, then. Alex was palming her off again with a nice little job for a girl. 'Hollywood stars who want something for *Picturegoer*?'

'Crikey, Anders, you can be real prickly! No, people who *make* movies, propaganda for the Republic, the stuff that brings in the money to provide more ambulances and trained medical teams. They need to get to villages, up mountain passes. Hell's bells! You know what I mean – people who want to go to some of the war zones. A substantial motor like a Mercedes is just the ticket.'

'I'd be no good, I don't speak any foreign languages.'

'God help us, Anders, nobody expects the English to speak a foreign language! These people have interpreters. You're the right man for the job.'

Disappointment welled up within her. She longed to be given something more heroic than this. 'Damn it, Ozz, I came here to drive ambulances.'

'OK. No skin off my nose. Go and ring Alex so at least we know what to do with these trucks.'

'I will!' Flicking out angrily with her wet towel, she stalked off, knowing that Ozz would be smiling and shaking his head as he watched her. Well then, *be* amused, I don't care.

Alexander answered with her usual efficient 'Alexander!'

'Driver Anders here.'

'Are you feeling better? Ozz gave me a very graphic picture. It must have been hellish.'

'It was. I'm feeling back to normal now that I've showered and changed, thank you. Ozz has tried to tell me that driving an elite few in this palace on wheels will help the cause.'

'I wouldn't agree on the elite few, but the rest is about right.'

'I drive trucks and ambulances.'

'I know that perfectly well, and very well. You're as good as any – maybe not including Ozz, but he's done more miles.'

'So why take me off the job?'

'Because I'm in a better position than you are to see which of my drivers is best suited to this particular work.'

She certainly had the capacity to put Eve's back up, but Eve decided to remain calm. 'It seems such a useless job.'

'I think I'm the best judge of that. I have the facts and you do not. What if your orders were to ride a pure-bred Arabian to Madrid for stud use – without a saddle, of course.'

Eve felt that she was being backed into a corner from which there was only one way out: Alexander's. 'I'd still want to know if it was worthwhile – for the cause.'

'Don't be such a prig, Anders. You aren't the only one with the cause at heart, some of us have it very close to our heart.'

'Twice in a single day. Would I still drive ambulances?'

'Of course. I can't see that a VIP car will be in use every day. What is twice in one day?'

'Being told I'm a prig.'

'Does us all good to be told that sometimes. Twice in a day is a bit much, though. Ozz?'

'Oh, never mind. All right, then, but on one condition.'

'Anders, you can also be very difficult. I don't bargain with my drivers.'

'I just don't want people calling it a VIP car, or referring to me as the chauffeur.'

Alex laughed. 'I think we could come to some kind of accommodation over that. Who is it politicizing you, Anders? I've never heard you on the subject of elitism and privilege before today.'

'You think I can't do it by myself?'

'I'm sure that you can.'

'A child on fire concentrates the mind wonderfully.'

'I'm sorry your initiation was so violent.'

Eve, suddenly, couldn't answer.

'Anders?'

'OK. What are we going to do with the trucks?'

'That's fixed. Now this car, the Mercedes, is a commandeered vehicle.'

'I'd never have guessed, all that red and black paint.'

'It belonged to some industrialist who couldn't take it on the plane when he scarpered to Italy. Now, Ozz can handle anything on wheels. The quickest way to get it on the road is for him to show you under the bonnet and then for you both to go for a good test run. Take a day's leave.'

Ozz was waiting outside the shed with the car, using his time to advantage by making up his twice-used cigarettes.

'How'd she change your mind?'

'Something she said about horses.'

'Horses. No wonder she's taken a fancy to you.'

'Fancy! She rubs me up the wrong way. Born-to-rule type. Even out here she's giving the orders and we're taking them.'

'Ne' mind, Andy, come the red revolution nobody's going to give the orders.'

'That's not socialism, that anarchism.' Ozz was about to say something. 'And don't ask who's been politicizing me.'

'I wasn't going to, I was going to ask what horses have to do with it.'

'It's too long a story.'

'She's quite a horse-flesh fancier, has some back home called Hipsen-horses or something like that.'

'Lippizaner. They're the most valuable horses in the world.'

73

'Oh, I think our Alex is loaded all right. I don't suppose you'd like a roll-up.'

Eve eyed the salvaged tobacco. 'I don't suppose I would either, but thanks for the offer.'

He winked amiably. 'You should taste it when you're out of ciggie paper and there's only your sheets of Izal.'

The events of that morning were not forgotten, but they were dealing with them as best they could by trying to return to normal.

Over the weeks at the depot Eve had grown to like Ozz for the good, reliable partner he was. She liked his nice, intelligent face, his broad-chested athletic physique and the soft, strung-out way he had of speaking.

They spent the rest of that day going over the car with a fine-tooth comb. Alex was right, he was a wiz with vehicles. 'There y'are, Andy, now you're a fully-paid-up bodger. Only thing you won't be able to fix is an empty gasoline tank if you forget to keep a spare can. So, can of gasoline, bottle of water. Tomorrow we see how she goes.'

'She says we should take a day's leave.'

He nodded. 'She's a wise lady is our Alex.'

She said, 'Lippizaner! Natural enemy of the people,' without rancour.

Just before they went in search of a place to sleep, he said, 'I have t' tell you, Andy, the little kid . . .'

He didn't need to say. She had known all along that a child with that severity of burns couldn't live long.

'His name was Luis.'

'I had thought he was a little girl.'

He shook his head. 'When you were in the shower, I saw Dolores – by the way, she's gone, got another lift – she knew all of them. Can you imagine!'

No, she could not. Who could imagine? It didn't make it better that Dolores was a nurse; they were her own villagers, and it was possible even that the bombers were of her own nationality. She wanted to tell Ozz the coincidence of the name

Luis, but that would mean admitting to her past, when her own name had been Louise.

That night spent at the hospital was unnerving. After washing in a kind of horse-trough, Eve again felt the same overwhelming need for sleep that she had experienced on most other nights since she had been here, what with the heat of the day and the tension of the job. She had expected, as the Villa Luna was run by the English, that the nurses with whom she shared a damp and crumbling room would also have been English, but they were Spanish. With smiles they offered *naranja*, not orange-coloured fruits but small, greenish ones which turned out to be the most sweetly delicious oranges Eve had ever tasted. The pungent scent filled the room, overwhelming the musty smell of several centuries of decay.

She fell asleep, but only on the edge of a restful sleep, jumping awake from time to time with the tail-end of a disturbing dream dissolving as she opened her eyes to the small steady flame of a primitive little oil-lamp. That evening she had asked a few people if they recognized Ken's name, but no one had.

Restless, she tossed and turned, then lay awake allowing her mind to drift. It had been stressful at first being Eve Anders, but by now she had no trouble in answering casual questions about herself, never being specific, stepping aside. The little lamp flickered and its flame expired. The room was very dark, but she sensed someone coming in quietly. Then she heard soft breathing close to her ear, as though someone was bending over her. She was not surprised, she had been thinking of Ozz and it was almost as though she had been expecting him to come. The mattress was very narrow, but she moved over to make room, and as she turned she detected an evocative and distinctive scent – the shaving cream David used.

David? It couldn't be, yet there was no mistake, it *was* David who was easing himself on to the narrow mattress. 'David?' she said quietly. 'Shh,' he said, and stopped her next question by closing his mouth over hers. David? His lips were soft, warm

75

and moist as she remembered. Joy and pleasure flowed through her body. She was glad that he had found her. Now she could have it all, freedom and love. Her lips parted to his firm and mobile tongue which tentatively touched the tip of hers, and she heard herself give a quiet moan of pleasure. 'Shh, Louise,' he said, speaking close to her ear.

'How on earth . . . ?' she whispered. 'I wanted . . .'

'Shh,' he said again, kissing her and making her nipples rise as his cool hands discovered bare skin under her shirt.

His clothes smelled of cars and cigarettes, his face and hair of the astringent sweetness she associated with him. She turned to face him. Moonlight coming in at the small, bare window allowed her to see his handsome face and tousled hair. She thought: I don't care if the others wake up. They don't know me and I don't know them. I'm a stranger in this strange land, making love in what was once a monastery. The idea of such a daring rendezvous was thrilling.

Even as she thought of what she wanted him to do next, his hand slipped down over her body and gently parted her thighs. He knew exactly what she wanted him to do, and anticipated her. This time he wouldn't stop as he had before; now she was older, experienced, liberated and free. This time David would be as confident as Duke had been. No restraints, no repressions, no being honourable.

She wanted to be on her back, to feel the weight of his body; she wanted to be facing him, wrapped in his arms and legs; she wanted him behind her, pulling her into the hollow of his body; she wanted to be standing against a tree as she had been when she and Duke had taken one another, desperate to relieve their hunger.

She held him, guided him, felt him slip into her as firmly as Duke had done, and imagined that she could feel the rough bark of the tree pressed hard against her back. Now she could scarcely move or breathe for the intensity of the pleasure. Over her, under her, above and below her, inside her body and on her skin. She was tantalized by a compulsion to extend this voluptuous liberation, and by the desire to give in to it. Soon she had no choice. The tidal wave of sensual pleasure crashed. Sensation flowed upwards. Breathtaking. Extreme. She was aware only of lust being tremendously transformed into ecstasy. She gave herself up to the great thump and pulse that surged through her body.

Fulfilment at last almost drowned her, making her gasp for breath. For the time it lasted, she had forgotten the lover who had detonated the explosion until, in the darkness, he spoke softly. He spoke not in the cultured upper-class accent of David, but in Duke Barney's plain country speech. He said, 'It don't signify nothing,' as he had said when they went their separate ways and he had thrust into her hand a gemstone still embedded in rock.

Suddenly, of its own accord, the flame of the little oil-lamp jumped back to life, startling her and causing her to sit bolt upright with her heart thumping.

The room smelled of orange peel and sleeping women.

She was trembling and breathless, her body slick with moisture still pulsed spasmodically. Clutching her shirt around her, she grabbed her things and rushed out along the empty stone corridor to the small ablutions room with its cold water in a stone trough. There she stood over a drain and tricked cold water over her sticky skin.

It was as well she had no mirror, for she would have been ashamed to look into her own eyes. She might have left her old life, but she had not been able to leave behind the effect of years spent in a church-ridden school. Her conscious self had no regrets at the way she and Duke had given in to their mutual lust, but this unnatural experience must have come from some unwholesome part of her mind, and she was afraid of it.

By the time she had combed back her wet hair, put on a clean shirt and swilled the other through with cold water, her more familiar self had returned sufficiently for her to go and look for something to drink.

Although it was not yet light, from the sounds that echoed

strangely along the stone corridors other people were up. She made her way through the passages until at last she found the kitchens. A woman, probably in her late thirties, with short greying curly hair and a trim figure, was watching a pan of milk and a kettle at the point of boiling. Eve's instinct was to slip away, but the woman had seen her and waved. 'Hi, nice to see another early-bird.'

'Is this the hospital kitchen?'

'No, those are way over the other side. Coffee?'

'Thanks.'

She grinned, showing good American teeth. 'Have yourself a seat.' She held out a hand, 'Sweet Moffat, been called Sweet since I was in first grade and said my name was Adeline.'

'Eve Anders. No need to ask where you come from.'

'You do too. I was born in Brighton, Sussex, England. Raised in the States and been married to the same American for ten years.'

'I'd love to see America. I've been a film fan since I was a little kid. I feel I know the Bronx, Staten Island, Monument Valley, even Tombstone Gulch.'

'It isn't all Hollywood, but it's a grr-eat country. Are y'always this early?'

'Not usually before dawn. I couldn't sleep.'

'Haven't seen you before, are you a nurse?'

'No, a truck-driver.' How legitimate that sounded, as though she had been a truck-driver all her life.

Adeline Moffat raised her eyebrows and made a one-thumb salute. 'Glad to hear it. I'm all for women doin' the thing they want 'stead of the thing they should. I've seen women truck-drivers, mostly they're pretty good too. Pity it takes wars to get us out of our kitchens.'

'Are you a nurse?'

'No, no, I work with the children, orphans and refugees.'

'Is your husband in Spain?'

'Oh, yeah, Will's here.'

'In the International Brigade?'

'No, Will is dead. Will and I are Quakers, pacifists, you know?'

'Yes, I do know. One of my best friends back home is a Friend, isn't that what you say?' 'Back home' slipped out unawares.

'Will and I came out here to set up a small aid station. We were on our way to Guernica but got caught up in the hills when the place was destroyed. Will died . . . heart attack. It's OK, I'm through it now. I continued with what Will and I intended, so I'm with the Society of Friends Spanish Relief Committee doing what we can for the children. You got family?'

'Two brothers, one is out here, with the IBs in the British Battalion.'

'How long has he been out here?'

'He left home a couple of years ago. He was going to walk and work his way across Europe, but I think he fell in love with Spain. It's ages since I saw him, or heard from him. I don't even know if he's all right.' Her voice broke and, although she pressed her hands to her eyes, she could not stop the tears that began to course down her face.

'Oh, honey, honey.'

The soft womanly embrace, full of concern and understanding, did for Eve. 'I'm sorry, I'm not really the weepy sort.'

'It's OK to cry, honey, it's something human beings do. Sure you miss your brother, brothers are pretty special. D'you want to talk about it?'

'No, it's all right. Probably driving too long without a real break. It just caught me unawares.'

'Hey, let me freshen up that tea. Like a dash of milk? It's goat's milk, really good for you. Maybe you just needed to cry. It's nature's way. I'm a great one for home-spun remedies.'

Oh yes, Eve Anders did indeed need to cry. About the child, and about the woman and about Florentîn who had done his Charlie Chaplin act, and the school-children, the idlers, the boy with the mule, and the soldiers who had guarded their little convoy. She needed to cry for herself, and for Ozz who had found that dreadful memento. But she was afraid to cry; afraid that if she did so then she might never stop. She turned her mind to her surroundings.

All kitchens have a unique smell, but this one was reminiscent of the farmhouse kitchen in which Eve had spent her happiest days. That too had old stone walls, a flagstone floor and a cooking range. It too had its efficient but easy-going woman, the aunt who, when life had threatened to run out, had wound Eve up and set her going again. The scent conjured up a memory of Ken coming in carrying a shotgun and a dangling pheasant, glowing and full of himself. He'd probably be carrying a gun now.

She helped Sweet Moffat for a while, then when the sky lightened she took her drink and sat curled up in the front of the Mercedes, and indulged herself a little by imagining how they were getting on at home. Thinking of her elder brother, Ray, was even more affecting because she had been closer to him than to Ken.

Ray hadn't really understood why she needed to get away, believing that she had been driven out by his unexpected relationship with Bar. People said two women in a house never worked, but it had, and for months she and Bar had shared a happy life with Ray. She and Bar had loved each other for a long time before Ray gave in and let himself fall for her. As girls, they had loved one another deeply, with the kind of perfect passion that only girls burgeoning into womanhood can ever know: mystical, romantic, physical, total. Without being overtly sexual, they had established their maturing sexuality, tested their enticing sensuality. It had been in that tender encounter with Bar, who had been the conjuror of spiritual experience with herself as the acolyte, that they had become for a while two halves of the same spirit. 'We are the one soul,' Bar had said. 'You the fair and I the dark. You the summer and I the winter,' except in her rites Bar, in her fey and wise role, was inclined to say 'Thou ist' and 'I be'.

There had been a Christmas when Duke Barney had stalked into the kitchen as he stalked into her thoughts now. Dark and proud, he had been so damned sure of himself, so damned sure that she desired him, which she did. In self-assurance she was his equal. She knew that she had a good brain and how to use it. She could do anything she wanted, be anyone she wanted to be. Duke Barney would never be the man for her, but he was the only person who knew who and what she was.

Ozz appeared with a bucket of water and some rags, and insisted that they do right by such a well-bred motor. 'Ain't she a beaut?'

They agreed to take Helan Alexander at her word and take a day's leave for Eve to give the motor a good run. She settled into the pleasure of being at the wheel of such a powerful car which was wonderfully easy to control. When Ozz encouraged her to increase her speed on a good main road, they seemed to be gliding along. Ozz, with a map on the dashboard, directed their route. Sharp corners, good roads, hair-pin bends, winding tracks where goats strayed, Eve took every change of road as though she and the car had been together for a long time. She loved it guiltily.

As the morning drew on, yesterday's experiences and the last vestiges of her disturbing night withdrew, closing the doors after them.

'Y' look born to the good life, Andy.'

'I know.'

He took out two new, uncrushed, American cigarettes, lit one and put it between her lips.

'Thanks,' she said. 'Don't light yours, we can share this one.'

He took the proffered cigarette and drew on it. 'Spoken like a good mate.'

That was how she felt when she was with him, not that she had any great wish that they should be anything other than good mates, but she was used to men eyeing her. She was puzzled by him. Her good mates had always been girls of her own age. Men? Well, they were the opposite sex, prospectors, predators, yet Ozz had so far treated her in almost a brotherly way. What would she do if he did make a pass? He was desirable, that was for sure. She heaved a sigh at her own perverseness.

'What's that for?'

'Take no notice, that's just me, sorting myself out. I'm leaving the route to you. Where are we headed?'

'Keep going till I tell you to stop.'

He handed her back the cigarette. 'Pull off the road just up here.'

She did so, and turned off the engine. Hitching one knee up on to the seat, and resting his arm along the plump leather back, he turned to face her. She clutched the steering wheel and kept facing front, even though she felt the first stirrings of interest. It would be the most natural thing, two young people who liked one another engaging in a mild flirtation.

'Listen, Andy, don't go off the deep end, and tell me to mind my own bloody business if you like, but it won't make any difference, I have t' say it.' He held up his forefinger. 'One. The driver is always in charge of the vehicle. Two. The driver must always know the destination. Three. The driver always checks the proposed route before setting out. Four. Spare tyre, can of gasoline, can of water – the driver is responsible.'

'I thought you put the cans in the boot.'

'How can you be sure that I did?'

She flung open the door, went to the boot and flung that open too. He came round, leaned against the car and smiled.

'OK. So you did see to it. OK, I didn't check. OK?' Back in the car she added, 'I won't forget again.'

'Good.' He took the cigarette, drew upon it and handed it back. 'There's another, but I don't want to get you mad.'

'Why should I get mad?'

'You don't take criticism easily because you don't like to believe that you're not perfect. It makes you feel guilty not to be perfect. Am I right, or am I right?'

'That's ridiculous. I've always been able to accept criticism.'

He was the most irritating man. 'OK, let's get the wigging all over at once.'

'Five. If the driver's a lovely young female and she's wearing a skirt that's too tight for driving, she should be sure that she can control the car if her passenger can't control his urge to find out how far up her legs go.' He took back the cigarette, but didn't look at her.

She sat very still, staring through the spotted windscreen. Her immediate impulse had been to pull her skirt down. I'm damned if I will!

He sucked on the last of the cigarette, blew a stream of smoke out of the window, then flicked away the stub. 'You said you wouldn't get mad.'

'I'm not mad.' She turned on the engine, but made no attempt to put it into gear. 'Let me see the map. Please.'

'You are mad.'

'I'm not! And if you don't hurry you're going to waste that half-inch stub of cigarette smouldering over there.' Such a childish remark. He turned casually to look at the thin trail of smoke. 'What the hell, let it burn. I'm in an expansive mood.'

He was needling her. She was determined not to respond, so she looked fiercely at the map. She switched off the engine and realized that the map was upside down. She traced the routes of their recent convoy journeys with her forefinger. He was right, she was mad at herself. She became as aware of her exposed knees as if they had been her naked thighs.

Ozz sat, half turned in her direction, seemingly quite at ease as she pored over the map. 'Six,' she said at last. 'Do you want to know number six, Mr Lavender?'

'Sure, Andy,' he said amiably. 'If it'll teach me anything, sure I want to know.'

'OK! Six. Drivers who are given a bit of sensible advice never allow themselves to get mad – it makes them feel so damned foolish.'

''Fraid that's not a new one, Andy.' Opening the door, he

said, 'I'll just get it before it burns right down. Shame to waste good tobacco.'

Opening the door on her side, she said, 'Come on, now that we've got that settled I'm going to stretch my legs for five minutes.' She had pulled off the road into the lee of some craggy rocks which shielded the view. When she walked round to the other side of the car, she was amazed to discover that beyond the rocks the land dropped away into a valley so beautiful that it might have been a fantasy. More than just beautiful, it was exhilarating, enchanting, and at the same time humbling and alien. Here was a landscape in which she knew she was a foreigner, the stranger in a strange land. Where had that phrase come from? Well, it suited her mood just now. Alienation invoked in her a sense of risk, of uncertainty. Tomorrow could bring anything at all. In the weeks and months ahead, she would become used to this exotic countryside, but not too soon, for she wanted to continue falling in love with this place.

She became aware of Ozz standing beside her, and he too was gazing reflectively over the red-earth valley striated with even rows of bright green narrowing into the far distance and ending in craggy outcrops, similar to the one where they found themselves. 'Makes me feel pretty homesick,' he said.

'Those are grapes, aren't they?'

'Sure. We got vineyards back home. Our place has good acidic soil, right amount of rainfall, hill-slopes open to the sun, what else but grapes could you grow on land like that?'

'I don't know. I assumed you were a truck-driver.'

He hunkered down close to the rough, dry ground, crumbling a handful of earth which trickled through his fingers. She sat beside him, covering her knees without making a point of it. 'I am, weekends, evenings and holidays,' he said. 'It's all I'm really fit for on my dad's spread. The big boys won't let me near the vines. I don't mind, I'd rather have grapes poured cool straight from a cool bottle. Château Lavender. It's true. My old man makes real good wine. Good as French, but it's fragile. Don't travel too well. You Brits turn up your noses at it, and

I can't blame you. Aussie wine should be drunk close as possible to where it grows.' He leaned back on his hands and stared up at the clear blue sky. After a few minutes of restful silence he said, 'In the real world, I'm a school-teacher.'

It was the last thing Eve would have guessed from his sun-burned skin, his unruly hair, his powerful physique. Her ear picked up the change in his vowel-sounds as he talked about his home. He dropped the stagey good cobber.

'Lavenders is a family wine business. You'd know Lavenders if you came from Down Under. Good stuff, not like this battery acid they drink in Spain. Dad and my brothers tend the vineyards.' He pointed to the green rows. 'I can tell you just what you'd find if you went down there. Thousands and thousands of sprays of little flowers, some still blooming, some showing the first titchy little grapes. You come back in a couple of weeks and they'll be neat little green grapes big as ... big as your fingernail. Seven Lavender brothers. Mam reckoned she always wanted to see one son in a white-collar job, so being the youngest I guess I was it.' He wagged his head and smiled a lop-sided smile. 'Just as well she didn't want a son in a dog-collar job, I'd have made one hell of a Father Lavender.'

'Did she mind you coming to Spain?'

'Mam? She was the first one to come up with the idea.' He smiled as he mimicked the Welsh tongue, 'Mam's a Thomas, you see.' He changed his tone. 'From Welsh Wales. Her da was a miner, but what is the use being in the coal if it's killing you and it is just a bit of sun on your back you need? So Granda took Nana and my mam and her brothers and sisters, and set off for New South Wales on a loan from some old auntie. My little mam still has the Welsh in her – clings to it like grim death. Granda didn't know anything about growing grapes, so he moved on to where there were people who did, and set up shop on his own until he met another Welshman – Bryn Lavender – with two sons and a variety of grape that was made by the Good Lord to blend with the one Granda grew. Ah, to hear the story properly, you should hear little mam tell it.'

'You love your mother a lot, don't you?'

'I guess I do, but your mam's always just your mam and you don't ask yourself that kind of question.'

'Do you take after her?'

'In looks? I suppose I do.' He grinned fondly. 'She's older, littler and a bunch of pregnancies hasn't done a lot for her shape. I don't know, like with the love bit, it isn't easy to look at your mam objectively. She's my little old Welsh mam, and she's got a sense of what's right and what ain't more than anybody I ever knew. You two'd get on like a house afire.' He looked at his wrist-watch. 'I was thinking we might drive as far as the coast. What do you think?'

She smiled. 'I'll just check the map.'

'It's not that far to Jávea, I wouldn't mind having a look now we're this close.'

'I'll go along with that. Do you know this part of the coast?'

He shook his head. 'In the classroom back home, there was a picture of a bay on a calendar that I inherited along with the ten-year-old kids. I'd give a lot to see the real thing. I'd like to write to the kids, tell them I was there. I expect the picture's still on the wall, they could mark it with a cross.'

'As good an excuse as any to cruise around like tourists.'

'To hell with your conscience. The war will still be there tomorrow and didn't Alex say that we were to give the Beaut a good test, and have a day off?'

They made for Chinchilla de Monte Aragón, halting briefly to take photos of its massive, sandy-brown castle which seemed to have thrust its towers and fortified walls out of a sandy-brown bed. The town itself was old and set on an isolated ridge over-looking the plains. Its streets radiated out from an old church and were so steep and narrow that at times Eve's heart was in her mouth, but that did not lessen her delight and curiosity.

Some miles further on, Ozz announced, 'Almansa,' and got his camera ready for anything that would please his mam. Here they stopped for a drink and some gasoline. This town too had its dominating castle, on a conical outcrop, looking as pictur-esque and dramatic as anything dreamed up for a Hollywood film. The church was gothic and imposing, and there was an ancient convent.

The day was now hot as hot, and the sky blue as blue. On the last few kilometres of the journey, the landscape oscillated, the red-and-black paintwork of the Mercedes shimmered, and those roads which were metal-surfaced seemed to be detached from the vehicles driving on them, giving cars and carts the appearance of floating a foot above the ground.

Tracing the map with his finger, Ozz gave Eve a series of directions, none of which brought him to the point from which his classroom picture had been taken. 'OK, I give up. Go south and it looks as though we ought to come to some small coves. If it's not too public, we might take a dip.'

They reached a point where it appeared they might get access to the sea. Eve manoeuvred the wide car along a road that dropped steeply down, becoming narrower as it went. Suddenly, they were confronted by a breathtaking view over the deep blue bay of Jávea, an expanse of still water enclosed within hills that sloped down to pale buff-coloured headlands and beach.

Ozz pushed forward in his seat. 'Hey! That's my picture. Would you believe it? It actually exists.' The sun was almost overhead, and as they got out the heat slammed into them.

'Smell the sea, Ozz?'

Ozz nods.

'My father was a sailor, we lived by the sea.'

Ozz peers at her, she seldom lets on about herself. Curious as he is about her, he knows better than to show it. Opening the boot he takes out a large green golfing umbrella. 'Bet you never reckoned there'd be a use for this. It's the real McCoy.'

'I'm surprised nobody's pilfered it.'

'C'mon, dig out a couple of bottles and let's go see what the beach is like.'

A spontaneous picnic. The feeling of elation as she unearths the red wine and fizzy lemonade and packs into her haversack some of the tomatoes she bought along the road, is straight out of her childhood: taking strawberries and honey-water in a bottle to sit with feet dangling in cool water.

There is a wonderful purple shade beneath the slender dark-green pines. Holding hands they scramble and slide down the deep litter of needles, fooling about and laughing as they stumble into one another until, hands still tightly clasped, they leap over a small outcrop of rocks and fetch up on a stretch of pale golden beach that in the brilliant sunlight appears dazzlingly white. He squeezes her hand and, letting out a low whistle, says slowly, 'Hey, hey. Will y' just look at that, sweetheart.'

The bay that they had seen from above is a crescent of rocky foreshore bordering a flat beach of fine, powdery sand. Behind the rocks the pine wood slopes steeply, dark against the deep blue sky. There is no sign of life, only birdsong.

'Listen, Andy.' They hold their breath, listening to the ribbon of song. 'D'you know what that sounds like?'

'Yes, but it can't be, can it? Not here.'

'Can't be what? Listen. Go on, say what you think.'

She laughs. 'It can't be, it's ridiculous, but I think – a night-ingale?'

'Yeah. I think a nightingale too. Can y' believe it?'

'Honestly!' Then she giggles like a happy schoolgirl. 'This is not real, you know, it's a Hollywood film set, and that's sound-effects.'

'OK. Scene one, take one!' He hurls one of his boots in the direction of the sea. The rest of their footwear follows in a kind of contest. Then he opens the huge umbrella, shoulders her haversack and with arms around one another's waists, they brave the hot dry sand in hops and leaps as far as the damp strand. There, Ozz angles the umbrella against the sun, and they sink gratefully on to the firm sand. They share one of the bottles of sweet lemonade that spurts over them as Eve opens it.

'Nectar of the gods. I'm goin' to peel off and cool down if it's OK with you? I'm decent. Athletic strip,' he explains as he reveals that he is wearing vest and running shorts. 'I went for an early run.' He removes the vest. In spite of the dream fantasy that had shaken her in the early hours, Eve finds herself responding to Ozz's marvellously athletic body and long bare legs, muscles shaped by the training specific to a hurdler and long, narrow, white, cared-for feet.

He grins happily. ''T' be honest, I wondered if we might just find a bit of quiet beach.'

She punches his arm playfully. 'I reckon you knew about this place all along.' His legs are beautiful. She never saw David's legs bare. He too had long legs, were they as firm? Was David's behind as tightly moulded as Ozz's? Were the hairs on David's limbs thick and golden? Did his chest have that silky sheen? She withdraws her eyes from Ozz's splendid body as he joins her in the umbrella's shade. She smiles to herself, recalling what her old teacher had said about lust being as dangerous as the first Mrs Rochester. Is it so terrible to have erotic thoughts? Why shouldn't she feel like this about Ozz, or any man? It was only nature at work.

She sits up and drinks some more of the warm, sweet lemonade, which satisfies her thirst. But the greater need won't be so simply satisfied. What would happen if she and Ozz did it together? So far theirs has been a platonic friendship, uncomplicated by sex. How easy it would be to demolish this quite extraordinary relationship. What is it that makes it so special? It wasn't as if they had known one another for very long. It was special for him too, she was sure of that. If he made an attempt to make love to her, and if she let it happen, they might still have a relationship worth having, but it would not be the same thing that they had now. Was it worth the risk? She doubts that she would stop him.

Ozz says, 'I shall try to promote the idea of *siesta* when I get back home. Great idea. I'm going to take a dip. Coming?'

'I was just thinking.'

'You'd be more comfortable if you'd unbutton or peel something off. There's nobody here but us chickens.'

She would like that. She remembers herself and Bar Barney as young girls, marvellously naked, dangling their feet in the chickweed-covered water, their bare hot skin catching the slightest movement of cool air. But to be naked so close to such a desirable man would be more complicated.

'I burn easily.'

He raises his eyebrows in amusement. 'Hey, you're not shy. And I know you're not a prude.'

'Of course I'm not shy.'

'That's OK then.'

'Really, I'm not. I'm cooling off nicely.'

'I shouldn't try to nuzzle you or anything like that.'

'Of course. I know that.'

'That's OK then.'

Sitting up and looking out at the blue water is relaxing, helps her resist more speculation about what would happen if he touched her breast or her Venus' mound. The sea is inviting.

'Andy?'

'Yes?'

'I'm . . .'

'What?'

He looks at her, smiles and pauses. 'Ah, noth'n', noth'n' at all that won't keep. Except that, it seems a bit of a waste if you're going to keep your knickers on and your tits covered when we could have a nice bit of a dip. I'm not the enemy, sweetheart, and I don't reckon you and me need to make a big thing about this John Thomas and pussy stuff.' He laughs. 'I could'a put that a lot bloody better.'

At that moment, all that she needs to do to change the nature of their relationship is to put out a hand and say something about Lady Jane, make an allusion to Lawrence perhaps. He was allowing her to make the decision.

'Them knicks ain't going to make much difference, but keep 'm on if you feel better. But I don't intend keeping my bum covered when I swim.'

'Ozz Lavender!' It takes her only seconds to bare her body. The ultimate freedom. It is wonderful.

Ozz looks at her appreciatively, she thinks, objectively. 'That is one hell of a body, Andy.'

He slips easily out of his running shorts, then stands up, holding out his hand to help her to her feet. 'C'mon, let's play the scene for the big production – Adam and Eve in Eden before the Fall.'

For a brief second she doesn't move but looks directly at his flat belly, narrow hips and then to his hairy groin where his penis hangs its head. He is as masculine as could be and isn't lusting for her.

The first Mrs Rochester stops rattling her bars. Eve takes his proffered hand and stands up. They run into the sea like children, splashing and kicking up the water.

The sea is soothing and wonderfully relaxing. As she might have guessed, Ozz swims gracefully, with an athlete's powerful over-arm action, his face turning sideways in the water only every six or eight strokes, always the same side, flicking his mouth clear of the water to take in air. The sea at home had not often been warm, so that much of her swimming had been in the woodland pool, thirteen strokes in one direction and twenty in the other, in fresh, green and glassy water shared on good terms with the abundant pond life.

Here the sea is warm as bathwater, and she plunges herself like a spear towards the sandy bottom which is further than it appears from the surface. As she touches the floor of the bay, Ozz, in a stream of bubbles, touches her hand and points to a shoal of tiny fishes. She shows him a creature that has burrowed in the sand but kept a single open eye on watch.

They surface together. She has never seen him look so happy. Like recognizing like, she has suspected that his cheerfulness is a bit of a put-up job, and now she sees that it is. This is the real Ozz. She likes him more than ever. 'If I take the chauffeuring job, do you think I get to keep the golfing umbrella?'

'Make it a condition when you see Alex.'

'I shall still keep pushing for my big truck or ambulance.'

'I never doubted that.'

Treading water, he holds out his hands. She takes them and they float facing one another, the hot sun on their backs, the cool bright water beneath them, gently letting the little wings of waves move them about as they might have moved seaweed or jelly-fish.

Soothed and happy, she at last gets out and sits patting herself dry with her skirt while Ozz takes another leisurely swim along the line of the shore. When he too comes out of the water, his normally unruly hair slicked to his head, she sees that he has a partial erection which is gone by the time he reaches the shade of the umbrella.

'Did y' ever feel this good?'

'Never.'

'I'm not as fit as I should be, I should stop smoking.'

'So stop.'

'What the hell, I enjoy the hunt for the weed.' He passes her the bottle of wine and then drinks from it himself. 'Y'know what I reckon, sweetheart? One day, when it's all over, we'll come back, shall we?'

She hugs her knees and joins him in his fantasy. 'You bring the umbrella and some of the famous Lavender wine. Choose a good year.'

'Vintage 1930, my old man's proud of that, didn't want to let it go. He's still got some put down.'

'And I'll bring a big basket of strawberries of my own picking. Red Gauntlets. I'll select the ones that reached their peak overnight and gather them just as the dew has dried and the sun has had time to warm them, and a little bowl of sugar and some heavy cream which I shall have skimmed myself.'

He rolls in her direction, his long body moving so beautifully. It does not arouse her sexually, nor does their closeness appear to do anything to stimulate him. Join me in Eden, he had said. For long moments they look into one another's eyes. 'Eve, sweetheart, I wish I could give you anything in the world you ever wanted.'

There is something so poignant about the moment that she feels lost in it. It is as though they have found a kind of love that is so extraordinary that it is more profound than anything they might have had if they had given themselves up to sex. It would have been so easy, the temptation to put out a hand and caress him had been there until she had plunged to the sandy bottom of the bay. Putting her arms around his neck, she kisses him gently on the cheek. 'I think you have, Ozz.'

He makes no attempt to hide the fact that his eyes are brimming with tears. He just continues to search her face as though it is important to fix every eyelash and pore in his memory.

They settled propped up, back to back, drinking warm fruity wine directly from the bottle. When the sun grew too hot for them they retreated to the pine wood and the car.

'What's with the strawberries, then?'

'Some people whom I love own strawberry fields. It was Elysium and I was a child invited to stay. You can't imagine.'

'Do you think we could have my little Welsh mam visit our umbrella? She'd bring figs and pomegranates.'

Eve laughed. 'Seedy fruit gets her in, I adore figs.'

He kissed her lightly on the cheek as she got into the driver's seat. 'Thanks for telling me about the strawberries, sweetheart.'

'Dear Ozz, you're a bright light in a naughty world.'

He gave her a brief smile before he turned to the matter of maps and routes. 'You ever meet my old man – you tell him that.'

Chapter Six

Ken Wilmott took his exercise, as he had done several times recently, by visiting *Las Cibeles*, statues that in peacetime foreign tourists to Madrid would make a point of visiting, though now they were hidden within a wall of sandbags.

'I say, Wilmott? Ken? It is you, isn't it? Remember me?' A tall, fair man holding a camera joined him.

'Dave Hatton, as I live and breathe. Good to see you again. How did the film go?'

'I'm told that it went down a treat in the provinces. Helped raise a hell of a lot of money, helped to raise awareness too. What are you doing in Madrid? Oh, I see. Winged. Bad one?'

'No, just one in the arm, but it's OK. I'm ready to get back, but I wanted to have one last look at the women coming back from the front. Amazing, aren't they?' He indicated the first of the young Madrileño women making their way back along the Gran Via from a spell of duty defending the Madrid front line, which was now close to University City. The road was so frequently under artillery attack that it was impossible for vehicles to use it, but it was a matter of pride for the young militia women to come back home that way.

'They're why I'm here. I hope *Picture Post* is going to do something on the militia, the Madrileño women. I want to get pictures.'

'That's just how my sister and her friends used to come home from the factory, arm-in-arm, looking as though they hadn't got a care in the world. You'd never think that these girls were quite likely toting rifles an hour ago.'

They came in little groups, chattering and laughing, cautious, but not cringing from the shelling. Their uniform consisted of khaki dungarees, a red *pañuelo* knotted about the neck, a tasselled militia cap and *zapatos* on their feet.

Hatton focused his camera on a group of chattering and laughing women who saluted with raised fists when they saw him. He said, 'An army of girls returning from the front shod in canvas and grass.' He ran across to one group, then beckoned Wilmott to join them. 'Do me a favour, Ken, I want you at the centre of the group.' Ken, with his arm in a sling and surrounded by laughing and dishevelled young women, would, the photographer felt sure, be a perfect icon for Aid to Spain people to sell at fund-raising events. 'Would you like some copies to send to your people?'

'I would. They won't recognize me, I haven't had a photo taken since I've been here.'

'Where will you be?'

'I'm going back to my unit in the morning.'

'With your arm in a sling?'

Ken Wilmott took his arm out of the sling and flexed his fingers. 'Just show. My trigger-finger works now, that's all I need. If I give you the address, do you think that you could send the photo to my brother?'

'Of course.'

The following day, Lieutenant Wilmott, his wounded arm dressed and bound, went back to his battalion. The battle ground was now at Brunete.

'Ken, owd man. Thank God you're back. I thought I was destined to pop off with bloody Greek and Polish in my ears. Hardly seems to be a bugger left who speaks English.'

Ken, having been away sufficiently long to forget how haggard they had all become, thought that Harry Pope looked sick with fatigue. 'You don't look too good, Harry.'

'I'm not the only one. Everybody's got something wrong with their guts. Bloody flies everywhere, filthy bloody things picking up our own shit and bringing it back to us. It's a vicious bloody circle. You get the runs till you feel your veins are pumping sand.'

'Still short of water?'

'Worse than ever. Same with the food trucks, they try to get in after dark, but ammunition gets priority. What water there is goes right through you.'

That night a food lorry did get through. The tailboard of the cookhouse truck was let down and was at once surrounded by men of all nationalities. 'See what I mean, owd man? Talk about the Tower of Babel. I don't know where they all come from, must have got cut off from their own lot or their own lot is all dead.'

Over the days that followed, Ken Wilmott spent his time choking on dust and firing at the enemy as the battalion fought on under the beating sun, and flies bred remorselessly on the filth and fragments of human carrion. When the battle ended, the battalion was sent for a few days to San Lorenzo de El Escorial to gather its strength.

Lieutenant Ken Wilmott and Captain Harry Pope were now the two senior officers. They sat and deloused the seams of their clothing, thankful not only to be alive, but to be out of the relentlessly beating sun, away from the stink of human corruption and decomposition, away from filthy, biting, contaminating flies and the acrid smoke of burning stubble. Water was still not easy to find, but at San Lorenzo there was at least a little for drinking.

The two men were withdrawn and silent, for there had been a roll-call of the battalion. Out of the six hundred who had gone into the attack, only forty-two paraded.

'What d'you reckon, Harry, were you and me saved so as we can pick fleas off each other like a couple of monkeys?'

'You and me were saved, me lad, for no other reason than we must have been better at ducking than the other five hundred poor bastards.' He inspected his nails and started on them with a sharp pocket knife. 'Did you ever see yourself as an officer?'

'Did I hell as like. My old oppos back home would give us

a good rollicking if they knew. Captain of the footie team is all I ever aimed to be. What did you do before you came out here?'

'I were a preacher.'

Ken Wilmott halted in his close inspection of trouser seams. 'You're joking.'

'No, it's true. In owd days they used to call us hedge-bottom vicars, no church, just God's good air for a church and a stile for a pulpit. Only difference these days is we has a factory for a parish and the works gate is where we preach.'

'But I never heard you say anything about religion, nor Jesus or God.'

'No, I preached socialism – fair shares and justice – equal pay for equal work – land belongs to everybody, nobody can own it – a better life here and now because there's nowt else to come after. D'you think we should shave our heads? It'd make a lot of sense, and you should get that beard off you and all. Ha' you still got that fancy self-stropping razor? Come on, let's do it.'

Ken Wilmott's thick, brown curls, hacked off with borrowed scissors, blew away on the hot wind, after which he sat wincing as the dry razor rasped over his scalp. Then they swapped places and Harry Pope lost his nit-packed hair. 'How about you? Did you have a job?'

'I had an apprenticeship.'

'Bie! They say it's better to be born lucky than rich. What's your trade?'

'Undertaker.'

The young captain laughed. 'You're having me on! I'd'a said you'd be a chap that spent most of his life in the open.'

'So I have the last couple of years, but that's what I am. Served all my time at the Co-op Funeral Parlour.' They sat side by side again, each from time to time running his hand over the strange head of pale skin. 'I thought about that several times back there.' He indicated with his head, meaning back at Brunete where the rest of the battalion had ended up dead. 'If any of those chaps had popped off in their home towns they'd have had all that stuff we used to do – combing them, sprinkling them with lavender oil and stuff – instead of which, because they stopped a bullet somewhere else, their bits and pieces are shovelled into a pit all together. I thought to myself, well, Ken Wilmott, that makes your job look pretty shittin'.'

'No, no, I'll not have that. Treating your dead with respect due is civilized, same as providing for your mental cases and owd folks decent-like. To me, that's what being a socialist is. Shovelling our own lads – and some of the others and all – into a pit is the best we can do under the circumstances.' He placed a handkerchief knotted at the corners on his bare head and with the knife started on his toenails. 'Did you wear a top hat for it?'

'No, pall-bearers go bare-headed, you couldn't do it in a top hat.'

'No, I suppose you couldn't. Bie heck, this place is an education, not a day goes by without you pick up something useful.'

'And you pick up a lot that's not.'

A quiet moment in a noisy war. Two young idealists did what would have been unthinkable in most other circumstances, they shaved one another of their pubic hair without embarrassment.

Chapter Seven

Nothing moved. The only sounds were small ones coming from the expanding metal of the Mercedes.

Although summer was running down, the weather was still very hot. It was quiet on the road.

Eve sat on the running-board of her car, her body still trembling from a violent vomiting attack, her face running with sweat, her hands cold and clammy. It would pass.

Nothing moved.

Drinking from a bottle of warm water laced with bicarbonate of soda, she shuddered as her stand-by medication touched her taste-buds. She hated the stuff, but it was the best antidote to these bilious attacks, the only antidote for most of the time. Bouts of sickness were as nothing in the greater orgy of disease, injury and death. Many of the foreign volunteers Eve met experienced the same day-to-day problems with their food. Although she kept in mind Sophie Wineapple's advice 'stick to the beans', meat of any sort was tempting. Other Americans she had met put all stomach disorders down to flies, and poor hygiene in the kitchens.

English admin said it was just the change in diet, it took time to get used to hot spices and horseflesh, or goat, or donkey, some of it too long dead before it reached the cooking pots, but it *was* meat. Food had taken on an importance way beyond being the mere means of nourishment. Sometimes, after dark in the Starlight Hotel dormitory, they would create fantastical meals composed of all the differing foods they longed for. Next morning it would still be bread and beans, sometimes bread and corned beef. Occasionally Eve was given treats by the VIPs she ferried around, but she often used them as barter for soap, or lavatory and writing paper.

Today she had delivered her charges, a two-man film team, and made a start as soon as it was light. She was on her way back from the hospital at Colmenar where she had spent the night curled up on the back seat of the Mercedes, while a transient nurse slept in the front. A couple of hours ago she had stopped off in a small damaged town to buy something to drink and found a *cantina* where the savoury smell of frying had been too much for her. She longed for something familiar and comforting and it seemed ages since she had smelled bacon frying. The meal had been a wonderful diversion.

Even now that the breakfast had gone and her stomach was empty again, Eve still considered that she got a good deal. It had been as close as she had come in months to a Sunday-morning breakfast. Perhaps she ought not to have drunk the local wine, but over the weeks she had come to like its sharp, rough taste. Ozz had said that the wine the peasants drank was full of tannin which killed off stomach bugs.

The nausea subsided. She lit a nub of cigarette and sat quietly smoking and looking out at where the violence of her stomach had forced her to halt. This was beautiful. Here, where a quiet, unravaged countryside dozed in the glare of the late summer sun, there was no sign that elsewhere there were two Spains viciously grappling with each other. She had stopped on the road from the Guadalajara region, and in valleys in the south where there were olive groves and orange groves and where, as now, there were moments when nothing moved, and she had felt herself falling for the country. Alexander had said, 'Wait till you've spent a winter here, then tell me you love it.'

Waiting for her strength to return, she took out the notebook that now had an essential place in her haversack and continued one of the accounts she now sent regularly to Sid Anderson, her sponsor in London.

Almost daily now, I drive through towns where churches have been demolished, sometimes destroyed purposely when the Republic was new and people wanted to obliterate signs of their past subservience and poverty. In many towns, centuries-old buildings are damaged beyond repair by bombs, and blocks of modern workers' flats, built since the Republic, are pitted with shell-holes and have their windows boarded-up. Both sides are convinced that theirs is a crusade, the Nationalists against communism, the Republicans against fascism.

I went through one town which has been held by both sides, tugged back and forth, and is now back with the Reds again. On a church ¡Fiexisme No! was daubed in red paint, then over-painted with the cross of Catholic monarchists and the yoke and arrow emblem of the right-wing Falangists. Then the Republicans returned, so that the most recent message is a new red ¡Fiexisme No! This raised my spirits because it gave me hope that, even if the Republicans are forced to give up a town, it is not the end.

A bit like the game children play piling their hands one on top of the other and the object is always to have the top hand. How many children's hands will be left to play anything when the fighting stops? The Republic must, *absolutely must*, succeed. Any other outcome is too dire to contemplate, for the German and Italian fascists will not stop at Spain. I sometimes wonder whether what we foreigners do is worthwhile, but then I tell myself that it must be, if only as a message to the Spanish people that although our government stands aloof, many of us will not.

Oh dear, Sid, if this sounds rather introverted, I expect it's probably because our food can sometimes be a little ... disturbing? Yes, that's the word. Stomachs trained to fish and chips rebel against olive oil and hot spices. Please believe that, whatever happens, I am very glad that I came here. I shall always be grateful to you for believing in a pushy young girl who burst upon you asking for the keys so that she could open up the door to the world.

The cigarette didn't last long, so Eve took another from her small supply. Each time she finished a pack she told herself it didn't matter if there were no more cigarettes, she'd be better off without them, but each time when she heard where there were some to be had, she bought what she could, as everyone did, chasing everyday items such as pins or hair-clips or soap. The Spanish cigarette was dry and squashed, but it at least tasted fresh. The smell reminded her of Ozz. She hadn't seen him since Jávea bay. He left her funny, friendly little messages, mostly about what he would do if she didn't take care of the Mercedes.

She took black sunglasses from her top pocket and a rolled-up man's Panama hat from the shoulder tabs of her workman-like shirt. She should move, yet still she sat on. Eager as she was to get back to the Auto-Parc, she was also putting off the time when she would need to explain her decision to Alexander and plead her case.

Before she continued her journey, she added a paragraph to her letter to Sid.

Yesterday – Colmenar hospital, talked with an Italian, a Marxist who was delivering supplies in an American truck. He had spent some time with the partisans. He was there when some fascist soldiers tried to give themselves up and come over to the Republic. Partisans shot them all. My truck-driver said, You couldn't blame them could you? Could I? Maybe I could, I don't know. With families split, brother against sister, father against son, it is all so complicated. I started out thinking it was Them and Us, but I am beginning to see how fragmented Us is. I am not sure which of the splinters I agree with. None and yet all I suppose. I believe that although they welcome foreign aid, the Spanish do not really want outsiders in their war except as symbols of international support. We don't understand the nuances of the various factions. It's true, we don't.

Her mission now was to pick up a small medical team, led by Mr Siel, who was, in his other life, a Harley Street specialist in reconstructing limbs, particularly of men who had crashed in motor racing. The others were his anaesthetist and theatre nurse. Mr Siel was legendary; he and his team divided their time between his lucrative London practice and the battle-zone hospitals. Eve had transported the Siel team several times before. She had supposed that all English doctors who offered their skills to the Republic would be young Marxists, like the one with whom she had travelled out, but she had been wrong. Mr Siel was urbane, Jewish and middle-aged.

Back on the road, she glanced at the open map on the passenger seat. Not far now. Her life had become hectic: maps, street-plans, place-names, some of them well-known, others isolated, orders and papers. Sometimes she hardly knew what day it was. The nursing sister from New Zealand who had slept in the car last night had said, 'Time moves so fast here, you grow up quick. When I left home I was my dad's good little girl. When I arrived here last year I was twenty-five, next birthday I shall be fifty.'

Another hospital. This one still bore signs of the convent that it had once been, a Moorish-looking building, probably as old as the presbytery where the burnt child had died. Not as suited to a hospital as that had been, but as near to the fighting front as this was, beggars couldn't be choosers.

She could tell at once that they were busy. She had come in on the road from the east, and so had not seen the line of ambulances and Red Cross vehicles coming in on the western road. At the gates she had to wait in line between two Bedford ambulances of the type she had driven when she first arrived. They were vehicles that looked as though they were on important work even when they were merely parked. She felt irritated with Alex and envious of the drivers. Lately, although she got great pleasure from driving the motor car, she had been dissatisfied with the uses to which it was sometimes put. If the thoroughbred horse she had ridden had finished up in the stewpot, it had at least served the Republic, but the thoroughbred motor car was sometimes pushed into doing what it had always done: providing an insulated cocoon to carry elite persons around so that they might look at what war did to other people.

Before setting out on this journey, she had again pressed Helan Alexander to take her off some of the VIP duties – the

Vipps. 'The trouble with you, Alex, is that you're too concerned with people of rank.'

'Not Mr Siel, he's a real Vipp. There are men walking on two legs who might not be doing so if it wasn't for Mr Siel.'

'You know I don't mean the doctors, it's some of the others. It's those who have just come to look: titled ladies who think they've been to the front if they walk through a hospital ward, and army officers who think they own the war. I can't stand them, they're useless out here.'

'Titled ladies are good at raising money, we can't do without them. High-ranking Soviet officers go home with a favourable glow around them and send out more of everything the Republic needs. If we had them haul their bags on and off railway trains, it might not endear the Republic to them. You and I have got accustomed to grubbing about, they have not.'

'You could soon get me off your back, Alex, by putting me on more valuable detail. When do I get to drive a truck again, or an ambulance?'

'You haven't been listening. The Vipp service is vital. I leave you with this thought: fawn on those with the wherewithal to keep us going.'

'You know that I'm as good as any of your men at driving heavy vehicles. If a man told you that you could keep your Vipp service, then you would. Alex, just give me a break sometimes. Ask Ozz, he knows I'm a good driver. I didn't come here to ass around with Vipps. I see why it has to be me, Alex – if a few blue-blooded liberals get a young woman courier, it looks good, equality of the sexes at work.'

'You aren't detailed to do the Vipps because you're a pretty woman, you are the best man for the job. Don't give me a hard time. I promise you, it's vital work, especially the delivery of X-ray plates. The hospitals couldn't function without them, and it would be profligate to use a truck or van that could be used for other supplies.'

'I don't mind the X-ray plates.'

'Mr Siel says he'd take you on as his personal driver any time.'

'Well, thank *you*, Mr Siel! My greatest ambition has always been to drive some rich doctor around.'

'D'you remember that first day here? I road-tested you, we went to look at the horses?'

Eve tried to look non-committal. 'Of course I remember, you said the poor things were destined for the pot.'

'I had you down as the daughter of some parson, a Fabian probably, raised in the country, been to a frightfully nice day-school where you did rather well – probably head girl or prefect or something, trained to care for people and animals, and come to Spain in a cloud of idealism, and looking for independence. A nice, well-brought-up young woman, quite shy and retiring, wouldn't say boo to a goose but sharp as a tack.'

Eve smiled wryly, wondering just what Helan Alexander had her down as now. 'But you changed your mind.'

'I dunno, except that I am aware that my infallible first impressions failed me.'

'So, what are your second impressions?'

'Not very shy or retiring, would say boo to a goose, quite often does. Caring, idealistic, that was right. Sharper than I first thought – as a blade. I don't know about the rest.'

'Good. That's my ambition, to become the greatest enigma the world has known.'

'That is exactly it! I can never tell when the real Eve Anders is there. Is she ever?'

'I wouldn't know, Alex, I'm only the driver.'

Enigmatic. Yes, that would do for now.

She switched off the engine and let other vehicles through. With all this activity she would have bet a bar of soap that Mr Siel wouldn't be leaving today. He'd stay on to mend as many casualties as he could. She had to admit one thing: it was possible to have an upper-class accent, and a practice in Harley Street, and not be a snob. She liked Mr Siel, although he seldom said much, because there was no side to him. In fact, the great man himself had less side to him than the anaesthetist, Dr Parragon, who treated Eve like a chauffeur. She had formed the opinion that perhaps Dr Parragon disapproved of Mr Siel's voluntary work, but in terms of the Harley Street practice, he knew which side his bread was buttered.

'There are injured coming in,' she was told, as soon as she reported and handed over the flat pack of X-ray plates. 'Mr Siel is still operating. He won't leave while men are coming in, so you'd best find yourself a corner somewhere.'

An orderly showed her a room that was at present unoccupied, but didn't make any promises about it staying that way. It was about the size of her own single bedroom at home, but here three beds had been crammed in. She didn't care, there was the back seat of the Mercedes, but it would be nice to stretch out. All that she could think of now was food and drink.

There was a terrible rush on. Orderlies were carrying stretchers, the nurses wore limp dresses and creased aprons, and rolled-up stretchers filled every available corner. And there was that same pervasive smell of blood, carbolic and cigarette smoke that she had encountered before. The difference here was that she had arrived in the midst of it.

'Stay with him, will you?' The nurse hung a bottle of blood above the injured man's head and put a bowl of water and a cloth on the floor. 'I'll only be a jiff. He's . . .' she hunched her shoulders a little, 'he's under morphine.'

'It's OK, I know what to do.' Abandoning her ambition of finding something to eat, Eve sat down beside her patient. He wore the uniform of the militia. Even though his features were obscured with dirt and blood, she could tell he was young. His eyes were closed, but was he asleep or unconscious? Was he dead? Judging by the colour and texture of his skin, almost like the big altar candles in the church adjoining her school, he must be pretty bad. A small stain of blood showed at chest level. Was it his blood? His eyes flickered, opened momentarily, then closed. With a little shock she knew that she had seen him somewhere, but couldn't remember where. In the last few weeks hundreds of people had come briefly into her life and then disappeared.

She squeezed out the cloth and gently wiped his face. He groaned, low and weak as though he had no energy left.

'Marco?' There was no response. The bloodstain had grown larger.

The mingled smells of blood and faeces caused her to give a little shiver of horror; she remembered that smell from a long way off. Death was never far away from that smell. Repellent and hypnotic, it stayed in the nostrils for ever.

As children, a gang of them would sometimes haunt the slaughter-houses after cattle and pigs had been driven from the cattle-market to await the stun. Animals and children alike sniffed the terror, the animals bucking and banging around. Children, held captive by barbarous scenes hidden from their view, shivered with excitement at being in the presence of violent death.

Where was the nurse? 'Marco, can you hear me?' There was no response. Eve delved into her top pocket and drew out the little talisman she always carried. 'Marco, look I have the . . . do you remember me? Sacred Heart?' She could have cried with frustration at her lack of vocabulary.

'Señorita Anders.' Marco's voice was barely there.

'Yes, Marco, yes. Look. Remember, you gave this to me?' She held up the little charm. A faint smile passed across her face. He brought his hand up, and she pressed the cloth into it. He held on to her fingers, but she didn't understand what he was saying.

'*Catolico* . . .' He closed his eyes.

'You want a priest? Is that it? A priest?' He had withdrawn again. She didn't know what to do. He looked as though each one of his short puffs of breath might be his last. She stopped a passing orderly and asked him to fetch a priest.

All that Eve could do while they waited was clean away the blood as best she could. When she went to return his hand under the cover, she saw for the first time what a fragment of shell can do to a shoulder and ribs. The extent of the damage was devastating. The top of his khaki dungaree uniform had been cut away, a field dressing applied and the jacket rebuttoned to hold the dressing in place. Dungarees and dressing were saturated with dark blood. She straightened the blanket and positioned the Sacred Heart talisman where the wound was.

The priest came, ready with his accoutrements. He was having a busy day. 'The orderly said you were English.'

Eve breathed a sigh of relief. 'Yes.'

'I'm Brother Nellis. He asked for a priest?' Brother Nellis wore plimsolls, a pair of what appeared to have once been cricket flannels and a navvy's shirt.

'Yes, at least I think that's what he meant.'

The nurse returned, apologizing for the delay. She lifted Marco's eyelids, and felt the neck pulse. 'He's still with us. Shall I leave it to you a minute, Father? Only two ahead of him for theatre.' She caressed his downy cheek with her knuckles. 'Hang on, laddie.'

The priest knelt at Marco's side and began the rite that might assure Marco's future in the next life. Eve stood back, watching the priest perform the rituals.

Brother Nellis got up stiffly.

'Thank you,' Eve said. 'He is so young, isn't he?'

'As are you.'

'I feel very old today. Poor little Marco, that's a terrible wound.'

'He may pull through. Young people are very resilient.' He looked directly at her. 'Is that a trace of the Hampshire Hog I detect?'

'Possibly.'

'It is just that my college, de Montfort, is in Hampshire.'

'I'm afraid I've never heard of it.' She wished that the nurse would come and say that they were ready for Marco in theatre.

'You know the boy?'

'Only that he was part of a company I drove south a few weeks ago.'

'Is that what you do, transport soldiers around the country?'

108

'It is what I *was* doing. I'm afraid that I am now a courier and chauffeur.'

'I hadn't realized there was such a . . . a service.'

'It's for special visitors, VIPs, we call them Vipps.' She squatted beside Marco, brushing his cheek with its soft down of black peach-bloom as the nurse had done. He had probably run away from the classroom to fight for his country. The awful, splendid ideals of youth.

'I see,' said Brother Nellis. He didn't.

'It is thought that special people require special transport.'

'Goodness, I thought that sort of thing went into exile with the King of Spain.'

'I probably protest too much. I also fetch and carry X-ray plates. Today I was supposed to be taking Mr Siel and his aides to the airport, but I don't know what will happen now.'

'I was with Mr Siel when you sent for me. He's very busy.'

'Do you know him well?'

He squatted beside her, the two of them watching Marco closely as they talked quietly. 'Not well, but he and I have spent quite some time together. He has quite a sense of humour – he says he likes to try his hand before he will let me try mine. He is a good man. He once said that I was the long-stop – it's a sporting term – to catch the souls that get past him.'

'I've never met a monk before.'

'Have you not? Perhaps you thought that we all went about with dusty feet and hooded robes.'

'Yes, I did, to be truthful.'

'Mine is a teaching order. I was on a two-year sabbatical near Jávea when the Nationalists invaded.'

'The presbytery that is now a hospital?'

'Yes. The establishment was closed down, dispersed.'

They fell silent.

'Marco gave me this as a keepsake, to protect me. His grandmother made it for him.'

'Ah, even the atheists like to have their little charms. Better safe than sorry, does no harm. Don't you have your lucky heather or rabbit's foot?'

'No. Just a pocket-piece.'

'You have a pocket-piece? How interesting.'

She was surprised that he should be familiar with such a pagan charm. Hers had been given to her years ago by Bar Barney's mother and, along with the uncut precious gemstone from Duke, she carried it with her always.

'Not many people know what a pocket-piece is.'

'I think of them as a kind of thought embedded in ashwood.'

'Ironic, isn't it? Marco *really* needed his sacred talisman. I tried to return it to him just now, but he wouldn't let me.'

'He must think a great deal of you.'

'He's still bleeding and the bottle won't last much longer. If you'll stay with him, I think I'll try to find Mr Siel.'

'Straight through, at the back of the building. You'll know when you get there.'

She did. The smell of ether was strong, the smell of blood and carbolic acid stronger. The smell of life and death.

As a nurse wearing a red rubber apron and cloth mask and a female orderly wearing a white overall and Red Cross armband came through a swing door pushing a wheeled stretcher, Eve recognized the voices of Mr Siel and Dr Parragon.

'Excuse me,' she said to a hurrying nurse, 'could you ask –?'

'You shouldn't be here.' The nurse made a shooing motion.

'All right, but could you ask Mr Siel –'

'Mr Siel is extremely busy. What is it?'

'I know he's busy. But I'm his driver, I'm supposed to get him to the airport.'

The nurse looked as though she had never heard of an airport.

'He's due back in London, and I want to know whether I am to wait.'

'Oh, well, you'll have to . . . down there somewhere . . . away from . . .' She disappeared with the name of Sister Pelham on her lips.

Mr Siel, peeling off his gloves with a peculiar squeaking

sound, came through the door of the operating theatre. He too wore a red rubber apron, plus a kind of white shift, galosh-like shoes, and a white, round cap tied with tapes.

'So. Right. You *are* waiting.'

'I just want to know whether you'll be going to the airport.'

They had to step aside for a trolley being pushed by an orderly and a nurse.

'Marco!' Eve exclaimed. His eyes were wide open now.

Mr Siel stopped the trolley. 'What is this?'

'Shell fragments. Ribcage, right shoulder.'

'Do you know this young man?'

Marco said huskily, 'Señorita Anders, *por favor* . . .'

The nurse said, 'Is he for you, sir?'

'Yes, be quick.'

'Please.' Eve bent over and gave Marco a light kiss on his pale forehead. He said something as he was being wheeled away. The orderly turned. 'He says, please forgive him.'

Eve bit her lip to stop herself from crying. Mr Siel said, 'It may be a long wait. I think we shall not be returning to London until tomorrow. Could you arrange something, a morning flight?'

'Of course. I'll see admin at once.' She turned to leave.

'Miss Anders?'

'Yes?'

'I can't save them all.'

'I know.'

'I'll do my best.'

'Thank you, I know you will.'

Next morning on the way to the airport, Eve told Mr Siel about Marco and the bullet that missed her. 'He insisted that I have the charm his grandma made him. It will always be at the back of my mind that he insisted that I have his shield.'

Mr Parragon put in tetchily, 'These superstitious charms are more likely to make them reckless, so he might have lost his head instead of only an arm.'

'Not *only* an arm, ribs and breastbone, Edward, and not lost, not entirely. You see, Miss Anders, much of the soft tissue was destroyed.'

'Mr Siel, I didn't even expect him to come through.'

As she helped to unload their bags at the little hangar that was the airfield waiting area, Mr Siel said, 'Perhaps you will be visiting the boy before he returns home?'

'I will try. I often have X-ray plates to deliver.'

'Tell him, say that we wish him well.'

'I will, Mr Siel, if I can find the right words in Spanish.'

'In my opinion, for what this is worth, the boy will not mind if you speak Hindustani. Warm hands and friendly faces say a great deal.'

As she drove away, Eve tried to imagine him in his other role, the Harley Street surgeon famous for treating royal skiing accidents and crashed rally speedsters. Benevolence and understanding had not been part of her idea of Harley Street specialists. She had thought of them as imperious men pandering to ladies such as David's grandmother, Lady Margaret Gore-Hatton, whose manner had once caused Eve to panic and hang up when she had tried to telephone David. If she had been wrong about Harley Street specialists, might she also have formed too hasty an opinion of David because his grandmother was high-handed?

She had grown to like and admire Mr Siel, but was the transportation of his team and the X-ray plates to be the best she could do for Spain?

Chapter Eight

There were times when it seemed difficult to remember where one was, but this wasn't so bad, it could be fixed in one's memory as one does with a telephone number: Operator, Sierra Pandols 666, please. Back from the front line now, at a rest camp for the unit he had been filming in action, dressed only in khaki shorts and a battered but very good Panama hat, David Hatton leaned back against a shady tree and wrote out a label to affix to his can of film – 'Hill 666: Pandols sector', then jotted down a script for the voice-over.

Hatton + Hatton Films. Report by David Hatton
We had barely taken over the Lincolns' position on the main heights of the Pandols when the enemy launched its biggest and most sustained attack yet.

An artillery barrage, the like of which none of us had ever experienced, crashed down around us, and flying shrapnel and rock splinters inflicted dozens of minor injuries.

When the barrage lifted, two fascist infantry battalions hurled themselves against us. Although still reeling from the shock-waves of the barrage, we repelled the fascists. The fighting was intense and the battalion received heavy casualties.

The battalion has now been relieved by a Spanish unit. The 35th Division seems likely to receive a citation from the Brigade for their efforts in holding the hill against incredibly superior odds. This report for 'With the 35th in Spain' is filed by David Hatton.

Smiling to himself, a tall, fair man, wearing only khaki trousers and the ubiquitous grass-soled *zapatos* like those worn by the Spanish militia, squatted beside David Hatton who looked up briefly and did a double-take. The similarity between the two was astonishing.

'Rich! By all that's holy! Where did you spring from?'

The two men clasped one another by the forearms and held on. 'From Hill Six, Six bloody Six.'

'I've just got a can full of that.' David indicated a film-carrier and the script he had just completed.

'Stuff for old Hatton Plus?' Their outfit had been given the name Hatton + Hatton, which in the early days they had thought amusing.

'Right. A series of short films for Aid to Spain. Fund-raisers. Great stuff, every one a winner.'

'Well, so they should be, you're the best movie reporter in town, Davey.'

'Only since you left. I mean, they're winners because I have only to point the camera and the story tells itself. No chance of a second take. Gives one a keen edge.'

Richard Hatton punched his brother genially on the shoulder. 'Modesty doesn't sit well on you, Davey old lad.'

They were twins, not identical, but extraordinarily alike, with greenish-gold eyes, wheat-coloured hair and eyebrows, and long, straight noses square at the tip. Six feet tall and handsome, they had always drawn attention, especially when seen together. In London the Hatton brothers were well known in the world of film and journalism.

David and Richard Gore-Hatton had both grown up with a passion for making movies since the day when an indulgent great-uncle introduced them to home-movie-making. Later, the same uncle and his sister – their grandmother Lady Margaret (who, before her marriage to a lord, had been a talented actress) – had shown sufficient faith in the boys' talent to make a small investment which had helped them buy equipment and secure a specialist niche in the film-making industry.

In 1936, when they were in Spain reporting on the first civil disturbances, Richard had met and fallen in love with Maite Manîas, a Spanish playwright, and decided to stay. At the outbreak of the war he had joined the militia, and when the International Brigade was formed, he volunteered.

'Do you hear from Maite?'

Richard Hatton shook his head and fell silent.

'Trouble, Rich?'

'She thought that she was pregnant.'

'Oh, God. And she's still in Orense?'

'No, we moved to the coast, to Vigo, then I had to leave her and get back into the Republic. The plan was that she would travel on to Rosal and try to get across to Portugal and on to London that way. But I haven't heard a word.'

'For how long?'

'Weeks now. I've used every last contact to try to find out something, but I have to be careful for her sake. They shoot first and ask afterwards and they imprison anybody and everybody who's the slightest bit suspect. And for God's sake, Davey, Maite wasn't exactly discreet in her work. You know what happened to Lorca and he wasn't even really political.'

'I'll see what I can do, Rich. I met Malou French on my last trip back to London, she might be able to discover something.' He smiled wryly. 'Met her passing through Biarritz of all places.'

'Why of all places? Biarritz is *exactly* the place to meet the French tart.'

'Oh, she's done with gossip and fashion, she's taken up with the Bishop's Fund for Relief of Spanish Distress.'

'That right-wing Catholic outfit?'

'That's right, she's in charge of the stocks for a kind of travelling hospital, I think that's what she said. Anyway she has the ear of some very important people in Burgos, that's how she got to be in charge of a set-up that's supposed to be entirely run by Spaniards. She has some nerve.'

'Then why in hell's name are you thinking of asking her to get information on Maite's whereabouts?'

'Why not? She and I recognize one another for what we are – political enemies – but she's not the type to do anything against one of her own.'

'Maite's not one of her own, she's a left-wing playwright and poet.'

'I'm one of her own, you and I both are. We did our duty at her coming-out ball. Look at the Mitfords, daggers drawn politically, but neither of the girls would hand the other to the enemy.'

'You're too nice, Davey. I wouldn't trust any of that set as far as I could throw them.'

'Rich, we *are* that set.'

'Were, Davey, were. I'd inform on Malou.'

'Would you really?'

'You know I would. So would you, young Hatton, so would you.'

David Hatton did not answer at first. He and Malou French had had a brief liaison. For both of them it had been sleeping with the enemy. ' "Play up, play up and play the game", ta-ra, and all that, Richard?'

'That was never honour. Honour is what's embedded in Marxism, honour's why I'm here. "Honour thy father and thy mother that thy days may be long in the land thy Lord givest thee." That doesn't mean nods and winks in the City, does it? That means take care of people, take care of everybody.'

David Hatton saw that something profound had happened to his brother since they were last together. 'You haven't caught religion, have you, Rich?'

Richard Hatton smiled, the ghost of his old handsomeness lit his face fleetingly. 'Not in the way dear old "MacDougall" Gore did.'

David smiled too, a flash of warm family feeling passing between them at the memory of one of their more eccentric relations. 'Douglas would have been fine if only he had caught some nice quiet Baptist variety instead of that drear Scottish kirk variety.'

'I haven't caught anything, old love, it's our legacy.' The legacy to which Richard referred was that same eccentricity that had manifested itself in religion in Douglas Gore-Hatton. It had always been something they spoke of lightly, perhaps to reassure themselves that their commitment to communism, in a family with blue blood in its veins, was not also mere eccentricity. 'The red Hatton blood might have curdled with the old Gore blue to produce Douglas, but ours is unadulterated Hatton red, Davey. Decent red blood.'

David Hatton uncapped one of his cameras. Knowing what was expected, his brother looked away from the lens and lit a thin roll-up cigarette, allowing the smoke to drift about his profile. 'That OK?'

'You're still a vain old sod, Rich. For two pins I'd make you turn the other way and take your bad side.'

'Haven't got one these days. Lost weight, uncovered the perfect Hatton facial bone structure. Look.' He grinned, lifted his chin and turned his face in the opposite direction.

David's concern as a brother almost outweighed his objectivity as a professional cameraman. Richard's bright eyes stared out from the deep, dark hollows of his gaunt features.

'Make a fist, Rich.'

Richard did so, looking directly in the camera's lens. '*No* fucking *pasarán!*' He took a long drag on his cigarette, then inspected the tip as he said fervently, 'That's more than just a slogan, Davey, you know that? We shall not let them pass, we *must* not. If we can't stop the jackboots here, they'll keep on marching and marching. And it will be the Hattons of this world who will be sent out to catch the bullets in their teeth; the Gores will stand back and urge them on as they've been doing for centuries.'

David had never seen his twin show so explicitly the extent to which he despised the Gore blood they shared.

The shadows were growing longer. People elsewhere in the rest camp began moving about again. 'Soon get a brew of tea, I should think,' Richard said. Neither of them moved.

'What about Malou. Shall I work on it?'

'I wouldn't trust the bitch as far as I could throw her.'

For a reason he would have found hard to put into words,

but it had to do with the possibility that Richard might not live much longer, David wanted to tell him secrets, perhaps to confess that he had not always confided in him as much as Richard might have supposed. 'Did you know that we once had a bit of a fling?'

'God help us all.' Richard stared at him. 'You and who else? How many to a bed? Or was it on horseback or a back-room in Chinatown?'

David was not fooled by the wry smile; Richard was troubled. 'Sounds as though you've been there, Rich.'

'Christ, Davey! No! And I never imagined you . . . I thought we were the only two in our set who *hadn't* been there. Anybody else involved? She likes threesomes and the odd dog or two, doesn't she?'

'Oh come on, Rich, Malou might be a bit of a mattress, but . . . no, it was just the two of us.'

'How innocent. For Christ's sake, she's not even a half-way decent journalist.'

'You've always said no experience is wasted – she wanted pictures.'

'Of the two of you? Christ, David, you never did them?'

'Why not? It was a bit of a challenge, really, making something more artistic than the regular crude stuff.'

'Dirty pictures are dirty pictures.'

'And Malou French is now hob-nobbing with the great and good of the Church of Rome. I think she's hoping to get an audience with the Pope.'

Richard snorted with derision. 'Saint Malou of Burgos! Sounds like blackmail, old son.'

'Blackmail has its uses.'

A few moments of silence ended the exchange.

'I'll have to muster soon. What are your plans?'

'I have to get these cans on a flight to Switzerland. They have to be in London the day after tomorrow.'

'Are you flying out?'

'No, there's some sort of motor car courier service. There

are drop-off points where stuff is picked up and taken to the airfield.'

'For cans of film?'

'No, it's a service for visiting nabobs. Nice motors too, requisitioned. They fly Republican pennants on the bonnet.'

'I came across a writer a few weeks back. English. He was at Eton – senior to us. Name of Blair.'

'Blair? Tall thin fellow who sneered down his nose? He's a writer, you say?'

'And a red. He's out here with the IB – forget which battalion – what I started to say was, he said something that stuck in my mind when we got to talking politics. "When people become equal, some will be more equal than others." See, Davey? Visiting nabobs require special motors, your use of them is abetting the system, confirms Blair's portent. It's the Gore in you still thinking it's OK being more equal than the rest.'

'Come off your high horse, Rich. This courier service is blessed by the state.'

'Many of whom still see themselves as the more equal.'

'So what would you do with abandoned and requisitioned Daimlers and Rolls, dynamite them?'

'It'd be a start, Davey. The anarchists have blown up churches because they symbolize injustice and oppression.'

'You always have had an answer for everything, Rich. Listen, *Tempus fugit*, and I've scrounged a lift in a lorry going to Madrid.'

'OK, but I'm reluctant to let you go. At least let's see if we can find a cup of tea or something. Are you still seeing Fiona?'

'Lord, no. Fiona married, she's gone to the States.'

'So what then, David, not leading a celibate life?'

'Are you?'

'It's different with me, I've got my woman, and, *Deo gratias*, she's carrying my child. I say, you aren't still mooning after that mystery woman?'

'Of course not.'

'Liar, Davey. I always know when you're lying.'

'OK, so I still think about her, but the odds against it coming to anything are pretty long ones.'

'She probably wasn't for you anyway. If Mags could scare her off, as you say, then . . .'

'Mags with her voice in full flight protecting one of her grandsons would stop a charging bull-elephant.'

'Maybe she was going to chuck you anyway. Arnold met her, didn't he?'

'I whisked her away from him pretty smartish. I had no intention of exhibiting our family, especially in the person of Arnold Gore.'

'He described her as a truly luscious totty.'

'I rest my case.'

'Did you never discover her true name?'

'Of course I didn't. If I had I might have had some chance of finding her again.' David Hatton paused and looked directly at his brother. 'I was really keen on her, Rich, really very keen, I still have dreams about meeting her.'

'Big dreams, at night?'

'Yes, damn it! If I didn't, then I imagine I might explode with unrequited lust.'

'That's bad, Davey.'

'Don't joke, Richard. I can't get the girl out of my mind. It isn't finished, I feel it in my bones.' The feeling in his bones, if he were honest, was nothing more than a fond hope that his love-life would be resolved in the manner of the novels his grandmother read to him, her favourite grandson, in his boyhood. Ah, Davey, she would say, how beautifully Jane Austen sorts them all out – each according to his or her deserts.

'I say, old son, have you thought that this might be a typical Gore affair?'

'I'm not a Gore, I'm a Hatton.'

'So you say, but our male ancestors have never been much attracted by their own kind. Perhaps you've been searching in the wrong places. Maybe she's on the stage, like Mags.'

Perhaps. For all her imperiousness now, their grandmother had once been an actress. It had stood her in good stead when she came to play the *grande dame* for real.

By now they were seated with mugs of tea at one of the long trestle-tables under the canopy of camouflaged canvas which was the cook-house. Richard said the smell put him in mind of the tea scrum at the Badminton Horse Trials.

'By the way, that reminds me. Did you know that Helan Povey – Helan Alexander as she now is – is running some sort of vehicle clearing-house for one of the aid committees? Down in Albacete, the Auto-Parc.'

'I heard. The vehicle bit doesn't surprise me, she only ever had two topics of conversation: horses and motor bikes. I didn't know that she had married.'

'Her chap, Alexander, he's a half-caste, more a quarter-caste. By all accounts, turned out to be quite a character. Got himself into some kind of trouble demonstrating at the Berlin Olympics, and was put on the first plane back to Berne. Black, you see. What with Jesse Owens winning gold, the Germans wanted no truck with an uppity black Jew.'

'Are we talking about Helan Povey of the prancing horses?'

'Absolutely. Half-black, quarter maybe, his mother is white, that's how he comes to have a Swiss passport. The Alexanders live there when they're not here.'

'Is he in Albacete too?'

'He came over here, got taken prisoner almost the same day he arrived.'

'Poor bastard.'

'Yeah.'

'Rich, you really have gone very red indeed. Is that Maite's influence?'

'I had a mind before I fell for Maite, I had my ILP membership card, and my Labour Party card even before you did.'

'But you never held a CP card.'

'It was a matter of time, Davey, you know that. After Winston Churchill ordered the rifles to be turned on people in Cable

Street, and the brown-shirts went through the East End like Cossacks . . . you saw it, you filmed it. Didn't it say to you, enough is enough?'

'Communism's not the answer, Rich.'

'It's a damn good start. Anyway, I don't know why you're being so argumentative, you couldn't put a card between our ideals when we were Hatton plus Hatton.'

'I'm not arguing. I haven't lost my ideals, I want no more Lord Gores or Lord Poveys blighting the lives of Joe Soap.'

'But you haven't yet picked up a rifle and faced the Moorish hordes.'

'True, Rich, but I've faced them with my camera. In fact, I was sniped at for five minutes.' He broke the strained mood by smiling, then chuckling, 'I was right down in a trench, with my camera pointed straight at the enemy line, and phut-phut-phut, the only bullets coming over seemed to be coming straight for me. I changed my position three times, and they still found it.'

Richard Hatton grinned, 'That silly sod was never you?'

'What d'you mean, "That silly sod"?'

'Well, that's what the chap called you, wasn't it, when he pulled you back into the trench by the braces? And saved your life? The camera it was that died. So it's true then?'

'The camera didn't die, but I did feel a damned fool not realizing that the sun was reflecting off the lens. But it was my first day at the front line.'

'Don't take it to heart, the story's apocryphal. It's the kind of story about visitors to our war that gives us a laugh.'

'Glad you enjoyed it.'

'The story wouldn't have stood up as a joke on camp-followers if the sniper had got you.'

'Don't needle me again, Rich. I shall not take up a rifle. Somebody has to counter the propaganda the other side is churning out. Desecration, executions, atrocities.'

'Atrocities? I'll tell you atrocities. Want to make a real horror film? I'll tell you where to go.'

'Calm down, Rich. Let me do things my way, and you do them yours.'

Richard sighed heavily, his inward breath catching like a sob. 'You're right, Davey.' He rubbed his face with the palms of his hands and sat for a few moments staring out over the tips of his fingers. 'Yes, yes, sorry, old lad. It's this business with Maite, keep thinking what they might do to her.'

David Hatton had nothing to say. Even as he had mentioned atrocities he wished that he had kept silent.

'This girl you seem so keen on, you don't really think she was scared off by Mags, do you?'

'She barks, Rich, she still thinks she has to reach the back row of the stalls when she answers the telephone. She doesn't like them, can't get the hang of them. If Louise wasn't actually scared off, she might have thought twice about leaving a message with Mags.'

'Mags thought that she was protecting you from some hussy of a fortune-hunter. I really do hope that you'll find her. I do know how it feels not knowing where the one you love is.'

'I have never said I love her.'

'That's true.'

David Hatton gave his brother an understanding clasp on the shoulder, leaving his hand there. Then he squeezed his fingers briefly and stood up. 'Maite's going to be safe, Rich. I feel that she must be.'

'You and your bones, Davey. I hope they're right. Once I hear that she has reached Berne or London, then I'll be OK and stop shrieking like an old queen. I'll not leave Spain, of course, I'll be here to the bitter end. This war is the first frost of a hard winter to come. If they aren't stopped here and now, Hitler and Mussolini will go for the whole of Europe, and none of us will be safe.'

Trained as they were in the ways of Englishmen, the brothers parted as though they were just off, as in the old days, to take pictures at a society wedding and would see one another the following day.

Before he left Madrid on his new assignment, David Hatton went to see an old friend, a man who knew more than even Richard about David's work for the Republic. A moving film was a great asset when one needed to send unofficial messages between countries.

Anyone wishing to see the man known as 'Cero' had first to be cleared by the tight security that surrounded him. Cero had no official title, no permanent office, but in all the many factions clashing for control of Madrid, he was the one person who had no political or religious axe to grind. Consequently he was trusted. He became an arbiter, a linchpin, a diplomat attached to no embassy. If anyone was able to discover what had become of Richard's Maite Manîas, it would be Cero.

Chapter Nine

As summer ran into autumn, Eve Anders was not alone in realizing that, as iniquitous as the invasion of a democratic country might be, it was possible that the invaders might be victorious. It was a disquieting prospect. In the north the Basque country and Santander were falling to the Nationalists. Having failed to take Madrid, Franco's generals turned their attention first to Vizcaya where, in two raids by the Nazi Condor legion on the small town of Durango, hundreds were killed. It was soon seen that terrorizing the civilian population was an element in the strategy of war because it demoralized those fighting at the front.

In the weeks that followed the Marco episode, Eve was very busy. Although she still thought she would be better employed driving an ambulance or a mobile hospital, she did as she was ordered to do. No sooner was she back at the depot than she would be given the ubiquitous slip of paper containing destinations, routes and times. She did a good many journeys to and from air-fields, carrying, as other couriers did, X-ray plates, cans of film and Aid to Spain organizers from many countries. Because she was a woman, she was often detailed to collect some important personage – at least, she supposed that was why she drove such a high proportion of male chiefs, heads and leaders.

Back at Albacete, heavy rains had started with the onset of autumn, but not heavy enough to wash away the accumulated dirt and rubbish in the streets. The town looked drear and dirty, and Eve had no desire to spend time there. She was glad to be busy.

At the depot she found a note from Ozz, written in pencil on sheets of Izal.

Do be careful, Eve sweetheart, there is some real rough stuff going on out there – but then you know that by now. I told Alex that you should be doing other things than the Vipp stuff. She has an old Bedford with a new engine (in Compound 1ON) ready to be fitted out as a mobile hosp. Make her give it to you. Tell me to mind my own business if you like, but it's time you had a spot of leave. I'll be back in a week, maybe then we can do something just for fun. I hope we shan't keep just missing one another like this.

Her spirits rose. A few days of Ozz Lavender's company would be a tonic.

By the time she greeted the other drivers and mechanics, and had checked in, refuelled, topped-up and checked the engine, she had a request for leave ready, but Alexander forestalled her.

'Oh, good, Eve, I was hoping you'd be back in time. No problems with the Senator? Good. Sit down, have some tea. Ozz scrounged me a packet of Earl Grey from somewhere. I didn't ask, just thanked whoever put it his way.' Eve nodded her acceptance of the tea. Alex's use of her first name was new. Earl Grey meant nothing special to her, but as part of her continuing education in a wider culture, she was always open to a new experience in the ways of people like Alexander.

'Look, I've even got limes.' Alex poured a stream of clear, golden tea, appreciatively inhaling the rising steam. 'If there were cucumber sandwiches,' she handed Eve the cup and saucer and offered a dish of lime slices, 'I could almost believe myself back in my Aunt Phyllida's little sitting-room.' Eve, not knowing how to use the limes, ignored them. 'I adored Aunt Phyllida, she'd been on the stage as a young woman – the family were pretty put out so I believe – but she redeemed herself by bowing out on the crest of the critics' approval and marrying an estate even larger than her brother's (that's my father). So that was all right then. I set out to model myself on her, to be a bit of a rebel, but I had no talent for acting or singing, so I did the most rebellious thing I could think of at the time, I went off to travel

America, in a car, on my own. The tea all right?' She took a lime slice and floated it on the tea.

Eve had never known Alexander in such an expansive mood. 'Delicious,' she said. She waited for Alexander to continue.

'They've gone – the horse and the mule.'

'Oh, I am sorry. They were such a marvellous pair.'

'I know. The one so well-bred and beautiful and useless, and the moke a cross-bred, ill-favoured hard-working old creature. I used to think, well, if those two can get along, then humans ought to be able to. Ridiculous tosh, of course.'

'It only worked for them because the "them and us" element was gone. Before that the horse contributed nothing but got the best deal.' Alexander might think that Eve included her well-bred family in that generalization. Perhaps she did.

Alexander smiled. 'Have some more tea, there's plenty.'

'Thanks. I think I'll have some lime in this one.'

Rinsing the cups and pouring afresh appeared to draw a line under that conversation. Alexander smiled. 'I think the ritual of tea is half the pleasure, don't you?'

'Absolutely. It can make an event a special occasion.' Eve thought of May's long kitchen table on a Sunday afternoon, a white, crochet-edged cloth at its centre and a round fruit-cake on a glass stand centred upon that, beside May's best bone china and little bowls of flowers. Did May and Ted know about scented tea with limes? Did Ray? Ray thought the ultimate treat in drinks was freshly made Co-op tea sweetened with condensed milk.

'Are you a committed red, Eve? I say, it's OK if I call you by your first name?'

'Of course.'

'Well, are you? I mean,' she smiled wryly, 'this is one of the few countries in the world where being red is totally acceptable.'

'I don't think that I'm anything.'

'Oh, I had you for one of the idealist types, but then I'm not really a judge of all the different shades of red. Before I met my husband, who put me right, I used to think that anyone who was against the status quo was bound to be red. Carl is deeply, deeply red, a card-carrier, his entire family are.'

'Communists?'

'I'm gabbing on. Tell the truth, I was a bit down, had a couple of gins before you came in. No good during the day. I'm sorry, you don't want to hear my problems. It's none of my damn business if you are all the colours of the rainbow.'

Eve had already been led into saying things she had planned not to, first by Adeline Moffat and then by Ozz. She would not do the same again, so she laughed lightly and said, 'Perhaps that is what I am. I do know that I'm against fascism.'

'I'm sorry. I don't normally get myself into a state, and it's not the thing to dump my mood on to someone who probably won't dump back. I don't believe fifty per cent of what I say and don't agree with the other fifty. Take no notice, I'm in a crabby mood.'

'You don't sound too crabby.'

'Want one?' She offered the pack of cheroots.

'It's all right, I'll have one of my own cigarettes.'

'No, don't. Keep them. Have these.' She took a full pack of twenty cigarettes from her desk drawer. 'I was going to give them to one of the doctors, but you have them.'

Eve took them, half-wondering whether she was being sweetened up, but not caring too much because she longed for a decent cigarette. She enjoyed the ritual of removing the cellophane and pulling back the silver and tissue papers and revealing the two rows of pristine cork tips. 'Almost a shame to remove one,' she said, but she did.

'Here,' Alex handed her a cut end of lime, 'do your fingers. They look as though you've been smoking down to the last half-inch. Ah well, let's press on. Look, I know you aren't happy driving the Vipps, but somebody has to do it, and you're perfect.'

'Don't you mean that I'm prettier than Ozz Lavender or Stavros or Frink?' She named drivers who were almost permanently on supplies or ambulance duties.

'There is that, but there's also that you are less likely to see the one and only car we have as a speedster.'

Eve could tell that Alex wasn't going to give her a truck to drive. 'I don't want to push it too much, but however you might see it, to me it looks like class distinction at work.'

'How can you possibly say that?'

'There are people who warrant being carried about in a posh car, while here we are supposedly fighting against that old kind of privilege.'

'It's just a car, damn it! A bit of machinery that moves people and fragile items efficiently.'

'It's a symbol. To be quite honest, it wouldn't surprise me if one day I'll get rolled off the road. Anarchists destroyed churches in Barcelona, a car would be child's play.'

'OK. I'll talk to people about it. I haven't heard any other complaints.'

Refusing to descend to petty arguments, Eve said, 'There's an ambulance with a new engine ready for fitting out. Put me on it, please, Alex. I have a brother fighting out there. I'd be surprised if people who contribute to the aid funds would think their money is put to good use running VIPs around so that they can be photographed with something significant as a back-drop.'

'For a young woman, you have become very cynical.'

'Ozz as good as told me that.'

'Do this run for me.'

'What run?'

'I need to do a run to Barcelona. After that we'll talk about truck-driving. Two Russian officers will be travelling with me,' she smiled. 'Quite handsome types. Your time's your own while we are there. You can still have a bit of leave when we get back.'

'Alex, you haven't understood anything about how I feel about that damned car. I don't want a bit of leave.'

'Damn it, girl, don't be such a Calvinist. There's a war here, but that doesn't mean we have to give up civilization. Give yourself a treat once in a while. You do yourself no favours by working yourself into the ground.'

Eve was shocked that anyone should see her in that light. She was an idealist but not the self-denying type at all. Alex couldn't know her or she would see that.

'If you think back a few weeks, Alex, you'll remember sending me careering round with Ozz teaching me to drive the blessed Vipp-wagon.'

'Nobody in Spain wants you to wear a hair-shirt for the Republic. If there's one thing Spaniards know, it is how to grab a moment and enjoy it.'

'You think I don't know how to enjoy life?'

'You don't have to always wear driver's clobber. Nobody's going to think less of you if you wear something pretty sometimes.'

Since Ozz's comment when her skirt had ridden up over her knees, she had almost always dressed in knee-length cotton shorts or loose cotton dungarees like women of the Spanish militia. 'You're a fine one to talk, Alex. In those dungarees you might have tree trunks instead of legs.'

Alexander looked down at her filthy, greasy overalls. 'Touché. Even points. Tomorrow I shall be dressed like a lady.'

Earlier in the year, there had been a great deal of animosity between various Republican factions in Barcelona. Each held some power it saw as its own and, even though it would be rational to sink their differences, no one would let go first. So an atmosphere of tension, aggravation and suspicion developed. The defence of the Republic was in danger of becoming fragmented.

If the Republic was to survive, then it was necessary to crush the antagonism.

To this end, a counter-espionage and political police organization, *Servicio de Investigación Militar*, known as SIM, had been created by the Republican government. Running on the same lines was an informal international group whose aim was quietly to investigate rumours of infiltration and suspicion of spying for the other side. The Spaniards may well have come up with a better name, but LOLO, *Las orejas los ojos* (meaning Ears and Eyes), had been created by an American.

Cero, the man who knew everybody and everything, played an unspecified role in the autonomous organization. Helan Alexander had become involved when she had tried every course open to her to get a prisoner-exchange made with her husband. Carl Alexander had been a colleague of Cero long before he and Helan Povey met. Because Carl was trusted, Helan was persuaded to be one of the Ears and Eyes. Now it had gone further; she had been asked to join in an investigation.

Infiltration was often through the volunteers. Lovely young women had always been used, and although Alexander did not seriously doubt Eve Anders' credibility, she wondered about her beautifully correct lispy pronunciation of certain Spanish words, in spite of her claim not to speak the language. Her records were scanty, yet her sponsorship appeared to be pukka. She had checked and it had been confirmed from London.

Helan Alexander slammed her papers into a pile. Why in hell was she looking for problems where none existed? Anders was a perfectly nice young woman whose only foible was that she did not offer any information about herself, nor give anyone much chance to enquire into her private life. In that respect she was very much like Ozz Lavender; he too was a lot more intelligent than he liked anyone to know.

Ozz and Anders left jokey little notes to one another. Alexander always read them. Yet, she wondered, was their wariness any different from her own need to keep people at arm's length? Slamming all her desk drawers shut, Alexander quickly locked them and ran out of the office.

I need a break. I *really* need a break.

On the morning of their departure, Eve received a letter from Sid Anderson. He was very enthusiastic about her description of the town which had kept changing hands between the Republicans and the rebels. He was sure that she wouldn't mind, but he had given it to some friends who wanted to publish it. Could she send more pieces?

Louise, my dear, [he still called her that]

Driving about Spain gives you a chance to see how working people are managing, which is what people here want to know. There are a few women reporting on the war, but mostly they are sent out with a specific brief – usually to write for a women's column or to plough their own political or charitable furrow. Also they are mostly society or college women.

I hope that you will take this on. Certainly (I have already asked) papers and magazines of the Left will welcome such personal accounts. I suggest you keep to that same style, like a focused camera thinking about what it sees.

You should realize that editors will go to work on what you write, but not to alter, only to tidy – so I'm told. You would, of course, be paid a fee.

If you decide to go ahead, then I suggest that, at first, you send any pieces to me and I will get them to the editors best suited. That way you won't become 'theirs', you can keep your independence, and anonymity too if you like. Not knowing what to do about the first piece, it was published under the name of E. V. Anders. Please say if you want to keep to this form.

The idea of being in print filled Eve with enthusiasm and ambition. Here was something that she knew she could do. She had been writing reports in a journal since she was a girl, when old Mr Strawbridge, who had been the first to prise open her dull little mind and allow the dormant seed of curiosity to germinate, had given her a book in which to record what impressed her. She loved writing. It had never occurred to her that there were women reporting on the war, for she had driven many newsmen, but never a woman. The only women she carried, besides the rare woman politician, were administrators such as Alexander, or nursing and Red Cross people from all parts of the world.

The idea of being a focused camera with a mind pleased her no end and gave her the idea of taking pictures to send with her writing. Film was a problem, but in every depot there was always somebody who dealt in goods in short supply. When she was offered a box of six rolls of film for the trip to Barcelona, there was no guarantee that they were not heat-damaged. The man offering the film took Republican currency and made no attempt to barter, which showed that she was taking a chance. It was worth it.

Eve drove to Valencia and then took the road that hugs the coast. The Russian officers, Captain Mintov and Major Vladim, sat in the back seat and spoke good English in attractive, deep voices and rolling accents. On meeting Eve, each bowed from the waist with a formality she had seen only in the cinema. She found them both charming and courteous, and Vladim impressive and attractive.

The Hostal Paradiso in Barcelona, while still functioning as a hotel, retained nothing of its former glory. Much of its famous mirror-glass had been shattered by bomb and shell-blast. Drapes and hangings were either missing or unkempt but although it was grubby, the carpet was of such quality that a good cleaning would restore it to its original pale plush. Amazingly, some small crystal chandeliers still hung, mostly without light-bulbs, but where large chandeliers must once have lighted the restaurant, there was now only metal hooks.

They arrived at the Paradiso in time for an evening meal. Eve had brought along her one piece of finery, the exotic gown from Lascelles'. Not that she expected to wear it here, yet as always when she packed, she had found space for it. It was so beautiful that even if she never wore it again, she liked to have it with her.

She had worn the gown only once, the time she and David Hatton had danced and danced, conscious of their attraction for one another. It was intended to be worn without undergarments to spoil its fluid drop from the shoulders. The silk was so fine that it had felt as if his warm hands were directly in contact with her skin.

Having shaken out the gown and draped it artistically over a painted screen, she put on a black cotton boat-necked frock that she had borrowed from one of the many admin clerks with whom she shared digs. They had a common pool of bits and pieces of clothing.

The evening meal was not greatly different from the daily fare they got in Albacete: tomatoes, pulses and hot spices. There was very little meat but this was compensated for by fresh herbs, and a great deal of flair in the cooking. The wine was very good, and there was an ice concoction, rather like a sweet vanilla custard, which the four of them praised as the treat that it was.

In her new role of freelance correspondent, Eve was more than usually aware of her own thoughts. She imagined this place as it must have been, and probably would be again. One of the most important hotels in Barcelona, it had once been the watering-hole of English upper-class families as they toured the high spots of the Continent.

Only three times in her life had she been inside a hotel. Once when Ray had taken her along to a union conference; then a brief stay in a hotel in Paris where, chaperoned by her old head-teacher, Eve had been taken by her employer to model a lacy corselette for the owner of Lascelles' who was likely to give the factory a large order. The third hotel was The Queen's, which she had seen from afar in her childhood as a luxurious palace, and where she had agreed to meet David on the evening he had taken her to a buffet dance in the Royal Navy officers' mess. Because of his obvious money and breeding, she was much too proud and insecure to let him know where she lived.

Had her family and friends known that she was secretly seeing a man she had met by chance in a seaside dance-hall and didn't know from Adam, somebody well above their own station, a man with a fast racing car, taking her to places like The Queen's and drinking and dancing in the naval officers' mess, they would have had something to say. A girl who had no mother since she was twelve, and no father ever, needed taking in hand, needed good hard reining in before she got above herself. What would a gentleman like that want with a factory hand? One thing, and then he'd be off. But the truth was that, on the occasion, when her youthful desire was threatening to get out of hand, it had been David who had called a halt.

Nobody except her Aunt May, who had been a surrogate mother, knew how complex Eve's life had become: ambition way beyond her station in life; head-on conflict with her employer; discomfiture when Bar Barney and Ray, who had always loved her, had begun to love one another more; restlessness when her role at home became ambiguous and excluded when Bar became pregnant. Ray and Bar and baby were a family complete without her.

Had her 'own kind' known of the extent of the high life she had tasted, then they might have understood better her sudden decision to leave. And had David Hatton known that the person she presented to him had no more substance than a character in a film, then he might have understood better the mystery she had created around herself. The night she had gone to meet David was when she had started to create a new identity, so to him she had seemed enigmatic.

'A penny for them, Eve.' Her first name, the sweet smile, and the inconsequential social tone sounded strange in Alex's mouth, as strange as the cigarette in a holder and the clean fingernails.

'Sorry, Alex, I was miles away. I was wondering about the days when this was a place for tourists.'

The talk was the kind of polite conversation of strangers treading on eggshells. Captain Mintov showed them pictures of his wife and children of whom he was obviously proud.

'You must miss them,' Eve said, determined to keep polite enquiry away from herself.

'I have seen the little one two times only since when she was born, and she is aged now two years. It is true, I do miss them.'

Eve remembered Ozz having said that the Russians were everywhere. 'They wear military uniforms, but their job is to keep an eye on their investment in the Republic. They only want to win those battles that will be of use to them.'

'That's a cynical thing to say,' she had accused him.

'Not cynical, just true. Stalin's aim is the same as Hitler's, to gain a foothold here. They ship in armaments and ship out gold.'

Eve did not know what the link was between these two and Alexander. For an English volunteer transport officer to have dealings with two Soviet officers seemed rather curious.

There was an amateur floor-show, of flamenco dancing and guitar-playing. Alex said she thought she recognized the dancer as the girl who had been at the reception desk earlier. A three-piece band of elderly men played dance music. Major Vladim asked Eve if she would dance with him. She accepted eagerly, for it was months since she had been on a dance-floor. He was not used to the kind of ballroom steps she was good at, but there was music and he was a good-looking, attractive young man who held her strongly and was light on his feet and, she guessed, a man who liked to enjoy himself when he was not representing the Soviet army. 'You do this very well,' he said. 'I have not learnt so much western style, but I like very much. You will teach me, Miss Anders?'

She smiled, 'Perhaps, if there is another chance like this, Major.'

'Chance?'

'Opportunity. If we are somewhere where there is music and a dance-floor. Another time.'

'We have three days here.'

'Three days? I thought just one.'

He shrugged. 'Maybe how long it takes. I teach you some Slav dances too, eh? It is good to be with a beautiful woman, very beautiful. My name is Dimitri, and you Eve? Is OK if I say Eve?'

'Of course it's OK.'

'Mrs Alexander and Captain Mintov have arrangements to make. They do not need us. Perhaps we should walk. I should like to see a little of Barcelona. I have to confess, I did not know at all of Spain until the fascist invasion.'

When the major made their excuses, Alexander's sharp eyes looked directly into Eve's. A warning? A query? Eve could not interpret it. 'Is it all right with you, Alex?'

'Of course. I did say that you weren't on duty while you were here.'

As they walked past derelict bomb-sites, Eve caught an occasional whiff of putrefaction. There were corpses, maybe only of cats and dogs but the foetid odour still clung, lying beneath the piles of rubble created in the rioting between communists and anarchists earlier in the year.

As they walked slowly through some neglected public gardens, she commented on how well certain shrubs and plants were thriving without the ministrations of gardeners. She thought of the open commons and contrived displays in the municipal gardens of her home town. Shrubs and flowers that were growing almost wild here could only survive in the municipal hot-houses there. Here there were no great open stretches of grass, no park benches or little kiosks that served tea and ice-cream. Here, although the shrubs and bushes of late autumn were still flowering, it was a wild and romantic place, beginning to return to nature. Some shrubs that had once been chosen for variegation had been almost wholly taken over by their strong green forebears. Pelargoniums that had flourished scarlet had burst from terracotta urns, becoming wayward and enormous.

'You like sitting . . . to sit?' The major indicated the stone surround of an empty formal pool with a stone figurine fountain, and spread an immaculate white handkerchief for her. Who had provided that? She couldn't imagine the splendid and handsome major with a flat iron, but surely a soldier in the Soviet army would not – as a British army officer would – have a body servant. She would have liked to ask him, but thought better of it.

'Thank you, it's a treat to be in a public garden. Do you have places like this in your country?'

'Of course.'

'I know hardly anything about Russia.'

'Cities in Soviet Republic also ver' beautiful. Not all.'

'Russia is a huge country.'

'I am born in Ukrainskaya. Pavlovka.'

'The Russian language does seem a very difficult one to learn.'

'Not difficult,' he laughed. 'Small children speak Russian ver' well.' She laughed too. 'What region of UK is your home?'

'Hampshire, in the south.'

'You are Party member? Communist?'

Ah. Was that what she was now? Her papers said that she was. 'I joined the Party to get here. The British Communist Party have been sending volunteers to Spain for months.'

'You have been here long time?'

'No. This year.'

'You drive well.'

'Thank you, but I did not come here to drive a limousine.'

'Limousine? I think is Mercedes automobile, no? Yes?'

'Limousine means a very luxurious automobile. Kings and queens have limousines, people have cars. A car like that we call a limousine.'

'Not all people.'

'Oh no! Not many people do.'

'People in Ham-shire.'

'Right.'

'Why come to España?'

'Why?'

'You are ver' beautiful woman. Why you come here?'

'Why not? Weren't there pretty girls in the Russian Revolution?'

He laughed and, in a seemingly natural way, took her hand. 'Russian women beautiful, yes ... I am curious to know beautiful English woman, why she come to the war.'

She did not remove her hand from his. The pleasure of his attention and warm touch were at that moment too seductive. She knew herself well enough to know how strong and impatient her libido might be in such a situation, yet still she did not move when he lightly kissed her fingers. She did not move because it was getting on for a year since she and Duke Barney had made love, and she wanted it again, not in erotic dreams but for real.

He removed his cap, loosened the knot of his tie a fraction and undid the buttons of his uniform jacket before turning towards her and taking her into his arms. With her own arms about his neck, she opened her mouth to receive his kiss passionately. When his hand ruffled up her skirt to caress her bare thigh, she tensed. A few inches higher and she would find it hard to stop him. 'No.'

'Please.' Renewing his kissing he kneaded her flesh urgently. 'Just to hold, please, to feel soft skin.'

Her mind said, No, but her body said, Yes, yes and yes. She held on tightly to his fingers. 'Not here. This is a public place.'

He released his hold on her thigh. 'Please. I think you are wonderful woman.'

Even though he released her, fastened his jacket and replaced his cap, even though they walked quite properly out of the overgrown gardens and into the thronging wartime night-life of Barcelona, the air around them crackled with their aroused sexuality. If they walked in silence it was because their senses spoke clearly to one another in the only language that mattered.

Without discussion he led her into the hotel through a discreet side entrance used by the staff, and up the back stairs. The only question was brief and unspoken. Eve chose her room because of the Dutch cap. Once lucky with Duke, she would never risk her future like that again.

For a minute or two, they smiled nervously at one another. She lit a lamp and he looked for somewhere to put his hat. He decided on the screen where she had hung the evening gown.

'Excuse me,' she said, and without explanation she grabbed her sponge-bag and went along the corridor to the bathroom. There she filled the springy rubber device with cream and, with one foot on the bathroom stool, slipped it into place. It seemed such a quick and simple thing for a woman to do to protect herself. The wheel wasn't the best invention – this was.

Dimitri had made himself quite at home in her room. He had put out the main light, removed his jacket, tie and shoes, and was standing by the window looking out at the dark night sky. 'Is beautiful . . . many stars.' She agreed that it was. 'This is beautiful also. Why you not wear?' He indicated the gown.

'It is too splendid. Do you understand "splendid"?'

'Understand, yes. Wear it, please.'

'It is too grand for a time like this. The war . . .'

'Wear it here, please. For Dimitri you wear this.' He laughed as he picked it up and allowed it to hang from one finger. 'For international friendship, OK?' He made a kissing motion. 'For Soviet and English peoples.'

Of course, why else were they in her room? Why else had she protected herself with rubber and cream? Taking the gown from him, she went behind the screen. He came to watch, silently admiring. She had never undressed in front of a man before, but in this situation of her own making, she felt powerful. She shivered as the gown slithered into place. It had not lost its magic to make her feel wonderful, exotic and beautiful. David Hatton had been the last man to see her dressed like this.

David Hatton was in the past.

Duke Barney was far away, making his fortune.

Dimitri Vladim was here, a Soviet officer, a lover of her choice. She was aware that inviting this almost complete stranger to make love to her was of more significance than her experience with Duke Barney. When he had suddenly appeared after years of absence, he had been confident that she would still be a virgin – and she had been.

This time, she would make the rules. She handed Dimitri

her hair-brush. As he stood behind her, making strong strokes down the length of her hair, they gazed at each other reflected in the mirror. Sparks crackled and her curls and waves bounced back into the only position they knew. She expected that he would kiss her neck, and he did. The sensation travelled like lightning down a conductor, except that the energy was not earthed.

She did not know what Dimitri's explosive exclamation was in his own language, but its meaning was universal. He knelt down and buried his face in the silk, and the dark green, minute pleating rippled against her warm skin with every move of his caressing hands.

He was not a gentleman like David, nor a pagan like Duke. Dimitri Vladim was like herself, a stranger in a strange land, hungry for sex, but wanting something more than immediate gratification. She sensed from the way he did not rush her that their encounter was going to be a more luscious experience than her first time with Duke. It excited her that he had the same ideals, that he was a communist. To be a red was to want to break with the old ways, with conventions. She would find it impossible to allow a Falangist or a fascist to bury his face in her soft flesh as Dimitri now did.

She unbuttoned his shirt and trousers.

He probably thought that she had done this many times. It didn't matter, she felt strong.

She slipped the khaki webbing braces from his shoulders.

While she was removing his clothes with one hand, she let the fingers of her other move over his face and ears and into his mouth. She was still wearing her treasured gown, but Dimitri was naked.

She had disarmed an officer of the Soviet army.

She had been born and brought up in a naval and garrison town, where uniforms signified male authority and strength. She had never expected to find that a man without his armour of stiff serge cloth, tabs, buttons and braid would look this vulnerable, and to have power over a man in uniform was exciting. Dimitri Vladim was a man with enough strength to take what he wanted, yet she knew that she could have made him beg had she had a mind to.

Now, she thrust her fingers into his thick, straight brown hair and, holding on tightly, pushed his head back so that she could take the initiative. He was kneeling, she was standing. Bending over him she kissed him for an unrelenting minute. Then, as he stood up and kissed her she saw, for the first time, a fully aroused man. She had once, momentarily, seen Duke Barney naked when they were young, but on that night when she and Duke had made love, they had done so under a dark November sky, so that she had never even glimpsed the erection that had taken her virginity and produced such immoderate passion in her.

When Dimitri tried to remove the gown, she said, 'No.' In Russian and English they said the same phrases to one another: Come to bed with me. Lay close upon me. Make love to me. Give me. Feel me. Have me. Take me. Enter me. Satisfy me. Stay with me. It was she who lay on him, it was she who made the sensuous, voluptuous pace, it was she who stiffened first and exclaimed at the first pulse of their first climax. Their second and third were not so hectic, but exhaustingly satisfying.

Dressed, he was once again an officer of the Soviet army. He left her room not long before dawn, whispering with a wry smile as he kissed her, '¡Salud! Comrade Anders. Soviet relations good with English – is very good surprise.' Wondering vaguely whether his English was good enough for him to have been using the word 'relations' wittily, Eve Anders turned over and slept like a log until the sun was up.

When, later, they met briefly in the foyer, they were correct and formal. In answer to Captain Mintov, they said that they had enjoyed the walk, but were sad to have seen so much damage to Barcelona's fine old buildings. Only briefly did their eyes lock then slide away, an exchange that neither of them had the words for. It had been good relations.

*   *   *

She had decided to try to find Sophie Wineapple, but when she telephoned the hospital, she was told in French-accented English that Sister Wineapple's name was not on the duty roster. Sorry, she was not available just now. Yes, she was still at the hospital. No, she was not on duty at this moment.

'She was ill the last time I saw her. Is she back on duty?'

'Not on duty at this moment. Perhaps you could call again?'

'When? I'm not here for long, and I should like to see her.'

'A minute please.' Eve could hear a series of exchanges muffled by the telephonist's hand, then, 'Who's calling, please?'

Eve told her and she was asked to hold again.

'Hello? I'm sorry, but I'm afraid I can't say when Sister Wineapple will be back on duty. You could try again tomorrow.'

'If she's not on duty, do you know where I could find her?'

There was dead silence. 'Sorry, I can't tell you anything about that.' From her tone of voice it was clear that she knew all right, so why wouldn't she say? Nursing staff were always on call in case of emergencies.

Crossing the foyer to return to her room and collect a map, Eve again bumped into Alex and the Russians.

Alex said, 'Problem?'

Eve shook her head. 'No, no, it's just I'd hoped to meet somebody but I can't get through to her.'

'I see. Take care. We'll be back here to eat this evening if you want to join us. Oh, by the way, it seems that we won't be finished here for at least a couple of days, maybe three. So, you know, feel free.'

Eve nodded. 'Yes, Alex, I already know. I'll try to fill in my time usefully until you're ready for me to drive you back to the depot.' The hard edge to her tone was intentional. If Dimitri had known that they would be in Barcelona for three or four days, then Alexander must have known too. For all Alex's attempts to be one of the proletariat, she couldn't stop her background surfacing. *Noblesse oblige*, and all that, but the Alexander types often assumed without question that Anders was there to serve without question, and Eve Anders had never found such an assumption by anyone at all congenial.

When she reached the gallery at the top of the staircase, she glanced out of a window and saw the three of them preparing to get into a car whose driver wore the uniform of the Soviet army. Her curiosity was a little aroused, but only a little. She had gathered from their exchanges in the car that they were here to interview some people, but their conversation was so guarded that even had she been curious, she couldn't have discovered what it was all about.

With three or four days to spare in this war-torn city, she might make her debut as a serious correspondent. She really did want to write about the kind of pressure under which nurses worked. She decided to go to the hospital.

On hearing that Eve had asked to see Sister Wineapple, the clerk asked her to wait on a bench while he made some enquiries. Soon another man came and asked her name and was she a friend of Sister Wineapple. Perhaps it was because he spoke broken English with a German accent, or perhaps it was the way he seemed to be watching her reactions, but Eve gained the impression that there was something going on which she didn't understand.

She felt guilty, like a child being questioned by a teacher, and the words tumbled out: 'I'm English. My name's Eve Anders. I'm a Spanish aid driver based in Albacete. I'm not really a friend of Sister Wineapple, but when I first arrived in Spain, several weeks ago, I was given instructions to drive her to a villa out of the city and stay with her until she was well enough to return to this hospital. Which I did.'

'I see.'

His attitude really did appear grave in the circumstances. 'How long were the two of you together?'

'About a week. Why do you want to know that?'

He looked at her without answering the question. 'I am a political commissar, you know?'

Eve nodded, 'Oh, yes, we call you red chaplains. You give lessons in politics, and I think you also help people with problems, people in the militia, and the volunteers. Is that right?'

He nodded. 'A commissar does those things.'

'I just wanted to say hello to Sister Wineapple. Is that a problem?'

'Perhaps you would come with me for a few minutes. You might be able to help.' She followed him along corridors. 'If you will please wait, I shall not keep you long.'

Eve heard voices from the other side of a door; questions, then answers by the commissar. Chairs scraped and the door was flung open by a tall man in khaki.

'Captain Mintov!'

'Please, Miss Anders,' he said in his thick accent, 'a little information and we may leave you to enjoy your free time in Barcelona.'

The room was furnished only with a table littered with files and papers, and some chairs. Alex was there. So was Dimitri Vladim, a woman in nurse's uniform with high-ranking belt and insignias, and two other men besides the commissar. Eve was greatly taken aback.

Alexander spoke. 'Well, Eve, small world.'

'Very small. I just came to ask about someone I knew – the woman I was phoning about this morning – and I find myself here.'

'Then we are in luck if you can help us. Just take a seat for a few minutes. How well did you know Sophie Wineapple?'

'If you remember, when I first arrived in Spain, I was supposed to be reporting to the depot but I was sent here instead to collect Sophie and take her out to the rest home. I stayed there the week and then came on down to Albacete.'

'Did you see a change in her while she was there?' The questioner was obviously a Spaniard.

'She seemed quite better by the end of the week. A little tense still, but really tons better than when I picked her up. I can't say that she was like her old self because I didn't know her, but I imagine that's what she must have been. Look, Alex, do you mind telling me what all this is about?'

'Just bear with us, Eve.'

Dimitri spoke. 'Miss Anders, did you spend time with Miss Wineapple?' She looked at Dimitri who looked back with an entirely neutral stare. His blank look unnerved her. How could a man who only hours ago had used his tongue to surprise and please her, now look right through her? But then she noticed that he was gazing somewhere beyond her left ear.

'No, not a great deal, Major Vladim. On the journey down she was terribly withdrawn, tired was what I thought. She slept a great deal of those first days. There were a couple of horses for people to use. She said she liked to ride and was pleased to find out that I did too, so we went out together. I wouldn't have let her go alone anyway because at that time she still seemed to me to be not right.'

'Not right in what way?' The matron wanted to know.

'She looked pale and I think that she was having . . . a woman's problem.'

'Was she haemorrhaging?' Eve looked at the desk. 'No need to feel embarrassed, Miss Anders, everyone here is a professional person.'

'I am not embarrassed, but I am a bit angry, because I think that you might have all been a bit more sensitive about hauling me in here and asking me intimate questions about a friend.'

'So she *was* a friend?' the commissar asked sharply. 'Did she confide in you at all?'

'There was nothing to confide. She was an ill woman. She was fatigued or perhaps she was taking something.'

'What something?' This questioner was American.

'How should I know? Perhaps something to make her sleep, I suppose. I have no idea. All that I know is she slept and slept and then she got up one morning and wanted to go out on the horses, then she slept some more, and then I brought her back here.'

There was a short silence, broken only by the click of Alex's cigarette lighter. Dimitri said, 'Miss Anders, the American nurse is dead.'

Eve stared at him, at first not taking in the full meaning of what he had said. 'Sophie Wineapple? If she's dead, then why are you asking me all these questions? Did she collapse again? I don't understand what it has to do with me.'

Captain Mintov started to say something but thought better of it.

Eve caught Alexander's eye and when she too did not speak, Eve stared her down. Then she looked at Dimitri who had lost his earlier stony gaze. He said to the matron, 'It would be good if Miss Anders had drink. Coffee, maybe?' Then to the rest, 'Is pretty good time to break right now. Return thirteen-hundred hours. Señora Alexander, remain if you please? Captain Mintov, we shall speak later?' Mintov left. 'Miss Anders, please.' Dimitri smiled, adjusted the knot of his tie a fraction and undid the buttons of his uniform jacket.

Damn you, she thought, you're trying to bring last night into it. Cups of coffee arrived and she accepted one from Dimitri who said, 'You are quite right, as you say we treat you not good, Miss Anders. Is not our intention. Right, Señora?' He turned to Alexander.

'Of course it was not intended, Major Vladim. I am perfectly sure that Miss Anders knows that, and I'm sorry if she felt that she was pounced upon, and that's the truth of it, Eve. OK?'

'It might be OK if I knew what was going on.'

Alexander said nothing. It seemed to Eve that it was Dimitri and not Alex who was the senior member of the panel or committee or whatever it was that the people who had just left the room constituted. 'I will explain to Miss Anders if maybe you like to eat. *Cantina* has *snoek* from USSR, good pie, much *el ajo*.'

Alexander rose. 'I'll try to find some corned-beef sandwiches; everybody's breath smells like coal-gas without any more *el garlico*. I'll see you before you leave, if you don't mind, Eve.'

With Alex gone, Eve felt at a bit of a disadvantage. If she had been the one to lay down the rules for last night's encounter, the rules here were very different. However, Dimitri Vladim made no attempt to change his earlier formal address. 'Mrs Alexander is embarrassed. You come to door, she does not know Miss Anders is connected with enquiry.'

'Please, Major, no more flannel. Why is everyone so touchy? What did Sophie Wineapple die of? Plague? Typhoid?'

'No, no, no. She drink . . . take? I forget what is the word,' he moved papers about, searching, but did not find what he wanted. '*Químico?* No . . .'

'She took *poison?*'

He nodded. 'No. I cannot think of correct word. It is work of commissar to understand. She is good nurse, good. Why?'

'Why should she kill herself? I have no idea.'

'Is my job to discover truth if possible. Understand questions?' He indicated the empty chairs.

'Yes.'

'Thank you. I make . . . atonement for your anger. Is right word, atonement?'

'Make amends? Put things right? Atonement is too strong, but I still think that you could have handled me a little more gently instead of pouncing on me.'

He frowned a little and then smiled. 'You did not handle Dimitri so gently, Miss Anders.'

She eyed him, a hint of a provocative smile at the corners of her mouth. 'You want me to make . . . atonement?'

'That would be most satisfactory, Miss Anders.'

'Damn it, Dimitri, what are we doing playing love-games in a room where you've been holding an enquiry about a woman who took poison? There are times when I can't believe the way I behave. What I shall be like when I have been here another year, I hate to think.'

'Another . . . ?'

The half-asked question hung in the air. Another *year?* Since she had been moving about the country daily, close to the war zones, seeing the growing dearth of even the most basic necessities, doubts had been growing in her unconscious mind. Now, when she came to think of a year hence, she could see the muddle of it all. How could the Republic keep going unless some of the democratic nations came to its aid?

Another year?

All the pieces suddenly fell into place. The Republic would not last another year. It was Dimitri who had made her realize this.

She could hardly get out of the hospital grounds fast enough. The tram she rode back into the city was slow, giving her time to look and think, mostly to think about what had happened at the hospital. What right had they to question her like that? It had been almost an interrogation. Who were they anyway? Why was Alex taking part? The whole episode was distressing.

Suddenly she felt hot. Her pulse began to race and her hands to tremble. Her heart thumped and raced as though going out of control. Perspiration was cold on her forehead. It was as though oxygen had gone from the air. If she did not get out quickly, then she would lose control. Pushing her way to the exit, she jumped off as soon as the tram slowed down, and held on to some railings.

This was not the first time that she had found herself panicking over nothing. In an air-raid, or under gunfire, or when negotiating a narrow pass with a drop on one side, she was calm and cool-headed. Alarm seized her when she least expected it; a terrible, frightening dread would surge through her body until she would have to fight against the urge to run.

A man of about fifty, wearing a beret, thick fisherman's jumper and workman's trousers and boots, peered at her through round-rimmed glasses. '¡Cuidado! ¿Mal? ¿Enfermo?'

Her mind was sluggish. 'No. Just a bit unwell . . . ah . . .'

'Will you listen to that? English, the only language I understand. Are you not well?'

'I just came over a bit faint. It was probably the coffee I had earlier, it tasted stewed to death.'

'That'll do it every time. Full of caffeine, y'know. D'you think you should sit for a bit? You could come along with me

. . . it's just here on the corner, the canteen . . . *cantina*. Y'see I'll get the hang of the Spanish given time.' He held out a hand. 'Michael O'Dowd. Pleased to meet a body who isn't speaking in tongues.'

'Eve Anders.' His kindly concern and warm Dublin accent were calming.

'So are you coming wid me? I have t'be there, t'lift the sacks around for the girls. You need a reviver.'

'I'll be all right.'

'You'll not, you're as pale as a ghost and I'll be for ever wond'ring if you didn't fall under a bus if I don't see the roses back in your cheeks. Ah, you're smiling already. That's better. Look, we're nearly there.' By now he was gently holding her elbow and guiding her along the pavement.

Outside the closed doors of a municipal building was a queue of mostly women and children who closed ranks and followed the man with their eyes as he nodded and raised a hand. '¡Hola! ¡Hola! Buenas tardes. Am I right, or am I saying something shocking? One morning I wished them all a Merry Christmas.'

'Michael, oh good, you're here. There's been rats in again . . .'

'Madge, Madge, will you just hold your horses a minute. This is Eve, she's from England, and she's in need of a cup of camomile.'

The woman was tall and thin, with short hair like a man. 'Dear man, why didn't you say. Sit you down, my dear, and we'll have you on your feet in two shakes of a lamb's tail.'

Eve was suddenly crying. 'I'm sorry. I feel such a fool.'

'Ah, go on, have a good cry while you're at it,' Michael O'Dowd said. 'Tears is good remedies, I use them all the time. Now you just sit there and drink Madge's brew, then if you've not'n better to do, you can give us a hand.'

At once, so it seemed, everything that had gone awry when she was on the tram, slid back into place. She was back in a world that she could make sense of.

So it was of this chance meeting that Eve wrote for the first short article that would start her brief career as a freelance correspondent for a London newspaper, and very soon for several others in English-speaking countries.

'We were so hungry . . .'

It is Wednesday and the food situation in this city is as bad today as it was Tuesday, Monday and all the days that have preceded it for months and months. Two hours in a queue for a single onion, 'not big enough to make tears'. That is what food-shortage can mean. But a single onion can brighten a thin stew.

Wednesday is the day I came to know something of the lives of the people of Barcelona.

A single onion and a turnip can be the basis of a stew, a little salt, a chilli and plenty of water. The Republic can survive on stew warmed with a determined spirit. None shall pass! And they mean it. *¡No pasarán!*

Wednesday is the day I saw hunger at close quarters. I spent this Wednesday helping distribute milk rations and bread. The *cantina* is run by members of the Society of Friends. On duty today were Madge Pickawa from Exeter, Mike O'Dowd from Dublin, Hélène du Bois from Tours, and Rachel Rozen from I never found out where.

Celeste, two Isabellas and Maria are housewives in Barcelona who come here every day to cook whatever is available, to clean, to knit socks for babies and darn elbows for orphaned children.

The *cantina* is housed in the courtyard of a municipal building. There is a huge canvas suspended beneath the courtyard's glass roof. It was originally intended to keep out the sun, but now serves as protection from splintering glass when the city is being shelled.

A child of eight, a thin boy, faints while waiting in line for his milk ration. Yesterday he had only turnip for lunch, then a little rice and some lettuce for supper. The cup of milk in the courtyard is the little boy's breakfast. Women fuss over him. He says: 'We have no bread because we have eaten the ration. We were all so hungry.'

A girl. Older, maybe thirteen, but self-possessed as a woman. Madge Pickawa says that she comes every day to collect her family's allocation of milk. She wears severe black like a widow, and she stands serenely, waiting, her long, fair hair, scraped back from her high golden-brown forehead, is tied with a black bow and falls to her waist. In a year or two, she is going to be a beautiful woman. I wonder why the women push her to the front of the queue. Is she the daughter of someone important?

'Marita? Marita is in a hurry and must get back to her children.'

'She looks young enough to be at school.'

'Marita *is* a schoolgirl, she is fourteen. Since her mother died last month, Marita is the mother of her brothers and sisters. She is worried to leave them alone in the house, because of the air-raids. She has so much to do, we see that she goes first.'

E. V. Anders – Barcelona, 1937

It was late afternoon when she got back to the Paradiso. She found Alex, wrapped in an old sheepskin jacket, sitting hugging her knees. 'It's bloody cold. Want to share it? I sent the little *botones* for something to drink. I asked for tea, but he brought wine. Gave him a good tip too.'

'What did you give him?'

'I don't know. Money. He's the bellboy, you give him money, he's supposed to bring you tea.' She sounded crotchety and imperious and was smoking furiously. Eve had seen her in this sort of mood on other occasions.

'Alex, there are times when I could cheerfully strangle you.'

Alexander looked quite shocked at the tone of her normally polite driver. Eve didn't give her a chance to reply but hurried off through an archway that she knew led to the kitchens and through which she and Dimitri had come in quietly last night. Dimitri had given the *botones* three cigarettes. Eve now gave him another two and, holding up two fingers, bargained with him.

When the tea with little dishes of milk and sugar arrived, Alexander said, 'Why wouldn't he do that for me?'

'Because you treated him like you're inclined to treat the rest of us at times. Hell, Alex, you don't know very much about the people with whom you are supposed to have thrown in your lot, do you? A bellboy isn't here just to please you.'

'I know that.'

'You need to stop being lady of the manor.'

'Who says I was lady of the manor?'

'Your entire style says it. When I held open the door for you, you got into the Mercedes but you didn't see *me*, you didn't say, "Thanks, Eve." You took it for granted that I would shut the door behind you.'

'Did I do that?'

Eve nodded, handed her a cup of tea and offered her milk and sugar. 'It's the way you are. You stick your head in the engine of a truck, talk with a roll-up pinched between your fingers, but that doesn't make you one of Us, one of the Popular Front, one of the common people.' Eve smiled. 'And you just took that tea as though you've had a maid all your life.'

'I have. When Carl, my husband, wanted to rile me, he would call me Baroness von Alexander.'

'Your husband?'

Alexander nodded. 'He's in a concentration camp somewhere over there.' She pointed in the general direction of the west, to where the front line now sliced the country almost from top to bottom – the greater portion being behind the fascist line.

'I'm sorry. That must be very tough for you.'

'Not as tough as it must be for him.' She plucked at the woolly coat collar. 'Carl's mulatto, a half-caste. The Generals do love the mixed-races don't they?' she said bitterly. 'Not true mulatto – American Negro and Swiss. Carl's mother is Swiss. Odd things happen when people fall in love. If they execute him, I wouldn't have any reason to live.'

You can be so wrong about people.

It seemed suddenly not to matter a damn that Alex's manner was irritatingly imperious. Her husband was a black man and he was in the hands of people whose dream for the world was of a pure, white race.

'I'm so sorry, Alex, I never knew. My little nigglings about driving the Vipps must have been a pain in the neck, with that . . .'

'I've always conceded that you have a point. OK, it may not have appeared like that, but you really don't see the whole picture. There are some visitors, MPs like Pollitt, who probably wouldn't mind at all being bumped around in the back of a pick-up truck, or being delivered to Madrid with a load of onions, but if we were to offer an onion-ride to an American Senator – no matter how Democratic – he's not likely to come back and then aid stops coming this way.'

'But if he's driven around in style, he might think that we don't want the aid.'

'Human nature being what it is, things don't usually work like that, Eve.' She smiled and took out her paraphernalia for making cigarettes on a little roll-up machine. 'Thank you for the tea. And thanks for the lesson on etiquette, or is that not the word one should use now.'

'The word is, good manners, Alex. Which is what etiquette is supposed to be. I believe the silly rules came about when people who wanted to be important started to put tall things on their heads.'

Alexander looked sideways at Eve, offered her one of the two cigarettes she had produced, and put a flame to them both. 'Explain, please.'

'Once a human being sticks something on his head – makes himself taller, more important, etcetera – he makes sure that everyone realizes that this makes him something special. But that's not enough; give a man a high hat and he'll add a rosette and then a plume and then a whole bunch of plumes. Then it's high boots, spurs, long tail-coats, swords and bucklers, breast ribbons and medals. It is impossible to approach such a man with mere good manners; one needs to know the rules. I've forgotten what we were talking about.'

'Etiquette.'

'Oh yes, good manners.'

Alexander suddenly burst out laughing, spilling a little of her tea over the coat. 'Leave it. If Carl ever claims it back, I shall remember to tell him that story.' Her cigarette had gone out, so she applied the long flame of her lighter again and sat quietly until, apparently apropos of nothing, she said, 'Who *is* Anders? *What* is she?'

Eve was more prepared than she had been a few weeks back to fend off questions about herself. 'She's a truck-driver, a good one, given half a chance.'

'Ozz thinks that you should have the overhauled Bedford.'

'He's right, I should.'

'Who will drive the Vipp?'

'You could. You don't have to be a mechanic to prove yourself one of Us.'

'Us?'

'Ordinary people.'

'So, Anders is one of the people?'

'Anders is a truck-driver.'

'OK, you win. You can have the Bedford and go on supplies, but not based at Albacete.'

Eve's heart leapt. 'You mean it, Alex? Wow! Thanks a million. Have some more tea.'

They sat side by side with Alexander's, or rather, Carl's, sheepskin motoring jacket round their knees, talking inconsequentially about the condition of the hotel and whether it ever was Paradiso, until Alexander in her sudden, point-blank way asked, 'Was it with you the major slept last night?'

'You have some cheek! What sort of a question is that?'

'A concerned one, for goodness' sake. Vladim did not return to his room until morning, or should I say, slunk to his room. I may not be much of a senior aid-worker, but it's what I am. You are assigned to me, and I don't want anything unpleasant to happen to you.'

'Nothing unpleasant did. Nothing will. I can take care of myself very well.'

Alexander went silent, frowning and fiddling with shreds of tobacco, nipping them off, balling them and flicking them into a flowerpot. 'Something unpleasant did happen to the American nurse.'

'Major Vladim hinted that she committed suicide.'

'He shouldn't have.'

'He didn't know the word. He said *químico* which I thought meant chemist or chemical. I suppose it must have been Aspirin?'

Alex shook her head. 'Wineapple was pregnant, many weeks so . . . She tried to abort it with a drug.'

'That's awful! And it killed her? It wasn't suicide, it was accidental?'

'She's still dead.'

Eve remembered grim stories of knitting needles, penny royal, concoctions brewed in back-streets, young girls and women dying of septicaemia, bleeding to death, incomplete abortions.

'Is that why that matron asked me about Sophie haemorrhaging?'

'Probably.'

Eve remembered now how concerned she had been when Sophie had got straight up from her sickbed and insisted upon riding strenuously over some rough terrain. Was that what she had been trying to do that day? 'She was a good horsewoman. She said that she was practically born in the saddle. What a terrible waste. What about the man? Wouldn't he marry her?'

Alexander began rolling again, but Eve forestalled her and offered her one of the few Spanish cigarettes she had left. 'What about the man? Oh, yes, what about him? That is what we should all like to know.' Eve waited, knowing that Alex had more to say. Alex was angry, she drew deeply on the strong cigarette, pulling in her cheeks and sending out a plume of smoke like a small volcano erupting. 'She reported that she was raped. All that she would say was that her attacker smelled of antiseptic.'

'Someone who worked at the hospital?'

'Possibly. Probably. Who knows now?'

'She must have told someone then?'

'Another nursing sister with whom she shared a room. She thinks it was a man Wineapple knew, maybe even worked with.

Possibly a doctor, possibly Russian or Slav. That is the extent of our information.'

'Why must it have been someone she knew?'

'Because her friend says that she wanted Wineapple to report him, but she said, who would believe her word against his. No one would believe a respected man would be capable of it. Which may well be true. I mean, who would believe that somebody one worked with every day would heave himself on to you like some wild beast? So, when you turned up today, I think we hoped that you knew something, hoped that she might have said something to you.'

Eve shook her head. 'Why would she have? She was quite a bit older than I am. I had only just arrived in Spain, I could have been anybody, a gossip. We were complete strangers.'

'It appears that when you came into the picture, she actually had taken an overdose of Aspirin, but vomited it up before any harm was done, then she collapsed during an operation. You know the rest. I really shouldn't be telling you all this, but I trust you. And Vladim has already said enough to make you curious. So now you know why we came here, and why you were jumped on when you mentioned being a friend of Sister Wineapple.' She felt in her briefcase and brought out a small phial with a red rubber stopper containing a red powder. 'I was given this today. Powdered chilli, the little fierce ones – *diablos*. They say go for his eyes or his willy. I guess I'd go for the willy.'

A medic? Could a rapist be a man like that, a doctor or an orderly? That seemed difficult to believe. She had always supposed that rapists were drunks or mental cases, not educated men. She had only ever known one girl who had been raped – it had been by her brother and his friends. At the time, it had been an open secret whispered and shuddered at. Everyone agreed that the whole family were disgusting, and lived like animals.

It was that incident which had fixed the image of a rapist for Eve. A vicious boy of low intelligence, he grew up to be a depraved man. At the time she had wondered briefly about her own brothers, not in relation to rape but rather as men with sexual needs. The blame had settled on the girl who had been sent away for years.

'Why you and the Russians? That seems an unlikely combination.'

Eve could tell even before Alex started to speak that she was not going to get a straight answer. And she was right. All that Alex would say was, 'There's a possibility that a Russian was involved and Wineapple worked in a British hospital.'

It was one thing to talk about the Wineapple affair which, if left unresolved, could quickly lead to nervousness among the women and a lowering of morale, but it was quite another to mention Vladim and the SIM, and herself and LOLO and the importance of secret intelligence. Alexander, mostly guided by her instinct and observations, had already suggested that Anders might prove to be a good LOLO candidate, and to that end had requested information about her. That was weeks ago, and so far London had reported nothing. Anders was certainly no gossip and, except for Ozz Lavender, she seemed to be a loner. Highly intelligent, friendly, personable, but still a loner. Alex had mentioned it to Vladim. Perhaps that was why he had got himself into her bed last night. If Carl Alexander had been able to persuade Helan Povey to left-wing politics in bed, then anything was possible when two heads shared one pillow. Sex was the most powerful weapon of all, but one must know how and when to employ it. Vladim would be good at that. He was the most virile and attractive man she had seen since Carl.

Still puzzled by Alex's part in this affair, Eve asked, 'Are you a political commissar?'

'No.' Alex smiled, making light of it. 'Nor Scotland Yard. Well, I think I'll go to my room and have ten minutes' rest. Shall I leave you the jacket?'

'If you don't mind.'

Eve sat on, hugging the jacket and smoking, adding water to the dregs in the teapot until it poured almost clear. She tried to think back to that week at the villa, but so much had happened in the meantime. Had she been aware of what had brought Sophie to that state, then she would have been more attentive. Fatigue from overwork. Sophie Wineapple had fallen into her bed, buried her head in the pillows and slept.

Had she been sleeping or only turning her face to the wall, trying to ignore the mess she was in?

What would I do? I'd want to tell somebody, make a fuss.

That evening, after the four of them had eaten together, Dimitri asked if she would like to go for a walk again. The evening was cold. During the weeks and weeks of sunshine, she had never really believed that Spain would have a winter. There had been rain and mists; she had driven through roads that had turned to mush in minutes, but always the sun had come out.

Alexander insisted that Eve wear the motoring jacket. It was bulky and heavy but she was grateful for its protection. Dimitri was perceptive enough to recognize that the coat was more than protection from the cold.

'You have not necessary be protected from me. This Wineapple is bad business, for men too. Men must keep woman from harm, is the work of men to do. I make *castrati* of such men.' He turned to face her and drew her hand into his long military coat. 'This must be for pleasure, not for violate. For nice, good pleasures.' 'This' was an erection. She flinched, but he held on to her hand. 'Do not let the bad thing that happened to Wineapple make a bad thing for us. I never would hurt you. I never would hurt any women. I like you very much. We like good sex together last night, yes? You like to do it some more? I like you very much to do sex with, very much.'

Darkness had fallen, but they had kept to the streets, away from the overgrown public garden, away from alleyways and bomb-sites. She was confused. As soon as she had felt the warm, hard prospect of good sex, she had wanted it, yet all that had happened today made her hold back. She hardly knew him, but that had been half the thrill of taking him into her room. Love with a stranger. Last night she had found the idea stimulating.

Their steps led them back to the Paradiso, which they entered through the front doors. The place was almost empty. The *botones* appeared, smiled broadly and asked Eve if she wanted tea.

'Tea, Major Vladim?'

He smiled broadly. 'This is only thing you offer. Please, tea. Sit here?' He pointed to the courtyard with its badly tended pots of climbing plants and groups of English-style wicker chairs.

Settled in one of the courtyard's pretty alcoves, she poured tea as he unbuttoned his great winter coat and skimmed his hat on to an empty chair. 'I think,' she said, wanting to get things settled between them without hurting his feelings, 'I think perhaps last night was a mistake, Dimitri. We really have no business getting involved – a commissar and an aid-worker.'

'I am not fool, Eve. Last night you were not involve with commissar, you involve with Dimitri. Is fear because of Wineapple?'

'No! Yes. It is not because I don't trust, well, I don't know you. You don't know me. I expect you think that I have been with . . . had, what you called games with fun, with a lot of men. It's not true. Last night was special, was new. I have never done such a thing before. You think I am . . . you understand "easy woman"?'

'Unmoral? Go with all the men?'

She nodded.

He shrugged as though he hadn't thought about it, or if he had then it was not important. 'You see,' he said, 'I know words. Not so good to put words together. I am good student of language when child. Speak French fine and German good, Spanish perfect good. Now I get better speak English. I like to speak words for bed for you to understand. I do not think that you are easy woman. No. Not go with all men.'

Suddenly it seemed important that he should understand that last night had been unusual. 'Only one.' She held up an emphatic forefinger. 'One man.'

'One man. I have four women, maybe five, six . . . Not one now. They marry . . . not marry Dimitri.'

'I want you to understand, I have only been with one man. One time, with one man. Only one.' To her ears it sounded as though her voice echoed in the deserted courtyard. How stupid! Why should it matter that he understand?

'One, two, four, is not problem. You beautiful, desirable. Men want much to sleep with beautiful women. I stay away tonight. I understand. We drink tea. You return Albacete two days. I not come to your room?' Narrowing his eyes and frowning, leaning close and lowering his voice, he asked, 'Is right this what I understand you say? Only one time you have man for love? You are virgin then you have one man, and then Dimitri? Is correct?'

She found his directness embarrassing. 'Yes.'

They sat silently together. She did feel at ease with the big Russian. What was the good of having instinct if you ignored it? Because of what happened to Sophie Wineapple, did Eve Anders have to suspect every man she met? Did she have to keep a phial of burning pepper powder to hand when she was alone with a man?

He was still in her bed when the sun came up.

She looked down at him and thought of the way he made love and how easy it would be to fall for a man with that kind of understanding.

Chapter Ten

By the time winter had settled in, Eve Anders was a heavy-vehicle driver stationed in Madrid. General Franco's forces were now occupying more than fifty per cent of what had been the Democratic Republic of Spain. They also now had the Canary and most of the Balearic Islands and Spanish Morocco.

One by one, during 1937, foreign governments recognized the occupied territories as a Francoist state.

The League of Nations was at long last forced to recognize that the policy of non-intervention had failed the Republic of Spain, one of its democratically elected members.

Arms now flowed in: from Portugal, Germany and Italy for the invading army; and from the Soviet Union for the Republic.

By the time Eve had been to the Auto-Parc to collect her big truck, the invading armies were surging across the country.

The Nationalists had set up headquarters in Burgos, and it was from there that the conquered part of Spain was governed.

The Vatican had blessed the fascist crusade.

Britain had diplomats and businessmen in Burgos.

The Texas Oil Company was supplying petroleum openly against the policy of non-intervention in the civil war.

Outside the frontiers of Republican Spain, the world was sure that the end was near. The people within the Republic would not accept that.

The Republic's problem was that there were weevil grubs gnawing at its roots. As General Franco had boasted when asked if four columns were sufficient to take Madrid: 'It is the fifth column within that will bring victory to the crusade.'

*   *   *

David Hatton sat at the desk of a journalist friend who worked on the *Daily Herald*, a Labour newspaper. He was looking closely at a series of pictures: a group of young men and women, looking for the most part ill-at-ease, receiving some sort of official send-off. He compared them with a passport photograph of Eve Anders. The friend, Archibald Archer, had provided the pictures from the photo archives of his paper. David had provided the passport photo.

Spreading the photos around again, David Hatton said, 'Do you believe in the Fates, Archie?'

'Coincidence and luck are more my line. Is that her?'

'Yes, without doubt. Look.' He ran a magnifying glass over the pictures of the group, holding it so that his old school-friend could see.

'I say, a real looker, Hatton. Not surprising you want to trace her.'

'Not me, Archie, LOLO wants her. You know LOLO, of course?'

'Yes, I do, but what, for God's sake, does it stand for?'

'*Los orejas los ojos*. Ears and eyes.'

'Oh, yes, a *very* subtle title for an information-gathering set-up.'

'You're not supposed to be privy to that information, so button up, Archie.'

The Hattons and Archibald Archer had been boarders at the same public school. It espoused, but did not necessarily adhere to, a gentlemanly code, but Archie was as good a man as they came, and David knew that tit-for-tat was a good way of trading in the information business.

'Looks as though she's traced, then. Trouble?'

'No. Somebody in LOLO wants her credentials checked.'

'For LOLO?'

'I imagine so.'

'And . . . ?'

'Can't tell you that. But I did know her once. I first met her quite by chance. I was covering a TUC meeting in

Bournemouth, went into a dance-hall for a bit of a break to get away from you lot . . .'

'What do you mean "we lot"?'

'You know what I mean – reporters and journalists as a bunch can only be taken in small doses, and Malou French was there all over me like a bag of fleas.'

'You have a turn of phrase, Hatton. Ever think of taking up this branch of journalism?'

'I can produce the equivalent of a novel in a single picture or a few yards of movie film.'

'Still as modest as ever.'

'About my work, of course. Anyway, to tell you what I know of her, I had most of what I wanted in the can, so I went for a drive along Bournemouth sea-front and I heard the siren call of a dance-hall. And there she was. Totally beautiful, hardly more than a girl, sitting at a table alone, itching to dance. As I now know, she was used to going dancing alone, but that place really wasn't the cream. If I hadn't have asked her to dance, some chancer would have.'

'Lucky girl, Dave. How long ago was that?'

'A couple of years, I suppose.'

'And you recognize this woman as the girl?'

'Damned sure I do, Archie. I've met her since but . . .'

'But what?'

David Hatton leaned over and took a cigarette from an open box of a hundred on his friend's desk. 'I knew her as Louise, not Eve Anders. She would never tell me her surname, nor where she lived, or anything about herself at all. Honestly, Archie, she was so wonderful I couldn't get her out of my mind. Twice, until now, she turned up in my life. The second time I couldn't chance losing touch again so, although she wouldn't agree to me getting in touch with her – maybe I frightened her off being too eager – I did squeeze out of her a promise that she would telephone me.'

'And . . . ?'

'She did, but I didn't take the call and I didn't know about it until too late. She left a terribly brief note that eventually got to me at the H + H office. I've been trying to find her ever since but it's difficult these days, Spain takes up most of my time. Yet here she is. And her name is Eve Anders.'

'Evelyn, do you suppose?'

'That's what I am hoping that you will be able to discover. It shouldn't be difficult for you, Archie. Your archives will show when this medical team went out. All that you need to do is to follow up on where she went, and which unit she is attached to, and where she is now.'

'And her background, her antecedents, her family, friends, what she was doing before she went out to Spain, etcetera. I know the drill, old man.'

'Well, yes, everything LOLO asks for. But once you have the first bit of information, the rest will be easy.'

'I'd have thought you would have wanted to do this one yourself, Hatton.'

'Can't be done, Archie. Plane leaves this afternoon. The loyalists are on the offensive for once. Teruel. Know it?'

'Yeah, read it on the tapes this morning. It'd be a shot in the arm for the Republican army, it's been too long on the defensive.'

'I know. I came across my brother recently. You remember Rich?'

'Of course, the great Hatton Senior by fifteen minutes.'

'Right. Well, later I got to thinking about his way of opposing the blackshirts, compared with mine . . . ours. My brother's way is uncomplicated, he knows who the enemy is and goes out to kill them.'

'Uncomplicated, except that he'll never get at the real enemy.'

'Off your soapbox, Archie. We agreed to differ and I told him that I'll fight my own way. You'll do it, Archie?'

'Leave it to me. You be off and catch your plane.'

'Good lad.' David Hatton gave his colleague a friendly slap on the back. 'Not too long, eh, Archie? It's going to be worse than ever now I know who she is.'

'Don't count your chickens, Hatton, she probably wrote you off the day you didn't take her telephone call.'

'I know, I know, and she might not prove to be either Louise or Eve Anders.'

'Funny thing, Hatton, the name seems familiar.'

David Hatton frowned. 'In what connection?'

'I can't think. Recent, though. Hold on.' He pressed a button on an internal telephone. 'Phil, name of Anders ring a bell? Of course. Of course! I knew I'd seen something. Real name? OK, Phil, if you can find it, I'd be grateful. Yes, now. Within a few minutes if you're able. Bye.' David Hatton waited expectantly. 'Well now, Hatton old man. E. V. Anders is some sort of a writer, been sending over a few pieces on Spain. Not the usual stuff but, you know, "A Day in the Life Of" kind of style. *Daily Worker* published two short pieces, a bit light for them, but good. They were sent on to me suggesting we might consider taking them. Not *Herald* stuff really. Ah, Phil, that was quick, thanks. Your dad going to sign him up?'

Phil had brought in a couple of sheets of paper.

'She's a her, Archie. E.V. stands for Eve, I think. Let's have the copy back when you've done,' he said and went back to his own desk.

Archie Archer skimmed one of the hand-written sheets, then handed it to David who read it quickly. 'That's not half bad, Archie.'

'Fresh at any rate.'

'Fresh be damned. E. V. Anders has the makings of a good journalist. Look to your laurels, old man.'

'On the strength of that piece alone I'd say your LOLO person shouldn't have any doubts about the loyalty of her protégée. That's always supposing that your woman and this one are the same.'

'I'm off, Archie. Do what you can to find out.'

The news coming into London that December indicated that the Popular Front of the Republic, although now united and disciplined, was constantly being undermined by hostility between its own factions – anarchists, communists and socialists – as they jostled for position and power. Persecution and assassination were commonplace. Subversives were, as General Franco had said, his secret army, his fifth column serving fascism within the city of Madrid. The communists, due to their greater discipline and rigid chain of authority, were in the ascendancy that winter.

The offensive strategy was, as David Hatton had told Archie Archer, essential to give the Republic a much needed boost to its morale, but no matter what season had been chosen for the fight to retake the town of Teruel, conditions would still have been bad for both sides. Teruel is situated at an altitude of 915 metres. It has hot, dry summers, and extremely cold winters.

Captain Ken Wilmott, his ears plugged with bits of chewed paper against the constant bombardment, made his way from blasted building to blasted building. Like a bloody ant, he thought, as he recalled the stop–go and zig-zag route an ant takes to reach its goal. One of 40,000 Popular Front ants. Rumour had it that there were less than half that number trying to hold on to the provincial capital. The street-fighting was bitter, fiercer than any Ken Wilmott had ever experienced, and the sub-zero temperatures were even harder to take than the sun. At least in Teruel there was no thirst to drive men mad enough to suck filthy mud; here in Teruel your own breath could freeze on your eyebrows. Here in the streets of Teruel, snow fell fast and thick and lay deep and treacherous.

With his platoon close behind him, using a ruined building for cover, Ken Wilmott waited for the next opportunity to advance another street length. What the hell am I supposed to do? He had gained officer rank by virtue of being next in line when others were killed or injured. If I get out of this, I'm going to get officer training, or give it up. Having tasted leadership, he liked its flavour.

'I thought this was supposed to be a walk-over,' a voice called from behind him.

The captain grinned. 'Still alive aren't you, Grimble?'

'Can't rightly say at the moment, Captain. I think I've got brass monkey trouble.'

Somebody else shouted: 'Stick a glove on it.'

'What, and have my fingers drop off?'

'Trust Grimble to make the intelligent choice, you can't fire a rifle with your prick.'

A voice with an American accent joined in. 'Can't you Limeys do anything about your sense of humour?'

'Nah, Yank, if we wasn't all idiots we'd be back home putting up the holly and mistletoe.'

'OK, my lot. Here we go again, "Out in the cold, cold snow-ow-ow . . ."'

Along with a burst of machine-gun fire came the blast and crump of a bomb or an artillery shell. Ken Wilmott was in no position to know which, for the roof of the burnt-out ruin he and six others had been using as a vantage point fell in on him. Had he not been the leader and already racing to the next bit of cover, he too might have been buried beneath many feet of rubble. As it was, he was blown clear.

Ken lay in the bitter snow for, it seemed to him, a very long time. At last, dazed and chilled to the point of strangeness, he was helped to a first-aid station set up in a shattered school some way back from the fighting. Scavenged wood was alight in an iron stove giving out a fierce heat from its sides. The walking wounded clustered around it, their faces burning, their backs freezing. From time to time they would rotate themselves like meat on a spit and roast the other side.

Ken Wilmott eased off his boots and socks, looked at the toes of his left foot and knew that this was frost-bite. He had already seen dozens of cases. A contingent of Republican troops had been sent directly from fighting in a warmer sector and were still kitted out in summer clothing. As he was trying to pull on a sock, a man, his left hand wrapped in a bloody field dressing, said, 'I say, old man, like to have a couple of these footie things? My grandmother sends me them. You wear them next to the skin, socks on top.'

'Thanks, they look all right.'

'They are, warm as toast. She makes them herself, buys skiver leathers and keeps her men-folk supplied. She recommends them for grouse shoots on the Scottish moors.' His laugh was strained and a bit unnatural. 'Grouse shooting. All that damned waste of shot, bloody birds never did any harm. I come from a long line of bird-shooters. The family's name's Gore. Gore bloody Gore, rotten to the core.' His laugh ended in on an hysterical cackle.

Ken Wilmott was intent only on his own state of mind as he pulled on the soft, chamois sock, followed by the two woollen ones. Two of his toes still felt dead, but at least he might not lose any more while he was waiting to get the bad ones seen to. 'That's better. Thank your gran when you write to her.' They touched fingers in lieu of a handshake. 'Ken Wilmott, acting Captain, Fifteenth Brigade.'

'Rich Hatton, British Battalion, but God only knows which bit of it. We keep re-forming.'

'Where were you?'

'La Granja. Brunete. Belchite. Now Teruel.'

'It looks as though we've been following one another around. Were you at "Mosquito Hill"?'

'What brigader wasn't at "Mosquito Hill"? God, the stink! I thought I'd never get it out of my nostrils. If I had the talent I'd paint a huge canvas and call it "Still Life with Maggots".'

'I got used to corpses years ago, part of the job before I came to Spain. Worst thing for me on "Mosquito Hill" was the thirst.' With the care of an old soldier, Ken smoothed out the creases in his socks.

'Why corpses? Were you a coroner, doctor or something?'

'No, nothing posh, I'm a time-served undertaker. I never got to be able to ignore that smell, but after the first couple of weeks it never turned my stomach. There were times when we would get a really bad one, a run-away from a mental home died in hiding, you know, that wasn't too sweet. When I was old enough to do pall-bearing, I could never hear that bit about "ashes to ashes, dust to dust" without it going through my mind that before it ever gets to dust it's got some pretty foul stages of decomposition to go through first.'

'First undertaker I've ever met. Interesting. Not for me, though. Poacher turned gamekeeper, is that it? Or the other way round.' He grinned, almost a grimace. 'Sorry, thought I was about to say something witty about your association with the dead. Not funny. Sorry.'

'It might be funny when you think about it. What did you do prior to joining the Internationals?'

'Photographer and film-maker. Factual stuff, not Hollywood.'

'I know another chap who does that, came across him a couple of times. Last time was when I was having a wound treated in Madrid, this chap was doing some photos for *Picture Post*. I asked him to send one to my brother. It was the Madrileño women coming back from the front line.'

'Hatton. David Hatton. That's who it would be.'

'You're right, it was.'

'I'm his older brother, by fifteen minutes.'

'You're twins?'

Richard Hatton frowned. 'You don't own a mirror, I suppose, Captain?'

'Just a bit of polished steel. My stuff's been blown up so many times, there isn't much I do have these days. Want to borrow it?'

Richard Hatton studied his reflection for about thirty seconds. 'Well, and no wonder. Davey and I aren't identical, but there's never been any mistaking that we're twins.' He handed back the little polished plate and grinned. 'You married or anything, old son?'

'No. Just as well when you see.'

'I've got a . . . she's . . . if you've got a Spanish girl who . . . you can't imagine what they do to dissident women. They keep them around for a while before they execute them.' He held up his wounded hand. 'That's my fucking trigger-finger gone. No more grouse shoots for Hatton Senior.' Tears were trickling down his face. He swiped them away with the dressing which left a gory smear right across his face. 'When they execute the women, they rape them first. The Republic's done for. You know that. I know that. Every man jack of us knows that. Even pregnant women . . . the Moors . . . the bloody Moors. You know what they do? They'll execute white women and rape them after. Every man jack of us knows . . .'

'On your feet, Private Hatton. Come on, man. Up! Up!'

Heads turned, but none of the walking wounded huddled around the fire could raise any real curiosity. Richard Hatton stood, his wounded hand held inside his coat. The captain picked up his own and the other's belongings and led the way outside. Ken had seen this before. It was one of the signs of breaking down. They called it shell-shock in the last war: men at the end of their tether, men who had looked over the edge and into the abyss. Often they didn't try to draw away.

He spoke briskly as he helped the distraught brigader. 'I can't think of a single reason why I shouldn't report you. Talk like that is treason. Do you want to end up dead by one of our own bullets? We are going to help these people hang on to their bloody country if it kills us.' It had only taken a minute standing in the blizzard for them to become snow-covered. His feet half-afire, half-numb, made him stumble, but he put a kindly arm around Richard Hatton's neck. 'Oh, come on, man, you look fit to drop. You've probably lost more blood than you realize. You're talking such crap. Come on, I'll see if I can get somebody to take a look at you.'

The captain, hefting all the bags and moving unsteadily on his frozen feet, led the way to where the field-hospital was set up. A nurse, her white apron hanging below an army greatcoat, was just disappearing through a canvas hanging. Ken called after her in his halting Spanish.

She turned, her Red Cross scarf, white against her black skin, sprouted incongruously from beneath a knitted cap. 'It's OK, Captain, I speak English real good.' When she smiled, it seemed to the captain that her large, dark eyes glowed warm enough to unfreeze him.

'He's a bit off his rocker,' Ken explained.

'An emergency? Yeah, you both look all-in. You want to let me take a look at that hand?' She threw the blanket she had been carrying around Richard Hatton's shoulders and then looked briefly at his blood-soaked dressing. 'OK, what say you come through to . . . just lean on me and we'll get one of the doctors. Like to sit and wait there, Captain? I'll be back in a couple a' shakes. Don't put your feet close to the stove.' Again that same smile of warmth and confidence.

The smell of death hadn't reached here yet, but the smells that preceded it – ether, carbolic and blood running, dripping and oozing away – pervaded the cold air. Ken Wilmott sat on the bags and wondered about his toes. If they were too far gone, they'd have to come off. If they came off, then he'd be out of the war, though not necessarily, unlike the other bloke whose trigger-finger was probably not there. There was always the field-kitchen. I wouldn't want to be behind the lines. Better the hole in the ground in Aragón, or the frozen trench he'd just vacated, than the cook-house. This was not the first time that his subconscious mind had sneaked in the question: Are you getting addicted to rifles and ammunition?

The nurse came back. 'Is he one of your men?'

'No, we just happened to be seated together over there, you know, where the walking wounded are waiting. I just know his name. I think he's with the Fifteenth Battalion. Is he badly hurt?'

'He should be OK, depends. Did he say when it happened?'

'No.'

'It looks a day or two old to me, could be infected. Dr Vogel is attending to it.'

'How bad? Will he have to go back home?'

'Two fingers are already gone, the thumb doesn't look too

good, he's lost a great deal of blood, but there are supplies of whole blood at the hospital. We'll get him there as soon as we can. Does some of that stuff belong to him? Guess I'd better get somebody to put it on his stretcher.'

'Right. Thanks, nurse. I hope he'll be all right.'

'At least he has another hand, that isn't always the case.' She made another note. 'Say, what about you, didn't you say you were over in the waiting-room?'

Ken Wilmott smiled. 'You mean the one without the roof and no windows?'

She smiled back. 'The one with the central heating. You waiting for treatment?'

He shrugged. 'Probably. Not urgent, I think I got frost-bite.'

He noticed that she wore a shiny new ring on her wedding finger. The gold band wavered and went out of focus. He might have guessed, they were always married, the ones who attracted him most. Maria Sanchez – not married, but betrothed, promised. Such a repressive and archaic practice in a country that was living its own revolution, that was giving women freedom. 'I am promised to José. José is gone to the front.' Perhaps he should have behaved with less decency and more passion. He had known hardly any black women; there was Lizzie Naylor who had been in the girls' part of the school. Frizzy Lizzie. A hundred years ago he had been at school with Frizzy Lizzie Naylor. Queer not ever thinking of Lizzie as being black, just as having all that hair.

For the second time in twenty-four hours, Ken Wilmott became unconscious.

Chapter Eleven

Eve Anders peered through the blizzard, the heavy windscreen-wipers battling against the build-up of frozen snow, so that every few minutes she had to lean out of the side window and scrape some of it away with her fingers clad in thick driving gloves. She wore a heavy skirt that met the tops of her solid lace-up boots two sizes too large to allow for the wearing of seaman's thigh-length socks. These she had recently received from home along with a much-delayed letter in which her brother Ray had written rapturously about the baby. She smiled. As if there was only one baby in the world. To Ray and Bar there probably was.

We have named her Bonnie. She has dark eyes, long eyelashes and thick black curling hair just like her Mummy's. Apart from the baby, we've been so busy moving to Wickham. It's coming up to Christmas, so we shall take baby Bonnie over to see her Granny and Grandpa Barney. Duke came up to the farm one day. I was on duty and he was gone before I got home. Bar reckons he's really in the money. Got some horses at stud apparently, and also got a training stable and looks after racing horses for rich owners, most of them Indians and the like who only come to England for the big meetings. You can guess how Aunt May is, you would think that there wasn't another baby in the world like Bonnie – well of course there isn't. We talk about you a lot. Bar doesn't say too much about it, you know her, she always looks on the bright side. She says it's good that you are leading the life you chose for yourself, but I know she misses you. We talk about our Ken too. We were sent a photo of him. Ted has bought it a frame to put on the mantelshelf. Nobody would recognize him. We were only saying, he looks so different that even though you are both out there, you could easy pass him in the street and not know he was our Ken.

The tyres of her heavy vehicle lost their grip on the icy surface for a second, sending her heart racing and forcing her to forget the lovely letter that held Ray's voice in every line.

Letters from Ken were sporadic and came without any reference to where he was. Over the last few weeks she had seen a lot of casualties, men and women who would never walk again, talk again or have children or be able to think straight. It would be so easy to lose heart. Too often now she would awaken in the early hours feeling low in spirits. Then she would tell herself what a wet she was and push herself into another day.

When she was being realistic, Eve could see that what had appeared to be such an idealistic and noble cause had become a muddle in which people's lives were tossed away. And yet, there was no way to stop the fascists taking over what was left of the democratic Spanish Republic except by fighting back. She hated the impossibility of the situation. It was in her nature – as her family used to say – to go off like a fire-cracker in all directions, but that had been when problems came singly and it was in her power to do something about them.

People like me won't make an atom of difference between winning and losing. So why stay? Perhaps what mattered was the presence of outside support to boost the morale of the Spanish people. Why not? I love it when I meet Italians of the Garibaldi regiment. It makes my day to be with Americans of the Abraham Lincoln.

The roads were treacherous and busy with every sort of military vehicle. The battle for Teruel was different, she had felt the optimism everywhere she went. At Teruel the Republic had taken the offensive. Tanks had recently arrived from Russia, raising the spirits of everyone who saw them roaring towards the front.

She no longer hankered after an ambulance or mobile hospital. The one she had been driving until recently had been hit by a shell and hauled back to Albacete. Now she was on almost permanent call, driving one of the big trucks she loved. There was never enough time, enough food, enough sleep; she was for ever being de-loused and had cut her hair again; she had chilblains and she was so thin and her diet so unbalanced that her periods had almost stopped and her skin often erupted. She did a regular run to some places, so that her truck with its crudely painted *¡No pasarán!* along the sides was easily recognizable. People greeted her with warmth and enthusiasm. If, as they said, it made their day to see her arrive with much-needed supplies, it certainly made Eve's; she had never felt so fulfilled in her young life.

As she peered out through the ever-reducing clear area of windscreen, she saw a name-board and direction arrow.

Thank God. In spite of the blizzard and dreadful road conditions, she had made good time. As she drove into the makeshift vehicle compound, a line of ambulances was leaving. She never quite knew how to take that sight – a lot of casualties, or a lot of saved lives? It was the other trucks she hated, the ones taking away the dead. Nobody had yet given her that task. She hoped they wouldn't, but if they did then that is what she would do.

As she opened the cab door, she heard sounds of gunfire and shelling coming from the direction of Teruel. At least the loyalists were on the attack this time, and an attack was a good sign. The Russian tanks on the road, and the battle being taken to the Nationalists were good signs.

The strangest things could change one's mood.

She jumped down and stamped her feet, trying to get her circulation going. No matter how well she tried to insulate her boots, her feet were always cold and covered in chilblains.

Her dream of bliss at this moment was a footbath of warm salt water. The load she was carrying was medical supplies. A small load for such a large truck – if only it could have been stacked to the roof.

She stopped a man wearing glasses; he might have been anyone, for glasses were his only feature in the huddle of mixed scarves he wore. 'Do you know who I see about this load of medical stuff?' These days she always tried English first; it was surprising how many other nationalities understood at least some English.

For half an hour she trudged back and forth between her truck and the first-aid station. 'Eve? That you under that gorgeous hat?'

'Kea! You're only jealous.' The two young women hugged. 'Things sound pretty rough out there.'

'For certain it's not a Labor Day parade. Hope you've brought in some sort of anaesthetic, we're getting low.'

'And some spirit for your sterilizer. Novac said you'd be down to sterilizing with candle-flames if I wasn't nippy.'

'Candles? We should be so lucky. Have you got a bit of turn-around time?'

'I can find a bit. You want me to do something?'

'Would you, hon? Just for ten minutes, then we should be over this flush, and there might be a mug of Oxo and maybe we can steal ten minutes just to say hello.'

Salaria Kea was one of the many nurses Eve met briefly but constantly on her supply trips. Trained in the Harlem School of Nursing, she was a devout Christian who had come straight to Spain from Ethiopia. Eve had met her soon after she had returned from her honeymoon with her white International Brigader husband. Many nurses were a bit sniffy and protective of their position, but Eve had found that most Americans, although very professional, did not put up barriers against an amateur like herself when help was needed. She had held up many a bottle of blood in an emergency transfusion, and finished off the dressing of a wound so that the nurse could go on to a patient more in need of medical expertise.

'A guy along there,' Salaria pointed, 'he's waiting to be taken into Madrid. He's lost some fingers and a lot of blood and he's in shock. Just keep an eye on him, talk to him, don't let him talk back. He's English.'

Eve pushed her fur cap back off her face, but didn't remove

anything, for even inside, her breath steamed in the cold. She halted a few steps away from the man, lying rigid, a field-dressing like a huge white fist already stained with fresh blood held to his chest. Her stomach clenched with distress, and she went cold with shock.

Moving to where she could see him better, she said gently, 'David?' There was no response. 'David. Wake up. I've come to sit with you till the ambulance arrives.' She wanted to weep. His handsome face was drawn and thin, a smear of blood was wiped across one cheek and there was a line where tears had dried. She wanted to hold him in her arms, he looked very ill indeed, but there was no mistaking his beautifully-shaped nose and lips. It seemed impossible that those lips had once pressed hard on her own, or that that nose had been buried in her neck as they lay on the grassy downs, both breathless with passion.

Taking off her gloves and kneeling beside him, she gently smoothed his brow. 'David, you shouldn't sleep just now. You can sleep when you've had your hand seen to. David.'

His eyes flickered, opened, focused and then closed again. A faint smile parted his lips. He had lost one tooth and another was chipped. He was still smiling when he opened his eyes again and spoke, his voice heavy with exhaustion. 'Odds of fifty to one that your name is Louise.'

Confusion. Her hand was stilled on his brow. The voice was not David Hatton's, she had never seen this man before, yet he had called her by her old name. He looked at her a long time, searching it seemed every inch of her face. 'Take off your hat, please.' She did so, and shook out her short curls still streaked gold from the summer sun. 'He said it was over your shoulders. He's a bugger for nice hair, is Davey.'

'Davey?'

'You called me David. He's the other half of the Hatton twinship. Now people will be able to tell us apart. Richard, the twin with only seven fingers and one thumb. Did your hair get lousy?'

Eve nodded. 'But I now have a secret weapon, so that when I can do without a hat again, I'll let it grow.'

'Davey lost you.' His voice had grown fainter, so she sat on the floor close beside him, her back against the chilly wall. 'Awfully cut up about that. Going about like Cinderella's prince looking for his lost Louise, 'cept that Davey has no glass slipper, not a single clue. Pity. Don't you want him to find you? OK with me. Shame for Davey.'

It would be so easy to ask about David, to make contact again. A word. A message. An address. Did she really want to know? What sense was there in opening up all that again? Her mind raced around like a rat in a cage.

He seemed to be drifting off again. Salaria had said, keep him aware, try not to let him sink into unconsciousness. 'You called me Louise.'

He responded with a faint smile. 'Davey's a good chap. Better than me. Younger, got more up top.' His speech had become slurred.

If Richard Hatton chose to tell his brother of this encounter, then it wouldn't be difficult for David to seek her out. Maybe that was what she would like. Duke's mother believed that people made their own destiny when they made a choice, and she had chosen to follow up on his mention of Louise. God knows, she thought about David, he still came into her best dreams. She even welcomed him to them. But God knew, too, how much she liked being Eve Anders, an independent, uncommitted young woman. Even the people she used to be so close to, so loving towards, even they had receded. It was hard to credit, but it was a fact that she was no longer a Wilmott. Indeed, she was no longer working-class. It seemed fanciful, but a kind of power had come to her: she wanted sex, but not love; she wanted men, but not a man.

Louise Wilmott, who had been as ambitious as hell, and had wanted the keys to the whole world, had found – in the guise of Eve Anders, and as E. V. Anders – a niche, a place where she belonged. She was alone yet part of something she could not yet understand fully. For the present she had found fulfilment in her driving and writing. If and when that was not enough, then she would look for something else. For the present she did not want any complications, not an affair, a romance, a permanent lover. She wanted her truck, to know that her reporting was effective in making people aware of the plight of Spain, the country she was beginning to love and feel that she had a stake in. She didn't care if that seemed smug – there was only Eve and Louise to know.

A big sigh from Richard Hatton brought Eve back. 'Are you all right?' He didn't look all right. She felt the pulse at his neck and watched his chest rising and falling hardly at all. She found Salaria disposing of a pile of soiled dressings on a little bonfire. 'You'd better come.'

Kea moved fast. She felt his pulse and looked under his eyelids. 'He needs a transfusion.'

'Can you do it here?'

'No, we aren't equipped.'

'Who is?'

'The main hospital, but we're fresh out of ambulance space. There's an amputation and a bullet in the lung which should get priority.'

'Couldn't I take him? The road's too iced up to drive at speed, but I'd try to see he didn't get a rough ride. We should be there well before dark.'

'I'll see what Doc says.'

'I'll warm up the engine. Find someone to travel in the back with him.'

Bearers slid Richard Hatton on to the bed of the truck, tied the stretcher to rope rings and covered him with a pile of coats and blankets, and requested that the coats be put on any ambulance coming back. Eve tucked her knitted knee-blanket around his head. 'You'll be OK, Richard. Do you hear?' He grunted a reply. 'You'll soon be tucked up in a warm bed.' She hoped that was true. She checked the petroleum carriers. There was enough.

Salaria Kea came back as Eve was revving up the engine. It sounded fine. 'I've got just the guy to travel with you.'

'Tell him to put a move on.'

'He's doing his best on his frost-bite. OK, Captain?' He confirmed that he was, in English.

For which, thought Eve, many thanks.

Kea, her head ducked against the shrieking flurries of snow, banged on the side of the truck and waved Eve out of the compound.

Once out on the road, Eve leaned her head against the little window at the back of the cab and yelled, 'All right back there?'

'OK, love.'

'Just try to see that the stretcher doesn't move. The roads are bad, but I'm used to them. Just hold on to your hat.'

She drove for half an hour, hardly aware of anything except the hundred yards or so in front. From time to time she asked if everything was all right back there and was told 'Yep!' Was the patient all right? Yep!' She caught a whiff of smoke and was suddenly hungry for the lift and a few moments of relaxation that a cigarette gave. 'I say, Captain,' she called, 'I've left my back-pack on your side, it's got my cigarettes in it. Can you see it? Hanging on the . . .'

'I see it.'

'Take them out, will you, and hand them through. Have one yourself.'

He did so and she lit up expertly, keeping one hand and her knee on the steering wheel. It was difficult to hold any sort of conversation over the roar of the engine and the noise of the wind, but nobody ever missed the chance of talking to another person in their own language. 'You got frost-bite?' she shouted.

'Just two toes, maybe three.'

'At Teruel?'

'A building fell on me, my feet got left in the cold.' His voice was strong and deep, and although he was having to shout above the noise of the labouring engine, she detected a Wessex broadness in his nice voice that reminded her of her brothers.

Their mother had never let any of them get away with the city whine. When they reached the hospital, she would ask him what other Hampshires he knew.

As soon as Ken Wilmott had heard her say, 'Tell him to get a move on,' he knew that the truck-driver was his sister. Until now, he had not imagined that she would be involved in this kind of front-line work, for supplies trucks were popular targets for the pilots who liked to dive and strafe. His heart thumped at the thought of it. Maybe they had been this close before and not known it. If he hadn't said that he would travel down to the hospital, leaving the first-aid men on duty, how would they ever have found out later that they had both been involved in the fate of the man who, as the black nurse had said, was missing coagulants in his blood and could bleed to death?

There was no point in disturbing her while she was driving. In any case, he hugged to himself the enjoyable anticipation of surprising her. How did she do it? This wasn't the first time that he had admired the skilful way the drivers handled their big ambulances and mobile hospitals, but he had never seen a woman behind the wheel of one of the huge supplies trucks. She had swung up into it as though it was a light van. He was proud and thrilled at the way she handled herself. And her voice . . . She had been a bossy kid, but her grown-up voice had authority.

She had never exactly been a shrinking violet, and she could pack a good punch, but this was something else entirely. Such confidence. You could tell that she knew that she was good at what she did; she oozed certainty in her own ability.

He would have loved to have watched her, but as soon as he moved away from the stretcher it slewed slightly. The soldier wouldn't stand much buffeting. So he sat and savoured the moment when they would reach the hospital, answering her questions briefly. He wondered whether she had received any letters from him since he had taken on the rank of captain. Not that it meant as much in this army as it would have in the

Coldstream Guards. Even so, she would be pleased when he said that he was an officer.

Mile after mile of rutted roads, but it was easier in the ruts than it had been earlier in the freshly fallen snow. She drove on silently. What could the soldier answer but 'Yep' to her enquiry about their sick charge? He could hardly say, 'It looks as though he's had it' – even if he had. She felt no more responsible than she would have for the life of any other man in his situation, but the thought of how the death of his twin would affect David certainly made her aware that she wanted to hand him over as soon as she could.

'About five miles now,' she called back. There was no reply. She knew how easy it was for most soldiers to fall asleep on a knife edge if there was five minutes to spare.

It was almost dark when they drove through the hospital gates but the blizzard had blown itself out. She knew this hospital, having delivered medical supplies many times before. When she tooted her horn outside the Emergency doors, a male orderly came out.

'Eve! Hi to you. I know is you under big fur hat? You been making winks with Soviet comrades? I do a good deal with lipstick and notepad for such a hat. What you do here at front door? You go trade people door.'

She jumped down and gave the Italian a friendly thump on the shoulder as she moved quickly round to the back and let down the tailboard. 'Milio. Move fast. Big emergency.'

Already he had hauled himself up over the tailboard and into the truck. 'I know. Blood transfusion. All ready.' He had released the ropes and in less than a minute he and another porter had transferred Richard Hatton to a wheeled trolley and were hurrying down a corridor, calling back, 'Lipstick, Eve. Good deal because I like you.'

Laughing both because she liked the tall Italian who was never out of humour, and because she wasn't sorry to be here, she leaned against the tailboard. 'Phew! I'm glad to hand him over. Thanks for your help, Captain. Hand me down my bag. Come on, I know this place and it knows me. I'll bet I can rustle up a Marmite sandwich and some English tea. Hand down the bags and I'll get somebody to keep an eye.' He passed the bags and she piled them inside the Emergency doors. 'How about your toes, do you want to get them seen to first?'

Pulling down his balaclava helmet and winding a scarf round and round his neck, Ken said, 'Tea and Marmite sounds good.'

'Come on, let me help you down, even if you can't feel your feet you can still do a lot of damage to them if you jump.'

He let her help him down, holding on to the moment when she would realize who the captain with frost-bitten toes was.

'Not in there, round the back where the kitchens are.' She led the way along a wall where warm steam was melting the snow which the frost at once turned to ice. Pushing open a door they received a wonderful blast of warm air. 'Mind you don't skid, there's a slope here, it's treacherous underfoot.'

Inside, she stamped her feet and whipped off the big fur hat, banging it to remove drops of water. She was smiling at him in such a warm and friendly way. When he removed his peaked cap and woollen helmet, her smile froze. She put a hand to her mouth and bit her lips. She hardly knew whether to laugh or cry. 'Kenny?'

He nodded, unable to speak as he took her into his arms and hugged her for a long time against his damp greatcoat. 'Well then, kid, how's tricks?'

'Kenny, I can't believe it.' She brushed flakes of snow from his beard and laughed excitedly. 'You're terrible. You knew I was the driver, didn't you?'

He grinned. 'Not until we were under way. I thought it best to wait.'

She grabbed him round the neck with great affection and kissed him. 'I can just imagine you savouring the moment when you would whip off your disguise, just like you used to like jumping on us girls to make us scream.'

'Did I ever do that?'

'You know you did.'

'I've always imagined my suave young self as being much too aloof and grown-up to play such tricks on my little sister. Now, come on, I've got my mouth all ready for a Marmite hunk. You'd better come up with the goods.'

She was concerned at the way he limped and hobbled as they made their way to the kitchens where she was greeted by the Spanish cooks and helpers.

'Any Marmite, Pet?'

The grey-haired Spanish woman turned up her nose and held her head away from the smell as she cut large chunks of bread and smeared them black with the salty, yeasty spread that so many of the English aid-workers rhapsodized over. They would do any kind of a deal to get hold of a jar. 'How you eat this stuff?'

'It's good for you, Petronella, you should know that with all your experience of cooking. Full of good vitamins.'

'You need vitamin, eat tomatoes, eat pimentos, eat onion. This your chap?'

Eve laughed. 'You know I don't have chaps, Pet.'

'Not because chaps don't try. That Emilio, he love you to bits.'

'It's my hat he loves. If I ever let him have it, he'd forsake me. Any tea? This is my brother, he's dying for some tea.'

'Tea, tea, tea.' The cook put the plate of bread and Marmite in front of them, then stood back with her hand on one hip looking as though she couldn't decide whether this was just a bit more banter. She had taken to this tall English girl. Not that she was anything like her own Carmen who had gone with the militia, but she loved her almost as a daughter. She looked closely at the IB captain who hadn't shaved for days. 'Brother?'

'Yes, Pet,' Eve said, her mouth full of the dry but delicious sandwiches. '*La hermana* . . . Captain Kenneth Wilmott.'

Petronella gave him a kiss and ruffled his hair. 'Is very hairy chin, this sister, need shave.'

'OK, OK, *el hermano* . . .' Eve grinned at her brother. 'I still don't know my *el*s from my *la*s. My God, Ken, I can hardly take my eyes off you.'

'So how'd you think I feel?' He took her hand and held it tight. 'You were just a kid when I left. What happened to the dancing, are you still the Queen of the Tango?'

She took a glimpse into the past. 'What flirty butterflies we were – especially you.'

'Ah, we had some good times. Do you miss it?' He noticed the dark rings round her eyes and her lips, although still young and full, were as dry and cracked as his own. Her mouth was set in a serious line. When she held a flame to their cigarettes, her hand trembled. He knew how it was: you held yourself together with your mouth, if you let it tremble you were done for.

'That's like saying do you miss your childhood, it's just something you look back on. Oh, but your feet, we must get somebody to look at them.'

'They've waited this long, they'll wait a bit longer.' Petronella brought two mugs of black tea and again he submitted to a hair ruffling. He didn't mind, it was a long time since anyone had done such a thing. Probably not since his sister had done it just to annoy him when he was ready to go out. They had never been close, not in the way that she and Ray had been close. What they had said about dancing wasn't how it had been, they had rarely gone to the same dance-halls.

But now? Now he felt very close to her.

As he looked at her from the other side of the trestle-table he thought how splendid she was, how fantastic to have a sister who was so full of life. She had a way with her, that was obvious. People responded to her, without her trying to impress them.

Wanting to be nearer to him, she moved to his side of the table. Theirs had not been a family which expressed their feelings for one another openly. Without the awkwardness she would have once felt, she took his hand and held it to her cheek. 'We got away, Ken.'

'Ah, we did, and look where it got us.' Briefly he kissed her fingers. Only the two of them knew what an extraordinary gesture that was. They weren't people like that.

'But you're not sorry.'

'You're joking! If I were to die tomorrow, I've lived more in these few years than the rest of the lads in Lampeter Street put together. God knows how it happened, but I'm a captain, I've got command of blokes, they respect me, look to me to know what's what.'

'And you do know. I can tell you do. Capability is written all over you. I'm so proud of you, Kenny.'

Raising one eyebrow, he said, 'You reckon? If I'm honest there's times when I don't seem to know my arse from my elbow.'

Eve laughed. 'Oh, Kenny, modesty doesn't suit you. Sometimes when I look back on those days, I think I see that you always knew where you were going.'

'Not where, only that I was.'

'Yet we were all dumbfounded when you went off.'

'It was seeing Dad after they fished him out of the harbour that really started me thinking serious. He might have been a bloody bad father – he *was* a bloody bad father – but he had been all over the world. I wanted to do that, but not leaving a wife and kids to fend for themselves like he did. And I could see all that looming up.'

'Marriage?' Kenny had always had a girl in tow, one after the other. It was the way most of his classmates had gone: the girl got knocked up, the families insisted on the wedding.

'It was called "settling down", wasn't it? God, how the thought of that depressed me.'

They sat for a few moments silently caressing one another's fingers until Eve turned their hands back and forth touching broken nails, hard pads, torn quicks and chapped skin, then she grinned at him. 'We could have stayed in Lampeter Street and got hands like these.'

He leaned away and looked at her for what seemed ages. 'I

sometimes can't help thinking what a narrow escape I had, do you?'

She shook her head. 'I always intended leaving. Now, come on, I must get your feet seen to.'

'Stop fussing, Lu. I've been looking after my feet for ages all on my own.'

She flushed and buried her face in the steaming tea. As soon as he'd called her Lu, he remembered the long letter of explanation about why she wanted to change her name.

'It's Eve, Kenny.'

'I know, kid, I know. I'm sorry.'

'Thanks. Is that why you're calling me kid?'

'I reckon I'll be less self-conscious about it. Eve's another person altogether, I have to get used to her. Don't worry, I will. I want to, it's just that she's bowled me over. Eve Anders is amazing.'

'You don't think it's, well, immature or something, pretending to be somebody you're not?'

'*Are* you pretending?'

'I don't know any more. In the beginning it was vital that I had to concentrate on making Eve live. I don't think I could have borne it if somebody had come up and said, "Hello, aren't you Lu Wilmott?" I knew who I wanted to be, how I wanted to look, dress and talk. Have you ever thought how much people of our age have picked up from the films? I never really had any qualms about which knife to use, or how to enter a room, book in at an hotel or hail a taxi, and I'll bet you didn't either. We were getting lessons in it twice nightly and matinées on Saturdays.'

'You could always put it over, I'll say that.'

'It isn't hard, just playing the part I've written for myself.' She looked at her brother who had always been overshadowed by Ray, the responsible one, the mature and serious one who had taken care of everything. She said, 'Nothing much wrong in making the best of what you've got.'

He smiled, his strong teeth shining in contrast with his grime and beard. 'Which is why I'm sitting here with nits in my hair and my toes going black.'

'Oh, come on, drink up your tea and bring that sandwich with you. I'm quite friendly with one of the doctors here.'

She had grown so beautiful, he could hardly believe it. He grinned at her over the rim of his mug. 'Bloody hell, who'd have thought our little old lanky-legs would have doctors for friends.'

Would it occur to him that she had had lovers? She took it for granted that Kenny would have. But what would he think of her affair with a Russian political commissar? And Ozz? How would Kenny view that eccentric relationship? She was convinced that once Ozz could get away from the codes of chapel ('My little mam would just love it if I brought you home to Sunday tea'), they would become lovers. She longed to see Ozz again. If there was time, she would tell Ken about Ozz, but not about Dimitri. She wasn't sure how Ken would handle a sexually active younger sister.

It was some months now since Eve and François Le Bon had come across one another again. He had remembered her at once, and even called her by name. She had said that she was surprised that he would remember her. 'You shamed me. I discovered that there was a streak of prejudice in me that I would have denied. When you picked me up at Barcelona station, I had expected a man to be driving. I was sure that we'd all end up rolling down a ravine.'

She had said, 'I don't believe you. You were really nice, you read the map for me.'

'Of course. I never expected that a brain capable of dealing with a lorry and a route map could be behind a lovely face.'

He hadn't been wholly serious, but each had been pleased to be remembered by the other. He was the senior English-speaking doctor in this hospital.

'François, this is my brother, he's got frost-bite. Would you mind taking a look?'

'Glad to know you, Captain Anders.'

'Wilmott,' Eve corrected. 'Ken Wilmott.'

'Sorry. Right, let's take a look.' As he supervised the careful removal of boots and socks, he said to Eve, 'Remember the nice lady who put us up for the night? Hey,' he smiled up at his patient, 'that isn't how it sounds.'

'You mean the teacher, Mrs Portillo?'

'Asked us to keep her husband and son in mind in case we ever came across them.'

'Eduardo and Paulo.'

'You remembered. (Feel anything there, Captain?) So did I, father and son. I removed shell fragments from Paulo's leg and he went back to Aragón. The father is a prisoner, either that or he's been executed. He was a POUM official. I sometimes wonder who hates POUM most, the fascists or the other comrades. (That hurt? Good, not too much damage.) Before I enlisted, it all seemed so simple: if you were against fascism, then you were with the Republic.' Her brother's toes looked bad to her, but she could learn nothing from François Le Bon's impassive, professional mask as he examined the damage. 'I think we should have you in for a few days.'

'No, I have to get back. I'm only here because we were bringing in a chap for surgery and there was no ambulance.'

'Bit of luck for you then, Captain. If you had returned to the front line, then I'll guarantee you'd have lost the foot with gangrene – even part of the leg. As it is, I think we might be able to salvage a full set of toes.'

'So my dancing days might not be over, then?'

'Probably not, if you'll let us treat you. I've seen worse than this respond to treatment.'

Ken Wilmott looked up at his sister and sucked his teeth. 'Have to keep the old toes in AI trim for the fox-trot.'

He wanted her approval.

'You were always light on your feet, Kenny.'

When he first entered Spain, Ken had felt that he had found his spiritual home. He would settle down here, in the south. Somewhere where the sun was warm. But seeing Lu – Eve –

had awakened a stab of homesickness. He had a niece now, and that had hardly registered until they talked about the family.

He would write to them all. With nothing to do for a few days while they pumped him full of stuff, he would write.

David Hatton sat in the back of a slithering lorry, his bags containing the portable filming equipment held in place by his knees. It had been a dodgy landing, and there had been a moment on touch-down when he wondered whether scrounging a lift on a plane with a Mexican pilot had been such a good idea. For all he knew of Mexican pilots, they might all be mad stunters. He was trying to read again the information Archie Archer had sent on. On the flight he had been seated next to a talkative, friendly passenger, so he hadn't really been able to take in the full meaning of the pages, but even so he had found them incredible, although their source was good. The lorry rocked and the light was bad. Even so, he was desperate to read and re-read the stark details of the woman who had flitted in and out of his life, but had become fixed in his heart and his head.

It was in the usual format, the details requested, but nothing more, no colour or speculation.

Eve Vera Anders née Louise Vera Wilmott: b. Portsmouth, June 1917.

Anders travelled to Barcelona in the company of a CP-sponsored medical team, continued to Albacete Auto-Parc, British Ambulances, Section Organizer Mrs H. Alexander (LOLO).

Birth registered as Louise Vera Wilmott. Birth Certificate dated July 1917, shows Father, Arthur Wilmott, Able Seaman RN; Mother, Vera Wilmott. Address: 110 Lampeter Street, Lampeter, Portsmouth.

Education: Lampeter Church of England, Lampeter, Portsmouth. Portsmouth Grammar School – unfinished course.

Profession/career: Factory worker/machinist. Ezzards

'Queenform' factory to 1937. Dismissed for Trades Union activities.

Political Activity: None (except the brief affair with the T&GWU).

Joined CP 1937 prior to enlisting as Aid to Spain ambulance driver.

Sponsor: S. Anderson (active).

Subject sometime chauffeur to visiting officials to the Republic, MPs, Senators and var. VIPs. Good reports. Personable, intelligent and well-spoken. Transferred to Madrid area supplies transport, at own request.

Subject recently on LOLO lists as 'Prospect Active'.

Subject's brother – Wilmott, K. Captain 15th Battalion Int. Brigade.

Subject was questioned in Wineapple enquiry (see sep. sheet). Cleared of any involvement.

Archie had scrawled across the bottom: 'Interesting, eh? Hope she doesn't go off in your hand when you pull the pin. Have second thoughts about suggesting we take up some of her reports. A female war correspondent could be good for *Herald*. Keep in touch.'

David Hatton folded the report, replaced it in the envelope and put it inside his camera case. As soon as he had read it the first time, some things fell into place. She had supposed that he had thought she was a pick-up that time in Bournemouth, and being the respectable working-class girl that she was, she had left him high and dry. That made some sense. He thought through their next meeting. Again that had been total coincidence. He had just happened to be whiling away an evening in a strange town, when for a second time he discovered her in a dance-hall. She had been more confident this time, and had let him walk with her to the railway station and accepted an invitation to an RN social affair. How absolutely stunning she had looked. She worked in a factory. He had thought of everything imaginable as her reason for being so mysterious, except that. Nothing she did or said had led him in that direction. He thought he knew an act when he saw one. Not this extraordinary girl, she was a natural. That gown would surely have cost a year's earnings.

Just before taking the flight back to Spain, he had gone to Portsmouth to satisfy himself about some of the details. He had seen the back-street school and the great prison of a factory. At lunchtime he had waited for the workers to come out. Had she really come out like the others, wrapped in an apron, scarf round her head, jostling and laughing, rushing to the house in that back-street? He had walked there, and been the object of curiosity; had tried to visualize the young Louise in the children he saw running up and down the street, playing hop-scotch, rushing into their homes for their lunch and coming out with hunks of bread. Had she come through that sagging door wearing the green silk gown? That seemed impossible to believe. There must be something else.

Was there a man? A man who had bought the gown? Did she have a place where she transformed herself from a girl in an apron to a woman not at all ill-at-ease with the high life? The more he went over those meetings with her, the more puzzled he became.

Where did the trades union activities fit into the picture? Why join the CP and enlist as an ambulance-driver? Rich had joshed him about her magic and mystery. Now that he had all this information about her, she was more magical and mysterious than ever.

It would be easy enough to find her now, but how should he handle it? If Helan Alexander had already approached her for LOLO, then Helan would have told her that her background would be checked. How would a woman like Louise react to that? He guessed that she would be as mad as all hell, as she had every right to be. It was a tricky one. Was he bound to pass on the information to Helan? No, why would it be necessary, just as long as Helan knew that Louise was genuine and not an informant for the other side, a plant. If he said simply, I've checked and she is OK, then Helan would accept his word.

OK. So what was his strategy when she discovered that he knew her true identity, and he came face to face with Louise. Straight away it became problematical. A potential explosion, as Archie had suggested.

The brother! He had quite forgotten that he knew him. The captain seemed to be the answer to his dilemma.

What the hell! All this work with undercover organizations had made him devious. He could find her and say simply, Hello, remember me?

Chapter Twelve

The new year came in with more blizzards, interspersed with days of sun. Eve Anders was now a seasoned and experienced supplies runner, covering the area between the hospital in the El Escorial area of Madrid, Valencia and the Albacete Auto-Parc as well as many little villages close to the Madrid front. She took to wearing a soldier's peaked cap and sunglasses; even so the sun off the snow could be blinding and the hours of driving with squinting eyes caused tension and headaches.

On the last day of 1937 she had been on one of her runs to distribute food and bundles of clothing to several small villages. How much longer would there be supplies to keep them going? She had heard that funds were beginning to dry up because of internal disagreements within the aid organizations. It seemed impossible that aid-workers who had, until recently, been so involved and dedicated to the kind of people she saw every day, could be so taken up with internal disagreements that it was a struggle to keep collecting aid.

It made her mad, but that was no good unless it produced the kind of articles that prompted people to send donations irrespective of the internal politics of officials. Berating readers would have the opposite effect. So, while still overlooking the panorama, she made a first draft of an account that she hoped might accompany her photographs. She had never tried to take pictures seriously until recently, and she was still too aware of not knowing where the next reel of film might come from to be too experimental. But she did want to learn. She knew from years of sitting in cinemas that pictures and words together produced something very powerful.

When I awoke early on New Year's Day I was so entranced by the sight of pigeons fluttering around in the courtyard of the hospital where I had put up for the night, that I used up one shot of my precious last reel of film, because a fall of snow during the night had transformed and made beautiful the area which is regularly filled with wounded men with bloodied dressings waiting to be admitted.

In my off-duty time, I climbed to the top of an old fortress (*see picture*). The panoramic view was spectacular, bare hills and hundreds of acres in small parcels, pleated by the plough under the covering of snow. It was a beautiful sight, even though I knew the truth of what closer inspection would reveal. I go almost daily to those small communities.

There is always some child who sees my truck from way off, so that by the time I reach the little community its poverty-stricken people have gathered. There is always a mixture of anxiety and excitement in the air. I always experience that moment of distress and helplessness when I climb down and see the pale faces of the ill-fed, inadequately-clothed children.

There is always too a mixture of anger and satisfaction on their behalf when I pass the villa owned by a member of the Spanish royal family who also owned these people. Yes, *owned* as slaves were owned. I have seen this palace, a most beautiful villa standing in twelve square miles of grounds within which runs a stream engineered to cascade spectacularly down rocky falls.

Within the villa, there is still crystal glass, fine wines and fine china bearing the coat-of-arms of the King of Spain. Walls are adorned with priceless paintings and tapestries which, before this palace was taken over by the Republican socialists on behalf of the people, was in use by its owners for only two months of the year. This short stay amid wealth and luxury was sufficient to give the owner the necessary qualification for collecting taxes from the villagers, many of whom still occupy their same dirty, sunless, cold and damp dwellings.

I hope that you who read this will be moved to do something to help halt what is happening to ordinary people who often work twelve or more hours a days, twelve months in the year, to produce crops and who, for the first time in hundreds of years, are doing so as a free people. Speak out before it is too late. Speak out before our democracy is taken from us.

E. V. Anders, New Year's Day, 1938

It was in Benicasim, near Valencia, once a millionaires' coastal resort whose beautiful villas were now in use as convalescent centres for the wounded of the International Brigade, that Eve ran in to Ozz Lavender again. They greeted each other like old friends of many years' standing. He still looked in good physical shape, and as handsome, but, like all chauffeurs and drivers these days, he was thinner and hollow-eyed, and his genial manner masked an underlying tension.

'Andy, sweetheart, will you just look at ya. That hair! You had it cropped off like a fella back when.'

'I let it grow again when I discovered a remedy for the nits.'

'Hey, you should bottle it and make yourself a fortune.'

'Old ladies in the villages make it from a weed – fleabane I think it's called in England. It smells terrible, but it works and the smell washes out.'

They sat in the cab of Ozz's big supplies truck and smoked Spanish cigarettes, halved and re-rolled. 'The last I heard of you, you had gone to Colmenar. I heard from Alex that you put your foot down. Good on you, sweetheart. How long turn-around have you got, Andy?'

'Twenty-four hours.'

'Do you fancy a trip out?'

'In?'

'In my truck.'

'We could go to the beach area, I'd like that,' she said, smiling.

'Like when we picked up the Mercedes?'

'We went to Chincilla de Monte.'

'And ended up on the bay of Jávea, swimming in the nudd.'

'I have to go pick up some fresh fruit and stuff, but we could have a couple of hours to ourselves.'

'OK. Maybe I could get some for an Englishman I was hoping to visit – he's in the English convalescent centre.'

They picked up fresh and dried fruits first, and then took the road along the beautiful coast of the Golfo de Valencia. On the drive they rediscovered the number of interests they had in common, and talked about books they had read, films they had seen and foods they would pounce upon when things got back to normal, but they did not talk about the war, or about what they had done and seen, each knowing that the other's experiences would have been equally distressing.

'We could just about fit in a bullfight, Andy, do you fancy that?'

'That's a terrible idea, Ozz.'

'Why?'

'Because there are more humane ways of slaughtering an animal.'

'It's not slaughter. Have you ever seen a fighting bull?'

'No.'

'They're great black devils, bred for the purpose, and they kill 'm real quick.'

'That doesn't excuse what goes on before.'

'Do you know what goes on before?'

'I can imagine.'

'That's how unintelligent people inform their prejudices, and you aren't unintelligent. If you won't go at least to see whether you are right, then how can you have an opinion?'

'I can have an opinion about the whole idea of killing for enjoyment. I've seen a fox-hunt . . .'

'I'm not suggesting we go to a fox-hunt. C'mon, Andy, I never took you as having a mind that goes snap as a rat-trap on a new experience.'

The seats cost only a few pesetas and Ozz got them a place at the ringside. There, the light appeared so clear and concentrated that it was possible to see individual grains in the raked sand. Even though this was a fairly small bullring, the traditional pageantry was impressive. The excitement was almost palpable, the colours invoked sexuality, and the noise and smells were erotic. If that had been the whole show, then Eve would have felt satisfied that she had experienced something new. But even as the crowd acclaimed the spectacle that it must have seen many times before, even as the toreadors and matadors paraded, even as the jerky horses champed and trotted, Eve tensed with anticipation.

Then the ring emptied of the opening pageantry, the spectators fell silent and suddenly, just below where they were sitting, a black bull bucked to a slithering, stiff-legged stance only feet away from a slim young matador standing in a pose of exaggerated machismo. The crowd applauded wildly, but his entrance proved to be the climax of the matador's performance. From here on, all that Eve could see was useless bravado, as the young man moved inexpertly and without grace.

When the matador eventually lunged, he missed and sliced the bull's neck. The bull bellowed and lashed with his tail as blood poured down his shiny black coat and spotted the yellow sand. As the crowd jeered, the youth tried again with the sword, but he had lost his confidence. The weapon fell, and he picked it up to catcalls. It sounded to Eve as if the crowd was cheering for the bull. She looked down at her shoes, convinced that when the young man's slim body became impaled on the curving horns, the audience would be satiated.

There was an outbreak of clapping, and her attention was again drawn to the bloody arena. Several young men had leapt into the ring, one with a sword, but made no attempt to finish off the bleeding, maddened bull who was thrashing wildly and going for everyone in sight, its feet sliding as it changed direction.

Suddenly Ozz was out of his seat and into the arena where he seized the bull's tail. The madder the bull became, the wilder the amateur bullfighters became. With more bravado than skill, they dared the bull, with Ozz still clinging to its blood-soaked tail.

Eve could stand no more. Nobody noticed her rush out; everyone was too intent upon the sordid and humiliating spectacle in the sand. As she reached the street she heard a great explosion of voices. Thank God, the humiliation of the bull and the poor little raw matador was over. She climbed into the passenger seat of Ozz's truck and waited for him to return. It was a much longer wait than she had expected.

At last, Ozz, filthy and smelling of sweat and animal, found her glowering and angry but not quiet.

'Sorry about the bullshit, Andy, I couldn't find a place to have a bit of a swill.'

'How could you! I can't believe you would do such a thing, such a . . . I . . .'

'Simmer down, it wasn't dangerous. The bull was probably not that well bred, it's all part of the show. The next fight is a stunner, and the local hero will leave the ring with his reputation a mile high.' Lighting a cigarette, he plumped himself carelessly into the driving seat. 'You didn't like it, I can see that, but at least you will be able to pontificate about bullfighting from your own experience instead of from someone else's.'

'Oh, you're totally wrong, Ozz. I *hated* it! I was appalled by it, as appalled as I was when I saw hounds bring down a fox. How could you? Of all people.'

'What is that supposed to mean, Of all people?'

What indeed? She really hardly knew him. Yet she had built up an image of Ozz as a gentle friend, based on the trust she had placed in him on that first outing together when they had taken off their clothes and gone swimming in the bay. 'I don't know. I thought you were different.'

'From whom, from what?'

'I don't know. From the general run-of-the-mill men, from the competitors.'

'But I am a competitor, you've known that from the first day. I told you that I was going to compete in the Berlin Olympics, but went instead to the People's Games in Barcelona. I *am* competitive, very competitive. If you don't know that, you don't know me at all.'

'I probably don't. It's my own fault for relying on my

intuition. I thought you were different, special, that you and I were friends, colleagues if you like.'

'So did I, still do, and I can't imagine that there is anything that you could do that would make me want to give you a rollicking. I guess there are things about you that I find surprising, but that's my problem for imposing my expectations on you. If so, I won't blame you for not coming up to the Eve Anders of my own invention.'

She felt like a child receiving a more-in-sorrow-than-in-anger talking-to by her elder brother or the school vicar. She felt too sullen to make excuses or even reply.

Ozz leaned back in the driver's seat and put his feet up on the dashboard. 'You're right about one thing, Andy. I am different. I'm homosexual.'

Her ears pricked up like an animal listening for an almost imperceptible sound. Had he said homosexual?

'You're what?'

'I'm one of your actual pansies. Just so's you know. Just so you know how much of a friend I hope you are. How much I trust you, as much as you trusted me that day at Jávea bay.'

She was flustered and blushed. He wasn't really serious. He was! But you could tell them a mile off. She had grown up seeing them hanging around the docks. Ozz looked normal, a real he-man.

After a long pause, she said, 'I don't know what I'm supposed to say.'

He looked at her and raised his eyebrows in a kind of plea. 'You aren't supposed to say anything, Andy. It's no big picnic. I don't go for girls, that's all. I happen to prefer fellas.'

'Prefer?'

'To go to bed with.'

'Oh.'

'I just thought I'd like to tell you, to kind of put a seal on our friendship. Anybody who knows that kind of thing about a fella has got him by the balls.'

She turned towards him slightly but did not look directly at him.

'C'mon, look at me, Andy. It's important to both of us. I never took to anybody straight away like I took to you. If I wasn't like I am, I'd have been in love with you. But I am like this and I do love you, but not in that way.'

She looked at him, her expressionless stare unblinking.

'Listen, Eve, you're intelligent, you're a breath of fresh air and a drink of cold water. I was just hoping we could be good mates. Something happened between us and we clicked, but you didn't fancy me as a bloke, which was good. It seemed to me that our being together after those kids got blown up, and things were pretty bad, pushed us together. It wasn't a sexual thing, and I was grateful for that. I felt as though we'd known one another years and years. I thought we could see a bit of each other and it'd be nice if we could talk, maybe go to the flicks. Mates.'

'But I've seen pansies about, since I was little. They walk funny, they dye their hair, and wear pink or purple shirts and long silk scarves round their necks. I've seen them hanging around the docks and dance-halls wearing more make-up than the girls. And now look at you, your hair's a mess, you wear a navvy's shirt, and you've got this astounding body, a male athlete, how much more masculine can you get?'

He smiled wryly. 'Most of the original Olympian competitors would have been homo. It was quite the done thing in those days. I shouldn't have tried to be flippant. Pansy isn't a nice word. I'm a homosexual, I didn't ask to be it, I didn't try to be it, I just am it, and there's nothing I can do about it.' He grinned. 'Well, nothing practical until I can find another one to settle down with, and if you was a fella, Andy, it'd be you.'

The girls she used to work with would have had a good laugh. Ho, just listen to him, that's a new line.

'My dad believes all his sons are red-blooded. He'd have been

202

proud to see me hanging on to a bull's tail. I think I'll send him the ear.'

'What ear?'

'The bull's bloody ear. I think the officials intended it as a bit of a joke, seeing I was a foreigner, so they insisted I have it. I guessed you wouldn't go a lot on that, so I chucked it in the back. It's OK, don't go getting your hackles up again, it's all wrapped up in newspaper.'

How perverse of nature to make such a perfect man and then give him a flaw. Perfect body, unthreatening manner, and always treating women with the respect of equals. Yet, in spite of him saying that he wanted theirs to be a perfect kind of platonic friendship, it was bound to be very different from female friendships. These were based to a great extent upon things women had in common: the functioning of their complicated moods and bodies for one thing, their female instincts for another. No female friend would accept a freshly cut-off ear for any reason.

She thought of herself and Bar Barney cuddling up in the same bed. That was sleeping with someone of the same sex, but that wasn't what Ozz meant. She couldn't imagine what two men could find to do that could give them anything like those wickedly sensuous explosions she and Duke had given each other and more recently she and Dimitri.

'Say something, Andy, even if it's only "So long".'

'You were wrong about me not fancying you that day.'

'Andy, I can't believe it! My antennae usually function better than that. I thought you were pining for some nice man, and I wasn't him.'

'No. I was probably still suffering from the shock of that awful day. I wasn't sending out any messages.' She gave him a tucked-lip little smile. 'But I wasn't sorry to see you without your clothes on.'

'Where do we go from here, Andy? I don't want to lose you.'

'You stand more chance of losing me by suddenly joining the bull-baiters.'

'Look, Andy. I don't know how other fellas feel about women, I assume they feel the same way I do about fellas, but as far as anything else goes I'm hardly different. OK, it's a mile wide difference, but I'm as competitive as the next bloke, I can be as much a crazy exhibitionist. I'm just the same as all those other idiots who jumped down into the bullring, and for all anybody knows, there's likely to be a percentage of them who wouldn't mind jumping into bed with the other idiots there.'

'Oh, Ozz. I wish I really understood what you are on about.'

He leaned over and took her hand. 'Andy, that young matador, I couldn't sit there and see him being humiliated, a kid like that. So what else could I have done to stop it? Eh?'

'Hanging on to the bull's tail was going to stop it? The creature was already half-dead from that pathetic little bullfighter. How many times did he stick it with his sword?'

'Too bloody many. All I did was to give it the kindest cut of all, so to speak. It wasn't very elegant, but I've killed a good many pigs and steers back home. You go for the artery and stand back.'

Her puzzled look was genuine. 'Are you saying that you killed the bull?'

'Finished him off, yeah. I thought that's why you were sitting here being so huffy.'

'No. I'm sitting here being huffy because you jumped into the ring and now, well, huffy's not the word for it.'

'I'm sorry about that. But that's me. All that's Clive Lavender. I've made a right dog's dinner of this, haven't I?'

Did his mother know? And what about his brothers? He was a competitive athlete, they could be proud of that. Maybe they didn't think twice about him putting all his energy into becoming a hurdling champion. It must have been lonely knowing that he wasn't like the others, not being naturally one of the crowd, always having to pretend. He must have been glad to get away.

'No, somebody else made the dog's dinner when they gave you this, this complication. Being different. I know what it means to be different. It's damned lonely.'

'How different?'

'From the time I was twelve, I've been different from everyone I grew up with. I'm now trying to be somebody else. But it's not working, I can't be the girl I was, and I'm not the woman I thought I could become.'

'What woman?'

'I suppose you might say, Unclassified. A person accepted for what she is, not what people think she should be because there was a label on her when she was born.' She went silent. 'That's it, isn't it, Ozz. You and I don't want to wear the labels.'

He reached out and put his hand over hers, squeezing it tightly. 'You're a good'n, Andy.' He took a cigarette from his breast pocket, lit it, drew on it then handed it to her. They were smoking cigarettes as though there was no shortage and a tobacconist's around the corner.

She turned to smile at him, but was arrested by his expression. She had seen the same look in her own eyes, only briefly, when she caught herself unawares. You're on your own.

She slipped one arm through his, drew on the cigarette and handed it over. 'Come on, we have to get back.'

'Wait, I'll dump that thing.'

'Don't, Ozz, send it to your dad.'

'You reckon?'

'You said he'd be proud, so why not?'

In Benicasim each of the beautiful villas was given over to a particular nationality, so that when Richard Hatton was sent there it was inevitable that he would meet up again with Ken Wilmott. Not that Richard Hatton was in good enough shape to call it a meeting. The doctors hoped that by sending him to convalesce in such good surroundings he would recover. He was very sick, very troubled. Ken Wilmott, on the other hand, was ready to return to his unit. A man who can't put his feet to the ground isn't much good on the battle field, so he had gone along with the treatment. He wasn't a good patient, fretting about being away from his men, but at least he was a step closer to getting back to his military career when he was sent to the training school at Tarazona.

Packed and ready, he went into the ward to say goodbye to Richard Hatton. 'I'm off then, Rich.'

If Eve Anders had once mistaken Richard for David Hatton, there was no longer any chance of that. The eventual loss of half a hand had been bad enough, but the lack of any news of the woman he loved had left him distraught and on the verge of breakdown.

'Then I shan't see you again, Will.'

'I'm Ken, remember?'

'Oh, yeah, you lost your toes and I lost my digits.' He gave a parody of a grin and his eyes filled with tears. Richard Hatton had chosen to forget that Ken Wilmott's toes had been saved and that he was ready to return to the fighting.

'Have you heard whether your brother is coming here?'

'The orderly said that he had phoned. He'll try, you can count on Davey to get here if . . .'

'Remember me to him. Tell him thanks again for the pictures. Sorry to miss him but, you know . . . Try to keep in touch, old son. Take care of yourself, and you'll soon be on the plane back to London.'

The reply came out, almost hissing with rage. 'I don't want to go to bloody London. I want to go where you're going. Who needs more than one and a half hands to massacre the bastards? I'll use my bloody teeth if I have to. I'm doing everything they tell me. I'm eating now.'

'That's good, Rich. Wasn't ever any good, you not eating. I'll have to go, mate.'

'Where are you going?'

'Training camp. Going to do the thing properly. Just a couple of weeks, then I'll be an officer worth having, I hope.'

'You're one now, chaps like yourself are what this country wants, not bloody public school arty types like me. Spain's got more arty foreigners than it knows what to do with. Not Davey, not my brother, he's doing fine work for the cause.'

'He's a decent bloke, I got on all right with him. He married?'

'No, never long enough in one place for that. He's always been the one for the gentle sex, could always elbow me out of the running, a bit love 'em and leave 'em. Now the tables are turned, poor old Davey.'

Although he knew that his sister was in the area and he would have liked to see her again, Ken Wilmott wanted to get back. 'Give your brother my best. I'll have to get going, Rich. Sorry to leave you like this, but, you know . . .' He shook the undamaged hand.

'Here's my grandmother's London address. If you hear anything, anything at all, let her know. I know I've been a pain in the arse to you, Captain . . .'

'Don't go upsetting yourself again, Rich, you aren't a pain in the arse. I knew a girl myself – she's active in POUM, so I see how you feel about these fearless girls.'

'She might be pregnant.'

'I know, and like I said, if I can get even a scrap of news from outside that might help, I'll send it directly to your gran. I'll put this in my wallet – not much else in there. I'll say so long, then.'

On his way back to collect his things, he looked at the scrawled card. Lady Margaret Gore-Hatton. Well, well. You met all sorts. First time he'd come across a bloke who had a double-barrel Lady Margaret for a gran. Not the sort of thing Ray would understand, he wouldn't go much on hob-nobbing with the Thems of this world. Ray would say that there must be something at the back of it, people like that were the natural enemy of the workers. Ray had never got to grips with proper socialist thinking, he had always been a straight up and down Labour trades unionist. It was clear as crystal to Ray. Them and

Us. He'd never believe that some of the Thems could see further than the end of their noses and might see that Marx knew a thing or two. And what about the Falangists – there's a lot of workers joined them. What about them, Ray? That's the influence of the Church, he'd say.

Would he? He was putting words into Ray's mouth and he no longer knew his brother. The mail service wasn't good at the best of times, and was getting worse. Getting married and starting a family changed a chap, and with a wife like Bar Barney, Ray might easily soften up a bit. Bar was a really nice girl. What did she think of Lu? *Eve!* Christ, I shan't ever get used to calling her Eve. Those two have been pretty close since they were kids, lived in one another's pockets when they were together. Never saw two such opposites, except for one thing: they both had a rod of iron up their backs. It was ages since he had seen Bar, but she wasn't the sort to change, she had been her own self from the start. Ray was going up the Southern Railway ladder now. There were times when he really missed his brother, but not enough to want to go back to England and the old life. Bugger that for a lark!

Thank the Lord he was back on his own again. Only himself and his mates, his comrades. He believed in the Spanish cause more than he had ever expected to at first. He needed the democrats to win, he belonged here. He had felt it as soon as he had seen the bare rocky landscape, the vineyards and olive groves. He had felt it again when he met Mariella in Barcelona on May the eighth, his birthday. It had been his first experience of all the different political factions, all dedicated to the cause of free Spain, all fighting almost as fiercely against one another as they were fighting together to save the Republic.

Mariella Redondo was a girl with a rifle. By the time the Assault Guards were sent in to settle the warring factions, he had become as close to the Redondo family as though he had known them all his life. Both parents, all four sons and Mariella were members of POUM, the reddest of the reds, the dissident reds who were against Stalin. The whole family had had a hand in the communal destruction of the images of the Catholic Church, the symbols of centuries of repression. The family had seemed to glow with pride as they had recalled that day of a symbolic breaking with the past, with the Church and the monarchy. He had envied them their family feeling. He wanted to be one of them.

When Ken Wilmott had finished his officers' course, he was trained to take charge of a company of 150 men of the British Battalion who would back up the Republican army on the Teruel front. He had special duties and a pass that gave him access to many sectors along the fighting front, but with the pass went the danger of a bullet in the head if captured while carrying it.

David Hatton was shocked when he saw his brother. The injury was pretty awful, but with a bit of practice, as he encouragingly told Rich, he would be able to resume his career. He wouldn't be fit to fight, but there were other ways of supporting the cause. 'No reason why the two of us shouldn't resume our old H + H partnership. We could make some bloody good documentary films, like the American travel films but we'd leave off the rose-tinted lens, not have any fades into the sunset. Hard-hitting stuff, like we always wanted. Studs Terkel on the silver screen.'

His brother's apathy was worrying, as were his easy tears and obvious depression. They had had a cousin like that. The family called it shell-shock, the physicians treated him for a nervous disorder. In the end he had thrown himself off a cliff in Devon. Now he really feared that his brother might do something like that. Twins they might be, but David had always thought that Rich had more of the Gore in him than he himself had.

Seated in garden chairs at a little table on a first-floor glass-enclosed balcony used as a recreation room by the recuperating soldiers, David Hatton was trying to rouse his brother's interest in some rough prints he had brought along. He happened to glance up just in time to see the driver of a big camouflaged truck climb in and drive it away. A woman. Louise!

Richard looked distressed and anxious. 'What's up? Don't go, Davey.'

'I'm not going, Rich, but I think I caught sight of somebody I know.'

Too late. She would be a mile down the road before he reached the ground floor. It was her. The hair, he'd never forgotten her beautiful hair. How many women truck-drivers were there in Spain? 'It's OK, Rich, I can probably find out later. Somebody in the admin here will know.'

'Who was it?'

'A truck-driver.'

'An Australian chap?'

David Hatton hesitated. 'No. A woman driver actually.'

Richard Hatton looked perplexed. They had always tuned in to one another's emotions, less so now that they were apart and were older, but they were still sensitive to one another when they were together. 'Is she the one you've been looking for?'

'I think so. She is in Spain, I know that much. Here,' he took a photo from a folder, 'remember this pic of the brigader and the Madrileño militia girls? Small world; seems that he's her brother.'

Richard looked steadily at the picture, not really feeling up to getting too deeply involved in his brother's complex life. 'I know him, his name's Ken.'

'How come?'

Richard recalled the matey exchanges he had had with the down-to-earth captain who didn't mind corpses. Not likely that Davey knew much about all that. 'Ken Wilmott, captain with the Attlee Brigade – the Fifteenth. He's been here until recently. They saved my life, the captain and your will-o'-the-wisp lady. She drove me from the first-aid station through a big blizzard in her truck, with Wilmott holding me together in the back.'

'He's been injured?'

'Frost-bite. Matter of fact, I gave him a pair of Mag's footlet things.'

'So that *was* her I just saw?'

'Probably. She's been wangling her runs so that she can visit her brother. Only thing is, I thought you said that your lady's name was Louise.'

'It is, was, it was the name I knew her by.'

'Louise Wilmott?' Richard knew very well that this was not her name now.

'I only knew Louise Vera, nothing else. But on my last trip to England . . .' He didn't really want to tell Richard the whole story.

'She's called Eve Anders.'

'I know.'

'And her brother is Captain Wilmott.'

'So it would seem.'

Richard paused, waiting for a response from his brother, but none came. 'Bit of a can of worms then, old chap?'

'Not at all. It's all quite simple really.'

'Good.' The dope he'd been given to help quell the pain of his injuries also helped to deaden his distress over Maite. Its effectiveness was beginning to wear off, and there was always that time between shots when he came face to face with the reality of his physical and mental state. Even so, he just had to say something to Davey, his idealistic and romantic brother, who had naive notions that things somehow came right if you believed they would. Going in different directions they might be, they were still Hatton + Hatton, still twins. He hoped that Davey could be spared some of the heartbreak he himself was experiencing. 'But I have to put my five eggs in, Davey. Don't build up your hopes. If she had wanted you to find her, she knows where you hang out in London.'

'I'm not building anything.'

'You are, I saw it just now.'

This visit was not going as David had hoped; nothing to do

with Richard was going as David had hoped. He could see that his brother was terribly ill and should go home as soon as it could be arranged, but Richard refused to leave Spain until he knew that the woman he loved was safe. And David had brought no news of Maite Manîas. It was going to be hard to have to admit this, when he still had the image of the golden head ducking into the cab of the truck. Sorry, Rich, found my woman, couldn't find yours.

A spasm of pain caught Richard unawares, making him grunt spontaneously. David got quickly to his feet. 'What is it, Rich? Pain bad? Shall I call somebody?'

'Just find my fags tin, Davey, do me a roll-up, will you?'

As David opened the lid he recognized the aroma. 'Hang it all, Rich, you aren't smoking this stuff.'

'What stuff? Oh, you mean good old hedgerow blend.'

'Hemp. Rots the brain and numbs the mind.'

'Eases the mind, numbs the pain.'

'You need medication, not stupefying. They're smoking this stuff in the trenches; men are facing machine-guns, doped out.'

'How bloody else can men face machine-guns? Stone cold sober? Heroically? If you don't want to soil your hands, then give it here.'

'It goes against the grain, Rich.'

'Don't be such a bloody prig. As soon as I get out of this place I shall simply chuck it.'

'That's what Lavinia Courtals said, what squiffy people always say.'

'I'm not squiffy, it isn't like cocaine and that sort of thing. It acts like a double whisky. If you can get me a couple of bottles of Scotch then I won't need to smoke the herbal.'

'You *need* to?'

Richard Hatton lit up the crackling, aromatic little cigarette and closed his eyes as he inhaled. 'Yes, little brother. I need to. It dulls the pain, and I don't mean just this.' He held up his bandaged hand. 'So. Did you get to see the French tart?'

'I saw Malou, yes, and a fellow who knows what's going on on both sides of the war.'

'Cero?'

'You know him?'

'Diplomat without a country, ambassador extraordinaire. Or is it that he runs with the hare and the hounds?'

'He's one of us, Rich.'

'OK, if you say so. So what's the bad news?'

'All that they know is that Maite Manîas' work is banned, and that she is no longer in Rosal. My guess is that she's making for London.'

'But Malou didn't think so?'

'She didn't know. She thinks she's well in with all the top brass – the generals and the bishops – she got her audience with the Pope. I think she thought that was really one up.'

Richard drew deeply on the failing cigarette. 'What's to do then, Davey? Don't want to go back home, no good here, nothing on the horizon.'

'Oh, come on, Rich, there's a hell of a lot on the horizon. There are a million stories to be told about the persecution of Spanish artists.'

'Then you'll have to tell them, old son. So why don't you clear off now and go after that lovely lorry-driver. Get her into bed, but don't make her fucking pregnant. Pregnant women revolutionaries are too hard to handle. They get raped before they stick bayonets into their bellies.'

'Stop that kind of talk, Richard! If you don't know about propaganda and the lies of war, then nobody does. She's not dead. You have to stop thinking that she is.'

'Dead I could handle.' He forced himself to look his brother in the eye. 'Now be a good lad, Davey, and bugger off. I'm grateful for you coming all this way, but I find it too damned hard to be civil to anyone.'

David looked at his wreck of a brother. How could he leave him like this? How could he stay? 'Would you see a psychiatric doctor, Rich? Just to help you through until you hear from

213

Maite.' Richard shrugged. 'I'll talk to somebody downstairs. You can't be the only one down in the dumps.'

'For Christ's sake, David! Call it a spade. I'm going out of my fucking mind.'

David Hatton collected his pictures and pushed the tin of herbals across the table. 'Have one, Rich. I'll send you down some Scotch, absolute promise.' Clasping his brother's good hand, he said, 'I'll be back, Rich, old son. I feel sure that Maite's OK.'

Richard nodded and put a light to another of his pain-killers.

When David Hatton reached Madrid, there was a letter awaiting him, postmarked Paris and date-stamped only two days previously. 'The little red ladybird has flown to Southampton. I've kept my side of the bargain. Does honour prevail in the realms of the unwashed where you now wallow, my love? MF.' Typical of the drama with which Malou always did like to surround herself. She saw it all as some kind of show. He had seen her once with Oswald Mosley when he was haranguing a crowd of workers outside a factory. She was got up in jodhpurs and black leather straps, her pale blonde hair cascading over one eye which was covered with a black patch. What the hell kind of a figure she thought she cut was anyone's guess.

Malou French's intelligence came too late. Richard Hatton's body, his wrists hacked open with broken glass, was discovered in one of the most beautiful areas of the millionaires' erstwhile playground.

Soon after Ken Wilmott got back, the British Battalion was assigned to defend the town of Belchite, a return to an old battleground for the newly trained captain. Among his 150 men there were hardly any faces that he recognized. Some had come with recent batches of volunteers, others from the remnants of other companies. The only familiar face was that of Jock Duncan who had also been at Teruel where they had briefly shared the protection of the same machine-gun.

'Ah heerd ye lost a foot, Kenneth man, but ah see you didnae.'

'Good to see you, Jock, you're not in my company, more's the pity.'

'No, but we're all dogs' dinners companies these days.'

'What do you reckon, then? Is the rumour right that they've got all this great concentration of tanks?'

'Aye, and artillery and infantry to follow through behind the tanks. And air support.'

'Ah, well, no trouble to us then, Jock.'

Having come to terms with the knowledge that, outgunned and outnumbered, they were bound to retreat, Ken Wilmott felt peculiarly at ease. If he died here, then he would have died for something worthwhile. Not that he had any intention of dying, for he still held faint hope that when the fighting was over, he would return to Barcelona. He did not think beyond that.

'Did you ever get news from yon POUM lassie you were telling about?'

'Not yet.'

'Ah never did fathom what all that was about, working man fighting working man. Assassinations and betrayals. You'd never think the reds had the fascists to go for if they were spoiling for a fight.'

'The POUMers wanted Stalin off their backs, and the Chinese weren't having any. Did you ever know why the Soviets are called Chinese by the Spanish?'

'No, but I dare say it's an insult so that they can have another shoot-up with one another. Why, man, I heard that upwards of a thousand were killed in Barcelona's May troubles. Whisht, Kenneth man, my big mouth never thinks before it opens itself.'

'A thousand, I know. Stalin doing Franco's work for him.'

'Hush, man. There's eyes and ears everywhere, the Ruskies have the best secret service organization in the world.'

'You know, Jock, when I left home I was filled with ambition to live in a Republic. It seemed that it had to be every working bloke's dream, equality, liberty and friendship. Isn't that what the Frenchies say?'

'Aye, man. That's our Sermon on the Mount. It's what makes us march to the same drum.' Smiling, he started to hum the *Internationale*, the anthem of leftists the world over. He had scarcely finished the first four or five bars, when it was taken up by everybody within earshot. It was extraordinary how a simple tune that any child could have picked out on a penny whistle could arouse such emotion in battle-hardened soldiers.

'It all seemed so simple when we came, didn't it?'

'Aye. Simple it was and simple it is. Them over there's the fascists, and us over here's going to shoot the shite out of them.'

All that Ken Wilmott could do was hope that Mariella and her family had survived. Like Jock, he found the ever-growing power-struggle within the Republic hard to come to terms with. For one thing, he didn't understand it. There was a revolution and a war going on at the same time. The origins of internal clashes were often ancient and complicated, only the Spanish themselves could understand.

As Jock Duncan and Ken Wilmott agreed, the thing to keep in mind was that they were there to blast the shite out of the fascists.

The headquarters of the Brigade was established amid the scars and ruins of Belchite. Bodies from the last battle still lay beneath the ruins, and the smell of decay was everywhere as Ken and his companies, together with thousands of other soldiers, marched to the front. The closer they got, the more remnants they saw of units who had gone before, until suddenly they were aware that there were no troops of the Republican army between them and the full force of the enemy. Attack came from air and ground. The terrain offered no defensive positions and there were no fortifications.

They fell back to Belchite.

Then further back.

Military discipline held. There was no headlong flight. There was no rout. At every stage of the withdrawal they covered their line against the enemy. They transported casualties to safety and tried to save as much *matériel* as could be saved.

If Ken and Jock realized this might be the start of a retreat through Aragón, they never suggested or even implied it. For one thing, Ken Wilmott was preoccupied with the state of his socks and boots. The long march to the front, followed at once by the withdrawal, was not the best treatment for damaged toes.

Chapter Thirteen

With every week that passed, the invading armies pushed the front further and further until, by the time the snows had gone, it seemed to Eve that the invaders were reapers slowly closing in on the eye of the cornfield. This fanciful idea came about because of the number of familiar faces she saw in and around Madrid. Ozz particularly, then Sweet Moffat who had come to help with refugee orphans. Then, one day, Helan Alexander, whom she hadn't seen since the episode of the enquiry into the death of Sophie Wineapple.

Eve's old truck had gone into the depot to be cannibalized by the mechanics who did wonders with ever-decreasing spare parts. But that was life in Madrid. Food was scarce, not to the point of starvation, but supplies were sporadic and unplanned. One day there would be only black-eyed peas, another only flour. Meat was more scarce than ever. Ration cards were prepared. A statement made by a government official warning that if there was no self-restraint in hoarding, then there would be food shortages and thus rationing, caused shops to be stripped almost bare. Wine was still plentiful. Oil was obtainable. Eve stopped smoking for the simple reason that it became too time-consuming to look for tobacco.

Eve had become a seasoned driver of anything and everything. Occasionally she looked back to last year when she had made such a fuss about driving a Mercedes. Now that she had seen the difficulties under which some visitors made their flying visits from front to front, she thought that there *was* a case for fast cars. Not that she would change what she was now doing, for she loved her big, thundering lorries. Her Spanish was now comprehensible in places as far afield as Murcia and Catalonia, not that she always understood their language, but there was always the language of the hands and nods. She liked the runs to the small villages where, in spite of the worsening conditions, people were amazingly cheerful.

Many of the more remote places relied on passing traffic for news of what was going on. The peasants would listen and nod. Eve had heard that many of them had always been against the Republic and were waiting for the day when they would be liberated by General Franco. The only indication that this might be so was when news of a Republican advance was greeted by a gob-spit, but, as many peasants were given to expectoration anyway, it was difficult to draw conclusions from this.

Because of artillery bombardment and air-raids, most of her supplies runs now were made as part of a convoy. On one occasion, when she had been driving in a line of close formation, they had all had to run off the road and into a grove when strafing planes were spotted. Suddenly she realized that the truck ahead was loaded with ammunition while Ozz, who was travelling in the rear, was delivering cans of kerosene. Having panicked for a few minutes, she calmed down and decided that wherever you were in Spain now, you stood a chance of sudden death. It did no good thinking about it.

With the onset of spring, the air-raids on Madrid become fiercer and more frequent. Despite this, whenever she had an hour off she would go out into the city and simply look. She always had something in writing ready to send to London. She now had an editor who handled all her work. Because her style was simply to record what she saw, a surprising variety of publications were willing to take her reports.

She was one of the team of drivers working the Madrid front. Like everyone else she turned her hand to anything that came along, from holding plasma bottles in a first-aid station to hauling potatoes to one location and returning with tomatoes from another.

It was when she was on her way back from wandering around the Gran Via and Calle de Alcalá in the city that she came upon

Helan Alexander, for the first time in ages it seemed. An air-raid warning sounded so she joined the crowd racing for shelter in the Metro where she squatted down among the Madrileños and rested her back against the wall. 'Alex?'

Helan Alexander was painfully thin and drawn, and looked as though all the stuffing had been knocked out of her.

'Anders?' She clasped Eve as though she was a long-lost friend. 'Thank God, a friendly face.'

'What are you doing here?'

'I don't know . . . actually what I'm doing is running around like a blue-arsed fly making a balls of everything.' From her top pocket she took two cigarettes.

'I haven't smoked for weeks.'

'So have one.'

The strong, Spanish tobacco was extremely satisfying, and numbed the hunger pangs that had been with Eve since the day before. 'Thanks, it tastes good.'

Alexander blew out a long stream of smoke, oblivious to the woman suckling her baby close by, and said casually, 'Carl's dead. Executed.'

'Oh, Alex, that's dreadful! I'm so sorry. When?'

'God knows. Probably as soon as he was captured, I should think. Not exactly the blood of the new master race – half-breed Negro Jew, married to white English woman from the decadent class.'

She was probably right, there was nothing Eve could say that wouldn't sound trite and crass. 'You're not giving up here? You're not going home?'

'I'm not much good here, can't think straight. I packed it in at the depot.' For a long pause she withdrew into herself. 'It's devastating, Eve. I didn't know how much I loved the bloody man until . . . I could keep my head above water when I could believe that he was in a concentration camp, my work had purpose. Now my reason for being here has gone. Pouf . . . bullet in the head. Gone.'

'Were you doing it only for your husband?'

'Yes.'

'Not because you believed it was the right thing?'

'No. I believed what he believed because he was such a good man. A man like that knows what is right. But it went against the grain, contrary to everything I'd ever been or known.'

'Why have you come to Madrid?'

'To hand over and go home, I think. I don't really know.'

'I think you will miss him more in England than you would if you stayed.'

'I miss him because he's stopped living in the same world I do. If I go home ... God! If I go home – what? Back to Mummy and Daddy – their naughty daughter who had a fling with a nigger? Back to the pretty horses? You see, Anders, I'm quite nutty.'

'I went nuts after my mother died. Grief knocks you off course.'

'I'm floundering. I think that I may be sinking. Just now, when the warning sounded, I thought, Stay where you are, Alexander, what in hell's name is the use of trying to save yourself. But then I got caught up in the rush for shelter. The instinct to survive, I suppose. What for I can't imagine.'

The air-raid over, they left the Metro. 'Where are you staying, Alex?'

She named a *pensione* that Eve didn't know. 'I know one of the secretaries, she bunked up a bit last night to make room for me. I came to see you.'

'Me? What's that about?'

They went into a small eating place and sat at a table away from the window, part of which was boarded up and part was stuck over with paper strips. Eve couldn't decide whether Alexander was pondering on what to say, or whether she had retreated into her own misery.

'David Gore-Hatton.'

Eve started and felt her cheeks flush. '*Who?*'

'Gore-Hatton. Has he been in touch yet?'

Eve sensed that whatever answer she gave would be the

wrong one, so she tried to keep a blank expression upon her face. Ozz had said that Madrid was the cross-roads of the world and if you hung around long enough everyone would come by. How could Alex possibly know that the name Gore-Hatton meant anything to her? David had no part in her life here, except in her dreams, and even there he was fading.

Dimitri, who probably had headquarters in Madrid, had come by the cross-roads since she had been in the city. He had sought her out when he knew that she was stationed there and they had met several times. As they had before, they made love with an explosion of repressed desire for a night or for an afternoon and then parted on good terms. Gratification? Pleasure? Lust, perhaps? Not love, no deep emotions, no strings attached to their hours of give and take. There might well be another side to Dimitri, of course there was; he was a commissar spreading the Stalinist line, or a member of the Soviet secret service – the GPU – reputed to be the power behind the government and paymasters of the Republic. It was no secret that for every shipload of weapons brought in from the USSR, shiploads of iron ore went back. But, if he was either of these, then she did not see it. He came, they enjoyed one another, and parted. Making love with Dimitri was a delight. She enjoyed watching him as he became transformed from the square-jawed, belted Soviet army officer, to the tousled and aroused, vulnerable white-skinned man. Afterwards she watched Dimitri the lover as he strapped on the accoutrements of Major Dimitri Vladim.

David Gore-Hatton. Suddenly hearing his name spoken aloud, it was as though he had been conjured up, vivid and real.

Alexander had now recovered her composure and was sipping coffee as though idling in a street-café with never a ruined building in sight, waiting for Eve to reply. She had probably learned the art of the stiff upper lip in her nursery, from nannies who trained little English girls and boys who were expected to rule the Empire. The display of feeling that Eve had seen in the

Metro shelter was under control by the time they were on their second cup of coffee.

Seeing that she would get no help from Eve, Alex took command of the situation. 'You may not like this, Eve. I would not like it, in fact I didn't like it when the same thing was done to me. Look. I know about Eve Vera Anders, and I have to talk to you about that.'

'You mean the newspaper reports?'

'Oh, no. Well, yes, I know about them, of course – and I have to say that it was disappointing to say the least that you did not consult me. After all – oh, what the hell! That's too petty for words. What I should have said is that I know about Louise Vera Wilmott.'

Eve didn't give herself time to consider Alexander's tone, which was not at all critical. Her chagrin detonated a burst of quiet fury. 'Oh, you do! Well, it's no damned affair of yours! People like you Poveys think they have a divine right to interfere in other people's lives. Well, you haven't got a right to enquire into mine!'

'For God's sake, calm down and give over on the people like me bit. I don't like the Poveys any more than you, but I'm stuck with them. Have a fucking cigarette and cool off.'

Eve took one, lit it and drew deeply, saving herself from wading further into a quagmire of pettiness.

'Why do you ask about David, Alex?'

Helan Alexander looked directly at her from beneath her straight brows. 'Sure you won't denounce me as one of the *Lliga Catalana*?'

'You are neither bourgeois nor even remotely Catalan.'

Alexander gave a wry little smile. 'Well, thank you for that.'

'Go on. What about David? I might explode sometimes, but I hardly ever do damage except to myself.'

'You called him David as though you know him well. I hadn't realized that.'

'Why should you?'

'Because the Gore-Hattons and the Poveys – my people –

are out of the same stable, but generations back, and when . . . oh, sod this for a lark! Look, don't fly off the handle again.'

Eve let out a slow stream of smoke, watching it on its way to the ceiling before she engaged Alexander's gaze again. 'I apologize. You have enough to deal with as it is. It was the last thing I expected.'

Eve had never seen Alexander non-plussed. 'It was David who, who, um, gave the information. I mean, told me that you used to be . . . that Eve Anders hasn't always been your name.'

Eve kept her self-control admirably. 'Actually, *that* was the last thing I expected.'

'I'm sorry. This whole thing is coming apart.'

'No it isn't. Just start again from Louise Vera Wilmott. I'll listen. I won't interrupt. But let's get out of here and walk.'

In the aftermath of the air-raid, the streets of the city were once more thronging with people getting on with their daily lives before the next raid forced them to pause. It was not a warm day, but the sun was shining, and spring was close.

'Does LOLO mean anything to you?'

'Not much. I remember Ozz once saying that there was some sort of equivalent to Franco's fifth column playing them at their own game, some kind of secret organization to look out for spies and fifth columnists within the Republic? I thought it sounded pretty far-fetched.'

'LOLO . . . ears and eyes. There are people like myself who are in a position to be able to keep our ears and eyes open.'

Eve felt anger begin to rise again. 'Was that what all the Sophie Wineapple questions were about? Did you think that I was . . .'

'No! Nobody thought that. But Wineapple was suspected of working for the other side, and it was later confirmed. You happened to come into the line of fire, so to speak, quite coincidentally. No one had any idea of the connection between the two of you.'

'But having found one, you checked on me.'

'Not because of that. I had hoped that you, well, I thought you were a good candidate.'

'For what?'

'For the Ears and Eyes.'

Eve was dumbstruck, again causing her thoughts to veer away from the David Hatton connection.

'You thought I would make a good spy?'

'Don't be so dramatic. It is merely a question of being aware of what is going on around you, being sensitive to things people say when they aren't on their guard.' She gave a brief, wry smile. 'Your explosions about having to drive the Mercedes were patently not smokescreens, and your antipathy to privilege like mine is only too honest – you are against us, no mistaking that. What I cannot understand is why you would want to do what you are doing by this ... why this false front? David wouldn't say any more than that you changed your name.'

'Don't call this a false front. It isn't. There is nothing false about me, I am what you see, which is all I ever intended.'

'Please, Eve, don't be so defensive. I don't condemn what you are doing, I only wish that I had been as successful in suppressing my early years. How many times have you said that I was patronizing or elitist when I argued for smoothing the path for visiting Vipps? If I had become the convinced egalitarian I am trying to be, you wouldn't have been able to talk about divine rights of my class as you just did.'

'David Hatton, where does he fit in to this?'

'It is he who obtained the details of Louise Wilmott.'

Eve felt as though she had been betrayed. She had taken David Hatton at face value and had fallen for him. She had run away from him, as she had run away from everything else connected with her first twenty years, but she had not suspected for a moment that he had seen through her – a factory girl pretending to be someone she was not. She felt mortified. 'Go on.'

'I had no idea that you and David knew one another. He doesn't make any reference to it. There's no reason why he should, of course.'

'We had a very brief romance ... hardly even that.' Eve knew that this bit of information must make Alex curious – did David Hatton know her before her life as Eve Anders?

'That has nothing to do with the question of whether or not you agree to join up as a listening ear or an observant eye, if you like.'

'As I said, a spy. Call it a spade, Alex. It's not something I would want to do. If I had known that Sophie Wineapple was a suspect when I spent that week with her, my loyalties would have been pretty stretched, because no matter what else she was, to me she was a woman having a pretty bad time.'

'You think her work for the enemy didn't give other women a pretty ... ?' She stopped abruptly, her attention caught. Eve followed the direction of her interest. Her mouth dried and even if her cheeks did not show it, she was blushing. Some men, one or two of whom were in the uniform of the Republican army, had jumped down from the back of a truck and were helping offload some luggage.

The man whose belongings were dumped on the pavement was David Hatton.

'Did you know, Alex?'

'That he was coming to Madrid, of course. I asked you if he had been in touch.'

Eve backed away into the comparative shelter of an entrance, but to no avail. It was as though, in the midst of waving to the truck-driver, David became aware of eyes on the back of his neck. He turned, slowly dropped a canvas tote on the pavement and raised his hand.

'*Hasta la vista.* This one's yours.' Without looking at its destination, Alexander leaped on to a tram that was just drawing away.

Eve did not move, mesmerized by the strangeness of the situation. David recovered more quickly. He abandoned his bags and dodged through the traffic. 'I can't believe it's really you!'

'Hello, David.'

The short silence was awkward. They were in a minefield of possibilities, neither knowing which way to step. Even mention of her name could blow them apart.

'I say, do you mind? I left my equipment over there. I don't want to . . .'

'Of course.'

He floundered. 'Will you come . . . or shall I . . .'

'Oh, I have to cross to that side of the road.'

He moved as though he might be going to embrace her; instead, he took her elbow gently and they dodged the traffic together. 'Um. I was just going in to deposit my gear in . . .'

'It's OK. I have to get back to the . . .' She waved vaguely in the direction of the hospital to which she was now attached. 'To my vehicle.'

'You are an ambulance-driver?'

'I drive anything, really.'

'Will you come up while I stow my stuff?'

'I'll wait here.'

If real affairs were to follow the rules of a romantic novel, then this meeting would be the one where they resolved the problems that had kept them apart. Life isn't like that.

He picked up his bags. 'You won't go.'

'No, but I do have to report in.'

'This won't take long.'

As she waited she was forced to face up to the reality of the situation. The years between eighteen and twenty had changed her. The David of sparkling and arousing memories, the sophisticated David in a tuxedo and driving a low sports car, the David who had thrilled her when she was eighteen, was not this David. Or, if he was, then he aroused and thrilled her no longer. She was too old for him now.

He laid a tentative hand on her shoulder. 'You waited.'

'I said I would.'

His reply could have been: You once said that you would speak to me. Hers: I tried, but I allowed myself to be intimidated by your grandmother.

'Yes. Um, do you know somewhere we could eat? I'm starving.'

Her reply to that could have been: So is everybody in Spain. (Although that was not the exact truth, shipping blockades had cut off the Republic from essential industries and supplies, resulting in terrible shortages. Eve, who had grown up in an area of great poverty and deprivation had, nevertheless, been one of the lucky children who had never gone barefoot or hungry. Destitution was becoming almost commonplace in the beleaguered Republic.)

'If you like chilli beans and pimentos.'

'I love chilli beans.' He smiled, as Ozz might have smiled when he suggested that they find a canteen, friendly and not caring about anything much except the moment.

As in Barcelona, the people's canteen had once been the banqueting hall of one of the city's most prestigious hotels. Extravagant light fittings were still suspended, but where there had once been long dining tables all a-glitter with crystal and silver, there were now dozens of small café tables at which were seated people who, in the glittering hey-day, might have worked in the kitchens. The aroma of garlic and tomatoes pervaded the air.

They collected their food and easily found a table. Eve ate a little of her rice and hot sauce, but she had no appetite. She had to tell him that the past was over, and it made her awkward and uneasy. She didn't want to hurt him. He was a nice man. They'd had fun together, they had kissed and danced, she had driven his motor car and he had briefly taken her into a more glamorous world than she had ever known.

'Aren't you hungry?' he asked.

'I've just eaten. Alex and I . . .'

'Ah, right.' He smiled. 'And Alex skedaddled and left you to it.'

They had talked about food in the officers' mess at the RN dockyards, when she had worn her green silk gown, and she had realized that she could never let him know that at the stroke of midnight Cinderella must return to her industrial sewing-machine. She could not meet his eyes in case hers revealed what she remembered. She said, 'I met your brother, you know.'

'I know. And I yours.'

They were treading on dangerous ground again. She gave him a puzzled look. 'Really?'

He nodded. 'Rich died.'

'Richard? But he was going to be all right. He was being treated by a friend of mine, everybody said he would be all right.'

'He didn't wait to find out. He killed himself.'

'Oh, David, how absolutely awful. I'm so sorry.'

'Thank you.' Absently he wiped a crust of bread around his plate. Eve watched him, wondering what his grandmother would think of that. Or his mother. She knew hardly anything about his parents, only that she stood in for them in their absence in South America or somewhere.

This attempt at formality increased the tension between them. Their well-behaved enquiries were at odds with their emotions.

'Please, could we go somewhere less public?'

She really did not want to prolong the inevitable end of the affair, but she owed him more than a blunt 'Sorry, David, but it's over.' 'There's a . . . it's just a kind of room where chauffeurs and ambulance drivers . . . no guarantee that there won't be people hanging around.'

'Can we go there?'

'If you like. It's only about five minutes from here.'

There were three male drivers there, including two who were English. Eve had seen them several times before, and today they were engaged in what appeared to be a critical discussion about poetry. They wore the short leather jackets and jodhpurs that had become the practical standard dress for those drivers who could bargain for the jackets.

'You recognized Rich was my brother?'

'I thought at first that it was you. Even though he looked dreadfully haggard and sick, I . . .' She trailed off.

He gave her a brief smile. 'I hope that you were going to say, that you would have known me anywhere.'

'I don't really know what I was going to say. To be perfectly frank, ever since I happened to meet Alex this morning, I've been in a state of confusion. I've swung from bewilderment to fury to chagrin and back again. When I said that I had met Richard, you said, I know. How did you?'

'I was at Benicasim, in that first-floor balcony place. I saw you get into a truck and drive away. I started to race out after you, but it was no use, of course.'

'And you said that you had met my brother. Were you at Benicasim when Kenny was there?'

'I'd met him before that. Of course, I had no idea that you and he were related. I've met Captain Wilmott on more than one occasion . . . sold his picture to . . .' That was the first step that he had taken towards the subject of her old name.

'The picture with the Madrileño women's militia?' He nodded. 'Ken showed me. It was a very good photo.'

'People thought so. It helped to buy some penicillin.' He leaned forward a little and said, in the same tone that he might have used to tell her he liked the hairband she wore, 'This may not be the moment, but I am very much in love with you.'

She sat back and clasped her hands tightly in her lap, not knowing what she thought, let alone what to say.

'I'm not expecting you to fall into my arms, but I do want you to know. Since that evening, the shindig in the officers' mess, remember? Well, I haven't wanted to look at another woman.' Eve gave him a doubtful look. 'You don't believe me? Rich knew, he'd heard all about it. Used to call you my magical mystery girl. That last time I was with him down at Benicasim, we talked about the way all our lives are governed by chance.

Rich believed it was Fate, part of a plan, a kind of play in which we have a part and we have to act it out.'

'You don't?'

'I shouldn't like to think that all of this was preordained and that we have no choices.'

'That is one of those philosophical subjects that takes you round in circles; maybe the choices too are preordained, and so are not choices. I don't like that kind of discussion.'

He reached out and laid his hand briefly upon hers. 'What do you like? I know that you like gardenias, dancing and driving.'

There could be no more skirting round the subject that was right there between them.

It was hard to keep her voice even. 'From what Alex said to me earlier, I imagine that you must know everything about me.'

'No. I know only what I see now, what I saw those other times, and a few unimportant facts that Alex needed to know before she showed her hand.'

'How could you agree to do it? How could you make enquiries into the background of this woman you've just said that you love? I can't understand . . .'

'I had no idea that Alex's protégée and you were one and the same woman.' He longed to tell her all the facts, how he had watched the girls come out of the factory and felt elated by the thought that she had once been one of them; to tell her that he had seen the house where she had lived, and the mean school she had attended; to tell her that his admiration for her knew no bounds. He longed to tell her that she was a woman in a million. But he knew that anyone who had worked so hard to obliterate what she been born to would find his curiosity unforgivable. He couldn't blame her.

He knew only too well that he wouldn't have had the guts to do what she had done. He called himself a socialist, yet he still used his own class to further his career. He knew the right people, knew whom to lobby, how the old public school network operated, how to call in a favour. To an extent, both he and Rich had rejected their own class, but not totally.

Her voice when she said, 'Well, now you do know,' was toneless.

'Yes. What do you want me to say? That I don't love you? That it is a matter of the greatest importance that you have chosen to be yourself? That it matters in the slightest that you've said goodbye to the kind of life that was imposed upon you? That it matters a damn to me whether your name is Louise or Eve, or Daffodil for that matter?'

'Oh that! A rose is a rose is a rose.'

'Yes, that! A rose by any other name *does* smell as sweet.' He laughed in a way that brought back memories.

'I am absolutely willing to believe that you are right.'

Before she could move away, he had grasped her hands and was holding on to them. 'Damn it, what have I got to say to you to convince you that the love of my life is this woman here,' he kissed her fingers, 'this woman with chapped hands, who dresses like a pilot in the Condor Legion.'

Not long ago she would have had a very different reaction to such a declaration of love. Now she was less certain. 'I . . . David, I don't know what to say.' She tried to lighten her tone. 'As they say, this is so unexpected.'

'I suppose it is. Because I have been thinking of you for months on end, I suppose I must have imagined that you had been thinking of me too. Pretty stupid. Just the kind of thing Hatton Junior would do.'

'I *have* thought about you, many, many times. I did keep my promise and phone you but . . .'

'But my grandmother answered. I know. She knew that I was expecting a call. I was on crutches, couldn't get to the telephone. She thought that you were . . . that you were someone else and that . . . Christ! Louise, it simply all went wrong. I've been every place I could think of to try to trace you, but you covered your tracks so well. I went to all the dance-halls in Southampton and in Portsmouth, because the only clue that I had was that you probably lived in Portsmouth and were a brilliant dancer.'

She began to feel guilty that, because his grandmother's authoritarian voice had startled her, she had cut herself off without leaving a message.

'I was only eighteen then, David. I've changed a lot since that time.'

'I don't think so.'

'I have, not only my name and so forth, I am . . . I'm quite different.'

'You are more a woman than then, which is why I can tell you how I feel about you, but all that . . . that enigma. I don't even know how to describe it, that sense of still waters running deep in you. I wish I could find a more apt simile but in the respect that nine-tenths of you is hidden, you are like an iceberg. Except that I know that you are the opposite of icy. You intrigue me, and I dreamed of spending a lifetime discovering what it is that enchants me.'

'Look, David, I'm sorry I was so silly as to have drawn you into my girlish fantasy. You were nice to me and, to be honest, I did have romantic notions. But the whole thing was a bit of a fantasy, you should have known that.'

'No. If I hadn't felt something more than that, then I would have gone ahead and . . . and made love to you that night out on the downs.'

'You didn't call it making love at the time.'

'I know. I hardly knew what I was saying. It . . .'

She watched as he floundered. She wanted it to be over, to be able to return to the life that had been hers before she happened to meet Alex that morning. But her past had caught her like a bramble, and unless she unhooked all the barbs, then she would have to keep dragging Louise Wilmott about with her.

'I'd been used to a different kind of girl. My own set, the set I've grown up with, the *fast* set, as people say. It's the clever sort of way we say things to prove that we are unconventional, not bourgeois.'

'Literary like D. H. Lawrence or earthy like Mellors?' She

233

heard an unpleasant edge creeping into her tone, and she encouraged it. 'Do you play Mellors when you are with your fast girls? In *my* set, as I'm sure you know, that sort of language is only spoken in the dockyard area – and I don't mean the officers' mess.'

He looked as though she had slapped him in the face. 'This is not to do with all that, is it?'

'No, it is not to do with that.'

'It is because I happened to discover Eve Anders' past life. If only you'll believe me, all that makes no difference to me. When I realized that I had found Louise, I went to see your street, where you went to school, where you worked . . .'

'You *what*! You went to see?'

'Yes, I couldn't not go once I had made the discovery. You must believe me, it makes no difference to my feelings for you.'

She felt her anger rise. 'Did you suppose that it might? When you discovered that a girl who could pass as one of your set had been brought up in a slum and worked in a factory, you had to go and look. Did you find the idea of Eliza Doolittle and Henry Higgins exciting?'

'That's not fair.'

It probably wasn't, but in her imagination she saw him standing outside the house, driving past the factory gates, looking at the poverty-stricken kids in the school yard, and she saw herself in those same locations. She should have been sad for their pinched lives; instead she was furious that he had inspected them. 'I'll tell you what's not fair. What's not fair is life at the bottom of the pile. You long for beautiful things, to be with beautiful people, to go places where nobody gives a second thought to where the next meal is coming from. What's not fair is for an intelligent girl with ambition to have to play-act to get a little bit of what people like you take for granted.'

'Stop it. Stop it. Why are you so angry? I'm way out of my depth, I just don't understand. I wish Alex had never asked about Eve Anders. I wish I hadn't been the one she asked. But it happened.'

'When you said that what you found out about my origins has made no difference, what did you mean?'

'That I can accept all that. We rise above the stuffy social differences between us. I don't care. I'm a socialist, for God's sake. I committed myself to the working-class cause long before we met.'

'You aren't a socialist, David. Perhaps you hold a party card, but if you really had committed yourself to the working class, as you call us, then you wouldn't have to insist that my origin is something to be risen above.'

Now he sounded angry. 'But isn't that what all this Eve Anders business is about – you getting away from that?'

'No. This Eve Anders business is nothing like that. It is getting away from the prejudice of people of your set, your class. I'm not trying to rise above anything, I simply want to be accepted for what I am. D'you know, that first time when I met you, I had travelled down on the train with a really fashion-plate woman – a journalist so she said – who complimented me on my style and then went on to make fun of the lack of fashion in women who were involved in trades unions. I let her go on until I could stand it no longer, then I told her that I was one of those figures of fun and swept out with as much dignity as I could muster.'

'Malou French. I know her. She told the story, she tried to make a joke of it, but it was obvious that she had been humiliated by . . .'

'One of the lower orders?'

'Don't, don't go on with that, please!'

'I saw her speak to you at that conference. I was in the visitors' gallery, opposite where the reporters were seated.'

'Doesn't that mean anything at all?'

'You surely don't mean Fate, David.'

'Maybe not, but we have constantly been lost and found. Don't let us lose one another this time. Believe what you like about me, the one true thing is that I do love you.'

'All that I was saying is that I wish that I could be part of it.'

Anything else they might have said was stopped when a

couple of women Eve knew came into the room and sank gratefully into low chairs. 'Hi, Eve. Have you seen Ozz? He wants you to go to that Marx Brothers film, I think.'

'Oh, right. I'll try to catch him before he goes out again.' She could see from David's expression that he expected her to say something about Ozz. Why should she?

David stood up, his face as rigid as his back. 'I'd better leave, then.'

It was all so easy with Ozz. Their relationship uncomplicated by sex, they were free to get close to one another and be honest. She told him the whole story.

'He would never be able to understand that even though I hated the surroundings in which I was born and bred, I'm not trying to rise above them.'

Ozz said, 'You are touchy about it, though.'

'Of course I'm touchy about it. I'm touchy because I had to leave home to be me.'

'Same reason I had to, sweetheart. The world's not ready for us yet.' He passed her his cigarette. 'I see you've got the old yellow finger again.'

She drew on the cigarette and didn't hand it back. 'Blame Alex. I've decided it has to be cigs or vino, and vino sends me to sleep.'

'Are you going to see him again?'

'No. One thing I've always been able to decide – and that's when something is over, it's over.'

'But you wouldn't mind him for the odd roll in the hay?'

'He's not the sort, Ozz.'

'Sweetheart, there's times when I wonder if you should be let out alone. Everybody's the sort.'

'Good old Ozz. What will I do if you ever take a hair-pin bend too fast?'

'I ain't one of them slick bastards in black leather and riding britches – saving your presence, ma'am – I come from the boots and corduroy bags school of driving.'

'Good. I thought, if I have to leave this place, I might like to try Australia.'

He paused before responding. 'And we are going to have to leave this place, Andy. You know that as well as I do.'

'That's defeatist talk.'

'That's realism, sweetheart, and you know it as well as I do. Don't mean we shouldn't keep on keeping on.'

She did know. It wasn't hard to see that, with all of northern Spain in Nationalist hands, a shipping blockade and no aid from any government except Russia, it would be hard for the Republic to survive.

Ozz Lavender thought about Andy as he negotiated the hair-pin bend with a full load of ammunition.

She was fantastic. If he hadn't been given this letch for athletic bodies that were like his own, she'd be just the sort of a girl Mam would have taken to her heart. He missed his mam, really missed her. Life'd be OK if he could take Andy home and say, Hey, look, no sex attached, but she's the big potato in my life. He hadn't heard from the Old Man lately. What had he made of the bull's ear? Would he believe that his school-teacher boy took it off himself, or would he think it had been a fix?

Another heart-stopping bend in the road took all his concentration. It was all right joking about these bastards, but a drop like that wasn't a joke. He kept as far over as he dared without actually scuffing sparks off the wheel-hubs. These narrow passes scared him shitless. The road widened a bit. He made a thumbs-up sign to the driver of the following lorry – he'd be scared shitless too. Awesome country, spectacular views if only you dared to look down at the plains far below. Back home he'd done a bit of driving into the outback, but back home you weren't carrying a bloody great load of ammo.

If his Old Man didn't believe his story, at least none of his brothers had ever given him a bull's ear as a keepsake. But they gave him grandchildren. Perhaps he should marry a widow out here and take her back to the Lavender place. It was a great life for kids and, Christ knew, there were enough of the poor little bastards here. That was quite an idea. An older woman with three or four kids, one who wouldn't much care if they didn't share a bed so long as he took care of them. It could be nice. He'd go back to teaching, have his own kids in the schoolhouse. He'd take up coaching. He'd bring some promising kid along and get him ready for the 1940 Olympics, no, there wouldn't be enough time. Train up a kid about fourteen now, he'd be in the Aussie Juniors at sixteen, international hurdler by twenty, and ready for the '44 Olympics.

He had never before let himself speculate about his future. It wasn't worth it. You might disappear in a cloud of smoke tomorrow.

Neither Ozz nor any of the other five drivers in that convoy heard the sound of the bombers of the Trechuelo squadron above the noise of their own labouring engines. The detonations were heard ten kilometres across the valley as the trucks exploded their way down the sheer drop, taking a huge section of the road with them.

Chapter Fourteen

Ken Wilmott and his men were now part of the force preparing to hold a strong point at Gandesa. On a halt on the journey to the front he again met up with David Hatton. They were both waiting for drinking water from the same tanker.

'Captain, we do keep bumping into one another. Nice to see you. Are you OK?'

For a moment Ken Wilmott was nonplussed by the likeness to Richard Hatton. 'Hey, Dave Hatton.'

'Always turn up like a bad penny.'

'I heard about your brother. I was sorry to hear . . . blinking shame, he was a good chap.'

'He said pretty much the same about you. Said you and your sister braved a blizzard to get through to the hospital. Saved his life and then he went and . . .'

'Don't blame him. Don't even try to understand. I thought about it when I heard. Look how fair-skinned he was, like you. You have to take care with sunburn and snowburn. There were some Swedish volunteers with us for a while – God, you should have seen them, blisters all over. Your brother was at Belchite, wasn't he? Well, there you are, the heat there was beyond belief. I sometimes think a lot of us went off our rockers for a while.'

'Yeah, could be. Like you said, he was a good chap.'

'Still taking pictures, then?'

'I've got leave to come along with you chaps. I'm doing some factual films, rather like the Voice of America. Short pieces, you know the kind of thing. I did have some notion about enlisting. You know, take on Rich's place kind of style, but I'd make a bloody terrible soldier. This stuff helps swell the coffers.'

'Trouble is, our side doesn't appeal to the supporters with the biggest penny.'

'We make up for it in numbers.'

'That's a fact.'

They were whistling in the dark. It was evident at every turn that the enemy was supported by every machine of war, and seemingly endless thousands of men. Even so, there was always the knowledge that the volunteers of the International Brigade were fighting for a cause, and not for the money.

Ken liked the chap. He'd probably been to Eton and all that, yet he always stood around with the blokes and mucked in. He didn't realize that he was a fish out of water – the blokes did, but they liked and respected him for working on their own newspaper, *The Volunteer*. 'My brother Ray used to believe that if you looked after the pennies the pounds would take care of themselves. I hated his blinking ideas then, because we were so bloody poor I could never wait to spend every penny I could lay my hands on. I was a bugger for clothes – liked dancing you see.'

For a second, David had a vivid image of Lu and her brother in that little back-street house, transforming themselves to go dancing. They were the two younger ones, he knew that, and the elder brother had been like a father to them. He needed to know everything about her if he was going to understand her. She was quite right, he really didn't understand people like her. Before he found her in Spain, he had thought about meeting her, courting her, perhaps marrying her, but finding her had killed off those fantasies because she did not want him. Yet, now that he knew who she was, he was more entranced than ever. He did not want to accept that she would always reject him.

'I heard this story about an extremely small mining village in Wales – no work, no hope of it, kids half-starved, no money for food – yet, apparently, they made a collection and raised two pounds. That's a lot of money in farthings and ha'pennies. I think about that when I wonder whether I should take up a rifle.'

'Somebody has to let people know what it's like out here.'

They paid close attention to securing the caps of their flasks. This might be all the water they would get until after dark, and the Aragón plain would be searing hot.

'Your sister is doing that; she writes some marvellous stuff.'

'You know her?'

'I was with her in Madrid not too long ago.' He tried to sound as though it was a casual thing, but he needed to talk about her. This opportunity of talking to her brother was God-sent.

'I didn't realize that you knew her. How is she?'

'As beautiful as ever. We shared a plate of chilli-beans, then she left to go on duty.'

Ken Wilmott smiled affectionately. What did he mean exactly, 'as ever'? She hadn't said anything about knowing the other brother during the time they were at Benicasim. The two Hattons were almost identical, she couldn't not have noticed, yet she didn't say. But then, there was a lot that he didn't know about her. 'Have you seen her in that bloody great lorry? She's amazing. I could hardly believe it, she couldn't drive pram wheels when she was a kid.'

'Was she pretty then?'

'Lu pretty? I wouldn't know, I used to call her Lanky-legs, that made her mad.' He trailed off. Damn! He had called her Lu. Taking a last swig of water he said, 'Sorry, old son. Have to get back to my blokes.' Sod it! He had let her down. He'd told her that she had no need to make him promise a thing like that. As far as he was concerned, she was Eve Anders, and their life before Spain was nobody's business but their own. 'Good luck, Dave.'

'Good luck, Captain.'

At first Eve had taken Alex with her whenever possible because she felt so sorry for her. Alex had become approachable. Eve had grown to like her once she realized that under the self-possession was a woman as uncertain and vulnerable as herself.

In their new close association, with their earlier positions of responsibility reversed, they talked their way through the thickets of assorted prejudices. A thing that surprised Eve was Alex's confession: 'I envy your composure. Confidence like yours must be bred into your bones. Mine was painted on at finishing school when I was seventeen. You were doing real work when you were seventeen.'

When just the two of them were working together, Eve no longer felt constrained to deny her early life. 'It was real, all right. My finishing school was the famous one of Hard Knocks.'

'It didn't do a bad job, you know.'

'Do you know what I was doing about a year ago?' She smiled at the memory. 'I was standing in front of my employer's desk as he told me that I was dismissed for organizing a trades union, and that I should never work in my home town again.' She laughed outright. 'How right he was! I told him that he couldn't dismiss me because I had already handed in my notice.'

Dissimilar as their upbringing was, it had given them both the conviction that an outward display of deep emotion was embarrassing. But war brings about drastic changes in disposition.

'Did your school of hard knocks teach you how one is supposed to mourn? Mine didn't, at least I never came across it. I suppose that we girls preparing for our night out in gardenias and white satin were not expected to think of anything that might crease our flawless brows.'

'When my mother died, my grief was mixed with such anger . . . I was so angry with her. Do you feel that?'

'Yes, yes. It's so bloody useless too. I want to kill him for leaving me like this. He didn't have to be a bloody sacrifice for such a bloody useless cause.'

'Wasn't that what made you fall for him? A man who was everything you were supposed to reject?'

She smiled faintly. 'Maybe I was ready for him. But, God knows, I wasn't ready for this. Are you still angry with your mother? I mean, if you think this is a bloody intrusion, just say so.'

'Give yourself a chance, Alex. If you ask me, when somebody you're very close to, OK, somebody you love, is suddenly ripped out of your life, it's a terrible thing. Terrible.'

Tears moistened Alex's eyes, and she appeared not to know what to do about them except to bat her eyelids. She nodded.

Eve avoided looking directly at her. 'I didn't stay angry with my mother for very long, but I have stayed angry. She died because she was a woman, because she was a poor woman, because she was a woman who fell in love with an unsuitable man and because women like my mother are expendable. Nobody in the whole country ever cared about women like my mother – only her children, and we didn't care enough.'

For a while they sat quietly, staring ahead. Eve was surprised that she could still be so affected by her old grief. Alex's tears were an embarrassment, and she looked to one side as she blotted them from the corner of her eyes. Eve laid a tentative hand on Alex's arm. Alex did not move away. 'Alex, if you can't cry when somebody you love dies, then when can you cry? People like us will never wail and rend our clothes but . . .'

Alex blew her nose and stretched her face. Turning to look directly at Eve, she said with a faint smile, 'I think that's all I can manage at this lesson. Could I ask you about your mother?' Eve nodded. 'Would it make her unhappy to see you doing what you are doing now?'

'In some ways, yes. She would have liked to see me in mortar-board and gown, receiving a scroll at some famous university – and that still appeals to me. What would have pleased her is that I am not ruining my life over some man. She never said a word against my father, but his neglect of her and us was shame-ful to her. I think that she thought that she was to blame, that getting pregnant was her fault, nothing to do with him, my father. It's just bad luck that men are made like that.'

'You sound bitter.'

'Do I? You should live in a street where every other house contains a woman hung about with a huge family – the results of the way men are made. There *is* contraception, but no one

243

will tell the women. Where I lived, the women abort one another, you know.'

'Where I lived, they went abroad, or to a surgeon in Harley Street, who would remove any kind of cyst from the womb for a three-figure cheque.'

Eve returned Alex's wry look. 'The going rate where I come from is half-a-crown.'

'My father was — is still, I suppose — a paedophile.'

'What's that?'

'Men who gratify their sex urges with children. Perhaps it's a middle-class male aberration. I know they do funny things at school.'

'You mean child-molesters. I never heard the other word.'

And so in the enclosed world of the cab, the two women gradually opened up to one another. They saw something unexpected and became closer than they would have imagined possible. They supported one another, and grew to appreciate qualities they had not been aware of for prejudice.

By July the Nationalists, having overrun Teruel, had reached the coast and effectively cut the Republic in two. Barcelona and Madrid were almost cut off from one another.

The casualties on both sides were high, but in the Republic there were ever fewer replacements. Conscription could not equal the huge numbers of trained soldiers and airmen flooding in from nations supporting the fascists, and although medical teams, aid and volunteers still arrived in support of the beleaguered Republic, they were not enough. Even so, in July, a confident army began to assemble with military precision and in secret. The plan was a surprise offensive. The river Ebro, broad and fast-flowing, needed to be forded. Then the terrain was rocky, giving waiting ambulances cover whenever enemy planes were spotted. Pontoon bridges were floated under cover of darkness, bombed the next day and refloated again.

The first troops to ford the great Ebro did so in rubber dinghies. Soon they were followed by more men, equipment, supplies and ammunition, which all went across on a pontoon bridge put in place with amazing speed.

'I say, aren't you the girl who lifted me when I left Albacete last year?'

Eve, on this journey driving a hospital supplies truck, looked up from her unloading. She connected the voice and face with her early days in Albacete. 'I think so. Sister Smart, right?'

'Actually, no. Smarty was the other one. I'm Haskell.'

'Of course. Is your friend here?'

'Typhoid. She was being sent back to England, but she didn't make it. Dear old Smarty, she was a bloody good nurse. Terrible waste. We'd knocked about together for years.' It wasn't difficult to see through the off-hand manner, a stiff upper-lip could never distract attention from what was in the eyes.

'I'm sorry. She seemed such a jolly person.'

'Thanks. Yeah.' Haskell straightened her back purposefully and rubbed her hands. 'Okey-dokey. I'm told that you're a pretty good general dogsbody. That right?'

'I don't like hanging around when I'm not driving. So tell me what to do.'

'Grab some of that stuff and just keep bringing it in. It might look a touch chaotic, setting up shop always does, but it works. Can't say I'm too keen on a cave, but it'll be the first bomb-proof hospital I've worked in for many a long day.' She guffawed. 'If anyone had said two years ago that we'd be setting up an operating theatre in a cave . . . I ask you, in the twentieth century!'

Haskell was a tireless worker. Her previously full-bosomed figure had become almost slim, and she walked as though every step she took pained her. Big veins showed on one leg, and the other was laced up in a crêpe bandage. Haskell was not young, but God help anyone who might think that she was past it.

'There's a rumour that there are hundreds of wounded on the other side of the river who can't be brought across.'

'Can't stop rumours. But it's probably the truth.'

'Why won't they let us go over and fetch them?'

'They're going to have to. We've already seen the chief. I dare say you'll get your marching orders any time.'

The ambulances, autochirs (virtually operating theatres on wheels) and trucks rolled across the newly repaired bridge just as dawn was breaking. Soon after, when they were toiling along a rough road, there came the increasingly familiar warning shout: '¡*Aviación!*' Ambulances pulled into the shelter of the cliffs and the medics and drivers lay under cover in hollows and ditches, but only a single plane flew over.

'Bloody observation planes, I hate them,' Haskell said bitterly. 'They're just like a bloody herald-symptom of some rotten bloody disease. Twenty minutes and the bombers will be here.'

It was twenty-five minutes.

Twelve huge bombers came into sight. The new autochirs and ambulances had already been drawn into the shelter of an olive grove and hastily camouflaged. All that they could do was lie and wait under the trees and bushes.

The planes bombed up and down the riverbanks and along the roads. Anti-aircraft guns fired constantly. This was the closest Eve had ever been to the fighting.

As she lay in the ditch, she thought of Kenny. The last she had heard on the grapevine, which worked pretty well, was that the British Battalion were in the rearguard of the Aragón retreat and had fought fiercely every inch of the way.

Then she went on to wonder where David was, and felt sorry that she had rounded on him for having been born with a silver spoon in his mouth, and guilty that he had gone away before she had explained. Not that there was an explanation, just excuses. They were both the products of their class, each of them pretending that they were not.

And Ozz. It wasn't unusual for her not to see Ozz for weeks at a time, but he usually left a message of some sort scrawled on any bit of paper he could find. The last message had been written just before he set out in a supplies convoy for the

Belchite sector, but Belchite had fallen to the other side.

Suddenly a machine-gun opened up, strafing anything in sight. Then six tiny fighter aircraft attacked the huge bombers. In spite of herself, Eve was thrilled by the dramatic dog-fight that went on for an hour. One bomber was shot down, and the rest soared upwards and disappeared. The raid was over and they could continue to push on to Santa Magdalena, a hermitage where they were to set up a hospital.

'Ah, splendid,' said Haskell wryly, when they saw Santa Magdalena from a distance. It was a landmark visible for miles around. Set high on the hills, its white walls caught in the afternoon sun, the place was lit up like a beacon. 'Nobody will ever know we're here.' It had been Hobson's choice, for there was no other building available that could be turned into a hospital.

Haskell went off to help set up another operating theatre. Eve got stuck in with scrubbing and cleaning. By eleven that same day the hospital was ready to receive the steady stream of ambulances bringing in the more severely wounded men.

The days that followed were very difficult. Eve's truck, parked after unloading, received a direct hit and was totally destroyed. Several ambulances were lost. There was little food. With no truck to drive Eve scuttled around helping the dedicated Spanish nurses and medical auxiliaries. Many of the latter had never had a day's schooling and were fast learning every skill the trained nurses could teach them. Eve fetched and carried, wrote up details and washed away blood; sometimes she held feeding-cups and blood-transfusion lines. Hard as she worked, with few breaks, she did not seem to be able to keep up with the auxiliaries. If she had grown up tough and poor, many of them had had a worse start. And if, as the outside world had been told, Spain was fast becoming a godless state, it wasn't evident from the blessings and quick pleas to 'Holy-Mary-Mother-of-God' the Spanish nurses and auxiliaries made.

At some time during the second night, Eve went outside the walls of the hermitage to try to rest. She longed to write, for her mind was full of what she wanted people back home to know, but it was too dark to see and too dangerous to risk a light. But she knew what she would write about when she got out of there.

A Front-line Hospital in Spain

This is a most extraordinary place. High up, overlooking a jagged terrain is a hospital that could be a model for the League of Nations.

The senior surgeon is Dr J. who is a Christian Socialist from New Zealand. Of the many nurses, there are Lillian from Yorkshire, Patience and Ada from the Australia, Nuala from Belfast, Consuella and Maria who escaped from Santander, Aurora from Barcelona.

Then there is Sister H. I first met her months ago when I was newly arrived, naive, and expected the invaders to be quickly expelled with the support of the League of Nations. Nurses such as Sister H. put on a hard-bitten act, which I have taken to copying. And no wonder. How on earth can these nurses and doctors live so close to extreme fear and unendurable pain? Do Lillian and Patience and Ada and Aurora and Sister H. ever give way to tears? Perhaps they fear that they might not stop, as I too might not.

My vehicle has been destroyed, so here I will stay until something happens to move me. It is far into the night, this is my second one here. I, with two or three nurses, have come into the open to try and get some sleep where it is quieter and cooler. Except for the faint glow of the white walls of this makeshift hospital, the darkness is complete. I am fatigued, but too tired for sleep, I can only lie and look up at the restful night sky.

If she went to sleep, she was not aware of it, her thoughts drifting back and forth, from missing eyes and shattered arms and legs to the cool green water of the Swallitt Pool where she had spent her twelfth birthday; from jagged bone and stretchers carrying bodies that didn't even make it to the operating table, to the meadow with poppies where the first photograph of herself had been taken.

There must be hundreds of trucks passing somewhere below – our men going to the front.

If today had been bad, they were all aware that tomorrow would be worse. This might be her last night on earth.

She didn't want it to be, she was only twenty and there was more to do now than she had ever supposed. Her writing case contained dozens of scraps of paper, each with a scribbled home address:

Come and stay when this is all over.
I'd love you to see my children/my wife/my hometown.
You'd like my Mom and Pop.
We could have a whale of a time.
I'd take you to see the Great Lakes/the West Coast of Scotland/
   the Empire State Building/Ayers Rock/Mount Tanganaua/
   the Yorkshire Moors.

Every time she had been given that assurance that there would be a future, she had said, yes she would love to. Every time she was sincere. Australia, America, New Zealand, Canada, South Africa, France, Germany, Italy, and of course this beautiful, terrible country that she felt owned her, but owed her nothing. Having no home address except care of her aunt's strawberry farm where all her close family except Kenny now lived, she cherished those names. She had daydreams of herself crossing and re-crossing the world in the way all those audacious Victorian and Edwardian women had done. On horseback, too, as they had. Or in a flying-boat or a car like David used to have, low and sleek and powerful.

From far below the crest on which the Santa Magdalena hospital had been set up, she heard singing. Soldiers' voices as the trucks took them to the front. The song was the *Internationale*, the one she had heard sung in a hundred places, in a dozen languages. She might have cried, but didn't, couldn't. It was too tragic for tears. She knew that although those men, and the others who would keep coming, would hang on to the bitter end, there was little hope left for the Republic.

It was becoming more evident to Eve that there had perhaps never been hope. It was known that anarchists had different views about women's education and freedom from those of the communists. She had worked with nurses who had laughed when they told how the anarchists, in an area where they were in charge, had said that the sight of women swimming in the river, even well away from the villages, even when dressed in swimsuits, would frighten the mules.

The communists, on the other hand, were generally believed to be controlled by the USSR. And, as Eve was already aware – not only from what she knew of Dimitri's increasing concern – Soviet intervention was not altruistic. She could not yet decide whether Dimitri was naive, which she doubted, or having seen the true situation was disturbed that he was a part of it.

The fractures in the left-wing parties that, in the early days of her involvement and in her youthful idealism, Eve had not even suspected, she now saw were opening up. She had gradually become aware that the differences between extremist left factions – the anarchist FAI, the Marxist POUM and what Ozz had called general-purpose reds, the PSUC – led them to fight for something other than the maintenance of the Republic.

Feelings between the factions ran high. Assassinations, revenge, punishment and retribution now split families and villages in a way that they had earlier split more simply between left and right, Republicans and Nationalists. To the world outside Spain, it seemed muddle enough for anyone who wished to wash their hands of the whole civil war.

But to Eve, it was no longer a muddle, and the clearer the situation became to her, a fascist takeover, in her view, seemed to be inevitable. The greater enemy of the Republic, though, was still a chronic shortage of both food and raw materials.

She missed Ozz. Of all the people she now knew in Spain,

Ozz Lavender was the only one with whom she could have discussed her growing disillusion. She wanted to know how he felt, what he had seen and heard. Was hers simply the view from the cab of her own truck, or had he observed a similar breakdown. Where *was* he?

It was an odd place to hear a cock crow and then a dog bark. Soon after that a bird started a song she didn't recognize. If it wasn't for the rumbling lorries and the soldiers' voices, she might have been awake under her aunt's roof, thinking of the day that lay ahead, driving a vanload of strawberries to catch the London train.

Sleep wouldn't come. One cigarette and then she would go back inside. She could see something light on the horizon – the river Ebro. Perhaps the next time she crossed it, if she ever did, it would be . . . ? She had lost track of time. Was it August? Good Lord, I suppose I must be twenty-one. Coming of Age. That meant something, she didn't know what. She'd had the key of the door since she was fourteen. The vote! Yes, she had become one of the great British electorate. She laughed aloud. It was quite funny. She didn't know why.

Captain Wilmott's companies were among some of the first of the 15th Brigade to cross the mighty Ebro. In small boats, rowed by local men who knew the river's currents and landing places, the first men crossed six at a time. The boats were small and each man carried a good weight of equipment, so that the surface of the water was close to the gunwales. Great care was needed to keep from shipping water in such strong currents. Six at a time, hundreds of them crossed to the south bank. A few at a time, thousands made a perilous crossing on the pontoon bridge.

They were taking the war to the enemy this time. Their route was westward, towards Cobera, and their objective was to sever the enemy's main route between Aragón and the front. Troubled only by minor skirmishes with Moorish troops and other enemy units used to delay their advance, the Republican army and the International Brigade surged on.

One of the singing voices Eve had heard in the darkness might have been her brother's, but they would never know. That same night Captain Wilmott and his men were part of the British Battalion on its way to fight for possession of a strategic hill, fortified with concrete bunkers.

Ken and Lieutenant Harry Pope were still, somehow, together. At Gandesa the lieutenant's scalp had been scraped by a rifle bullet. The wound had bled profusely and left a scar like a parting in the wrong place. Near miss didn't say the half of it. Indicating their objective, Harry said, 'Look familiar to you, Ken old man?'

'God above, Harry, there can't be two of them.'

But there were. As at Brunete, they were again confronted by bare, rocky, exposed terrain with the enemy at the top within a concrete bunker. Again there was blazing heat, the problem of drinking water, and the same sweat, flies and excrement.

'If you couldn't laugh, old man, you'd have to fucking cry.'

For two days they tried to inch forward over the few acres of rocky ground, while bullets constantly rained down upon them. When the time came for Ken Wilmott's company to lead an ascent, they were all exhausted and weak from the heat and lack of sleep. Some of his men had been wounded, but it was impossible to move them except under cover of night when they had to be dragged off by stretcher-bearers to ambulances waiting to carry them to the hospital. Many did not make it.

Just before dawn the company started its cautious ascent, keeping low, crawling from rock to rock, but they had not moved far when they were pinned down by a fusillade of machine-gun fire. Ken could not move his men either forward or back.

Harry's voice came from behind a bit of craggy rock. 'Fancy our chances, old man?'

Well aware that their only water was what each man carried in his flask, and with scarcely any food, the captain could only give the order to lay low till darkness fell. There was no option but to lie in the shallow trenches in the full heat of the day.

At about midday, Ken Wilmott called to Harry Pope, 'Harry. Try to keep me covered. I'm going to see how scattered our blokes are.'

When his lieutenant gave the signal that he was ready, the captain cautiously raised his head. When nothing happened he slithered to a new position to look for his men. Before he could move further he felt a blow in his neck that laid him flat on his back. Beautiful shooting! Two of his men dragged him back into their cover. 'Only a flesh wound, passed right through,' a corporal said cheerfully, as blood poured from the wound. 'A lot of blood cleans out the germs.' He unwrapped a sterile field-dressing and applied it to the wound.

It was a minute or so before he realized that, although the bleeding was stopping, he could not move his head; it was immobile as was his company, and neither they nor he could move until dark. He handed over command to Harry Pope and waited. The day seemed endless.

At last, those who, like the captain, could walk began to make their way to a dressing-station and after that back to the river Ebro. A pontoon bridge over which supplies and men had crossed had been under constant attack and was no longer safe until engineers could again work on it under cover of darkness. When he began to wade into the water, he heard the shouts and warnings, but there was only one way to get to the north bank and that was hand to hand along the line of boats that composed the pontoon bridge.

In a little room in what had once been a small convent, Ken Wilmott saw how desperate the situation had become. Little food, few medical supplies. The wound in his neck was not bad enough to warrant using even that small amount of material to make stitches. He could have cried for Spain. But he had healed quickly before and he would heal again.

News came by way of a mail-lorry driver. The hill had never been taken. They had been forced to withdraw. The battalion was now in a reserve position. 'Want to come with us? We can hide you in the back.'

In his pyjamas, with the driver carrying his nicely laundered uniform, Ken Wilmott was hidden under some sacks and driven back to take command of his men once again.

For four days work carried on at the Santa Magdalena hospital while enemy planes droned overhead. Roads were bombed and more ambulances destroyed or disabled.

Haskell flopped down on a chair opposite Eve. 'What's this, still that bloody roasted wheat stuff? I'd sell myself for a decent cup of coffee.'

'Dr J. says it's better for your health than coffee – no caffeine.'

'Caffeine's the only bit I need. Strewth, here they come again.'

It never stopped: the drone of the planes, the banging of anti-aircraft guns, the crunch of high explosives. There was a constant bombardment of the roads and bridges and crossing points all along the Ebro. Haskell quickly ate a small dish of white beans and tomato, and drank her roasted grain beverage. 'Actually it's not all that bad. Old Grandma Haskell would never drink anything except her American Postum, which is the same as this.'

There was a whistle and an explosion, quickly followed by others. Eve jumped up. 'They're shelling us!'

'The buggers! If they start on us with their heavy guns we'll have to move out.'

The hospital evacuated at two a.m. Eve took over the truck of a driver who had received a shell splinter and was now himself a casualty. Going ahead of the ambulances and the autochirs, she drove in a small convoy of supplies trucks which composed the vanguard of non-medical people, the wonderful hard-working auxiliaries who had rushed back and forth collecting anything and everything to clean up the new place before the wounded arrived. The road to a safer place was along ten kilometres of shell-potted roads, driving without lights. Someone had the idea of taking over a disused railway tunnel at Flix.

The tunnel, which was near the river, was reached just as dawn was breaking. It was a mass of ruins, the grime of years hanging from its walls. Tired and hungry they stumbled along in the dark. But for all its drawbacks, it was ideal as far as safety from shelling was concerned.

So, having recently scrubbed and cleaned Santa Magdalena, the advance party started to convert the railway tunnel at Flix into an enormous ward lit by candles. Three operating tables were lit by electric light generated by ambulance and truck engines, but fuel was in short supply so some operations were performed by oil-lamp light.

Since the truck's original driver was in no position to argue, Eve drove back across the river at one of the constantly shattered and rebuilt crossing points, and started once again to ferry supplies to the front.

On a morning after she had come across the Ebro under cover of darkness, Eve was in Madrid signing herself out for the two days' rest-leave due to her, when the duty clerk said, 'A man is waiting,' adding confidentially, 'GPU. An officer.'

'How do you know he's secret service?'

'You think I don't know? My home is Ukraine. For sure he is GPU.'

He sat on a low wall waiting for her. Impressive in his uniform, he was good-looking and appeared very desirable to a young woman whose libido could easily get the better of her good sense.

'There is entertainment at *taberna*, you come, Eve?' Taking her elbow he guided her to a nice-looking car painted camouflage green.

'I was on my way to the *cantina*, I haven't eaten all day.'

He helped her in and said something in Russian to the driver, who started the engine. 'What is English to say pig leg, smoke pig-meat, is slice thin?' Actions accompanied his struggle for the word.

'Bacon? Ham?'

'Is ham, yes. Is ham at *taberna*. I know . . . I take ham there. We eat there. You again teach some dances.'

'Dancing in these clothes?'

'These clothes I like. Women in pants, I like.' He pursed his lips in a provocatively fake kiss.

She smiled at him, it was easy to smile at such an easy-going and persuasive man and pleasant to let somebody else take over for a short while. 'I thought you liked women in silk dinner gowns.'

He grinned and put his arm about her shoulders, lightly, friendly, making no advances. 'I like this woman many ways.'

Good as his word, they ate the most amazing tinned ham served by the proprietor of the small restaurant herself. There was only bread, fruit and wine to accompany it, but it seemed to be one of the best meals Eve had had in a long time. It was such a pleasure to be out with him, and an indulgence to spend the night with him at his hotel where there was soap and shampoo.

After such daily deprivation, breakfast consisting of a small amount of toasted bread and olive oil and plenty of orange juice became a kind of orgy when he produced a packet of Swiss chocolate and offered it to her a square at a time between his teeth. She lay back against the headboard, taking in his nice face with its alien features and noticing again how often he smiled. 'Dimitri? Can I ask you something?'

'Of course.'

'Are you GPU?'

'GPU? I am Dimitri, is all that I am. And happy lover. You want to do some more now?' He broke off more chocolate, teasing her with it. 'What for you ask about GPU?'

She snatched the chocolate, bit it in two and pushed the other half into his mouth. 'I heard a rumour that you were and I wondered whether you had any pull. Pull? Influence? A friend of mine. I was going to ask whether you would be able to find out what has happened. GPU are reputed to know all the right people.'

He paused before responding, perhaps trying to decide whether the question was as casual as it sounded. 'Most people like to make mystery. Your friend is English? Is volunteer brigade?'

'An aid-worker. Driver like me.'

'Is possible I could discover something. Maybe. I could try. Is she missing?'

'Not she. He's a man. An Australian. I haven't heard from him in ages. I've tried all sorts of people. Last thing anyone seems to know is that he was taking ammunition up to the front just before it was overrun by the Moors. I just wondered . . . perhaps he has been taken prisoner, but they say the Moors take no prisoners.'

He did not respond to that speculation, as it was well-known that the Moorish mercenaries took no prisoners and treated no wounded. 'Perhaps is not possible, but I try.' Dismissing the subject, he said, 'Now eat. I like for you to have fat here, and here, and also here.'

He was such fun, such a good lover, this was such a wonderful break from the ever-growing tension and stress of daily life as it now was. She had heard stories of soldiers, in the zone of a ferocious battle, without food for days, retreating and dispirited, eating the leaves of a tree reputed to lift the spirits and curb hunger pangs. As she returned to duty she felt that the effect of such a narcotic could never equal last night. In a world that wasn't so set on curbing natural pleasures, she thought, people would be able to spend their lives enjoying one another. As things are now, people don't value one another. If children were seen as the wealth of the next generation, which is what they are, how different everything would be. She imagined herself with a child of her own, perhaps living within an extended family. She smiled to herself – maybe not such a good idea with some of her grim-faced, censorious aunts and uncles.

As she drove out of Madrid, her mind slipped into thinking about home. How had those aunts and uncles who had despised her mother for having airs and graces, and who would have called Eve a 'tart' for sleeping with Dimitri, how had they managed to hold up their heads after the Mary 'trouble'? The Good Name of the Family was their icon; it was what gave them the assurance that they were better than the rest. Perhaps they were, and it was her own values that were impoverished. Certainly, she had been an embarrassment to them the year before she left home. Mary, her cousin, Eve's own age, had Gone off the Rails, with a marine who had a wife in the North of England. (Any man from the North was a bit of a foreigner; it was a hard and unknown country.) This must have happened before Eve had left home, as in Ray's last letter he had said that Mary had 'nice little twins, but nothing near as pretty as our little Bonnie. Mary's gone back to the factory, and her mother is looking after the babies and cleans Barclays Bank in the morning for a bit of extra money now she can't work herself.' In that situation, it was always the grandmothers who stopped work, the nimble fingers of the daughters being able to turn out much more work which was paid by the piece.

How remote that life was now.

Her conscience prompted her to use her turnaround time to write home.

My Dears, all,

It did not matter that I forgot my own birthday, but to have missed the first birthday of my one and only niece does. At the moment, life is so hectic that, even with my pocket diary, I cannot remember where I was on that day in August. Not that I imagine she is wanting for yet another adoring female telling her how wonderful she is. I should like to send her something significant, but of course there is very little of anything. I had thought of sending her a box of the dusty dry Republican soil that follows the tyres of my truck on many of my journeys, but the Republic has lost enough already. So, I send her this beautiful set of buttons as a keepsake. Not Spanish, yet they tell a story, which I will tell now, and hope one day to tell you in person.

When I was in Paris on my way to Spain, I helped sort and pack some clothes sent out from England as comforts for refugees. Among these was a splendid waistcoat which the aid-worker recognized as once having been Lord Lovecraft's. We were amused that such an exotic item should appear among the mounds of practical clothes. However, it happened that on a journey when I was transporting some young volunteers we stopped at an orange plantation – oh, so different from the strawberry fields which loomed so large in my young life. To me an orange grove is a wonderful place, blossom, dark-green glossy foliage and perfume. This was my first real encounter with a Spanish family, my Spanish almost non-existent and my ignorance of the country appalling, but they shared their meagre stew with us and were happy to do so even though their entire crop was rotting on the roadside for want of transport.

All that we could give was some of the clothes I was taking to the depot. The young mother appropriated Lord Lovecraft's waistcoat – it was more suited to her anyhow.

Now to the buttons. They are, as you see, more like miniature works of art than mere waistcoat buttons. Also, they turn out to be currency in the market where everything has its barter price. I don't know what the Spanish woman from the orange groves got for them, or who had exchanged them before I saw them, but there they were again, on a stall that had a greater assortment of items than the church bazaar. I must say that my heart leapt when I recognized them.

It's a strange thing, but for the first time in my life I have a surplus of money. Plenty, in fact, for I get paid a decent wage but have little upon which to spend it. You see, it's all barter, barter, and I have to confess that I do occasionally exchange one of your homemade cakes, perhaps for a supply of toilet paper, or some marvellous delousing shampoo. I can say that to get Lord Lovecraft's buttons for Bonnie, I literally greased the stall-holder's palm as I had a packet of butter that I had only that morning acquired in exchange for a toothbrush and half a lipstick.

I hope that one of you will make Bonnie a party frock and sew the buttons all down the front. How I would love to make the little dress myself. Do you remember how good I became at sewing fine fabrics? I couldn't do it now, my hands are in a terrible state.

But this is my job. The ingrained oil, callouses and nails broken from all the loading and unloading, remind me that, however little my contribution is, I do it because it is perhaps the most important thing I may ever do. I don't know how you view it from where you are, but you must surely see that Spain is being used as a practice ground. This war is a dress-rehearsal. If the fascists are not turned back in Spain, then they will not be turned. And those nations – our own being one – who refused to help the Republic, will regret that they behaved with such indifference to the future. Everybody goes to the pictures, so everybody *must* have seen Hitler who is surely mad as a hatter. He intends to take over the world. Most of my friends here believe that he could. Spain could still be our salvation, but time's running out.

There are people trying to get this message over and I think if I were back home I would have to get on a soap-box in Hyde Park. What use would that be? So I stay here and drive my supplies trucks or transport injured men from the field-hospitals whenever there is a shortage of ambulance-drivers.

I have to chance whether this letter will be selected for examination and then arrive with you heavily censored. But I feel a need to say these things to you who are dearest to me so that you will understand why Ken and I will cling on to the bitter end. Disillusioned we may be, but we have seen the planes of the German Condor Legion raining bombs on civilians and know that huge numbers of Italian fascist soldiers have been brought in on the side of the Nationalists. Then there is Russia, pitting *its* tanks and guns against them.

Here in the city, we have seen the killing machines turned on schools and hospitals. They can wreak as much destruction and spill as much blood in a city as they may in a battle on some bare mountainside.

I may not send you these last few sheets, but I must write and if you do not get them now, then I shall send them from a place where you are sure to receive them. The dress-rehearsal is almost over, three big nations have tried out their weapons, their armies and air-raid plans.

Dimitri had not been able to discover where Ozz Lavender was. It was well into autumn before she heard that he had been killed. She overheard the news as just another item of gruesome gossip offered over a mug of coffee and a cigarette.

'. . . they found that Australian driver, Ozz Lavender, well what was left of him, Ozz and a whole lot of others . . . they were carrying explosives. Direct hit on a mountain pass . . . couldn't have known anything about it. Not enough left to bring back. I heard that they put what was left of the whole convoy into a single grave. Well, that's what I heard . . .'

Eve was devastated by the news. She would miss him very much. In total, their time together was not that much, yet they had packed so much into odd days and hours. She had come to understand something of what it must be like to live as two people, one the manly athlete, the other a pariah. When they didn't see one another for long stretches at a time, she would often talk to him in her head, using his image as a sounding-board for ideas, or as a confessor for her guilts and ambitions. Ozz never judged.

For months now, she had lived with the starving and the dead and dying and it had been Ozz who had helped her keep her nerve by talking about the unspeakable sights and the gross misery instead of denying them. When she had said, 'I don't know what I'd do without you,' he had given her a big bear-hug and said, 'Ah, come on, sweetheart, you're same as me – tough as old boots.' But that was just what Ozz was not. Within the self-assured, bronzed and beautiful athlete, Ozz had been tender and vulnerable and alone.

Haskell was a pillar of strength in her stiff-upper-lip way. Unlike Ozz, Haskell never made sympathetic noises, her advice was, 'Pull yourself together . . . Keep on keeping on . . . Swim for the shore.' In her case the shore was alcohol. When Eve told her about Ozz, she said, 'I've got the evening off. Go out and find some decent cognac and we'll send a message home in the empty bottle.' They had holed up in the nurses' quarters. Eve had cried for Ozz, they had drunk the cognac and Eve slept like the dead until next morning and it was time to go back on duty. It was one way of coping.

Eve was on her way now to a children's house that Helan Alexander was setting up in Murcia. Alex refused to call it an orphanage.

The power money gives you, Eve thought when she saw the place. Once Alex had decided on the project, there was nothing to stop her carrying it out. She had money in Switzerland, transferred it to Barcelona and bought the house, some distance north of Alicante.

'Come and see.' Alex seemed to be back on form, but she had changed. Perhaps she was not so arrogant, or perhaps it was that now she no longer had to take orders from her, Eve had lost her prejudices.

The house was large, with a great deal of white plaster and tiles, built round a rear courtyard with a glass roof. An iron-railed gallery ran round the first floor overlooking the courtyard which seemed to be filled with babies. 'There!'

'Christ, Alex! I never knew that you meant it to be on such a large scale.'

Down in the well of the courtyard, Eve looked into a score of makeshift cots containing little bags of bones. She had been born and bred among children who were dreadfully under-nourished, often hungry, but she had never seen anything like these babies. It seemed impossible that they could live.

'There is only so much one can do,' Alex said. 'We do it.' There were cages of canaries and finches, and baskets of pro-fusely flowering plants hanging by ropes overhead. 'Stimulation,' Alex explained. 'I believe that seeing and listening to pretty things can only do good. These are all orphaned or abandoned.'

'Are there older children as well?'

'Oh, yes, I want you to meet them too. Did you manage to get leave to stay over a couple of days?'

'I have the weekend, but I must be back in Madrid by Monday afternoon.'

In the kitchen three Spanish women chattered as they

worked. Alex touched and hugged them briefly as they showed Eve the stove and the charcoal fire and the plate-rack as though these were modern conveniences. The perfection of the tiled surfaces attracted Eve as she thought of the dreadful draining-board and partition walls of her old home. How much easier it must be to keep sweet and clean, no scrubbing down with hot soda water in the constant battle against infestation.

'Well? What do you think? You hold yourself so close, Eve, one can never tell.'

'It's a small miracle, Alex. I've never seen anything like it.'

'You mean that? You can see that it's working, can't you?'

Eve thought how strange it was that a woman who, back in England, had lived in the world of the rich and powerful Poveys, idle and pampered, remote and unapproachable to Eve's kind, how strange that such a woman hung on *her* approval.

'Of course it's working, Alex. If you saved a child from drowning, you would get praised to high heaven. You are saving them by the dozen. Alex, you are amazing.'

Alex grinned, a rare sight. 'I know, bloody amazing.'

'Your husband would be pleased.'

'Wouldn't he just. Odd thing that, if they hadn't murdered him, then this would not have entered my mind. There's something about saving the lives of children, do you know what I mean?'

For a moment, Eve wondered just what the lives of these pathetic little babies were being saved for, but Alex was right; any human life was valuable, but a child's life was an unknowable part of the future.

'I want to set this place up so that, whatever happens to this country, the children's house will survive. No politics, no race, no religion. Any sort and kind of kid can come – even if its name is Baby Franco. Now come and see the chickens – we keep them upstairs on the roof and a few on various balconies. It's terribly sensible, no fear of them being taken by wild animals.'

Eve admired the nesting boxes and was at once transported by the smell of warm straw and feathers to the first time she saw live chickens. 'Can I look in the nests?' She slid her hand under a sitting hen and withdrew a warm egg.

'How do you do that? They scare the pants off me with their beady eyes, and pecky beaks. You look as pleased as if you had laid the thing yourself.'

'I was remembering.'

'Of course, don't I remember you being brought up on a farm?'

They strolled outside to inspect the goats.

'We don't keep them in the house, but I wonder whether we ought, they are so vital for those poor little stomachs. They shrink, you know, it's terribly difficult to get the digestion going again. The body feeds upon itself, did you know that? That's why their little limbs are down to skin and bone. I'll tell you something, when I'm trying to get one to start taking an interest in the bottle, I look down at my tits and wonder what in hell's name is the use of us women having to carry the bloody things around empty most of our lives. Fault in our design, don't you think?' She patted a kid as though it were a dog. 'I suppose that you know about milking goats too?'

'Fetch me a pail and I'll show you.'

'Good God! I wasn't serious. I say, you wouldn't like a job, I suppose?'

'As I said the last time you offered me a job, Alex, I'm a truck-driver. Do you need help?'

'No, no. Plenty of local people. In any case, I want the children to be in the care of Spaniards. All those thousands of Basque children distributed all over the world, will they ever know who they are if they grow up in Canada or Russia?'

'Better than not growing up at all.'

'Of course, but to grow up with no knowledge of the ways of one's own country, one's own culture. No, one thing I do have is money, which means that the children can have local people around them.'

'Isn't there any difficulty in getting money from England out here?'

'England! That's where the Poveys keep the petty cash. There isn't a country in the world where Povey money isn't available. Well, perhaps not Russia, though I shouldn't wonder if there were bars of Russian gold stacked away in Siberia. You haven't got any smokes, I suppose?'

Eve produced the 'emergency' pack that she repeatedly found it necessary to replace and they both lit up.

'Thanks. I don't encourage cigarettes in the house. Can you stand the rest of this squalid tale?'

'Having too much money may be squalid, but it is fascinating to the rest of us.'

'Believe me, it is squalid. I come from long line of money-grubbers, and I am the last in line. I am pretty rich already, and when Daddy darling goes to meet Old Nick, I shall become seriously wealthy. You understand the difference? Of course you do. That is the difference between you and me, you understand the way the world works. Carl did. You are a leader like Carl. I am a follower.'

'What was wrong with the way that you ran your bit of the Auto-Parc?'

'My dear, I just happen to have the voice for it. We learn to use it early on. You've seen me in action. I say "Jump" and people jump.' She took a long look at Eve. 'But you didn't, and I liked that. You didn't sulk or mutter into your beard. I knew on that first time out with the ambulance that you would never jump. I knew that you were one of those with a rod from your arse to your neck. When I was eighteen I was dressed up in white satin and taken to curtsy low before the King and Queen. I would have bet my life that Anders would go to the wall rather than perform such a demeaning act. I'm right, aren't I?' A smile hovered round Eve's mouth but she didn't reply. 'You see. You read me like a damned book, yet I know as much about you as I did the day you arrived in Albacete. I almost wish that I had read that damned intelligence report of

David's. Not that he would have let me. My guess was that you were some MP's daughter, or you had come from some terribly famous libertarian ménage.'

'I'm neither.'

'Don't tell me. I don't wish to know who you might or might not have been. I know who you are, and your people must be proud of you.'

Eve felt almost intoxicated with success. She had achieved what she had set out to do a year ago, to be accepted for herself alone. To hide her elation she said, 'So, about the children.'

'Yeah, well. I've been thinking that, eventually, I shall start up other houses like this one and work to get them recognized as non-partisan in the way Switzerland and the Red Cross are. If our people lose this war, I want the other side to understand that this is a non-partisan orphanage – damn! I vowed I would never use that word. Oh, call a spade etcetera, and an orphanage is what it is. As far as anyone knows, none of my kids have kith or kin.'

'But you aren't non-partisan, Alex. You are working for Aid to Spain, and you are a card-carrying Marxist. They murdered your husband, they must surely know about you too. There's no way that you can stay in Spain if the Republic goes under.'

They were walking slowly through a citrus grove that had gone wild. Alex sank to the ground, and patted the place beside her. 'Sit, Anders?'

Eve could see that behind Alex's eyes, thoughts were gathering, and she recognized the almost furtive look that she and Ozz used to exchange as they took each step in the direction of mutual trust. In the end, she had told him everything. Would she come to terms with the loss of Ozz? In many ways, Alex was as unlikely a confidante as Ozz had been, but they were growing easier with one another.

'I'll tell you why I can survive in Spain, Eve. Because I'm a Povey. Because Daddy, that decadent paedophile who sired me, is third generation PEC. Do you know the PEC?'

'Vaguely, the something Electric Company.'

'Oh, how the Poveys would like to be another General Electric. Great-grandfather Povelli – Italiano – was the Povelli Engineering Company. Grandfather was Precise Engineering; Daddy is Precision Engineering. Weapons of war – some of the most precise engineering going. A nice little war, anywhere in the world and PEC sells to both sides without fear or favour, so whichever side wins, PEC is in favour. Neat, isn't it?'

Eve did not respond because she didn't know how to. Finally she said, 'I'd like to write about your set-up here, Alex.'

'Good, I was hoping you would, but wait until you've met the other children.'

That day the world turned around for Eve.

Chacolatti Children

This, I warn you, is not a traditional bedtime story, for all that you might be reminded of Hansel and Gretel or of jelly-babies, sugar-mice and gingerbread-men. Chacolatti Children are quite, quite different.

Chacolatti Children are not born, they have been made. Made in Spain. In Madrid and Barcelona, in Valencia and Murcia, and although they have all been made in Spain, and bear the same trademark, they are obviously not from the same mould. They all have bits missing.

Thus they are rejects, and like broken biscuits you get a lot of them for your money because nobody much wants a product with bits missing.

I did say that this is not a traditional story told at bedtime to warn children against wandering alone in the woods or visiting gingerbread houses. In this story ordinary little Spanish children were leading their good and naughty little lives as children do, when they see chocolate bars falling from the sky, or they find them hidden in odd places as in a treasure hunt. And what treasure, for until now chocolate has disappeared from their lives. They scramble for it, pounce upon it, grab and scramble for it.

Another surprise, the chocolate bar goes BANG!

What inventiveness, what imagination, what skill and

planning and raw materials must have gone into making a bar of chocolate that is booby-trapped.

You get a lot of Chacolatti Children for your money.

E. V. Anders, Murcia, 1938

Chapter Fifteen

Of the 150 men who had crossed the Ebro river under Ken Wilmott's command, there were now just two dozen left. He looked at the exhausted and emaciated little band around him trying to gather strength for the inevitable next attack.

He scratched his itching seven days' growth of beard. 'Give us a bit of a haircut, Harry?'

Harry Pope giggled. 'You daft bugger, Ken. Next time we go back up there, they'll take it off at the neck for you.'

'Fair enough, I hadn't thought about that.'

They had been on the hill. No sooner had they relieved the Lincoln Brigade who had been holding on to their positions, than the Nationalists launched a massive and sustained attack. They threw everything they had at that bit of the Pandols sector. An artillery barrage of fantastic power crashed into rock, sending splinters and shrapnel everywhere and inflicting dozens of injuries. As the barrage lifted, two fascist infantry battalions had been hurled against them. In all the war, Ken Wilmott had never been so shit scared as on the hill.

He and his men had willingly scuttled back when they were relieved by a Spanish unit.

Now they were supposed to be resting for a few days, but the continued artillery fire on the front line marred the break. His men had been no less scared at the ferocity of the attack, yet they had not wavered and the battalion had fought bitterly and repelled the enemy.

But not for long. Ken Wilmott was under no illusions. The enemy had more men, more planes, more artillery, more of everything. They must believe themselves invincible. Perhaps they were, but it did no good to let yourself think so.

Back in the fray. Do or die. They had held on to the line for forty-three days; they would not give up now.

Two hundred enemy guns along a one-mile front opened up and were supported by huge flights of bombers. The Republic could not match such a weight of attack. The front wavered and broke and the entire 15th Brigade retreated along roads under steady bombardment.

Almost without respite they were sent into the attack again. They fought, and again rested.

Ken Wilmott hacked away at his hair with small nail scissors. Harry Pope was gone now, another idealistic young volunteer in a shallow grave scraped in the dry, rocky earth.

Georgie Green, who was leader of a machine-gun crew, said, 'I heard they were dropping 10,000 bombs a day on us.'

Ken said, 'Is that all?'

By the end of September they were so battle-weary and fatigued that there were times when they could hardly drag themselves from sleep and climb into the trucks that would take them to the front line under cover of darkness. Their ranks had been swelled by a number of young Spaniards whose only training for front-line battle was learning how to load and aim a rifle. But they were determined and courageous and would fight for their country to their last breath. There were times when it was hard to believe that on the other side of the line there were other young Spaniards equally determined to fight to *their* last breath for the same country.

It was not often these days that Ken Wilmott had either the time or the strength to think about such things, but when he saw how young and raw these Spaniards were, he wondered how a country could survive without such vast numbers of its young men. How many had he himself killed?

First light showed the enormity of their position.

Georgie shouted, 'Christ a'mighty, Ken, how's your bowling arm?'

Any fairly competent cricketer could have lobbed grenades right into the enemy line. Once the enemy turned its guns upon them, there would be no chance to bring up any more men, ammunition, food or drink.

When the attack started, Ken shouted, 'If they go for us here, they'll hit their own blokes.' It was true, they were that close. As the bombardment started they could do nothing but lie low and try not to imagine the carnage that was being visited on the Brigade Headquarters in the rear. Pinned down in a trench for hour after hour, Ken Wilmott's company of assorted nationalities lay pressed close to the earth. Planes strafed, shells stormed and screamed without let-up and bombs rained down. It was any infantryman's nightmare – they could neither advance nor withdraw.

At about midday there was a lull. Ken peeped cautiously over the parapet towards the fascist lines. He yelled in the direction of George Green's machine-gun, 'Tanks!' Five tanks were advancing ahead of infantry. George turned his guns on them. He was a good gunner; three of the five were knocked out. Enemy infantrymen, who had been sheltering behind the steel hulks, were now forced to face the Republican lines without protection. As the rifles of the 15th Brigade were directed at them with ruthless accuracy, the enemy fell like flies. But then so did the men all around Ken.

Suddenly, amid the crack and roar of the battle, there was a lot of shouting from the direction where he had positioned some of his men. They were standing with hands up. He couldn't believe what was happening. They were mad.

Not mad. They had seen what Ken Wilmott had not. The enemy troops, hidden by a bank of tall bamboos growing along a water-course, had worked their way behind his right flank. More were advancing on his own line. He shouted a warning to Georgie Green, but too late! They were entirely surrounded. Whatever happened next, bullet in the head or a trek to a prison-camp, he knew that this was the end of the war for him. With great cool and calm, he removed his jacket with its incriminating pass that permitted him to move freely on any part of the eastern front, placed it at the bottom of the trench and pulled part of the parapet down to bury it. Without insignia he was just a foot-slogger. The pass, which he had gained after officer training, would have guaranteed him a date with a firing squad. It would be no use Georgie trying that trick, it was the policy of the fascists to shoot machine-gunners on the spot.

David Hatton had been filming at Brigade Headquarters. The shells that had gone over the heads of Ken Wilmott and his company when they were pinned down close to the enemy lines, had landed all around him. He knew that he had got some remarkable film, but it seemed doubtful that it would ever reach London. When it was known that the enemy had broken through and surrounded a large area, the brigade withdrew and he with it. There was talk of a negotiated settlement, but the increasingly triumphant General Franco would have nothing but unconditional capitulation by the Republic.

So the battle continued for four months. It claimed 100,000 casualties. David Hatton was not one of them, but he was captured and joined a long line of troops of the International Brigade on their way to one of the many prison camps. His last act as a free man was to set light to his film and equipment. A British civilian would probably be shot as a spy, so he became Richard Hatton, a private in the British Battalion of the International Brigade.

Under interrogation, he lied like the rest. 'I have never even fired a bullet. I have only been driving trucks.'

'Where is your lorry?'

'It was blown up in the bombardment.'

'You will join the stretcher-bearers and carry your wounded to the first-aid post.'

There was a prison train waiting at Gandesa. By morning David Hatton was one of hundreds of prisoners-of-war disembarking on Zaragoza railway platform. Zaragoza, which the Republic had striven for so long to prise from the hands of the fascists. He kept his eyes skinned for any familiar face in the assembled lines. Suddenly he found himself looking across at

Ken Wilmott whom he had last seen at the water tanker before the battle for the hill. As they were herded along, they gradually manoeuvred their way towards one another until they were walking side by side. Before he could say anything, Ken Wilmott said quietly, 'Remember me? *Private* Ken Wilmott.'

'Yeah, of course. Remember me? *Private* Richard Hatton. I was a driver – food supplies.'

They each raised a small smile of acknowledgement.

'Will you just look at them?' Ken nodded at the well-fed, well-clothed, lightly-armed guards. 'They haven't gone short of much.'

Throughout the journey from Gandesa to Zaragoza, they had become ever more aware of the full extent of their captors' transport and weaponry.

David Hatton asked, 'What do you think they'll do with us?'

'Send us packing over the border into France.'

'No reprisals?'

'Why should they bother now? They've won the bloody war. It's only a matter of time before it's all settled. These buggers are favourites at the League of Nations, it wouldn't do them any good to do anything unpleasant, would it?'

That did not stop his captors singling Ken Wilmott out from the line of prisoners and taking him to the military barracks while the others were marched off to a civilian prison.

The letter Eve received from Sid Anderson, her sponsor and friend in England, pushed her first into a black mood, and then into a rebellious one.

My dear,

This is the first of your commentaries that seems too hot to handle (not me, you understand; I would put this in front of every MP and citizen who refuses to see that what happens in Spain could happen all over Europe). Nazi Germany is what stirs them now, everybody sees that there will inevitably be a war that will go far beyond the boundaries of Spain. There are newspaper and journal editors here who would like to publish your Chacolatti Children, but the proprietors will not allow 'scare-mongering' as they call it. In my opinion, scaring is what is necessary – no, more than that, people need to be terrified of what could happen. They need to know what Herr Hitler and his cohorts are capable of. But please, my dear, do not let this one episode stop you sending other pieces for publication. I will continue to pester all the right (Left) people. I think you might be surprised to know how well thought of and well-known E. V. Anders is. Still a bit of a mystery, but that is intriguing to readers. Some people know that you and I have some sort of connection, but I have no intention of satisfying anyone's curiosity.

Word has got through that one of the Hatton twins, whom I believe you know, has been killed and the other has been taken prisoner-of-war and is now in a French concentration camp.

I wish that your parents could have lived to be rightly proud of you. Recently, when I was attending a conference in Winchester, I took the opportunity of going out to the farm where I know you have spent many happy times. Your brother and sister-in-law are a splendid couple. I know that he is torn between wanting to join you and your other brother out there, and his family and the farm on which he works hard after his day job on the railway.

I have to say that I was entranced by the little girl, Bonnie, who is learning to talk and who babbles constantly. Your uncle says it comes from living in a family of all women. Your aunt says, it only seems like that, because the women have more to say. They talked about your 'transformation' into Eve Anders, and I believe that they are more at ease now that we have talked about you and they begin to understand that your intention is not to deny your roots, but to be independent and free to use your talents, and that leaving your old self is probably the only way to do so.

Your affectionate friend, Sid

'Alex, I want to join you here. Permanently, I mean.'
'Doing?'

'Anything you like. All that can happen now is for the Republic to wait for the *coup de grâce*.'

'You should leave.'

'No. I can help with the children.'

'Would you drive a truck?'

'You're not thinking of evacuating?'

'No, no. I shall stay whatever happens.'

That 'whatever happens' sent a shiver through Eve. The rumours of the huge numbers of committed reds being shot in every town the Nationalists conquered were not without foundation. Every town and city had, as General Franco had suggested, its fifth column waiting in the wings to inform and denounce.

Alex continued: 'But there is a Friends International refuge in Barcelona which is in dire need of help. The man who drove for them went down with typhus.'

Eve remembered the time she had spent helping in one of the Barcelona *cantinas* with Madge Pickawa and, what was his name? O'Dowd. That would be something worth doing.

Unable to get a seat on a plane, Eve took a lift in a supplies truck to the coast and then sailed on to Barcelona.

The craft was small and hugged the coastline, so that the waves and tide flipped it about making her feel queasy. There was the smell of oil and diesel and engine fumes. The view from the open deck, where she sat on a box, was a dismal one. She had seen the shapes of all the sunken supplies ships from a distance, but as the captain navigated between and around them, the full extent of the devastation hit her.

These ships had been carrying aid to the Republic – food, raw materials, armaments, vehicles – much of it paid for out of funds collected by the penny and sixpence from people all over the world who had wanted to do something against the fascist invaders. What had started out as coins in collecting-boxes at fund-raising meetings had ended up this close to the shore.

The thought of all those necessities feeding fishes and all those tanks and lorries providing lairs for sea-creatures made her ache with bafflement. Sid had sent her a cutting of a speech made by Helen Wilkinson, a fiery little woman MP whom Eve admired. The MP too had been baffled by the international agreement which allowed Germany and Italy to control the non-intervention scheme and consequently put a blockade on any vessel carrying supplies for the Republic. Britain, which had always been looked up to for its tradition of democracy, had concurred. As she looked at all the hulls and sterns sticking up out of the water like so many gravestones, she thought, This is crazy, no, worse, it's immoral.

The only other passenger was an elderly woman with a black shawl covering her head. She spoke a Spanish dialect Eve did not understand. Who the woman was or where she was travelling Eve would probably never know. It had been like that ever since she had been in Spain. People came close for an hour, a day, a month, and then they were gone. There were lives here that would always be entwined with her own: Marco, Sophie Wineapple, Ozz, Alex, Dimitri.

And there were fleeting glimpses of people who had left a deep impression on her, and had probably been part of the changes in herself that she recognized, like the young schoolgirl whom the women had pushed to the front of the queue because she had to get back to see to the children. Was she still surviving? And the woman with the orange grove who had accepted Lord Lovecraft's waistcoat, a chance meeting out of which had come a link that led directly to Bonnie and the strawberry fields at home. Would she ever see them again? The odds against it seemed quite heavy. Especially now that she was entering a city under fierce attack.

The miserable light in Ken Wilmott's prison cell burned night and day. There was no bedding, and the chill of the stone floor struck through his thin trousers and rope-soled canvas shoes. There was nothing to sit on except the floor. There was nothing to do except to pace from the wall with the small barred window to the cell door. There was no one to talk to except the large crucifix above the light. The guards must have thought him a devout Christian. Perhaps he was, for he found no difficulty in talking to the icon.

'The only logical answer is that somebody denounced me to curry favour. Do you reckon? No, neither do I. My own blokes wouldn't, and I can't believe those poor young Spaniards would, can you?'

It was obvious from its grievous expression that the icon could not.

'I don't know who painted your loin-cloth in the fascist colours. Did that hurt? More than a crown of thorns. If you've got so much say in things, why didn't you stop them? What I was saying earlier, I'm sure it wasn't the Spanish boys. Do you know, I came to Spain because I wanted to see it. I had heard that the sun always shines in Spain, and I love the sun. I didn't know about the snow. I got frost-bite, you know. That's why I walk with a bit of a limp. See?'

The icon's expression did not change, but Ken felt sure that, in spite of the red-and-black loin-cloth, this chap who had been so much against oppression agreed.

'Do they ever feed you in this place? The guards didn't look as though they're going short of anything. My admiration for the Spanish workers (of course, I only know the ones fighting for the Republic), my admiration has grown a lot since I've lived close to them. I know, I know. Some of them have done some terrible things, but if you put people in danger of losing their freedom, then they are going to fight dirty, and you couldn't have wanted all those great churches to stand there when so many people didn't have a roof over their heads.'

He tried to look out of the window, but it was too high even when he jumped. He tried to see out into the passage along which he had been led, but he could only see the wall and a bit of another cell door. He heard the voices of the guards from time to time, but the only time he had seen one was when food had been handed in. Good *gazpacho* and bread, the best soup he'd had in ages. It had gone down better than anything he could remember since he was last in hospital.

'What I can't understand is why, in the name of God, you let it happen. The Republic started as a splendid ideal, you should have been on its side. It should have been an example to the rest of the world, but you let the ordinary people down. All we ever wanted was for things to be fairer. I know an old man back home who always said that the first true socialist was Jesus Christ, he really believed that. Maybe you were, but if you were you didn't get the message over very well. Do you know what? I think that's not a loin-cloth at all, it's the fascist flag.'

They had all gone to an English Church school, but none of them had ever taken to religion. Even so, he had often thought how comforting it must be to have a moan at, or try to twist a promise out of, some great father who could do anything. Comforting, but damned childish.

He had grown so used to the sound of his own voice that he jumped when a guard appeared at the door. Every four hours, day and night, when the guard changed, this happened. He sprang to attention and stood against the wall furthest from the door. He saluted and said 'Franco' as he had been taught by his captors. He was quick off the mark, he had enough bruises already that no amount of decent soup would compensate for.

Ken gave his salute. The new guard gestured with his rifle butt. Ken quickly followed him out of the door to where a sergeant and some other guards were waiting. With the sergeant in front and flanked by two guards, he was marched across the parade-ground to what turned out to be an administration block.

Seated at a long table in a spacious room were officers in beautifully tailored uniforms decorated with braid, impressive medals and epaulettes. The sergeant went forward and answered questions asked by the most senior officer present, both, it sounded to Ken, speaking partly in English. Was that for his benefit? Was this a trial? He felt dread creep through his loins and he most desperately wanted to pee, but he tightened his muscles and held his head erect. If there was any last request, then he would ask to empty his bladder. He caught the words '. . . is no doubt. He is English.'

The sergeant instructed, 'About turn, quick march.'

He was marched to the latrines and then back to his cell. Well then, he thought, as he marched as smartly as he could in his canvas shoes, I've had it. His cell was now occupied by another prisoner, a Moroccan, still wearing the uniform that his own side had feared to see more than any other. The Moors took no prisoners. This one sat glowering, a blanket clutched around him.

'Well then, mate, what have you done to get yourself in here?' He didn't expect an answer. He didn't get one. The Moor sneered, turned his back and sat facing the wall.

'Well, if that's how you feel, I'll go on talking to this block of wood. I just wondered why they've put you and me in here together.' The Moor dropped his head on to his knees and pulled the blanket close about his head. Ken's forced levity was to keep his spirits up. He needed to; his knees still felt like jelly from his sudden brief appearance before the panel of immaculately uniformed Nationalist officers. The brevity could well have been because he knew that he must stink. He must have been as offensive to the nostrils of the officers as his new cellmate was to him.

Ken stood silently staring up at the wooden crucifix. Had that been one of the infamous 'hearings' they had all known about? Death by firing squad. No appeal. There was no time to collect his thoughts for the guards were back. He put one foot in front of the other, the last bowl of *gazpacho* coursing through his bowels. His legs did not want to function, but somehow he managed to pull himself together. As he faced the firing squad, he was determined to be defiant: '¡*Viva la Republica!*' God above, what if his bowels let him down at the last moment. He'd seen it often enough in dead and dying men. The next to last indignity, the last being heaved into some shallow grave.

At the main gate of the barracks a party of captured

Republican soldiers was already drawn up. He was ordered to take a place with them. It was bewildering. Nobody knew where they were going except the guards and they said nothing. At the railway station they were ordered into what could only be cattle trucks from the smell and lack of any kind of fittings. As the train wound its slow way through Aragon, they relaxed and began exchanging stories of the various battles in which they had been engaged, some shaking hands at discovering that they had fought in the same sector at the same time.

At Burgos they were ordered to disembark and march, their destination still unknown. At least, Ken reasoned, they probably aren't going to shoot us, they could have done that at the barracks. After several hours they reached San Pedro de Cardeña. One of his compatriots said that El Cid was buried in the church in the village. Ken had only the vaguest notion about the hero; perhaps he would live long enough to find out.

Their place of captivity was a neglected palace, stripped of its splendours. It stood, a pile of decaying architectural beauty. It was filthy.

Well, Ken thought, I'm suited to this place. He was still wearing the clothes in which he had been captured, and had been given no opportunity to wash or shave. What had once been smaller rooms had been knocked into one, and into each of these modified spaces were herded hundreds of men. The days passed in the most dreadful, insanitary conditions, the men plagued by lice and infected wounds. At any time Ken Wilmott would have almost exchanged it for the hill. *Almost*, for in spite of being among long-stay men whose diet of garlic-flavoured water, bread and a few beans once a day indicated scurvy, he was at least alive and had hopes of eventually being part of the exchanges of prisoners being made between the two sides.

Amazingly, some mail caught up with Eve almost as soon as she arrived in Barcelona. There was a parcel from her aunt who ran the strawberry farm containing packet shampoos, some hard sweets stuck in their wrappers, and a letter in which she gave a detailed account of Bonnie's progress. There was also a photograph. When Eve saw it, her heart leapt; the picture was obviously an attempt by her uncle to re-create one that he had taken of herself when she was a girl. The pretty toddler was standing in a field surrounded by poppies. From the squinting eyes and the shadow thrown by the brim of a straw bonnet wreathed in poppies and ox-eye daisies, it was obviously a hot day. As it had been that day ten years ago. There was another of Bonnie and her mother, again a re-creation of that day. Bar's great buzz of black hair was studded with flowers, and she was wearing a sleeveless, black top and long black skirt. Eve, sheltering from a strafing and bombing raid, ached to be back there. If she could choose a day to relive, then it would surely be that one.

No. That was maudlin and sentimental for, unbeknown to herself, her mother had already been dying of cancer. Her unforgivable father was probably already planning to kill himself rather than have to retire from his life at sea. The thwarting of her ambition to go to university was there in the shrubby background, as were four years of working in a factory.

No. Nothing is as sweet as the life being experienced now. All the rest is memories and daydreams.

The other two letters both held an Australian stamp and the name and address of Ozz's parents on the envelope. She read them in sequence.

Dear Miss Anders or Eve if you don't mind,

Thank you kindly for the letter you wrote about Clive. The news has just about floored his mother, and it has knocked the rest of us sideways too. He had told us that he had met a nice English girl who was driving lorries same as he was. It seems hard kind of work for a woman, but seeing as you feel same as we do ourselves about politics, it is a great thing that you are doing.

The kids in Clive's school had a special memorial for him, he had been sending them pictures and letters. He says that you were with him when he took the bullfight trophy he sent me. It was about the queerest keepsake any boy ever sent his father,

281

but I still got it in the box with all the medals he has won for sport. The Lavenders are proud of their youngest son.

You could do the whole family a great favour if you could ever find it possible to come to these parts, we should give you the biggest welcome ever. Clive's mother says she won't rest until she sees what sort of a girlfriend Clive had. If you have a picture, could you please send it. Seeing's believing as they say, so if you could get the lorry in too we could take it down to the school and show them.

She sent them a photograph similar to the one she had sent home to Ray. Ozz had taken it before the tragedy of the villagers at the bus stop in the Alcaraz valley. She was wearing her old cords and shirt and smiling happily at the camera. She knew that now she was much thinner and more haggard than she had been then. She had shared in more terror and grief, and seen more tears and blood than she could ever have imagined. Ozz had written across the bottom: 'This is for you, Sweetheart.' It put a seal on Ozz as a normal son with a girlfriend. That was all right. A man friend was what Ozz had been, her best and only one.

Dear Eve,

We hope that you will take this in the spirit we mean it, but we just wanted to let you see how sincere we are about you. Lloyd (my son next up from Clive) is going down to the shipping office to see if he can make arrangements and pay up front for you to get a passage out here any time it suits you — that is if you would like for to have a stay with us. I expect your own family will be longing to see you, but a visit from you would be such a great consolation to us in our grief over the loss of Clive.

Your affectionate friend, Jess Lavender.

Her own feelings of grief for the loss of Ozz must pale into insignificance compared to theirs, especially to that of his mother. Theirs was a really nice offer. Would she ever dare take it? The only people in the world to whom she could talk about her best friend. If they thought that they'd had a romance, never mind. To his mam he would live for ever as her lovely, handsome boy who had won at the People's Games and had stayed on to fight for an ideal that had emigrated with them from Welsh Wales. And to his mam, as to Eve, he would never grow older than twenty-four, would always be good-natured and cheerful, never mean-spirited or depressed or old or sick.

It was satisfying to be driving a truck again, but she felt less free than she had in the early days. When she was not driving she helped at the Friends International centre, sewing and mending clothes for refugees and orphans. When a warning of approaching enemy aircraft sounded, they would head for the basement where they continued to patch and darn by the light of hurricane lamps and candles, but as these were both in short supply they would quite often sit it out if the sound of the planes was not too close.

Eve could not fail to see the irony of her situation. For years she had sat in a roomful of women and spent her working day stitching garments at an industrial sewing-machine. For years she had worked at educating and making something of herself, and planning to escape. And so she had.

One day she would go home and tell Bonnie that there was an extraordinary world out there if only she would tear herself away from the poppy fields, and break the bonds of the pretty daisy-chains and give up the narcotic love of a protective family. Until recently, her understanding of what had transformed her from Lu Wilmott into Eve Anders had been only subconscious, but now that she had grown more contemplative and less likely to live up to Lu Wilmott's reputation of going off like a firecracker, she was better able to think clearly about how that transformation had worked.

She had escaped to the country of – as Mrs Lavender had said – splendid ideals, and here she was again, sitting in a roomful of women stitching garments. Yet, here was the difference: the girls at the factory had not experienced feminism, or the kind of equality that the young Spanish women had come to expect. As they sat and sewed, these women whose language she could now understand and speak, many of whom spoke better English than her Spanish, gave her a potted history of their transformation through education. She had at last found an encampment in which she felt that she belonged. They were, as she was herself, butterflies recently emerged. They wanted to fly.

'Six years ago almost half of the population was illiterate, we were starved of education.'

'*Si*. The Republic recognized this hunger for education. We now have schools in even the poorest villages.'

'*Si*. More schools in a year than in all the years of the monarchy. We know the value of our schools. We shall never let them take our schools. Before women were educated, we were nothing.'

'*Si*. Nobodies. Whores without pay to our men, even our good husbands. The men, the unions, say we shall have equality. We women say, and so shall we.'

The older women said, but not in such good English as the younger, educated women, 'So different. When we were young, we were told everything by the Church.'

'*Si*. The Church, the King, the big landowners. That was the old Spain.'

Eve, with her miserly, poverty-stricken schooling wished that her own government could see the extraordinary standard of education here. In peacetime, with money and supplies, such a standard would be an achievement, but these people were doing it now, with the enemy almost at the door.

She made up her mind that she would stay on to the very last.

Chapter Sixteen

Early in September, news came from Geneva that the Republican Premier had offered to withdraw the International Brigade under the supervision of League of Nations observers. Pain and relief were equal. Pain at being forced to recognize that this was not just the beginning of the end of the Republic, it was the ending of the end; relief at knowing that if there was now no hope of winning, at least no more young men of the IB would end up in a shallow or communal grave.

Eve had heard nothing of Ken for a long time. There was little chance that, even if he *was* in the farewell parade, she would see him. The International Brigade was to be sent off with a great show of affection. Their numbers depleted by hundreds of thousands since its formation, the volunteers marched through the streets of Barcelona to assemble in a huge arena.

Eve, in the company of some of the Spanish women with whom she shared a room, wanted to see Dolores Ibarruri – La Pasionaria – their great idol. Everyone hoped at some time in their lives to hear La Pasionaria in full flight of inspiration. She wondered whether David might be here. If he was, she did not see him anywhere in the crowd of journalists, photographers and newsreel men. Even so, she would send Sid Anderson her own view of the returning Brigade.

It was only when she came to put it down on paper that she found that it was about as difficult a piece of writing as she had ever done. She was not up to capturing the mixed emotions of knowing that one is present at a great moment in history. If editors didn't want it, never mind; she still felt compelled to mark the day.

Today I took part in a small bit of the history of the ordinary decent people of the world. I stood with an aching heart and tears running down my cheeks as these men from all corners of the world left Spain with the cheers of its people ringing in their ears. People who themselves have stood at the barricades, have joined the militia, have, in just the last few days, seen their streets and homes bombed into piles of smouldering rubble.

This, the International Brigade, of all the armies ever assembled, was the only one ever composed of truly selfless and moral soldiers. None came to Spain for the money – a few pesetas a day worthless outside the country. Nor did they come for the blue skies and the sun – there were times when the sun was the enemy, burning the fair skin of the northern races, drying the water-courses on the battle fields so that tongues swelled and throats barked with thirst. None came for glory – which was not to be had in trench warfare, in deep snow on precipitous mountain passes.

Many came against the laws of their own countries, others came from countries such as Germany and Italy where their own brothers may well have been conscripted and sent to fight on the side of the fascist Nationalists. They came because when the democracy and freedom of one country is threatened, then the democracy and freedom of the world is in danger.

My tears were for them, for Spain, for its people and a little for myself, for I had come as the men who were leaving had come, to help a democratic country whose splendid ideal was attacked. It will never be possible to know how many died for the splendid ideal. The terrible truth is that even those countless thousands have not been enough to stop the onward march of the jackboot.

My later tears sprang from a different emotion. La Pasionaria's face is a familiar one in the newspapers all over the world. It shows her high forehead, beautiful cheekbones and long, straight nose, perhaps a typical image of a noble Spanish woman. Classical perhaps. No picture did, or ever could have, prepared me for the explosion of emotion when she spoke. Her emotion and mine.

Hundreds of men who had fought on all the battle-fronts of

the civil war stood unashamed of their tears. She said, 'Goodbye my sons. Come back to us. You have made history. You are a legend.'

E. V. Anders, Barcelona, October 1938

When she had finished, she read it through. It was not good; it was too emotional. A journalist is supposed to be able to stand back and be objective. She felt that she would never be able to do so. If she wanted to become a journalist then she would have to learn to be uninvolved. How was that possible? If only she could paint or write music, those were the passionate arts. Words were inadequate, too restricting, they stood there on the page blocking the way. What she wanted was a means of saying: This is what it was like, this was what I felt, this is what I saw. She wanted to write about how important the defence of Spanish democracy had been, but she was aware of attitudes towards women journalists. Politics was for the men.

Even so, and inadequate as they were, words were all she had. As she checked and corrected, she became aware that she was already thinking of the war in the past tense.

She would stay on with the Friends International – in some ways the worst might be yet to come. When autumn comes, is winter far behind? Anyone who was in Spain that autumn knew that a bleak winter was now bound to come to Europe. And yet, and yet, somehow what was left of the splendid ideal of the Republic kept on going and going. Barcelona went hungry, under constant bombardment. Many of the beautiful old buildings were reduced to smoking ruins.

The concentration camp of St Cyprien, in which David Hatton found himself, was near Perpignan in France. It was a stretch of sandy desert surrounded by impregnable barbed wire.

Had he not seen it for himself, he would never have believed in the callous indifference of the hundreds of armed guards towards the men, women and children refugees and soldiers who poured into France. He wished that he had not been forced to get rid of his equipment. The experiences he had undergone on the way here and now inside the camp he would never forget, but he wanted to record the appalling suffering on film and shove it in the faces of the Pontius Pilates of his own government.

The camp at St Cyprien was the underbelly ... no, it was the arse of France.

He was weary and hungry, but this did not stop his anger from bursting out. He remonstrated with an armed guard who, with the butt of his rifle, had clouted a man who had tried to get outside to post a letter. For his interference David Hatton received a prod with a bayonet. The wound festered and swelled and throbbed, but his unwashed wound was minor compared with those of the many other unattended casualties.

Fifteen to twenty thousand refugees were supplied with water from a single spring, and they were without food for five days. No one would explain why nurses were not allowed to tend the wounded, and they were left for six days. More and more refugees seemed to come, but none ever seemed to leave. Some must have, for from time to time there were little flurries of people gathering, forming anxious lines, stretching their necks to see what was at the head of the queue.

Ken Wilmott had arrived in the camp a couple of days before David Hatton and, having spent two years frequently living in conditions far worse than those in St Cyprien, and being still fairly fit in spite of his time in the military prison, he walked round as much of the camp as he could, looking for familiar faces. In spite of the dire conditions, he was so glad to find himself alive, that he didn't grouse.

He came upon a black American from the Abraham Lincoln Brigade, Enro Peters, who had been in officer training at the same time. Like Ken, he was a poor boy who had risen from the ranks to officer class. It could happen in Spain, where ability counted for more than class or race; it could be done, and they and hundreds more had done it. They each understood the other's pride in his success. Now they greeted one another with emotion, and set off together reconnoitring as any two hardened soldiers would.

It was the American who saw David Hatton first. 'Say, I know that guy. He's English, but he ain't no soldier. He's the guy who done good pictures of my company in action.' He called, 'Hey!'

'What's up with the arm?' Ken asked.

David said grimly, 'You've heard of war-wounds – well, this is a fucking peace-wound. I got it from a non-interventionist guard.'

'Sit down and I'll clean it up for you.'

From a capacious pocket, Enro Peters produced a hussif-roll that contained small items intended for first aid and began cleaning the wound. He smiled, 'Ain't had no chance to use this till now, seemed such a shame to break it open seein' how pretty it was and all. When I said I was going away to fight some bad folk my little niece, Selma, stitched this with her own hands, and went to the store and got stuff with her own money. See, she even stitched on a little red cross.'

'It won't be too long before you're back there again,' Ken said.

'Well, yeah . . . I guess. That feel better? This stuff's called Tiger Balm, never used nothing else in my family. Sure-fire cure-all.'

'It feels better all ready – quite soothed.'

The three men had hunkered down while the wound was dressed, so they stayed there, there being little point in going further now that they had made contact with each other.

They stayed together for another two days waiting to be told something. The two brigaders exchanged information about their different battles, while David was hanging on to their stories trying to fix their words in his memory, hoping that one day he would write a book. Although over the past twenty-four hours they had all tested the water, it was Enro Peters who took the plunge: 'Our comrades are still fighting their asses off over there, while we're sittin' around telling war stories. It seems a dam' waste of two trained men who hoist theirselves up by their boot-laces to get to be trained officers.'

'I just want to get out of here and see if the Spanish army will have me,' David Hatton said.

The other two looked at him; he was the bloke with the camera.

'OK, maybe I won't make much of a rifleman or whatever, but I've had it up to here. I say, fuck trying to tell people that if you show them what a mad dog can do, they'll do something about putting it down. I say, fuck that and give me a rifle.'

Enro Peters made what was, for him, a long speech. 'I guess that's how it's goin' to be back home if my people don't get the same rights as white folk does. We got mad dogs there too, comes out hiding theirselves under bed-sheets and sets fire to homes of anybody steps out of line. But I don't know . . . is gunning them down the way? Maybe I'm going opposite direction to David here, maybe I'm thinking of more peaceful ways. Don't want to see fighting on the streets like it's been in Spain, but if decency don't break out in the white population back home, then . . .' He paused. The other two sat silently; Enro's experience of Them and Us was something they had never encountered.

He went on, 'I been out here long time. The Abr'am Lincoln Brigade, no black 'n' white there. First time in my life I been with white men and haven't been a nigger. It's just ordinary respect for another human being, nothing big, just fit and proper. How it ought to be.'

'It's how it will be,' Ken said. 'Has to be. If nothing else comes out of this bloody war, it's shown that, given half a chance, an ordinary bloke can do as well as a university-educated one like Dave. And as you say, a negro as well as a white man.'

David Hatton nodded. He felt out of this. Even though he had seen what was wrong and had joined the socialists to try to change things, his experience was not theirs; he had always been at the top of the pile, but he wanted them to know that even if he was not of them, he was with them. 'Given half a chance is what you'd never have got in the British army.'

'Fat lot of good it's doing me sitting around here scratting for the odd bit of bread, waiting for some arrogant Frog to tell me when I can go home.'

Enro Peters smacked his palms together. 'OK! What we go'n to do. Break out?'

'Have you been back there beyond the latrines?'

David Hatton shook his head. 'I never felt compelled to explore.'

'You should. Looked to me as if the constructors thought so too. The barbed wire just fades away in places. You can see what's happened. Lorry drivers who had to come in and out couldn't be bothered replacing it properly, so in places there are gaps where it must have been shoved together and it's now sprung apart.'

'Why'nt you say so before, Ken?'

'Wasn't too sure you blokes would want to risk it. I had to be sure, I don't reckon it's a thing to try on your own.'

'OK, and then what do we do?' the American asked. 'It's one-way traffic, and we're kind of short of cash and papers.'

'It's been done plenty of times over the mountains,' Ken said.

'I've done it, twice,' David said. 'Once each way. I wanted pictures, but the enemy hold everything on the other side of the Pyrenees.'

The two soldiers smiled. Ken Wilmott said, 'He wanted pictures!'

'You two keep straight faces or the guards are going to take an interest and want to know what's the good news.'

'So what *is* the good news?'

'I know this part well enough. Once we're out of the camp, if we keep clear of St Cyprien itself, we go south to Argelès – I know people there – if we can't get a boat going to Barcelona from there, then we'll carry on down to Banyuis, where we are certain to be able to get somebody to take us.'

'Yeah, it sounds good, but can you trust these people? Those guys who stuck your arm ain't goin' to just kick our asses if we're caught on the loose in France. They're mean enough to hand us over to the Nationalists.'

'My contacts in Argelès, they're good comrades.'

'But are they good enough, Dave?'

'Trust me, Captain, they are better than just good enough. I'd trust them with my life.'

'You sure as hell are goin' to have to.'

David said, 'The difficult part is getting out of here.'

'No problem,' Ken said. 'We join the latrine detail, trundle some buckets down there, and we're away.'

'If it's that easy, why isn't there a stream of people leaving?'

Ken laughed in spite of himself. 'Why? How many silly buggers do you think there are in twenty thousand?'

Enro sucked his teeth, trying to mask his need to smile. 'By my reckoning, there should be at least three.'

They entered Barcelona in what had once been a rather splendid yacht, but was now quite run down. David Hatton's 'contacts', as he called them, kitted them out in warm clothing with money in the pockets. It had all gone as Hatton had said it would. Ken wondered how this chap had come to know his sister, but the truth was, he didn't really want to know. He had seen enough of David Hatton by now to know that there was something reckless about him, something that went against the grain of his class and style. He had met blokes in the brigade who had been to Eton and university, and they were good blokes, really committed to the cause, but Dave Hatton? He was deeper than he made out.

Their plan was to enrol in the Republican army, two ex-brigade officers would be welcome. David Hatton said, 'God knows if I'll be any use, but somebody has to dig the trenches.'

Eve, now part nursing aid, part kitchen-maid, and part driver, was skilled at getting food on the black market. She was seated in a roomful of little children. As always, it had taken a long time to settle them after hearing the air-raid warning. It always sent them into paroxysms of terror, and they would leap up and cling to the nearest adult. Eve had shepherded seventeen stricken children down to the basement and brought them back to the nursery where the toddlers slept and were fed. She was nursing a little girl who weighed about the same as a young baby, but who was probably about Bonnie's age. Where her leg muscles would have been were ulcerated sores that were just beginning to heal. Margarita, a trained nurse, and Concha, a soldier's young widow, watched as Eve spooned a vitamin mixture into the child's mouth.

'She took all the baby food, see, and now she is taking the vitamins.'

Margarita smiled warmly as she watched Eve concentrating on the baby. 'Eve make very good wife, eh, Concha?'

'Me?' Eve laughed. 'Not on your life, Margarita.'

'Is different now. Womans is more equal with mans.'

Eve frowned. She had seen the equality they all talked about and the women cherished, but in all her time here she had still only come across one female Spanish doctor, and no English ones at all. 'Don't count on catching them up, Concha. In the human race, we run with a handicap.' Concha was puzzled. Eve looked down at the little girl. 'You think she can be premier?'

Concha nodded vigorously. '*Si*, La Pasionaria.' She spread her hands, resting her case.

'If she lives, I'll be satisfied for now. A seat in the *Cortez* can come later. What do you think?'

Margarita felt the stick-like legs encased in thick woollen socks. 'This child will live. Tomorrow you give her a little fish, is easy digest.' Although fish was still being landed here, it disappeared in a flash. Eve, who now knew several fishermen by name, was always waiting with a small van, or a boy with a handcart, when a catch was about to be landed. Fish, plus the dried milk supplies that were still getting through in a variety of ways, were the main items of diet for the children suffering from malnutrition. The rest got bread, and an unchanging diet of tomato, onion and bell-pepper soup, and a small amount of beans for protein as well as oranges, most of which had to be brought in by sea from the south. Not an ideal diet, but in a city where there was not much food it kept them free of the scurvy-like symptoms with which many of them had arrived. Its reputation meant that the accommodation was bursting at its seams.

Margarita and Concha were the experts on malnutrition. When two-thirds of their home city of Málaga fled before the German and Italian contingents of the Nationalist army, they fled with them. Ignoring the doctors who had ordered the usual treatment of injections into the wasted muscle, Margarita had started the child on vitaminized fluid a few days ago. 'She is responding?'

'She is. Look, she is beginning to take notice.'

'These city doctors, they all know hunger, but they have not experienced malnutrition.' Concha, not being a trained nurse, was not in awe of doctors.

Margarita, who was a most dedicated nurse, did not like going against orthodox treatment, but it was obvious that if a child had no muscles, then to try and inject fluid was to create a problem, which was why her limbs were ulcerated. 'Is best treatment, for sure. Return to vitamin injections when she more fit.'

This was *siesta*, and once the two Spanish women had gone to continue their rounds of the nurseries, the whole place was silent. Eve continued cuddling the little bag of skin nicknamed Posa, whose name had stuck after someone had commented that she weighed no more than *una mariposa*, a butterfly.

Although she had still as yet not seen two complete cycles of seasons, she was familiar enough with them to know that they were predictable. When warm weather started in springtime it kept going and never returned to winter as it often did in England; when the sun rose in summer it was pretty certain to be visible throughout the day. Strawberry season back on her aunt's farm, you might pick in baking heat one day, and see the fruits spoiled by rain the next.

These days, she scarcely gave a thought to anyone or anything outside her work with the refugees. There was never time; the flood of people trying to escape the oncoming enemy grew so huge that it seemed impossible to imagine that it could continue for much longer.

People escaped by various means. If little Posa could be got back to a reasonable state of health, then Eve hoped that she would be accepted as one of the orphans going to Mexico. The Mexican government had been considerably more generous in giving asylum to refugees than Eve's own. To Eve, who had become almost obsessed with getting Posa back to health, the fate of this one child was a kind of talisman for all the others. Bar Barney would understand. You imbued one thing with a good spirit, which affected everything around it. In the 'sacred grove and sacred pool' of their childhood, Bar had cast a spell which had purified the whole place. In her saner moments she was aware that any good spirit that may once have lived in Barcelona was being bombed out of existence. But, as she had said to Alex with whom she kept in touch, a little madness is what keeps us all sane.

Alex's experience with her Children's House was no different from the Friends Refuge in Barcelona. It was as if the whole landscape of the Republic was on the move. People were fleeing from the rumours of the atrocities being committed as the Republic shrank daily; nobody wanted to discover whether there was truth in the rumours. Better to die from strafing in a refugee column than in the streets of your hometown. Thousand upon thousand of them took what they could carry and left.

Inevitably there were lost, abandoned and orphaned children. Nobody could estimate how many there were. Many children were too young or disturbed to know who they were, or where they came from. Many died before a refuge could be found. Many, like the Chacolatti Children, were maimed. It seemed to women like Eve and Alex and Margarita and Concha, and Leah, who ran the place, and the hundreds of Spanish people who tried to cope with the sea of unclaimed children, that they all ended up on their particular doorstep.

'Hsst, Señorita Eve, is . . .' Eugenia, who spent as many waking hours as possible as Eve's shadow, gabbled an excited and unintelligible message. Two words, 'come pronto', were enough to indicate that visitors were waiting.

Still wearing an old rubber surgical apron she wore when feeding the babies, and carrying a bundle of ragged muslin used for mopping faces, and a pap basin, she put her head round the door. It was her brother. She flung herself at him.

'Kenny . . . oh, Kenny . . . I thought you must be dead. I'm sorry, oh God, I don't want to cry.'

By now she was hugging him and burying her wet face into the side of his unshaven neck. The feel of his hard, strong arms was wonderful, the rancid smell of sweat and stale tobacco made her want to laugh.

'Come on, let's have a look at you. I've come all the way from France to see you.'

She pulled back and looked through tears. 'From France?'

'Yeah. We got away in a posh yacht, belongs to a friend of Dave's.'

She sensed him there, handsome and desirable as ever. Wiping her nose and eyes on the bundle of soiled muslin, she looked round and saw David Hatton and a large, smiling, black man she had never seen before. David held out a hand and shook it formally.

'Great to see you again, Eve.'

The black man snapped to attention and held out a hand that was warm and dry when Eve took it.

'Enro Peters, Captain, late Abraham Lincoln Brigade, ma'am.' Eve had seen *Sanders of the River* three times because Paul Robeson spoke with that same quality in his voice.

'I'm proud to meet you, Captain. I've got several friends in the Lincolns.' She smiled. 'If I accepted every invitation to visit America, I would need five years.'

'You should try it, ma'am. One day we goin' to have our own revolution.'

'I thought you already had.'

'That was white breakin' away from white. Next one will be my folk doin' the breakin' away.'

'I'll drive a truck for you, it's something I'm quite good at now.'

'Eugenia, coffee, *por favor?*' Eugenia, wide-eyed at what must have been a puzzling drama, rushed out, offering David Hatton a big smile.

'You don't have to, Eve. But we couldn't leave until we had seen that you were OK.'

'Leave? Where are you going, Ken? What were you doing in France?'

'It's a long story, and I'll write to you all about it. Now that the brigade's stood down, the three of us are going to join the Republican army.'

There ought to be something that she could say, but she could not think what. 'I saw the parade, I wondered if you would be there.'

'No, I went straight to St Cyprien.'

'You've been a prisoner?'

'We all have.'

Enro Peters said, 'An' we didn't think it was too hot, so we going back to get even.' He smiled, suggesting that it was just a bit of a playground fight.

At last she had pulled herself together sufficiently to turn to David and ask, 'You too, David? I thought you were no good with firearms.'

'I'm not. I've always been a decent bowler, so I dare say I can lob a few grenades.'

Eve could have hit them for their *machismo*. If they had been at St Cyprien, then they had been almost home and dry, yet they had decided to come back and fight on. The feeling passed. Now she wanted to hug them.

Eugenia came in with a tray she had obviously taken some trouble over; there was even a tin of condensed milk and a spoon which she offered round like a hostess.

Although David had taken a seat a little away from the table where Eugenia had placed the tray, Eve was aware that he hardly seemed to take his eyes from her. Suddenly conscious of her rubber apron, she slipped it off and pushed it under her chair, and could have kicked herself for caring how she looked. She said, 'I should have thought the last thing the army wants now is a left-handed cricketer.'

Ken said, 'You a left-hander, Dave?'

Suddenly, Eve started to laugh, one of those inexplicable fits that is difficult to stop. The three men and Eugenia looked at her. 'I'm sorry . . . but you men are so strange. You are going off to this dreadful war and you talk about your cricketing techniques.'

'Yeah, well. Listen, what are *you* going to do? You're going to have to leave before long.'

'*Have* to?'

'Look, Eve, if this goes on another six months it will be a miracle.'

'OK, then pray for a miracle. Damn it, Kenny, pray for a thousand miracles. You should see the state of the kids we have here.' She put an arm about Eugenia's waist. 'When I was Eugenia's age, I spent the summer with Bar Barney, traipsing the country lanes, and swimming in that lovely green pool in the birch woods, you know the place.' David Hatton was obviously taking in every word, but so what! He knew everything else about her life. It was mortifying to think of him poking around on the streets of her childhood, the factory. Her pride had been hurt, she had felt herself as very shallow and foolish. 'You remember that summer, Kenny?'

'You'd had diphtheria and went away to get better.'

'When Eugenia was twelve, she was on that great exodus from Málaga. She got separated from her mother and grandfather, the only people of her family left alive. Somewhere along the road she was molested . . . she was *raped*, damn it! At twelve years of age she was raped by a youth from her own street.'

The men were silent. Here was something beyond their experience, a casualty of war who could not be comforted by a show of comradeship and a shared smoke. It was the American who asked, 'How did she get this far?'

'Women. They took her under their care and,' Eve smiled affectionately at the girl who blushed, 'here she is, all ready to grow up and do what we all did. What I want to do, is to try to see that she gets her chance.' Eve was aware that Eugenia had done her growing up, but that didn't mean that she should not still experience something that would compensate for the innocence she had lost.

This was an awkward meeting. Nobody appeared to know what their role was, so they took cover in a kind of cheerful formality that was posing as naturalness.

David said, 'Does that mean that you will stay on here?'

'Where would I go?'

Her brother said, 'You could take Eugenia back home.'

'And leave my baby?'

Three male minds seemed to spring to attention. Ken said, 'Not actually *your* baby?'

'She is now, but whose she was, Kenny, God only knows.'

Ken was puzzled by the tension there was between her and Dave Hatton; she didn't really want him there. In the awkward atmosphere, they all seemed to be waiting for somebody else to say something. It fell to David.

'I read a piece about the Chacolatti Children. It was impressive.'

'You did? I thought no one would publish it.'

'It's out in a little pamphlet. Somebody sent me a copy. I'm surprised you haven't received one yourself, but so many mail trains are . . .'

'It doesn't matter, I know what I wrote. It only matters that people back home will be reading it. Come and see our children here.'

Eugenia led the way into one of the big nurseries, empty of everything except mattresses and assorted cribs and the babies who were asleep, but filled with the smell of milk-fed babies wearing well-washed woollen clothes.

Eve lifted Posa from her mattress and, having taken a moment to decide, placed her in David Hatton's arms. 'This is Posa, David. I want you to remember her when you get back to London. Maybe you could tell your grandmother about her.'

He didn't appear to have been thrown off balance by Eve. 'There's not much of her.'

'The doctors say she is probably two years old.'

Enro said, 'She minds me of a new-hatched bird with big eyes and all, always seem too big for their heads, you know what I mean? Kin I hold her?'

Eve was surprised. She had supposed that the men would have been repelled by the unattractive little creature, which was why she had chosen David as the recipient of a lesson in yet another kind of war casualty. She felt that they must understand that war wasn't just between soldiers; they must understand that *because* they were soldiers, at least Kenny and the American were. 'Have you got children, Captain?'

'Enro, ma'am. No, not so far as I know.' He grinned, ducking his head and raising his shoulders. To Eve, he seemed to exude warmth and geniality. And he was honest and open, not afraid to show that he had a gentle side to him. There was something almost feminine in his attention to the baby. She had seen Kenny handle a shotgun, she could visualize David with a rifle, yet she could not imagine the big, black American in his soldier's role. But then, neither her brother nor the man who said that he loved her could have imagined the girl they had known before she came to Spain pouring everything she had into a houseful of sick children.

'Peters family is a big one. I got five sisters and four brothers older than me, and they all got kids. Guess they miss good Ol' Uncle Enro. I always been a fool where kids is concerned. Would you like to see the first aid kit one of my little nieces made? Saved Dave's arm, I reckon. She'll be no end pleased when I write and tell her.' He handled Posa with the assurance of a man who revelled in being Ol' Uncle Enro. 'Say, you goin' a be a pretty little thing, when you get them muscles filled out.'

Eve could have kissed the American for his praise. 'I think so.'

They made their way back through the house, Eugenia hanging on one arm and the baby cradled in the other. Eve turned to David. 'You see why I can't take you up on your offer to get out of Barcelona, David?'

He nodded. 'I'd say you have your hands full here, Eve. However, I'd like it if you'd . . .' He tore a scrap of paper from an envelope. 'Here's a number to ring, in Tarragona, just say you're one of Hatton's friends.' He looked straight at her and smiled.

Ken said, 'You can rely on Hatton's friends.' He grinned. 'They seem to have boats and things just when you need them. Being in the know isn't at all bad.' Strings had tightened again, she looked ready to twang. What had he said?

She said, 'Well, that's nice. I'll use anybody and anything these days if it will help these kids. When you write home, tell your friends we need things. Does your grandmother knit, David?'

He looked perplexed. 'I'm not sure.'

'Most grandmothers love to knit baby socks, maybe you could ask her if she could make us some.' To Ken, 'I think they must have got a real knitting circle going back home, we've had quite a lot of baby clothes.' She smiled. 'You can tell which are Bar's, unintentionally lacy from dropped stitches.'

Posa picked up the tension in the arms holding her, and gave a cat-like wail. 'I'm sorry, Kenny, but I have to . . . Ah well, you wouldn't know about such things, but milk has to be scalded and feeding bottles sterilized. Will I see you again before you go?'

Ken wasn't sure whether she was asking himself or David. 'I'll try to come again, but, you know . . .'

'I know.' She kissed him and held on. 'I want you back when . . .'

'Come on. I've got a hide like a rhino. Two wounds and frost-bite didn't stop me. You take care. And, listen. You do as Dave says, get out before it's too late.'

She smiled, but made no promise. He didn't expect one. She kissed Enro Peters' cheek. 'You just make sure that you get Uncle Enro safely back, children need their uncles. Goodbye, David. I feel sure that you will get a book out of all this. Kenny, what I said to Enro goes for you too, the only uncles Bonnie has got are you and Duke.' Her voice cracked. Brother and sister held each other tightly for a few seconds and then let go.

It was not long after that visit that the last of the Republic began to crumble before the onslaught of the combined forces of the Right.

In posters that had been pasted up in the early months of the conflict, the enemies of democracy were shown as ridiculous figures afloat in a toy-like boat with a gallows for a main-mast on which dangled Spain, and over which a vulture had settled in the crow's-nest. There were five passengers – a fat capitalist with his bag of gold and wearing a swastika on his lapel; a priest in a biretta; a haughty soldier with a ceremonial cannon; a white-turbanned Arab; and an armed Moorish mercenary. The monarchy was not represented, as it had already fled. Below decks, pinched, anonymous faces peered from portholes.

That was then. This was now. The five were on their way back to rid that part of Spain that was still free of its freedom. The five of the Right were safeguarded and upheld by planes and tanks and a great army of foreign mercenaries swelling the ranks of the haughty soldier. The five were no longer comic. The imminent return of the old oppressors sent hundreds of thousands of people looking for a means of escape. Those who had proudly acclaimed 'They shall not pass!' were now under threat of death, torture and years of imprisonment.

Dimitri Vladim saw how few options he now had. He had seen his once great hero, Stalin, from outside the USSR and had come to the conclusion that his country had used Spain as cynically as the right-wing nations. Soviet armaments and supplies and men had not been given without forfeit. On several occasions he had hinted to Eve how disillusioned he was becoming. She neither encouraged nor discouraged him in his dilemma.

'Could you guess, Eve, what it is that I have been doing today?'

'Something that gives you a sour face, Dimitri.'

'Also a troubled mind.'

'Ah, poor Dimitri, you want me to kiss it better?'

'Is not a joke, Eve. You may kiss me, but it will not make better. Russian soldiers all day loading on ship, what is it? *Hierro*. Iron! Natural i-ron stone.'

'Iron ore?'

'Is this, yes. We steal this i-ron. We say we give aid. No, is not so. We have surplus tank, we send. Not needed. I-ron ore, yes! Russia very much need i-ron ore. Spain not give this, my country send no tanks, guns. I go home too.'

Sometimes during the autumn Dimitri had turned up at the refuge bringing vodka, and tinned fish for the children. Only the food was welcome under a Quaker roof, so the good-time Russian officer took Margarita and Concha for an evening of dancing and laughter, and Eve for a night of immoderate sex.

'The people here get bad deal from USSR. Is wrong. I love my country. Is being made bad by so many bad things. Is not communism, is state too powerful. Leaders forget people.'

'Doesn't only happen in Russia – leaders always forget they are supposed to be leading their people. When I came to Spain, I was innocent enough to believe that here it was the people who held the power.'

'Eve?' He didn't finish, but enclosed her hands within his. When he held her gaze she was startled to see the depth of sadness in his own. That look scared her. She was going to lose him. Suddenly the loss of yet another person who had been so close to her seemed too much.

At last he said, 'Eve, I bored of politics. Forget state for moment. You hear me. I say I am in love, Eve, with you. When you leave Barcelona, please I must go with you. I cannot leave you and the children.'

He had said what she had never dared to hope he would say. He was a rare man, a political commissar born and bred under communism, yet he was sufficiently his own person to have an opinion about it. She herself had come to see that the ideals that she had seen as 'red' or socialist when she came to Spain, actually covered that part of the spectrum from pink to purple.

At that moment she was so full of feeling for him that she would have said anything. David, Duke, Ozz. They had all stirred up intense emotions in her. She had mistaken it all for love. It had been something, but not the intense passion that she could now admit she felt for Dimitri Vladim.

'Is not necessary that you say anything to me now about love. Please say just that we shall take the children and leave Barcelona together.'

'That is what I want more than anything else.'

They kissed with great tenderness. They had known great moments of passion and lust. This was something else. This, Eve thought, is probably what makes it love, but she could still not bring herself to say that it was.

Days, weeks, months passed in an almost routine sequence of air-raids, until it was hard to believe that there could be a building left standing. In the outside world, only the Vipps who had been in Spain and the brigaders who had fought there understood how it was that what was left of the Republic still hung on tenaciously and fought fiercely.

In Eve's small world of women and children, orphaned children came and stayed for as long as it took to get them away to any country that would take them.

A boat left carrying refugees to Mexico, but Posa was still far from being robust. The decision not to select her had been taken by others, and it was with a kind of relief that she heard that Posa was still too weak to make the journey. Bad as things were in Barcelona, Eve was convinced that she could bring her back to health, given time. There was no problem as far as Eugenia was concerned, she was attending school regularly, and for a pre-pubescent girl who had been raped when she was still a child, she had become as near normal as anyone could expect.

During the difficult and troubled months of autumn and winter, Eve felt wonderfully at ease in spite of the turmoil around her. It was becoming increasingly obvious that it would not be possible for her to remain in the country after there had been a settlement between the two sides. The Nationalists were not magnanimous in victory; at every step of the way they eliminated anyone with socialist sympathies. As a foreign aid-worker, she would be known to the Falangists and other right-wingers in Barcelona.

At one of the regular meetings of contemplation and discussion, it was decided that they should gradually wind down the refuge by getting children into places of safety, send the foreign aid-workers home and take with them any Spaniards who wished to go.

Eve made a plan and talked it over with the others. She would try to adopt the two children, give them British passports and take them with her. It would be hard to leave. This had become her country by virtue of what it had given her: friends all over the world, two children to care for and a Russian lover. The tragedy being enacted all around her every day was so great that the only way to cope with its consequences was to be fatalistic. She could plan, but she was not in control. Whatever will be, will be.

She started writing longer pieces than before, but sent none of it to London because of a vague idea that she might try to write a serious novel. The journal she had managed to carry with her wherever she went was filled with her uncharacteristically neat writing. There were cigarette burns on the cover, mug rings, and addresses scratched on the leather with a hairpin when there was no pencil to be had, but within there was a scrupulously honest account of her experiences. The journal was written for herself alone, so there was no point in being anything but honest, no point in not admitting that she had been unfair to David. Had she been given the job of looking into his background because he was trusted enough to be asked to join an undercover group, she knew very well that she would not have resisted the temptation to go and stand outside his home, look for the street where his Hatton + Hatton offices were sited.

In December, a parcel addressed to 'The Babies in the care of Miss Anders' arrived at the refuge. It contained a dozen or more pairs of beautifully knitted little stockings of fine rainbow wool. Also enclosed were three lengths of wide satin hair-ribbon. The letter in a Christmas card read:

Miss Anders,
My grandson, David Hatton, has mentioned that these few items would be of use to the children in your care. If you would like more, perhaps you would let me know as one gets ever more useless in old age. Also, I have been pleased to discover that I have the facility to turn a neat heel, something every young girl was taught. I remember how well children love bright colours. I do myself. You may not know that my grandson was quite badly injured, and has been with me since October. He is unable to hold a pen, so has asked that I send you his kind regards and as soon as he is able to sit at his typewriter, he will write you a letter. May I add my good wishes, and say how greatly I admire young women like yourself.
Yours most sincerely,
Margaret, Lady Gore-Hatton

Eve, her emotions already heightened by painful and frequent departures as members of the refuge got out of the city, was brought to tears by the humility of this old lady. She remembered their one telephone conversation: 'Can I speak to

David, please?' 'No, I'm afraid that you may not!' Eve would never forget that imperious voice, yet behind it had been an old lady who liked rainbow colours and who felt useful to be knitting babies' socks.

What if David's grandmother had replied, 'Of course, my dear, he's got a broken leg, but if you'd just hold on . . .'?

Bar Barney's mother had said that there appeared to be many possible paths, but there was just the one true one and you were bound to follow it. So was Dimitri bound to be waiting somewhere along Eve's path?

Shortly afterwards she at last had news of Ken. It had come in a letter from Ray. Ken had once again been taken prisoner of war, but arrangements had been made for his repatriation.

Then came a letter came from Enro Peters bearing a Louisiana date-stamp and containing a photograph of himself at the centre of an enormous gathering of the Peters family. All of them, even the littlest child, held their fists in the people's salute. He had written across the corner, '¡No pasarán!'

To Lady Margaret she sent a little note and pencil drawing of a row of socks that one of the boys had made. It had not been spontaneous, it had taken an extra handful of peanuts to extract it. A reply came from David, who said that he felt rather a fraud about his injury, which he had not received in battle, but was from a reinfection of the bayonet wound he'd received in the camp at St Cyprien. He said that he had lost touch with her brother somewhere along the Ebro. It was good to know that he had been repatriated; he had the greatest admiration for him and, if it were possible, hoped that they could meet. He asked her whether she had heard anything about Peters, would she please let him know. He had been commissioned to make a series of films about the southern states of America, and would like to make contact with the Peters family. He had signed it, 'Yours, David'. She replied at once, knowing that there was little time left. Now that Dimitri was part of her life, the part that David once had played lost any importance. It proved easy to write to him.

Dear David,

Thank you for writing. I am so pleased to hear that you are beginning to get back the use of your hand. I hope that the injury will not prevent you from returning to your camera work. I have probably never told you how much I admire your work, but I do.

It was nice of you to offer help through your friends, but if I do need it I shall not be too proud to ask – it is a long time since I had any of that kind of pride.

My brother reached home safely and at once joined the regular army. His rank in the IB of course stands for nothing there, in fact he has had to fight prejudice against the brigaders to get accepted at all. I expect to hear that he is wearing 'pips' on his shoulder before long.

When the three of you left to enlist that day, I felt certain that the odds were against you all surviving the same war twice, but you have. Not entirely whole, but you *have* survived, and it makes me very happy to know that. Ol' Uncle Enro's artificial leg provides endless interest to his nephews and nieces. He says too that he is ready to join in that other revolution, the one for equality for his own people. He says that it will come from within the church – the ministry as he calls it. Did you know that he had been a Pentecostal Minister before he enlisted in the IB?

In answer to your query about my trying to follow a career in writing, I have thought about it a lot, but have decided that it is time for E. V. Anders to think about her future.

You and I have had the knack of turning up in one another's lives, I have no doubt that we shall again. Thank you for mentioning the children to your grandmother, she has obviously been rounding up her friends. Such comforts and pretty things for the children here are appreciated.

Eve.

Chapter Seventeen

A terrible silence fell when, on 26 January 1939, just a month after the start of the Barcelona offensive, the Nationalists entered the city. That night she went with Dimitri by train to a small town on the coast and came back with documents that said that she was legal guardian of Eugenia and Posa Rodrigez, aged twelve and three, orphaned daughters of unknown parentage. She suspected that documents obtained in such a clandestine manner might not stand up to close scrutiny, but with a million people on the move, who would care?

With the last months of unrelenting deprivation and anxiety, and constantly living with the knowledge that Catalonia must be the last battleground before the Republic was finished, Eve, feeling the rot of defeat seeping into her mind, was already prepared to leave with a group of other English-speaking refugees.

The few possessions they had – a few items of clothing, a couple of blankets and some strange dried meat that Dimitri had brought – went in a bundle which Eve slung over her shoulder. Posa and Eugenia wore warm undershifts made of the green silk gown that had travelled so far in Eve's sponge-bag. Posa's scarred and thin legs were encased in two pairs of Lady Margaret's rainbow wool stockings. Eugenia, clad in Concha's good boots, a long black skirt and a thick jumper and shawl over the silk, carried Eve's haversack containing everything Eve now owned: the notebook written in Spain, her old journal, the keepsakes she had brought from England plus a new one – the gold star from Dimitri's uniform.

The exodus from Spain was too hectic for any but the briefest of farewells with Dimitri. Their one farewell kiss, a brief brush of the lips on either cheek, given and taken four days before Eve left, revealed nothing of the wrench they both felt at parting. He smiled with his mouth only. 'My heart is too much hurt.' He gave her the gold star from his uniform. 'I love you, very much I love you, Eve.'

There was a feeling of exuberance growing among those who had no fear of staying under the fascists, or who had been waiting for their coming, which eventually burst forth in a kind of mad joy that the war was ended. Many did not care who had won, only that it was over. Those fleeing before the Nationalists made up a steady procession, carrying their belongings, as Eve and Eugenia did, on their backs, or by any means available; as well as those on foot there were mule-carts and a few cars. All day and night the parade of fear and despair wended its way northwards in the direction of the border with France, through streets littered with documents and torn-up membership cards of the many and various left-wing parties and unions.

It was said that there were half a million refugees in that same trek, and that within a couple of weeks the Nationalists would have fought their way to the French border. Eve had no reason to doubt it.

They joined the trek of people as they passed by the harbour which was filled with masts and funnels of bombed shipping. The children had been marvellous, doing everything they were told. For the first stage of the journey, little Posa was hoisted up on a loaded mule-cart to sit beside an aged grandmother and two children, part of a family of Spanish women who had constantly warned their crazy old grandfather about giving the clenched fist and the ¡No pasarán! salute.

The first two days were the worst. Eugenia's boots made her feet sore until Eve packed them with several pairs of socks. And although Posa was still very skinny, her dead-weight hanging from Eve's shoulders was tiring. But Eve was fit, the sparse diet and being on her feet all day long had given her stamina. For miles she and Eugenia trudged along, holding hands, the young girl frequently looking up at her for reassurance.

On day three, after they had rested for a short while, Eve noticed Eugenia looking furtively over her shoulder.

'There's no need to worry, Genia. It is a long walk, and we shall be hungry and cold, but we will be safe. I shall never let any one harm you. If I tell you something, it is a secret, eh?'

'*Si*, Eve, secret.'

'Look.' Eve opened her jacket a fraction and let Eugenia see the handle of a long, thin kitchen knife slipped into her belt.

After another four hours of walking, Eugenia said, 'Is *el cabron*.'

Although Eve understood why an abused girl had taken to referring to men as bastards, Dimitri had dealt with it gently, referring to himself as *el cabron*: 'Genia, come, *el cabron* brings can *snoek* for good fish stew,' or, '*El cabron* and Señorita Eve will go drink coffee, come back. *El cabron* like hug.' The most that Eugenia would ever offer was the tips of her fingers as a token of friendship. But over the days, when Dimitri had been helping them prepare to leave, Eve had noticed the girl becoming more at ease with him. With a bit of time and patience, she thought, they might draw out some of the poison of the horror of her family's deaths and the subsequent rape.

'*Ruso el cabron*,' Eugenia whispered and again half-looked over her shoulder. 'Eve, *el amor*, you understand?' Eugenia covered her face with a corner of her scarf and looked around her suspiciously.

Eve's heart gave a bound of excitement. Dimitri had made it! His plans were so fraught with difficulties that she feared all along that his mood might give him away to his fellow-officers, particularly Mintov with whom he worked closely. But they were all – these Soviet commissars – well trained in keeping their cards close to their chests. However, it was essential to be cautious, for Mintov was a solid product of the Soviet Republic.

'I have come.'

Eve felt the blood rush to her face as his voice whispered close to her ear. 'Dimitri?' she asked in a low voice, not that there was any doubt, in spite of the peasant clothes and two days' growth of beard.

'No,' he said quietly as he took Posa to carry. He spoke in perfect Spanish. 'Josep Alier. You like for me to walk with you? If you will tie this little child on my back, I will carry her.' It was the children's acceptance of his sudden appearance that made Eve realize how used they must have become to him, but his transformation from Soviet officer to working man she found difficult to accept.

Eve looked at Eugenia. 'Shall we take him with us?'

'Have you a knife? Eve carries knife.'

'Better than that, Genia, money. I am rich bastard.'

When she asked him why money was better than a knife, he told her conspiratorially that, although he would not be able to fight their way through the guards, he sure as hell could buy their way through. This seemed to be the guarantee Eugenia needed. 'I take your hand.'

When they reached the pass leading into France there was a solid block of refugees. A few thousand at a time, they were allowed through. Although Madrid was hanging on by its nails, the Nationalists had already set up government under the dictatorship of General Franco.

Slowly, slowly, they were carried along in the dense tide of humanity. The closer to France they got, the slower the pace. There was nothing to be done except sit and wait, anxious that the French might decide to close the border again, fearful that the Condor Legion might decide to mow them all down as they waited.

Night-time on the road was the worst. Along with other groups they gathered what they could find to burn. Small fires flickered as far as the eye could see. They were sitting ducks, all packed along the one pass. An air attack seemed inevitable. Dimitri insisted that they would be safe now because the new dictatorship had nothing to gain by offending the League of Nations and attacking women and children.

'You think that they won't bomb us because there are mostly

women and children in this trap? It hasn't stopped them in the past.' There was a fierce bitterness in her quiet voice.

Dimitri said nothing, but wrapped his big coat closer around the dozing Eugenia who was flopped against him.

Eve became aware of his hand, warm over her own, then of the strangeness of their situation: a soldier of the Soviet army – perhaps even an intelligence officer – disguised as a peasant, comforting a tormented Spanish girl, and an English woman truck-driver cradling a malnourished Spanish baby who had never had the strength to toddle a single step. She leant across the children and kissed him gently. 'I love you very much, Josep.'

As night wore on, rumour and speculation heightened the tension but the attack never came. Eve thought that a more likely explanation than Dimitri's was the rumour that the convoy of several large vans that had gone through the border post during the night were carrying paintings by Velázquez, El Greco and Goya en route to the Duke of Alba in London. Who knew such things? How did these rumours start? And yet, someone, somewhere, knew how to drive past the guards with scarcely a check.

There was also speculation that when they reached the border they would all be put on trains and sent back to work as slaves under the new regime; that the men and women were being separated on the French side, the men going to Argelès, and the women God knows where. Everyone hoped that they would be taken to Mexico – the haven most of them wanted to reach. In Mexico they would be welcomed. All these pretty Spanish girls, Eve thought, will be welcome anywhere. There were women who swore that they would rather go on the streets than return to Spain.

Only the children slept that night as Dimitri put forward his plan of how they would get through if they did not have permits that suited the guards. His own was quite authentic: Josep Alier was a half-Slav Spanish labourer. His fingernails were easily broken by delving into the rain-sodden rocky earth and his well-cared-for skin was soon rough and chapped enough to match his face.

The next day they reached the border. Although there was a great crush of people desperate to get through before it closed again, the guards still made an attempt to inspect every document thrust at them. Eve was so apprehensive that she trembled until Eugenia took her hand and squeezed it.

With no proper food and exposure to the wet and cold, the journey had set little Posa back weeks. She hung about Dimitri's neck in a state of sick torpor.

They had arranged that Eve should hold back and not make any sign that they were together until he had spoken to a guard. What they had not arranged was that he should take Posa with him. Eve and Eugenia stood together and watched stiffly and silently from a distance. At first the guard waved Dimitri away, but Dimitri persisted, pointing over his shoulder at Posa. People around were becoming agitated until the guard took Dimitri into the guardhouse. What if he never reappeared? Eve felt the bile of hunger rise, burning her throat. What if they were separated? Eugenia would never stand another emotional shock, and Posa was so delicate that there were times when Eve felt that her frail life still hung in the balance. Without the children life would be unendurable. Without Dimitri?

She didn't know. Until his sudden reappearance in the exodus from Catalonia, she had told herself that a line had been drawn under that affair, as it had been drawn under Ozz, Alex, Haskell and the scores of others whose light had burned so brightly in her life for a short while and then gone out. The chances of ever knowing what had happened to Alex and Haskell were slim.

But suddenly there was the possibility that hers and Dimitri's story might have a different ending. What had prompted him to put everything at risk and come with her and the children? The three of them would have managed somehow, but his presence made all the difference. In the great thronging mass, the four of them had taken on an identity. People travelling alongside them supposed that they were a family. At this moment that was all she wanted in the world, to be a family with the girls and Dimitri.

The waiting seemed endless. Suddenly Dimitri reappeared, cradling Posa in his arms. It was apparent from his positive stride and the set of his jaw that he might have succeeded. Eve and Eugenia breathed sighs of relief and squeezed hands, then went forward to meet him.

'Is OK. I have paid three gold rings and one good wristwatch for our sick child to be taken through to Friends.'

Dimitri had apparently been referring to Quaker Friends, for as soon as they were on the French side of the border, almost collapsing with relief, she saw a familiar face.

'Sweet! Sweet Moffat.'

'I say, if it isn't . . .'

'Yes,' Eve quickly put in. 'Señora Alier. This is my husband Josep and our children, Eugenia and Posa.'

'My, my, if young Eugenia here don't make me think how well you've kept your looks.'

Eve smiled wryly, but felt so old at twenty-one that she was sure that she could easily pass as the mother of a twelve-year-old.

'Here, give me that wee thing. We have very little here, but at least the children can have a drink of warm milk and a bite of bread.'

Although their escape was now secure, they were still made to jump through bureaucratic hoops before they could get a train across France. Where, at the border, Dimitri had worked the miracle, in Paris it was Eve who was able to take over. The O'Dells accepted it as an everyday occurrence that a young woman who had left them nearly two years ago carrying a vanload of clothing, should return with two solemn children and a husband who spoke bad English with a Russian accent, and perfect Catalan.

Eve was as proud of them as though they had been her family. For two weeks, while arrangements were being made for all four of them to obtain the documents they needed to enter

England, the children were fed and petted and taken shopping for clothes. Dimitri, although he accepted some better clothes than the rain-shrunken dank ones he had travelled in, decided to keep the beard.

Fran O'Dell took Eve to a beauty salon and then to buy some feminine clothes. Eve felt apprehensive and out of her depth to be suddenly in the midst of such luxury. It was time to consider the future.

'Fran. I can't go back home.'

'I can understand that.'

'You can?'

'Of course.'

'It seems such an awful thing not to want to go back to where you belong.'

'Come here, sit down.' Although it was still hardly spring, the tables were out on the pavements. Fran ordered café-au-lait and they lit cigarettes. 'So, where is this place? The one where you belong.'

Eve stirred sugar into her coffee before she answered. 'I don't know. I don't feel that I belong anywhere at the moment. Not with my relations. You said you understand.'

'I was born as English as you, my dear, yet I am a Parisienne, and I shall always be. This is where I belong. If France goes to war with Germany, then I stay with France. One's place in the world does not have to be where one's mother happened to give birth.'

Eve, smiling, reached across the chipped enamel table and clutched the other woman's hand. 'You don't know what a relief it is to hear that, Fran.'

'But I do. Frankie had to tell me much the same thing. Before that I felt all sorts of a traitor loving France more than England. But I do. I should die if I had to go back there. I hardly ever do.'

'My family will be hurt.'

'Perhaps. But you may be surprised how easily the place you left has been filled. They would have to fill it. How else can any family keep going when one member is removed? Families survive deaths. Your family will survive your defection – I expect that they already have.'

She was probably right, but she and Ray had hardly survived Kenny's empty place and she did not like to accept that they could do without her. Yet if she returned, she would be smothered. It would be like slowly drowning in warm honey. Would Dimitri survive? Had Ray? It was tempting to crawl back to the place where there were magic groves and strawberry fields, to unquestioning love and allowances made for all things.

But she had seen such pain and misery, hunger and fear in children that no one should ever see. She needed to go where she could try to come to terms with such overwhelming evil. She needed to digest her anger and bitterness and put it to some use. Above all she was responsible for two children who were victims of the war that they had never had any say in. They needed to be cared for by people who had experience of how they had come to be injured mentally and physically.

'Do we have time to do some more shopping?'

'In Paris there is always time for that, and it is good for the children if you are not always hovering over them.'

'Do I hover?'

'I'm afraid you do. You'd be surprised how well they manage when you're away – if it is not too long. Posa is everybody's sweetheart, but Eugenia is only yours – and Josep's.'

Eve nodded. 'She is. Dimitri is so patient with her.'

'He has such a nice nature. Shall you marry him?'

'Now that I've decided that I shan't go back to England, probably not. In any case, why make changes to something that works perfectly? Come on, Fran, drink up your coffee, I want to find a bank. I should have royalties from my writing piled up and I want to spend some. Where can we find summer clothes at this time of year?'

Fran laughed. 'Now that April is around the corner, in almost every boutique and shop in Paris. Am I to take it that you have decided not to be the prodigal daughter returned?'

'For now, yes. If Dimitri agrees. Hell, even if he doesn't agree I'm going to take the children to visit the Lavenders.'

They stopped off in Cape Town. The days spent there were like a stay in Paradise. Dimitri and Eugenia held hands with Eve, while Dimitri carried Posa to the unconcealed amusement, or disapproval, of black nannies. They spent hours window-gazing and entering street cafés just for the joy of asking for the food they fancied and finding it brought to them. Seeing the way the Europeans used the blacks made Eve think of Enro Peters and the future he now saw for himself working for the freedom for his own people. An active Christian, he had written to Eve: 'I shall work for my own people now, not with guns and fire, but with the vote.' But, she had thought, wasn't that where it had all started in Spain? A democratic revolution. Spaniards had voted for their freedom; yet it had turned into a tragedy so immense that it looked as though there might be no end in sight.

On midsummer day, as they were putting the children to bed in the hotel, she said, 'This is my birthday.'

'How old?' Eugenia asked.

'As old as my hair and a bit older than my teeth.'

Eugenia grinned. 'So, how old is your teeth?'

Eve gave the girl a hug. There were times when she saw a glimpse of her own girlish self in Eugenia and promised herself that she would do her damnedest to see that the worst of Eugenia's life was now in the past. 'You, girl, are catching the Russian bastard's sense of humour. My teeth is about eighteen.'

Out of the blue, Posa said, 'Posa-Posa-Posa', which left them speechless. It was a moment of great triumph. Dimitri said, 'Say again. Posa.' Once started there seemed to be no stopping her. The sudden appearance of something normal in the little girl was astonishing to them.

Looking out over Table Mountain later, Eve began to get cold feet. 'Supposing it's all a great disaster, Dimitri?'

'It will not be.'

'It's not that, it's the Lavenders. It's all very well saying this and that in a letter, but are there really people who will give a home to people they know nothing about?'

'Is it only Eve who has compassion for lost people, for poor children?'

'But this is different.'

'Is not. These people are good. They need to help, because of Ozz who died.'

'Will they really be able to take to Spanish children?'

'This son dies for, what you say?, for beautiful ideal of freedom?'

'For the splendid ideal.'

'Yes. Is splendid, I think too. If the children have food and love in new country, is not enough if there is not freedom. In my country I have plenty food always, warm things; in army I have good friendships. But no freedoms to *say*. Think, but not say. Even to think is now dangerous.'

She looked at him closely. It was almost like seeing him for the first time – not the exuberant lover, not the generous soldier who liked a good time, not the children's protector, she was seeing a good man, an admirable man even.

Had she really met this good man so casually? At what point had they each made a choice that would lead them here? Had there been a choice, or was it simply serendipity? Chance? If not that, then Fate? She had met David as casually, and he had been the subject of her thoughts and dreams for a long time, yet what she felt for Dimitri was not at all the same. If Dimitri disappeared from her life it would matter very much.

'Dimitri? Listen. When you said that you loved me . . .'

'Is true!'

'I know. I –' She hesitated to say the words. She still wasn't sure that she could handle such commitment. 'I'm glad.'

He looked straight into her eyes, not allowing her to be evasive. 'Tell me how.'

Why was it so difficult?

It was difficult because in telling him that she loved him, she felt a kind of failure. Until that day when he had joined the exodus from Spain, until he had picked up Posa and given Eugenia the protection of his arm as she slept in the rain, until he had put himself in danger of being exposed at the frontier checkpoint, she had been the independent new woman she had set out to make of herself. She had done it, thrown off the conventions of her class and escaped. She had vowed never to become like her mother and her grandmother.

'I'm glad because, because I have fallen in love with you, Dimitri.'

'Is wonderful, Eve. Say to me, "I love you, Dimitri". Is this possible to say?'

It was possible. She went across to where he was sitting on the hotel veranda under the clear bright stars of the Cape Town night. She put her arms round his neck. 'I love you, Dimitri. Truly, I do love you. I love you very much, Dimitri.'

Epilogue

Jess Lavender had said that she would bring a lilac-coloured scarf so that Eve could pick her out. Eve, aware of the scrawniness of the children, was tense with apprehension that these people might not take to them. Dimitri lifted Eugenia on to his back, and Eve sat Posa in the crook of her arm. 'Can you see her? Look for an old lady with purple scarf.'

'She is old?'

Eugenia said, 'Old as her eyes.'

Dimitri said, 'Is clever, Genia.' He turned his happy brilliant smile on her and gave her a kiss. 'Is good to make jokes.'

It would be all right. Whatever happened with the Lavenders, it would all be all right. Eve and Dimitri and the two children were as complete a family as any other. More complete than her own had been. But she wanted the Lavenders to like the children, so that there would be time to give Eugenia back her mental health, and to allow Posa to develop physically in peaceful surroundings with plenty of food.

And, if only for Ozz's sake and for the loss of him she still feels, she wants to give the Lavenders something. He had said that she was the sort of girl they would have wanted him to take home to Sunday tea. The picture of Jess Lavender that Eve has held in her mind was not from a photograph, but drawn by Ozz in loving and funny sketches. Eve looks for a fierce little Welsh lady who smiled and laughed, and was soft as butter inside.

Suddenly Eve, waving a lavender-coloured scarf, sees the large lilac square as big as a pillow-case being waved. Her heart leaps. A tall, sinewy, handsome woman with golden hair that is beginning to fade from the colour that had been Ozz's. There is no mistaking Ozz's mam.

'Look, look! That's *her*! She's seen us . . . Eugenia, wave. Dimitri, it's her . . . It's Ozz's mother. I mustn't cry, Dimitri . . . just don't let me cry.'

He gives her a peck on the cheek. 'Is OK to cry, maybe Dimitri cry . . . Is very moving. Future is hopeful, Eve. Is good we come to Australia with children and make more.'

She almost can't bring herself to tempt fate and be happy. Too many times in the past she has been slapped down for thinking that she could be happy. Yet this moment is marvellous. 'We couldn't have made it without you, Dimitri.'

'Ach, you modest. You would have make it OK.' He gives her a friendly squeeze. 'I come because I know I shall never wish to live any place without this woman. I love very much this beautiful woman who is so concern for little children.'

A snatch of words flashes into her mind from the last time she had heard La Pasionaria speak. What was it? 'We shall not forget you, and when the olive tree of peace puts forth its leaves again, entwined with the laurels of the Spanish Republic's victory – come back.'

One day the children would go back. She must never let them forget that they were Spaniards. In time Eve would tell the girls about La Pasionaria, tell them that they should be proud to be children of the Republic. There would be ways to give them their own history.

The Spanish Republic, as they had last seen it as refugees on the escape road, might as well be on another planet, and already the Republic was history. If Franco's new regime ever tried to excise those years, Eve is certain that she and thousands like her would each have to be the custodian of their part, and the time would come to tell it. Dimitri's would be different from Eve's, Eve's different from Eugenia's. Would Posa remember anything at all?

Eve hopes that she will not. She hopes that Posa's memories will begin here, with Ozz's exuberant mother holding out her arms as though to gather them all to her.

'Dimitri, what a long way from Spain we are.'

'Also from USSR and UK. Is good this new world for us.'

Suddenly she is overwhelmed by their good fortune. She laughs as she turns towards Jess Lavender, waving. Eve Anders has not experienced such light-heartedness in a long time. 'Is good, Dimitri.'